I Heard Your Voice in a Dream

by

Jennifer Juárez

To everyone and anyone going through hardships they think will never end...your black coffee will taste just the way you want it to taste soon.

CHAPTER ONE

"Excuse me!" a voice rose in the busy and rampant hallways of the school she was completely unfamiliar with. Unfortunately, no one was being much help. Elena sighed in frustration as yet another one of her fellow alumni completely ignored her desperate request.

Great.

Not only was she completely new to New York City, but the high school monarchy too. Either that or it was *Ignore Elena Day.* Now more than ever did she want to ship herself in a box back to Miami, her home.

Back in Miami she had a life with the beautiful beaches that intoxicated her nostrils, the wonderful smell of sea salt, the warm sand covering her feet, beautiful and warm weather where she didn't have to bundle up at all, and a home she'd lived in for the past 16 years up until this point.

The point where her father gathered up the family of four and announced excitingly that he'd gotten the promotion at his job he'd worked his butt off for.

And of course, Elena was happy for her father—excited even. That is, until he came up with the lovely catch: moving.

And it wasn't moving across town—no—across *states*. Now she left behind her old life in Miami to begin one here in New York.

And so far? Not really working out for her.

The tiny brunette approached another student walking by the hallway. "Excuse me!" she exclaimed to the boy moving down the busy hallway. "I really need help getting to this classroom—"she didn't even get to finish her sentence when a group of rowdy jocks accidentally pushed her to the cold floor, her belongings flying everywhere.

Groaning, she attempted to gather up all her belongings while students navigated around her down the hallways with no one taking the time to help her retrieve her things.

Except one.

"People can be so rude sometimes..." A voice trailed off. Elena looked up to see a girl decked out in urban-styled clothes kneeling down beside her, helping her collect the scattered notebooks.

"It's New York's trademark, isn't it?" Elena spoke up.

The other girl looked up at her and snorted at the reply. Standing up, the girl used her free hand to offer Elena a lift and Elena took it gratefully.

"That's the nicest you're going to get." The girl replied, handing her the fallen belongings. "I take it you're new?"

Elena nodded. "Yup." She popped the 'p' and sighed. "I'm from Miami."

The other girl hummed. "Miami…must've been one hell of an awesome place. New York has its good qualities too. You just gotta hang around the right people." She winked. "I'm Phoenix."

Elena smiled. "Are you suggesting I hang around with you then?" she retorted. "Elena, nice to meet you."

The girl Elena now knew as Phoenix laughed, shaking her index finger to Elena. "I like you, Elena. You've guessed correctly, I'm the greatest person you'll ever meet!" Phoenix exclaimed, throwing her hands up dramatically.

"Correction: *I'm* the greatest person you'll ever meet." A dark-skinned girl butted in the encounter. "Is Phoenix annoying you?" the girl turned to Elena. "She tends to do that a lot. That's why she lacks friends."

Phoenix sent the girl a playful glare and rolled her eyes. "Rude." She replied simply.

Elena chuckled. "She wasn't annoying me. In fact, she's the only one that's acknowledged my existence up until this point."

The dark-skinned girl nodded. "So you're new then? I haven't seen your face around these halls..." she assumed. "I'm Maya." She introduced herself.

"Elena. Nice to meet you, Maya." The girl nodded. "I'm definitely new here. I have no idea where to go."

Maya reached her hand out. "Let me see your schedule." She replied.

Elena looked through her messy pile and pulled out the sheet with her schedule. "Of course, if you'll help me not look like a lost and sad-looking puppy...then be my guest."

The two girls laughed and Maya took Elena's schedule and scanned over it. "You have first, fourth, and seventh period with me." She announced. "I could take you to first period, so don't even worry."

"And you have third and sixth with me!" Phoenix added. "You'll enjoy me in class." She winked. "I am the highlight of everyone's day."

"On a good day." Maya teased.

Elena grinned, she was so happy to have made friends already. Or at least she hoped they'd become her friends. But from they were starting out, she was coming to think they were. "You two are my

heroes. I would've looked ridiculous walking into the wrong class."
She chuckled.

"It's no problem. And even if you did walk in the wrong class, you could just walk out like this," Phoenix strutted halfway down the hallway like a runway model and then back.

"I think the point is to *not* be ridiculous." Elena laughed.

Maya nodded in agreement. "I like her, can we keep her?" she asked Phoenix.

Phoenix thought for a moment before smirking. "Well it looks like you've joined the greatest group you'll ever meet."

"In other words, you're with the greatest people in this school." Maya added.

"That doesn't sound like a bad deal, as long as you come to realize I become less shameful and more ridiculous as you get to know me more." Elena told them. She tended to be a total goofball around people and never missed a chance to completely embarrass herself—most of the times unintentionally.

"We're okay with that. We'll join you." Maya replied. "We're experts at carrying no shame."

"It's true." Phoenix nodded. "Especially Maya."

Maya raised an eyebrow. "Says the girl who thought she was a runway model five seconds ago and failed horrendously." She retorted, imitating Phoenix's strutting dramatically, taking longer steps and stomping on the floor.

Elena burst out laughing as Phoenix pretended to look annoyed and rolled her eyes. "The nerve I tell you, the *nerve!*" she exclaimed.

The newly formed trio spent the next couple of minutes making small talk and getting to know each other, finding themselves to like each other way more than they expected. Their meeting had to come to an end eventually as the first bell signaling to head to their first period rang.

Elena pouted. "Stupid bell." She whined.

"Girl, I know I got English first. I hate reading." Phoenix scrunched up her face in disgust, not one to willingly pick up a book unless she needed to.

"I can tell… your grammar's as terrible as your modeling skills." Maya teased, and Phoenix stuck her tongue out making the three laugh.

"Your banter is going to be the reason I wake up in the mornings." Elena commented, giggling.

"You're going to sit with us at lunch, right?" Maya asked.

"Does it look like she's got anyone else to sit with Maya?" Phoenix questioned.

Elena sent Phoenix a playful glare and then laughed. "She's got a good point. If you guys didn't invite me to lunch, I'd be stuck eating in the bathroom." She replied, referencing the film *Mean Girls* even though she was completely serious.

Maya scrunched up her nose. "God, *please* don't ever do that. The bathrooms are kind of disgusting here." Maya laughed.

"Can't be worse than the food." Phoenix commented, shrugging. "Seriously, *never* get the freaking meatloaf. It isn't meat, but I'm pretty sure there's some kind of loaf."

Maya and Elena looked at her with a confused expression. "What does that even mean?" Maya asked. "Your logic gives me a headache Nix…" she laughed but then turned to Elena. "We should get going, don't want the new girl to be late to her first class." Maya told her.

"All right, abandon me then!" Phoenix exclaimed.

Maya rolled her eyes playfully. "You'll pull through." She teased.

Elena only laughed, turning to Phoenix. "I'll see you third period?"

Phoenix nodded. "It's a date." She winked. "With physics." She pouted. "But I'll see you, Lena! I should go before the teacher bitches at me for being late on the first day. I should *at least* try to be on time today. Bye, May." She said in an annoyed tone for Maya before waving cheekily and walking away.

"And that is Phoenix Hale everyone." Maya said, shaking her head and laughing. "Come on, let's get to class. It's the wonderful world of Geometry." She said sarcastically, linking arms with Elena's and leading her to the classroom right on time.

Upon entering class, Maya squealed. "Emma!" she exclaimed, dragging Elena along with her. Elena saw a tanned and tiny girl squeal twice as loud as Maya did and embraced her tightly.

"Hey girl! I missed you!" the small girl exclaimed.

"I missed you too! How was your summer?" Maya asked.

Emma shrugged. "Oh you know, same old thing. I went to visit family in Texas and hung out with my man." She blushed.

"The flame continues I see." Maya teased, nudging the girl. She turned to Elena and then to Emma. "By the way this is my friend, Elena. She's new here from Miami." She introduced.

Emma turned to the other girl and grinned. "Hey! I'm Emma!" she hugged Elena and Elena hugged her back, though a little taken back by the girl's sudden hug.

"Hi! I'm Elena. It's nice to meet you, Emma." She greeted back.

"So what brings you to New York?" Emma asked curiously as the three took a seat beside each other before the bell rung.

"My dad got this promotion at his job and it required him to move here. It sucks since my life was all in Miami but I'll get over it." She replied.

Emma nodded. "Well you seem to be making friends already so you should be fine. New York is amazing—kind of tough—but still amazing. You'll get your way around here in no time." She said optimistically. Emma was a literal ball of sunshine, Elena thought. She was so sweet without even knowing Elena for five minutes.

"Thanks Emma, I appreciate that." Elena smiled, with Emma quickly returning the smile.

Maya turned to Emma. "So I'm surprised to see she's not in class with you this time." Elena kinked up an eyebrow.

Who was *she* and why was Maya surprised *she* wasn't in here?

Emma exhaled. "She's taking a special class for this period. She's too advanced for this class anyway. She's always been good at math. And it's nice taking a break for one period—not that she bothers me, because she doesn't." Emma replied. "It's just she's…"

"Rude, snarky, sarcastic, and kind of a bitch?" Maya questioned.

Emma playfully pushed Maya. "Hey now! She's actually really nice once you get to know her!" she defended.

"When she sat with us, she called me an uncultured swine when I didn't know who Edgar Allan Poe was. And then told Phoenix she sounded better when she wasn't saying anything." Maya argued with a smirk on her face. "Now tell me, Emma, where's the niceness in that? Because I don't see it."

Emma laughed. "It takes a while for her to open up to you. She's nice, I swear. Don't let the words fool you."

"Who are you guys talking about?" Elena asked curiously, causing both Emma and Maya to turn to her.

"Emma's friend. Her name's Autumn." Maya answered. "She's…quite the girl."

"Care to elaborate?" she asked, raising an eyebrow.

Maya shrugged. "There's not much to say. She's pretty mean and sarcastic and just all-around not the person you want to hang around with."

"You don't know her the way *I* do though." Emma defended. "She uses it as a defense mechanism because she's...you know..." she mumbled.

"She's what?" Elena pushed Emma for an answer.

Emma pursed her lips and replied. "She's blind." She said softly, uncomfortably shifting.

Elena immediately felt terrible for pushing Emma for an answer. She had to stop being so damn curious. "I'm so sorry Emma...I-I shouldn't have asked." She apologized immediately.

Emma shook her head. "Don't worry about it. We all get curious. Just...don't let her attitude get to you if you ever meet her. Don't take it personally; she's the same with everyone." Emma advised.

Elena nodded and soon the teacher began going over what to expect in class for the year and passed textbooks to all the students. Not much was going on and Elena found herself wondering about this Autumn girl. She seemed to have an interesting story and if there was anything Elena liked, it was a good story. But from the looks of it, it didn't seem like this Autumn girl would be very interested in sharing her story.

She took out her sketchbook while the teacher assigned everyone a textbook. Maya and Emma began gossiping about their summer adventures and Elena really didn't feel like inserting herself into the conversation, even though the girls attempted to sneak her into the conversation. She began finishing up the drawing she'd been working on in sharpie pen last night. It was clear how concentrated Elena had to be to complete the drawing. It was filled with intricate patterns that ultimately created a flower-like drawing.

Maya glanced over at what Elena was doing and her eyes widened in surprise. "Oh my god, Elena!" the girl exclaimed. "Did you do that?"

Elena looked up and nodded slowly. "Yeah. It was just something I started on last night. It's not that great—"she tried to say.

"Not *that* great?!" Maya exclaimed. "Elena, it's freaking *awesome*! Never in a million years could I make something like that." She assured.

Elena turned red and smiled sheepishly. "Thanks. It's still not my best work. I've done better. I'm better at painting."

And truth be told, Elena was indeed a great artist. She had won a good amount of rewards and recognitions for her artwork that she'd submit to contests and was even featured in a gallery once. Of course, it was a gallery in her art program at school…but it was still a huge honor for her.

Art to her was everything. It was like she could pick up a paintbrush and with the swish of a paintbrush, the world slowly disappeared and all that mattered was colors, patterns, and shapes.

"If that's not your best work then what the heck is the best?" Emma butted in, an impressed look on her face.

Elena chewed on her lower lip, contemplating for a second on whether or not to show more of her artwork before taking out her phone and opening up pictures of some of her artwork. She showed them only two.

The first one was an oil painting of a brunette girl sitting on the bus. But you only saw the back of her head. She was the main focus while everything else Elena had made slightly blurry but still visible enough to see.

The second picture was a painting of a shadowy-like tree. It was purposefully messy and with smudges, making the colors pink and black display more.

Emma and Maya were wide-eyed and mouths wide open. "Well damn." Maya said simply.

"These are good. Like really, *really* good. Wow." Emma said, baffled. She looked up at Elena. "You should go talk to our art teacher, Mrs. Freya. She's an amazing art teacher and she runs the art program. You should try to take one of her art classes she offers, you'd do more than great there." She told Elena.

"Thank you, I'll definitely think about it. I might try looking for her during my free period." Elena replied, smiling.

"Do it. You have some serious talent going on there." Maya insisted.

The rest of the period, the three girls talked amongst themselves. For the most part, they talked about Elena's artistic talents which Elena couldn't help but act sheepishly over.

After class ended, Elena spent the next couple of periods anxiously waiting for her free period to come. Though she knew the classes she'd be spending with Maya, Emma, and Phoenix would be the ones to look forward to.

That and her possible art class if the art teacher liked her enough.

Finally, sixth period came and Elena couldn't have dashed out of that classroom faster enough.

Going to her assigned locker, she began putting belongings in and taking belongings out.

Elena brought out her sketchbook and began flipping through the many filled pages of drawings Elena had created, picking out the ones she'd want to show the teacher in hopes to impress her enough.

Suddenly, she began hearing piano playing coming from across the hallway. But it wasn't just *any* piano playing, it was *beautiful* piano playing. The kind of piano playing where you feel the need to just close your eyes and listen to it closely.

Closing her locker, Elena slowly walked over to where the music was coming from. Elena stopped at the entrance of what appeared to be a music room and stared at the person playing in the grand piano.

Wearing black Ray-Bans, the pale girl's fingers delicately pressed each key. Like every note she played mattered. And it did to her. It truly looked like it did.

She wasn't even looking at the keys she was playing, she was simply staring straight ahead. She must *really* know the piano to be able to play without looking.

The girl swayed slightly to the music playing, clearly getting lost in the music. The way she played the song is what fascinated Elena. It was as if this song was the last song she would ever play in her life and she was playing one last performance.

Elena loved seeing people lose themselves in something they loved so much, and it didn't help that the girl was beautiful too. Even though she couldn't see her eyes, the rest of her features were easily seen.

But Elena couldn't help but feel curious about her eyes. They seemed like a mystery to her. Were they colored? Dark? The girl herself looked like a mystery.

A mystery worth solving for.

The girl finished playing and sighed in content with the effort she had put.

Elena smiled softly, her slippery hands suddenly dropping her sketchbook and other contents and Elena cursed silently.

The girl's head snapped towards where the noise came from and called out. "Who's there?" she asked.

Elena didn't reply, instead scrambled up her belongings and gulped.

"I *said*...who's there?" the girl said, anger now clear in her voice. Elena looked up to see the girl grab a white cane she had on next to her and slowly getting up, using the cane to help guide her. "I know you're here. Stop being a creep and identify yourself."

Elena still didn't utter a word, staring at the girl walking towards her. But Elena soon realized she couldn't see her. The glasses. The cane. It all connected instantly. She was that Autumn girl Emma and Maya had talked to her about.

"I know I'm blind, but I'm not fucking stupid." Autumn said, annoyance presence in her voice.

"Tha—that's a really bad...joke." Elena blurted out suddenly. There were a lot of things she could've said, but she chose instead to say *that*. Great.

Autumn quickly became more alert. "If it was a joke, I'd be laughing." She retorted, now a couple feet away from Elena. "So why would I joke about the fact that I can't see a thing? Not something to laugh about clearly."

"Good point. I should...I should go." Elena muttered awkwardly, backing away from the entrance and back out to the empty hallways.

"You should. You just wasted two minutes of my already dark life." Autumn licked her lower lip. "Now *that* one was an intentional joke." She pointed out, but no change in expression.

Elena laughed awkwardly. "Funny—kind of. Unless it was supposed to be funny…then ha." She replied nervously.

"You're very weird." Autumn told her.

"So I've been told." Elena agreed. "I'll…see you around." She said finally.

"I'm surely glad I won't." the girl said, monotone in her voice.

"Right. Yeah…" Elena said, beginning to walk away.

"I was playing 'Moonlight Sonata' from Beethoven by the way." Autumn suddenly said.

Elena turned around and smiled softly. Even though the girl had been rude to her, she still saw a hint of kindness in her. "Thanks." She replied.

Autumn shrugged, fiddling with her white cane while her head turned to where her ears last heard the other girl move. "Figured you needed culture in your life since you sound like the kind of girl that listens to shitty boy bands or any other variation of bubblegum pop."

Autumn smirked. "You're welcome." She said before walking back inside the room.

Elena scoffed before shaking her head and walking away. But she remembered not to let her words get to her; she was like this to everyone. She heard the piano playing once more and smiled to herself.

"Moonlight Sonata." She said to herself.

She headed to the art department and saw many forms of art hung around the walls. The art department definitely had their share of talent and it intimidated the heck out of Elena.

What if her art was trash compared to this work? Shaking her head she continued walking to the classroom Emma told her to go to.

Walking inside the classroom, she was surprised by how chill and relaxing the classroom was. There was work of art by other students. Sculptures, sketches, and paintings hung around the classroom and it just gave such a relaxed vibe. And The Beatles were playing as well, so she had a feeling this teacher would be pretty cool.

"Um, hello?" she called.

"I'll be right there!" she heard a voice reply.

Elena silently waited, fidgeting with the hem of her flowered skirt. A woman in a gray pixie haircut and very bright clothes came out.

She looked around her 50's but the way she dressed looked like she was stuck in the 70's era still. She had feathered earrings and a large amount of beads danged across her neck. She definitely gave the impression she was an art teacher.

"Hello there, dear, I don't think I've seen you around these halls. And this noggin here remembers every face she sees!" she chuckled, tapping her head.

Elena smiled, laughing. "I'm new here. I moved from Miami." She explained. "And a friend of mine said you were the art teacher." She said. "And I was wondering if you could take a look at some of my work and hopefully you could put me in one of your classes?" she asked.

The graying teacher nodded. "Of course! Come! To my desk! It's kind of a mess but the best artists are the messiest." She winked as she walked to her desk, Elena following.

Elena grinned. "That's what I say!" she exclaimed as she set her sketchbook down to the art teacher's table.

"Well great minds think alike." She joked. "What's your name, sunshine?" she asked.

"Elena. Elena Díaz." She smiled.

"Nice to meet you, Elena. I'm Mrs. Freya. Or Freya. I don't like being called Mrs. all that much. Makes me feel old." Freya scrunched up her nose. "Although my soul is far from growing old. It's still 24 years old."

"Nice to meet you too...Freya." Elena smiled. "I think my soul's six years old still." She chuckled. "But anyways, here's some of my artwork." Elena opened her sketchbook and flipped through her many sketches. She didn't seem to be able to find the perfect picture to show the teacher. She really wanted to impress her.

"If you're only trying to show me your 'good' work, then you're not passionate about your art. Show me the ones you like most. *You*." Freya told her. "This is *your* artwork, not mine. Don't hide it."

Elena nodded, flipping one more page before showing a pencil sketch of a girl who had her hands around her face, a single tear falling down her cheek. "Why did you pick that one?" the art teacher asked.

Elena bit her lip and shrugged. "I don't know—"

"Yes. You *do* know. Never tell me you don't know. That's the lazy answer. You know why you picked it out and you know why you drew it. So tell me. 'I don't know' is never the answer in art. In art, there's *always* an explanation for it." She told Elena, smiling encouragingly. "Now tell me why."

Elena chewed on her lip. "She had just found out she was pregnant that day and she was only 15. She was scared and frustrated and teary-eyed. She had no one to listen to her. So I sat down next to her and talked to her. I had her say everything she wanted to say but no one gave her the time of day to do it. So she was thankful that someone had finally seen she needed help, and instead of pushing her away I decided to pull her in. I asked if I could draw her and she agreed. And…this is what I came up with."

"Why did you draw her?" she asked softly.

"Because it shows the human emotion of vulnerability. It's hard to ask for help and when someone gives it to you without you asking…you're grateful. Or sometimes, you're usually harsh when someone gives you help because you don't want to be dependent on someone else. But this girl showed the softer side of vulnerability. And it was a different wave of emotion I'm not used to seeing." She explained. It came out so naturally to her, Elena was surprised she even came up with that.

The teacher nodded. "Welcome to my AP Art class."

Elena's eyes widened. "What? Are you serious?" she sputtered out. "I just showed you one of my artworks…"

"That's all I needed." The teacher shrugged. "Your explanation is exactly what I wanted to hear. It's one thing to make art, but it's another thing to *know* it. And you…you know your art."

Elena was at a loss of words, so she simply nodded. "I—thank you. Thank you so much." She smiled. "What period is AP Art?"

"Fourth period. Is that fine?" she asked.

Elena nodded. "It's just another science class. It shouldn't be a problem." She shrugged.

"Then welcome to class, Elena. I expect great things from you." The art teacher smiled.

"You do?" she asked, surprised.

The teacher nodded. "I do." She closed Elena's sketchbook and handed it to her. "And you should too. You're fantastic. Once you start seeing it for yourself, you'll be shocked at how great you are."

Elena fidgeted for a moment. "And how will I see it for myself?"

The teacher thought for a moment. "By living. Get out there. Make mistakes and then make 10 more. Smile more. Cry more. Get angry more. Fall in love and then get your heart broken. Make friends and lose friends. Start making adventures for yourself and drag along others with you. You'll never see the greatness in life unless you search for it yourself." She advised. "So get out there kid, *live.*"

CHAPTER TWO

After school, the newly formed trio was walking out of the school talking animatedly. They had only met each other that morning and already were acting like they've been best friends since birth.

"So I met Autumn." Elena spoke suddenly, causing the other two girls to look at her with worry.

"Shit, did she eat you alive?" Phoenix asked with her eyes wide. "Every time I force myself to associate with her I pray to everything possible. She's the ice queen. *Literal* ice queen. Her soul is cold. That, or non- existent."

Elena chuckled as she recollected the awkward and brutal moment briefly. She wasn't as bad as Elena thought.

Sure, she did look like she had a mean streak…but a part of her still wanted to see Autumn again. Especially to hear her play the piano. "She wasn't *that* bad…"

"Key word: *that*." Maya butted in as they crossed the street. "But what happened? You still look fully intact."

Elena shrugged. "I was just making my way to see Mrs. Freya, and I heard piano playing. *Brilliant* piano playing might I add." She said, smiling. "And then I just followed the sound and found myself in the music room I guess. So I just kind of stood there watching her play and she was just so...*fascinating*." Elena told them. "And then I dropped my stuff and she heard me and I freaked out. She was definitely not pleased that someone was watching her. So we exchanged words briefly...hers weren't very kind. But I didn't take it to heart." She looked at her two friends. "I don't know, it was weird..."

"Why weird?" Maya asked.

"Because..." Elena chewed on her lower lip as she thought of what to say next. "She told me what she was playing. And I felt like she doesn't just tell anyone that, you know? For a brief moment, I think she was glad someone was there." She shrugged. "But that's just my opinion."

Phoenix and Maya exchanged looks, both their eyebrows raised. "Sounds like Autumn caught your attention there Lena..." Phoenix trailed off, smirking. "You sound like you got a little crush." She teased.

"What?" Elena asked in confusion. "I mean—yeah—she seems interesting but I'm not into her. I talked with her for, like, five minutes." She retorted. "And in those five minutes she wasn't doing anything that would make me like her in that way."

Maya shrugged. "Whatever you say...for the record, I hope we didn't offend you by making the assumption that you're a lesbian or anything." She said quickly.

Elena shook her head. "No, you didn't. Because I am one." She shrugged indifferently.

"Oh." The dark-skinned girl said simply. "Then I take it back."

"You guys don't mind, right? That I'm gay?" Elena asked, chewing on her lip again.

Elena was pretty open when it came to her sexuality. It took her a while to fully accept who she was, but she's been out of the closet since the middle of her freshman year. Both her parents supported her and found no problem of who their daughter loved, as long as she was happy. And her classmates didn't seem to mind either. But of course, there were always those few individuals that found something wrong with it, but she would shake it off.

Phoenix and Maya shook their heads. "Not at all. You do you, Lena." Phoenix smiled. "Besides, I felt rather flattered when you checked out my ass fourth period." She smirked.

Elena blushed. "Shut up." She muttered. "It's huge, that is not my fault."

"So is yours! It's pretty nice if I do say so myself." Phoenix smirked, blatantly checking out Elena's butt just to tease her.

The Miami native shook her head and laughed. "You are terrible."

"Get used to it, it gets worse from here." Maya laughed. "Phoenix carries no shame in her body."

"It's true." Phoenix nodded in agreement.

"Oh! You guys finally agreed on something." Elena pointed out, a smug look on her face.

"This happens once every two days. But for the most part, I'm trying to rip off her weave." Phoenix teased, ruffling Maya's hair. Maya quickly swatted her hand away and fixed her hair.

"It's real, shut up." Maya laughed. "Besides, you're one to talk. Your hair looks like a wig used in *The Lion King* over at the Minskoff Theatre. So bite me, *Mufasa.*" She smirked, obviously proud of her comeback.

Phoenix gave a fake laugh, a second later giving a playful glare to Maya. "*So* funny May, how long did it take you to come up with that? A century?"

"Not as long as it takes you to come up with something even remotely *close* to hurting my feelings." Maya teased back.

Phoenix pushed her, causing Maya to stumble and laugh. "The *nerve* you have!"

Elena was cracking up as she watched her friends interact with each other. "You guys are idiots." She commented in between laughs.

Phoenix pushed Elena as well, causing her to stumble and fall. She was always so clumsy.

All three girls burst out laughing, Elena holding onto her stomach that was aching from all the laughing.
"Phoenix...you...little...shit..." she said in between laughs. This only caused Maya and Phoenix to laugh even more. Elena was beginning to love their newly formed friendship even more. Maya helped Elena up as they continued walking.

"But anyways, I'm going to have to keep heading straight. I take the subway back home. I'm on babysitting duty once I get home." Phoenix told them. She had to watch seven kids once she got home, including her younger siblings. She lived in a house with 22 other people, so needless to say she grew up with a huge family. "I will text you both later." She promised as she continued walking straight when Maya and Elena turned left.

"How far does she live that she has to take the subway?" Elena asked, never have taken the subway herself.

"Pretty far. She lives around 24 blocks from here. Not really walking distance, you know?" Maya shrugged.

"Whoa—yeah. That's…pretty far." Elena agreed. "I live only a couple of blocks from here. Like…8. Still a little far but not Phoenix far."

"I live four blocks from school so my stop is coming pretty soon." Maya said apologetically. "However, I will be texting you. Especially to tell you all about Autumn." She teased, winking.

Elena blushed. "I don't have a crush on her!" she exclaimed.

"Sure you don't." Maya laughed. "I don't blame you though, Autumn is pretty. If she only took off her shades every so often…"

Elena rolled her eyes playfully. "I'll admit, she's really pretty. I've been wondering what the color of her eyes look like. I'm curious." She told Maya. "I imagine her eyes are gorgeous, it's a shame she hides them behind a pair of glasses."

Maya stared at her with a smile. "You like her." She stated.

Elena scoffed. "I do not!" she exclaimed. "I *just* met her! And like I said, when we met it wasn't something very fun to experience." She retorted.

"The way you talk about her Elena..." Maya trailed off. "No one talks about a person with that much curiosity. You want to know more about her, don't you? Because that's what it looks like to me."

Elena stopped and thought for a moment. Perhaps Maya *was* right. Not that she had a crush on Autumn, but the fact that she was curious about her.

"She has a story." She told Maya. "A *really* interesting story. And a part of me wants to hear it, but to get her to share it sounds pretty hard to do. She's closed off, it's easy to see that."

Maya hummed in agreement. "I don't know much of her story, but it looks like a really interesting one. Maybe if you try to get to know her more, she'll tell you it. However, no one's ever tried to make friends with her. Emma because she's known Autumn since they were babies. They've been friends for so long, it's impossible not to be friends with each other. But Autumn's...mean, really mean. Her words sting a little. And she comes with a lot of package you know that right? I get it," Maya said understandingly. "Autumn comes off as mysterious and interesting, everyone wants to know the story behind the blind girl. But don't think simply because she told you the name of a song, she wants to become besties with you. She's filled with complications."

"I know, I know. But...I think she *wants* to make friends. I think she's lonely." Elena assumed. "Imagine living in a world full of darkness...how hard that must be. She's angry about that of course, because who wants to live in darkness? A world where you can't see all of life's beauties and wonders? She's lonely in that dark world of hers and...I don't know...maybe I can be the person to let some light in there. Metaphorically, of course." Elena said. All this talk of Autumn had her growing more and more curious of the girl behind the glasses and behind the cold demeanor.

Maya shrugged. "You can try, whether it works or not I cannot confirm. Autumn may want friends, but she'd never admit it or go looking for it herself. Good luck is all I can say." She smirked. "And by the way, if you have any luck with Autumn...I might even start shipping it."

Elena put her hands on her face. "Oh god...Maya!" she exclaimed.

Maya laughed. "I'm kidding! God, can't take a little teasing can you?"

"Go home, Maya." Elena stuck her tongue out playfully.

Maya shrugged. "Fine. I need to turn here anyways. I'll text you later, keep me informed on your Autumn fascination." She winked as she waved goodbye and turned.

Elena blushed but waved goodbye back, shaking her head. She continued walking straight ahead for three more blocks before making a right turn and heading to her Brownstone-styled home.

All the homes in her street were connected together in rows and Elena had to admit it looked pretty cool. It was something she'd consider drawing in the future.

She walked up the steps of the front of her house and took out her keys, fidgeting with the keyhole before opening the door, stepping inside the new home. There were still boxes everywhere, but slowly they were adjusting. At least they had furniture.

Elena walked more into the house, walking in the kitchen to see Liliana eating an apple by the island. Lily's face immediately lit up at seeing her big sister and she jumped off her seat and ran over to Elena, hugging her waist tightly. "Elena!" she exclaimed.

The eldest Díaz sister grinned as she hugged her little sister back. "Hey Lily!" she kneeled down to Lily's level. "How was your first day?" she asked.

Lily grinned, showing off her missing front teeth. "It was *awesome*! I made two best friends today! And my teacher, Mrs. Castillo, is super nice! Even after I accidentally called her Mrs. Castle a couple times." She giggled.

"I made two best friends too." Elena kissed Lily's forehead affectionately. "They're very funny and kind of crazy but that's just the way I like them." She winked. Elena laughed when Lily talked about her teacher. "Mrs. Castle sounds *way* better in my opinion. I don't know why she's not calling herself that." She agreed. "Does she live in a castle?"

Lily laughed. "They're crazy like you then! I want to meet them!" she exclaimed. "I thought the exact same thing! But she probably doesn't live in a castle—I asked. It would've been *so* cool though if she did!" Lily rambled.

"You will." Elena assured. "And they'll think you're *so* cool." She grinned as she stood up again and reached for a banana in the fruit bowl, peeling it and taking a bite. "Teachers who have castle names or live in a castle are automatically awesome, that's a rule Lily." She said as if it was the most obvious thing in the world.

Lily nodded in agreement and her mom, Ana, walked in the kitchen with a box that had scribbled in sharpie *CAUTION: VERY FRAGILE* on the box.

"Hi honey! How was school?" her mother asked, putting the box on the counter and running her hand through her bob.

Elena shrugged. "Okay. I made friends." She said, a small smile. "And I'm going to be taking an AP Art class." She said, excitement in her voice.

"Oh!" Ana clapped her hands together. "That's so great mija! I'm glad you made friends and you're taking a class I know you'll do so amazing in!" she hugged her daughter. "I know you weren't very happy to move here, but see? Things are turning up, right?"

"Yeah, it is. I'll get over it, don't worry. I like New York more now come to think of it." Elena smiled. "I feel like it's going to be a good year."

In Emma's car, Autumn crossed her arms. "This is going to be a terrible year." She spoke up from the silent ride to Autumn's house.

"This should be good." Emma muttered.

Autumn played with her white cane, scoffing. "No! You don't understand, I am surrounded by complete idiots."

"Ooh, *shocker*. Tell me more." Emma said sarcastically.

"You're lucky you're driving me, if not, I'd beat the living crap out of you. However, I don't want to be blind *and* paralyzed if I get in a car accident. I can't pull that off." Autumn told her, always the one having a dark sense of humor.

"You can't pull off being nice either." Emma teased.

Autumn protested. "I'm nice to you!" Autumn paused. "Sometimes…" she mumbled.

"I come with benefits, that's why." Emma told her.

Autumn shrugged. "True." She paused. "No, but seriously… this year's going to be terrible." She threw her head back, hitting her head on the leather seat. "The classes that I don't have with you, are for the most part special classes. Except for AP Art, that's probably the only thing I'm looking forward to." Autumn told her.

"But anyways, the special classes basically are 'Boo hoo, you're fucking blind let's accommodate you even more despite the fact that we know you are capable of being in normal classes with assholes and bitches who are going to become Wal-Mart greeters and strippers because they peaked in high school!'" Autumn exclaimed, sighing. "They think I'm an idiot when in reality, I'm smarter than 95% of the school population. I'm blind, not fucking stupid." She scoffed.

Emma glanced at Autumn sympathetically. She knew Autumn since they were babies, and seeing Autumn hurt so much made her hurt.

Emma was Autumn's best friend and ever since Autumn lost her sight completely, she dug herself in a hole of anger and bitterness. She found no use in being happy when she couldn't enjoy what the world had to offer completely.

But Emma tried, she really tried to have Autumn experience what the world had to offer. But Autumn was pessimistic, finding no joy in anything for the most part.

"Those special classes are to *help* you." Emma tried to reason.

"Bullshit. I can take a regular class, I *have* taken regular classes and done just fine." Autumn pushed her black sunglasses up the bridge of her nose. "I don't need fucking help. I'm not useless, you know." She mumbled.

"I know you're not. Just let it be. Take advantage of the classes, they might help you in the future." Emma replied.

"What they teach me, I already know. It's like having free periods." She retorted.

"Then use those free periods to…draw or play the piano. I don't know, just quit whining, Autumn. It's not that bad, you're making a big deal out of nothing."

Autumn scoffed. "Right. *I'm* making a big deal out of nothing. It's not like I have it bad, right? I'm just blind. Nothing big about that."

Autumn was the queen of sarcasm. "It just gets in the way of everything, but no biggie. Just let it be, right?"

"You know I don't mean it like that." Emma said quietly.

"Whatever." Autumn muttered. "Forget I said anything."

Emma sighed, nodding. "Okay." She agreed as they parked in front of Autumn's house. "We're here."

"Yay." Autumn replied in a monotone voice as she opened the car door and clutched onto her white cane.

"Do you need help?" Emma asked.

"I'm fine." Autumn insisted. She stepped out of the car and placed the white cane in front of her, having it guide her to the front steps of her home.

"I'll call you later?" Emma called out.

"Yeah—sure." Autumn replied, her hand reaching the doorbell and pressing it. "I have an appointment with my ophthalmologist today, so call me after seven."

Emma nodded. "Got it." She waited until the door opened, Autumn's dad waving at Emma with a smile as he led his daughter inside.

Once the door shut, Emma sighed. She wanted her best friend back. There were days where parts of the old Autumn came back, but most days it was like talking to a stranger in the body of her best friend.

Autumn lost her eyesight completely when she was 10 years old, and since then the old Autumn slowly disappeared. Emma opened her glove box and reached into it, taking out a flask filled with vodka and taking a swing of it. She exhaled as she turned on the ignition and taking another drink before driving off.

"So, how was your first day?" Joseph, Autumn's father, asked.

"Uneventful." She replied simply.

"I'm sure there was something…" he urged on, desperately wanting some kind of interaction with his daughter.

"Where's Gabe?" she asked, changing the topic. Gabe was her guide dog. He was a three year old golden retriever that was probably the *only* living thing Autumn treated nicely.

Joseph sighed, another day of his daughter shutting him out. "In your room. He doesn't have his vest on, just so you know."

"That's fine, he doesn't need to help me with anything. Thanks." She muttered before heading to her room that was on the first floor.

Her old room was upstairs, but they had Autumn move downstairs after she fell down the stairs when she began losing her vision. They couldn't risk her getting hurt.

Even though Autumn hasn't stopped being hurt.

Upon entering her room, she was greeted by Gabe who was wagging his tail, feeling the soft fur hitting her leg. She smiled as she walked to her bed, sitting down so she could properly pet her dog. "Hey Gabe!" she exclaimed, scratching behind his ear.

Gabe licked her hand and she giggled, petting him some more. "Thanks for that." She grinned, a genuine grin.

Cora, Autumn's mother, was leaning against her daughter's door. A small smile was on her face as she watched her daughter interact with her dog. She loved just staring at Autumn, seeing her smile.

It was so rare to see Autumn act truly happy, and she wanted nothing more than to have Autumn be happy. And if she could give Autumn her eyes so that she could see, she'd sign that deal so quickly.

"Hi." Cora greeted softly.

Autumn turned towards the door where she heard her mother's greeting. "Hey." She said, smile disappearing.

"The appointment's not until an hour." She reminded her daughter. "Maybe we can go get some ice cream." She offered.

The younger girl shook her head. "No thanks. I just want to get the appointment over with." Autumn answered.

Cora sighed, stepping inside the room and sitting on the bed next to Autumn. "You can't keep living like this, Autumn." She told her. "Hiding from the world doesn't make this any better."

"Drop it, please!" Autumn snapped. "Stop trying to pretend like you understand what I'm going through because you don't. You're not surrounded by pure darkness, *I am*. *I'm* the one that comes with baggage, *not you*." Autumn petted Gabe's head. "So I don't want to go out for ice cream, it won't make the fact that right after I'm getting things poked in my eyes in hopes *some* vision comes back. But you and I both know it's not going to as hard as we try. The doctor's said there's a 15% chance that my vision will come back completely. That's a pretty low chance so why bother wishing for something so impossible?" she gulped.

Cora stared at her daughter sympathetically, placing her hand on Autumn's shoulder only to have it shrugged off. "I wish I was in your shoes instead, Autumn. I always do. You know I hate seeing you like this, we all do. That's why we have to keep trying every trial and every shot—no matter how small—to get you back your vision. We have to try. It's a 15% chance, I know, but it's a chance so we're taking it. I'll fight if you fight, all right?"

What sucked more than being blind? It was being the parent of the blind girl. And Autumn knew that, that's why she reluctantly did whatever her parents asked of her. Because they hurt just as much as she did.

Autumn's cold hand reached out for her mother's warm one and Cora smiled softly, taking it and squeezing it. "Thank you." Cora whispered.

Autumn said nothing and simply squeezed it as they sat in comfortable silence. "I think I'll take that ice cream offer, mom."

CHAPTER THREE

Walking to her fourth period the next day, Elena couldn't take off the big smile on her face. She was excited to start her AP Art class, because not only was it taught by the most awesome teacher ever, but she got to have that one class where she knew she belonged.

Granted, sometimes she thought she wasn't good enough to be an artist but she knew that if there was anything Elena did know, it was art. It was one of the main things her thoughts occupied.

That and the pondering question of the mystery color of Autumn's eyes.

Walking inside the colorful classroom she looked around to find a spot to sit in and the only available spot was in the back. She noticed long, dark locks in the back, but couldn't recognize the face straight away. She walked over to the seat next to the mystery girl.

"Hey, do you mind if I sit here?" Elena asked softly.

Autumn turned her head where she heard the voice and shrugged. "Whatever." She mumbled, not really caring who sat with her and who didn't. But she did appreciate the vacancy while it lasted.

Elena's eyes widened when she noticed it was Autumn occupying the seat next to hers. "Okay." She replied, sitting next to Autumn.

Autumn furrowed her eyebrows together as she recognized the voice. "Wait…are you the creep that was listening to me play?"

Elena gulped. "Uh, yeah. That was…that was me." She muttered sheepishly.

Autumn hummed. "Interesting."

"Yeah…"

Autumn didn't say anything else and pushed her sunglasses up, placing her sketchbook in front of her and some sharpened pencils and charcoal pieces. She opened the sketchbook to a page where a charcoal drawing was brilliantly created.

"Wow." Elena whispered to herself when she glanced over at the page. It was a charcoal drawing of a girl, parts of her face smudged with the black color.

What Elena found so amazing was that Autumn managed to draw something so brilliant yet she was unable to see the work she created.

All of Autumn's drawings came from Autumn's mind, so it was as if Elena was catching a glimpse of what went on in Autumn's head. And it was dark like the hole Autumn had dug for herself.

Mrs. Freya suddenly stood from her desk and clapped her hands together with an excited grin. "All right! So, I let you all get adjusted to starting school again by letting you guys be unproductive. However, that changes today." Some people groaned and she mimicked their groaning.

"Oh no! Mrs. Freya you're making us do work at school! Why would you make us learn at school? Who even learns in school?" she mimicked, chuckling. "I've heard it all sunshines, now, I have your first assignment for you all!" she exclaimed.

Everyone stared at the teacher expectantly for their first assignment. "You guys will be pairing up with the person seated next to you and you are going to get to know said person—if you already know them then that makes your assignment much easier. However, you're not only getting to know them, you're going to draw them. Or paint them, or sculpt them, or whatever you want! Point is that the person seated next to you is going to be your muse for the next couple of days." The art teacher explained. "Yes, you can draw them and know their favorite food is pizza but that's not the point of this assignment. I want you to mesh in what you've learned about them in your art piece."

"So we could draw the person holding a pizza?" someone commented, and the class burst out laughing including Mrs. Freya who chuckled

"If you want to remain inside the box, sure. But the point is to think outside of it!" Mrs. Freya exclaimed. "Impress not only me, but impress yourselves at what you could come up with. And who knows?" she glanced over at Elena and Autumn who were completely avoiding each other. "Something could come off of getting to know your partner." She smiled softly. "You have a week from today to get this assignment done. Starting…" she paused. "Now!" she waved them off to get started and sat back down on her desk.

Elena looked at Autumn for a moment. She didn't know whether this partner assignment with her was a good thing or not. Autumn wasn't exactly the most open book out here. She'd be lucky if she could get Autumn to tell her what her favorite color was. Elena had a feeling this was going to be a tougher assignment than she originally thought.

For starters, it had been two minutes already and Autumn still hadn't uttered a word to her about the assignment. She was simply drawing something in her sketchbook.

"Elena?" Mrs. Freya called out, staring at Elena. "Can you come to my desk for a second? I want to talk to you."

Elena nodded, standing up and walking over to Mrs. Freya's desk. "What do you want to talk to me about?"

"Well, I have come to notice you're paired up with Autumn for this assignment." The teacher noticed, glancing over at Autumn.

"Yeah…" Elena sighed. "It's not going to be easy."

"I understand that. Autumn's not the easiest person to talk to, I know, but I think you've got the best partner here." Mrs. Freya told her, smiling.

Elena quirked up an eyebrow. "Really? I don't see that. I mean, she won't even acknowledge my presence. How am I supposed to get her to talk to me so we can get the assignment done?"

"To do just that." Mrs. Freya paused. "Talking to her. Autumn's still human, I hope you know that. Human interaction is a vital part to our lives. Sit down and just talk to her. She's blind, but that doesn't mean she lacks human emotions and thoughts. Autumn's an interesting girl. Not only a great artist, but an interesting soul. Just talk to her. The worst she could do is say something insulting in order to push you away. But don't give up easily. If she won't talk, make her talk." She smiled. "I expect something great from both of you." She told Elena, putting on her glasses. "Good luck."

Elena nodded as she let all the words sink in. Of course, she'd just talk to Autumn. How hard could that be?

She walked back to her desk and turned to Autumn. "So," she spoke up. "it looks like you and I are partners for this assignment."

"You don't say." Autumn replied sarcastically, still working on the sketch she'd began working on since the class began.

Elena suppressed the urge to roll her eyes. "Hilarious." She mused. "But in all seriousness, I think it's great that we were paired up."

"So you can creep on me for longer periods of time?" Autumn questioned.

"I wasn't creeping, I was…" Elena chewed on her lip to think of something. "I was captivated by you—your piano playing I mean." She quickly added.

Autumn turned to her, not really staring at her but Elena knew she got her attention. "You were?" she asked, no longer displaying any sarcasm.

Elena nodded. "Yeah. You were really good. You were…fantastic. I've never seen someone play so passionately before. How long have you been playing? "She decided to ask. It was a start.

Elena saw a blush creep up Autumn's cheeks and she turned back down to her drawing. "Since I was six." Autumn replied simply.

"Wow, that's a long time. Now wonder you know it so well, it's like a part of you now. I say that because that's how I feel when I play the guitar. I've been playing since I was 11. Not as long as you've been playing piano, but still pretty long." Elena shared with Autumn.

Autumn didn't say anything else and simply focused on the task she was working on, which was that drawing she'd been fervently working on since the beginning of the period.

Elena sighed and looked back at Mrs. Freya who had been watching the short interaction. She smiled sympathetically but gave her a look that urged not to give up so easily.

But as hard as Elena tried to initiate another conversation, Autumn wasn't budging. She simply ignored her. Did Autumn dislike her so much she wouldn't even talk to her? She sighed in defeat as the end of the period came and it looked like everyone had a head start but them.

Autumn ripped off the page she drew in and scribbled something below it before sliding it over to Elena and standing up to leave, using her trusty cane to help her exit the classroom.

Elena raised an eyebrow at the sketch but picked it up anyway. It was a sketch of an eye with two hands holding the eyeball.

Under the sketch, Autumn's messy handwriting had written something.

You have five minutes exactly to meet me in the music room so we could go to my house after school to work on the assignment. If you're not there in five minutes, I'm leaving you.

Five minutes.

Elena smiled softly as she collected her things and glanced over at her art teacher, giving her a thumb up.

Mrs. Freya smiled and nodded approvingly before Elena left the classroom with a grin on her face. Maybe there was a chance for her to get to know Autumn's story.

Phoenix and Maya waited for her outside the classroom so they could head over to lunch. They quickly noticed the grin plastered on Elena's face and exchanged a look to each other.

"You seem happy." Phoenix noticed, a smirk on her face.

Elena grinned even more. "That's because I *am* happy."

"Well...I did see Autumn coming out of here too so that must be it." Maya observed, smirking as well.

Elena rolled her eyes as they walked to the cafeteria. "It actually is."

"Talk. Now." Phoenix ordered.

"We're partners for this assignment Mrs. Freya assigned us. And we're going to work together after school at her house." Elena showed them the drawing Autumn had made with the note written below it.

Phoenix and Maya took it in their hands and read the note, smiled creeping up their faces.

"She wants your ovaries, Elena." Maya told her as if it was the most obvious thing in the world.

Elena blushed. "It's a note with a drawing, calm down." She rolled her eyes. "The reason I'm happy is because I didn't think she was going to put any effort in working with me, but she is." She took the drawing from Phoenix and Maya's hands and waved the paper. "And this proves it. I guess I might get to hear her story after all." She smiled.

"Well good for you. But I still wish you all the luck in the world. Just because Autumn's inviting you over to her house, doesn't mean her cold demeanor is going to go away. It's just an assignment, don't get your hopes up." Maya advised.

The trio sat down at the table they had claimed theirs since yesterday, taking out their individual lunches they had brought from home.

"I know." Elena agreed half-heartedly. "But anything can happen, you know?"

Across the lunchroom, Emma was seated with Autumn. Her fingers rubbed her temple as she had one too many drinks the night before.

"So—um, how was your last class?" Emma asked. "It was AP Art, right?"

Autumn shrugged. "It was okay. I'm working on an assignment with this girl after school, so you don't have to drive me home like always." She replied.

Emma perked up. "Really? Tell me about this girl." She asked, intrigued.

"Well, all I know is that her name's Elena. And I only know that because I heard Mrs. Freya call her over and she responded. She really likes art, I guess, and she plays the guitar. But that's about it." Autumn told Emma, turning to her.

"The assignment is to draw each other but incorporate what we've learned about them in our art. That's why she's coming over after school, so we could learn stuff about each other." Autumn shrugged.

Emma grinned excitingly. "Elena? Ooh! I know her! I have her in my first period class. She's really nice and sweet. I think you'll like her." she paused. "It'd be nice for you to make some friends outside of just me and Ethan. You need to get out there, Autumn. Live."

Autumn's head turned forward again. "I stopped living a long time ago, Emma. You know that. I'm alive, and that should be enough."

"It isn't enough. Because you're still here Autumn, and you deserve to be happy." Emma insisted.

"How can I be happy when the world has given me a million reasons not to be?" Autumn retorted.

"By pushing those million reasons to the side and finding one reason to be happy anyways. You're blind Autumn, yeah, but that doesn't mean the world stops spinning. Just because the world to you is dark, doesn't mean it actually is. There's brightness if you seek for it. And quite frankly, you're not looking for it. You're burying yourself from seeing it."

Autumn sighed. "My world is dark, deal with it. I never asked for you to keep being friends with me. You don't have to stick around with the poor blind girl. Go find some friends who can actually see you. You're better off with them. I'm perfectly fine on my own." She snapped.

Emma frowned. "I don't want those people, I want my best friend." She replied. "And I know she's still in there somewhere, bring her back Autumn."

Autumn pushed her chair out, making a scraping noise. "I'm going to the music room." She muttered to Emma, standing up.

Emma sighed. "Autumn...don't do this. Don't push me away."

"I'm not doing anything. I'm going to go play the piano. Like I always do." Autumn replied.

Emma grabbed Autumn's arm. "I'm trying to be there for you but you're not letting me." She pursed her lips. "Just let me be there."

Autumn clutched onto her cane. "I don't want you to. Just keep being my caretaker, that's all you ever are anyway." She said coldly before ripping her hand away from Emma's clutch and walking away.

Emma sighed, gulping to push away the sob wanting to escape. As hard as she tried, Autumn would never fully come back to her. The old her anyways.

Emma cursed everything that led to she and Autumn losing their friendship, because it was fading. The more time that passed with Autumn being blind, the more she could feel herself losing Autumn as her best friend.

Her boyfriend, Ethan, sat down next to her and noticed his girlfriend in distress. "Hey, where's Autumn?" he asked, kissing her cheek.

"She left. To the music room." Emma answered, smiling softly when he kissed her cheek. "I'm losing my best friend."

Ethan shook his head. "No you're not. Autumn loves you, you know that. She just has a hard time expressing her feelings since she lost her vision completely. Don't give up on her Em, she needs you even if she doesn't want to admit it." He told her.

Emma felt a tear escape her eye. "I try so hard to get her to open up to me. I work my butt off to try to make her smile, at least once. But as hard as I try, she's still miserable and she's still hurting. And the more that happens, the more she pushes me away. I just want my best friend back…" she said sadly, her head looking down.

Her boyfriend wiped the tear that escaped her eye. "I know it's hard, Emma, but don't give up on her. She's going to come back, I promise. I have a good feeling she will come back. Just keep trying to be there for her. She may not show it, but she appreciates it. Because you're an amazing person, Em." He smiled softly.

Emma couldn't help but crack a small smile, leaning her head against Ethan's chest. "You're amazing, you know that?"

"Well...I have been told once or twice." Ethan said jokingly.

Emma playfully pushed him. "You're so modest." She teased. "But really, thank you for telling me that. I think I needed that."

They shared a quick kiss and Ethan hugged her. "I'll always be here to remind you. Autumn will come around, I know it."

"I'll be right there with her when she does."

"That's more like it." Ethan smiled.

———————————

School came to an end and all the students rushed out of their classes immediately, trying to escape the torture that was education.

Elena was one of those students, quickly running to her locker and collecting her things. She did not want to be late on Autumn. Not after being given this chance.

Shutting her locker, Elena sent a quick text to her mother that she'd be coming home later than usual because she was going to work on an assignment with a friend. Her mother gave her the okay and she clumsily made her way over to the music room across the hall. Her black high-tops squeaked as she ran across the hall, nearly missing the entrance to the music room from running too fast.

"Made it with 45 seconds to spare, impressive." Autumn spoke up, having heard Elena walking in.

"How do you know it's me?" Elena asked, out of breath.

"Because no one else would come in here to look for me." Autumn replied, standing up from the piano bench. "Let's go. The quicker we get this done, the quicker I get rid of you."

Elena rolled her eyes. "Gee, thanks for that."

Autumn shrugged. "I try."

The two walked out of the music room and Elena stopped. "Um, do you want to…grab hold of my arm? It gets pretty rowdy when everyone tries to leave the school." She offered.

Autumn stopped and thought for a moment before nodding. "Sure."

Elena stepped next to Autumn, holding her arm out for Autumn. "I'm holding my arm out." She told her, looking up at Autumn.

Autumn reached for Elena's arm, holding onto it while still guiding herself with her cane. "Thanks." Autumn said softly.

Elena felt small tingles when Autumn took hold of her arm. Like tiny sparks igniting on her arm by the other girl's delicate touch. "N-no problem."

"Have you considered seeing a speech therapist for that stutter?" Autumn asked, a smirk on her face as they walked out of the building. Autumn felt the warm sun hit her face and she sighed in content.

"Have you considered wearing a plug for that mouth?" Elena retorted, reflecting Autumn's smirk that disappeared.

Autumn definitely wasn't expecting that sort of reply. But she appreciated the girl's gall to talk back. "My voice is one of the few things I can use to get the attention of others. Being blind makes people think you're an idiot when in reality you're the same as they are. You just can't see for shit." She replied. "So no, I haven't considered it."

"I don't think you're an idiot." Elena told her. "You're rude, yes." She chuckled. "But not an idiot. "

"I know." Autumn said simply. "I just like reminding people what I am and what I'm not."

The rest of the walk to Autumn's house was silent. Not an awkward silence, a comfortable one. They only spoke when Autumn gave a direction of where to go so they could reach her house quicker. But for the most part, they didn't utter a word. Autumn still clutched onto Elena's arm and Elena didn't mind for a second.

It was weird, because she seemed to like the way Autumn softly held onto her. For a girl with such a cold demeanor, she was careful at the way she held onto Elena. Like Elena was fine china and she had to make sure she wouldn't break her. If only Autumn treated herself like fine china.

Walking up the steps of Autumn's house, Autumn finally let go of her arm to ring the doorbell. Her father opened the door and smiled warmly at both girls. "Hey there!" he greeted jovial. "I didn't know Autumn was going to have a friend over. The only person she ever has over is Emma."

"Classmate." Autumn corrected. "It's for an assignment. She won't be here for too long." She said as she entered inside the home.

Her father nodded. "All right, well that's fine." He turned to Elena. "I'm Joseph, Autumn's father." He introduced himself.

"Elena, nice to meet you." She smiled shyly, shaking his hand.

"Don't be shy, come in." Joseph insisted.

Elena nodded, walking tentatively inside the home. It was a comfortable home, not too big but not too small either. It was a beautiful home, but it didn't look new. It had that lived in kind of feel, which made it less hard for Elena to settle in.

"If you girls need anything, don't hesitate in letting me know." Joseph told them as Autumn walked over to her room, Elena in tow.

"Fine." Autumn replied simply, stepping inside her room. Elena only smiled softly again to him before stepping inside the room.

Upon entering Autumn's room, Elena looked around. The walls were colored a light blue, giving a relaxing feel. There were posters of artists and other famous people and art pieces hanging around the room. Autumn sat down the bed and Elena sat down beside her.

A golden retriever walked over to smell Elena, looking up at her and studying her before licking her hand. Elena smiled. "Hey." She greeted the dog.

"Is he wearing a vest? If he is, he's at work and you can't pet him. It distracts him from doing his job. He's my Seeing Eye dog. His name's Gabe." Autumn explained.

Elena shook her head, seeing no vest on him. "No, he's not wearing one." Elena took that as a sign to pet him.

"All right then."

The two remained silent. And not the comfortable one from before, it was an awkward one.

Elena coughed. "Um, we should probably get started on the assignment."

"Right, right." Autumn agreed. "So…um, how should we do this?"

Elena pondered for a moment. "Well…a little 21 questions never hurt anyone."

CHAPTER FOUR

Autumn raised an eyebrow. "What's 21 questions?" she asked.

"You don't know what 21 questions is?" Elena asked, mouth agape. She grinned. "This is going to be way more fun than I expected…" she smirked.

Elena swung her legs from the edge of the bed. "So basically, 21 questions is when we take turns asking each other questions—21 questions each." She explained simply. "Do you get it?"

"Oh." Autumn said stupidly, nodding. "I see now. So we just ask each other any question?"

Elena nodded. "Yup. We just ask each other questions. It's easy, you'll get the hang of it."

"You start then, I can't think of anything." Autumn replied, leaning her head against the headboard.

"All right," Elena furrowed her eyebrows together as she thought up of a question. "Who's your favorite singer?"

"Lana Del Rey." Autumn answered without a second thought.

Elena smiled softly and nodded. "I like some of her music. I've been listening to 'Brooklyn Baby' since I got here. Mostly because I was moving to New York so I figured anything that had to do with this place should be in my playlist." She chuckled.

Autumn looked amused. "That's one of my favorite songs from that album. It's brilliant." She raised an eyebrow. "So you're not from New York? Then where are you from?" Autumn asked.

"I'm considering that a question, just so you know." Elena teased. "But no, I'm not from New York. I moved from Miami. My dad got a promotion at his job and it required us to move here. It sucks, but it's whatever." She shrugged.

Autumn chuckled, shaking her head. "Fine then. It saves me the trouble of coming up with a question anyways." She paused. "Can you describe how Miami looks like to me?" she asked softly.

Elena thought for a moment, closing her eyes and thinking of what to tell her to describe her home. "It's...tropical. There's...palm trees. The leaves are so green and the trunks brown. And when you touch them, they're so warm. But not as warm as the sand. The sand in your feet is the best feeling in the world, honestly. It's like...when you feel a warm blanket fresh out of the dryer. It's warm and makes your feet feel awesome." She grinned.

"And the ocean, god, don't get me started on the ocean. It smells amazing, with the sea salt and all. It's so blue too. And when you swim in it, it's refreshing. Not too warm but not too cold either. It's a perfect temperature." Elena opened her eyes and looked at Autumn who seemed to be paying close attention.

"At night, you could see all the lights coming from downtown. They're so bright and colorful. It's like a lights show, with the lights just shining at your face. The beach at night is incredible too, because the moon is beaming down on the ocean making the blue water look so beautiful. It's wonderful. I would sometimes sneak to the beach at night and lie on the sand and stare up at the starless sky. It felt nice." She finished, still staring at Autumn. "Do you see it? In your head?"

Autumn nodded, a small smile on her face. "Yeah...I do. It sounds beautiful." She paused. "Thank you for describing it for me."

"It is. So beautiful." Elena agreed. "No problem, I kind of felt like I gave my eyes to you so you could see it for yourself." She shook her head. "It sounds stupid, I know—"

"It's not stupid." Autumn disagreed. "I think it's nice." She coughed. "So, um, it's your turn to ask a question."

Elena nodded, tucking a strand of hair behind her ear. And so they began throwing each other questions back and forth. Both of them learned a bit about each other.

Like Elena's undying obsession for art and pizza. And Autumn's love for Edgar Allan Poe.

Elena shared that she hated odd numbers and that she owned exactly 106 scarves (her go-to accessory). Autumn shared that she hated open doors and if she didn't hear the door close, she'd throw a fit. And that beanies was her accessory of choice, owning a variety of them.

Elena thought it'd be hard to initiate a conversation with Autumn, but it was easier than she thought. They just bounced off each other during their conversation, she even got to make Autumn laugh a couple times.

This Autumn was so much different than the one at school, the one that was rude and sarcastic and everything in between. But here, it was like she was witnessing the authentic Autumn.

Deciding to dig a bit deeper once they reached question number 20, Elena licked her lips nervously. "So, how did you—um—how did you lose your vision?" she asked tentatively.

Autumn immediately tensed up at the question, visibly gulping. "Why do you want to know?" she said quietly, almost defensively.

"I'm just curious. If you expect me to get to know you more, then I need to know something that has deeply impacted your life." Elena replied. "But you don't have to tell me."

Autumn shrugged, crossing her arms. "Whatever." She paused. "I was diagnosed with Retinoblastoma when I was five years old." She told her. "It's, um, it's basically cancer in the eye. Specifically in the retina which is the sensitive lining inside your eye. I had tumors in both my eyes." She explained.

"Due to the aggressive treatment I had to endure, my eyesight began to plummet. I lost my eyesight completely when I was 10. By that point, I was already getting better. They say I'm lucky though, I still have my eyes. Usually, they're removed to remove the tumor if treatment doesn't work. Because the eyes are basically useless after treatment. But I was the rare case, my eyes still have a 15% chance of gaining eyesight back. It's small, but it's there." She shrugged.

"I don't have tumors in my eyes anymore, but I still have to check-up monthly for my eyes and in general because I have the risk of getting cancer to other parts of my body. So...yay."

Elena felt her heart sink hearing the story. It must've been so hard enduring all of that at such a young age. It made sense why Autumn had so much pent up anger and sadness inside her. "I'm sorry."

Autumn shrugged. "Life can be a bitch. It throws you all this shit to you, expecting you to catch it when you only have two hands. And there's only so much you can carry before you just drop it all and just...not care anymore." Autumn sighed, pushing her sunglasses up.

Elena didn't know what to tell her, so instead she said. "It's your turn to ask me something."

Autumn pursed her lips and thought for a moment. "Why were you there? You know, when you listened to me play the piano?"

"Honestly? It was coincidental. I happened to be by my locker getting something when I heard you playing. And it just caught my attention. I had to see it up close. And then you were there and you looked so passionate about it. Like it was the last thing you'd ever play. I love that about a person. You looked...radiant." Elena responded, a small blush creeping her cheeks.

Autumn raised an eyebrow. "Radiant?"

Elena blushed even more. "Yeah, radiant." She smiled, staring at Autumn. "What color are your eyes?" she whispered.

Autumn stayed quiet for a moment, not making a single movement.

"Autumn?"

Autumn slowly removed the tinted frames, her hand reaching to touch Autumn's cheek so that she could face her. Elena's heart beat quickly when Autumn's hand gently touched her soft skin, feeling little jolts of electricity when that pale hand touched her.

Elena looked at Autumn awestruck at the greenness of her eyes. It was like looking into a gorgeous green forest, and Elena was sure she could get lost in that forest for centuries.

What struck her the most was that Autumn's eyes had an opaque gloss to them, and they were staring intensely at her. Even though Autumn wasn't really looking at her, Elena was.

"They're beautiful." Elena said breathlessly.

Autumn felt a blush creep onto her cheeks and she looked away, quickly slipping her sunglasses back on. "Thanks." She mumbled.

"It's a shame you hide them behind those glasses." Elena said, feeling disappointed when Autumn hid her eyes again.

Autumn pursed her lips. "Last question." She paused. "Why do I get the feeling you're about to mess up my entire life and turn it upside down?"

Elena broke out into a smile. "I'm not about to mess it up."

"Then what are you going to do?"

"Fix it."

Later that night, Elena lay in her bed with a grin on her face that she couldn't seem to wipe off as she dialed Phoenix.

Phoenix sat outside the steps so she could hear Elena better since it was so rowdy and loud inside her home. "Why is Ms. Elena calling me in these late hours?" she teased when she answered.

"Hush, it's only nine. You'll live." Elena replied, giggling. "Can you add Maya to the conversation? I have something to tell you both."

Moments later, Maya entered the three-way phone call in the comfort of her room. "Someone better give me a good reason why I'm being thrown into a three-way phone call in these late hours." She teased.

Elena laughed. "It's only nine. You'll live!" she exclaimed. "Unless you both don't want to hear me admit that you both were right..." she trailed off, playing with the ends of her hair.

"Wait, what were we right about?" Phoenix asked.

Elena paused, raising an eyebrow suggestively. She waited for them to catch on with a grin.

Maya was the first to catch on." Holy sweet Jesus you like Autumn!" she exclaimed. "Are you serious, Lena? You legit have a thing for her?"

Elena nodded as she blushed. "She was just so different from what I saw in school. She was so nice and genuine and amazing…and her eyes. Holy shit, they're beautiful." She smiled.

"This is crazy." Phoenix spoke up. "I didn't think you'd actually start liking her. Just be careful, Lena. This isn't just any crush on any person. This is Autumn Castillo. She may be a certain way one moment, but she could drastically change the next. You don't know it with her."

"I-I know, but I felt something with her. I felt a million jolts of electricity when she touched my face. And when she held onto me when we walked. Not only that, but there was a connection between us both. Something's there. I don't know what it is, but it's there. Maybe I could be the person that changes the way she is in a good way." Elena said optimistically.

"I hate to break it to you Lena, but you can't just fix a person like Autumn from one day to the next. Are you sure you like her? I mean…don't take this the wrong way but…" Maya trailed off. "Autumn is a mess. And I think you want to clean it up for her. You want to rescue her and save her from herself and all that romantic bullshit we hear in books and movies. You've listened to part of her story so now you want to hear the rest." Maya concluded. "Simply because things went well today, doesn't mean they will tomorrow. Your heart's beginning to trick you, Lena, watch out."

Elena gulped. Perhaps there was some truth in Maya's words. But she was wrong in one thing, and that was her feelings for Autumn.

"My heart's not tricking me. I like her. I really, truly like Autumn. And you can't tell me otherwise because what I feel, I haven't felt in a long time. Yes her story intrigues me and I want to help her, but I also want to know Autumn. I want to know Autumn behind the glasses. And she showed me a part of that today. And I think I have a chance at seeing more parts of her."

Phoenix smiled into the phone. "I think it's cute." Phoenix spoke up. "I call captain of this ship here. What do we call you two?" she pondered for a moment. "Alena! SS Alena is setting sail ladies and gentlemen!" the girl exclaimed.

Elena blushed, putting her hands on her face. "Oh god..." she muttered, putting her free hand on her face.

"We should ask Autumn and Emma to sit with us at lunch tomorrow." Phoenix suggested. "It can't go so bad, right?"

"You forget that the last time Autumn sat with us at lunch, we were insulted heavily by her. My god, that girl has insults coming back and forth…" Maya retorted.

"Also coming out of her ass." Phoenix mused.

"That too." Maya agreed.

"Still here you know." Elena spoke up, chuckling.

"We know. But you must agree, Autumn has her little attitude. Regardless what you saw today at her house, Autumn's not planning on changing that part about her any time soon. She's going to be hard work Elena." Maya told her, looking at her pink nails.

"I know, but she's worth the hard work. And even if nothing happens between us, I still want to be her friend. She only has Emma to lean on, and she needs more support. So I want to be that support for her." Elena replied as she placed her sketchbook on her lap and began sketching something in pencil.

"You're adorable when you're in love, Elena." Phoenix piped in, grinning. "I'm genuinely happy for you. I'm not saying it's going to be easy, but if Autumn's the girl for you then go for it. Anything can happen, you know?"

Elena coughed. "In love?" she squeaked. "Love is a very strong word." She told her. "Let's go with smitten. Yeah…smitten sounds much better." She agreed with herself.

"Whatever floats your boat." Phoenix chuckled. "But good luck, I wish you the best. The captain is granting permission for you to proceed with your plan!" Phoenix saluted. "Wait…do you even have a plan?"

Elena suddenly stopped what she was doing and paused. "Fuck."

"There you have it." Maya laughed. "I'll pray for you girl, you're going to need it."

"I'll come up with something, I'm sure. I'm going to take things slow." Elena told her. "I'll be friends with her first, get close to her. And then…I'll just take it from there." She grinned, going back to her sketch.

"Well, that's better than nothing." Maya shrugged.

"It could be worse May, she could be saying she's going to kiss Autumn and see where that goes." Phoenix added. "Wait, you're not thinking that are you, Lena? Because that's assault and Autumn will kick your ass blind or not."

Elena shook her head laughing. "God no! I mean, I'm curious about how her lips must feel like...but I'm not going to kiss her without her permission!"

"Just checking."

The girls continued talking, with Maya and Phoenix teasing Elena about her crush on Autumn. When suddenly, she felt her phone beep that she had another awaiting call and Elena checked to see who it was.

Her eyes widened when she saw who it was. "Holy shit."

"What?" Maya asked. "What's wrong?"

"Autumn's calling me."

"ANSWER THE PHONE ELENA! ANSWER. THE. PHONE." Phoenix shouted into her phone, an excited grin on her face.

"Well, I should say bye I guess then—"Maya and Phoenix had beaten her to it and hung up themselves. She huffed. "Well goodbye to you guys too!"

Elena stared at the caller ID for a couple seconds longer before answering. "Hello?"

"You left your scarf here." Autumn told her. "I think it's a scarf anyway..."

Elena felt her heart flutter at hearing Autumn's voice. "I did?" she questioned, thinking for a moment before realizing she did. "Oh yeah, I did."

"What color is it? Describe it to me."

Elena grinned. "Is this going to be our thing now? You asking me to describe everything?"

"Don't feel special, I ask everyone. You're just one of the few that actually does it." Autumn replied.

"In other words, it's our thing." Elena grinned even wider.

"Fine. Sure. Have it your way." Autumn rolled her eyes.

"It's red with white polka dots on it. It's an infinity scarf, so there's many ways I can wear it. The fabric's soft and thin so if you touch it, you could feel how thin it is. So thin, it'd probably rip if you tangled it somehow onto something sharp." Elena described the scarf.

Autumn touched the scarf in her hands, closing her eyes. "I see it."

"You do?"

"Yes. It's pretty nice." Autumn complimented. "Can I wear it?"

Elena turned redder and grinned. "Yeah—sure. Of course. It'd look nice on you."

"You think so? Well if it looks nice on me, I just might steal it from you." Autumn chuckled.

Elena laughed lightly. "There are a lot of things you can steal from me."

"Like what?"

"*My heart.*" Elena thought to herself. "My buttons collection…" she said instead.

Autumn scrunched up her nose. "I'm not very into buttons. Not my thing. But thanks for the offer. I'm perfectly content with this supposed red polka dot scarf in my hands that I have stolen from you."

"It's not stolen if I give it to you."

"But stealing it from you sounds much more daring. Let's stick with that story."

"How about instead of pretending to be daring, you act daring?" Elena suggested, hoping what she would say next wouldn't leave her embarrassed.

"Explain in further detail."

"Let's go on an adventure."

Autumn quirked up an eyebrow. "Define adventure."

"Let's discover New York City and all it has to offer. On Saturday. You and me. And Gabe too, if you need him." Elena explained.

"Give me five reasons I should say yes." Autumn commanded, taking off her glasses and placing them on her nightstand.

"Why five?"

"Because I know odd numbers piss you off."

Elena broke out into a grin. "You remembered?"

"Five reasons." Autumn insisted.

Elena thought for a moment before answering. "One," she stuck out her index finger as she listed off the reasons. "you need to get out more." She stuck out a second finger. "Two, I need to get out more." She stuck out a third finger. "Three, you'd benefit heavily from this because I'd describe everything I see. Consider me your eyes for the day." She paused before sticking out a fourth finger. "Four, I'm fun to hang around with. I'd make sure it'd be a day you'd never forget." She assured before sticking out the fifth and final finger." And five, a crazy art teacher once told me that in order to be a great artist you needed to live. And if you can, drag people along with you. So Autumn, you appear to be my victim of dragging along. I gave you five reasons. Are they valid enough?"

All Elena heard was the soft breathing from the other line for a minute.

She gulped nervously. Had she been too quick to ask? Should she have waited? Oh god she was ruining it already, wasn't she?

"Autumn?" she spoke up, nerves clearly present.

"By what time should I be ready?"

Elena internally breathed a sigh of relief and her lungs and heart functioned normally again. "11 am." She replied.

"That's pretty early."

"We have a lot to see."

"You mean you have a lot to describe to me." Autumn corrected.

"Same thing." Elena shrugged.

"I'm probably going to bore you or piss you off an hour into this so-called adventure." The pianist assumed.

"Is that a challenge?" Elena taunted.

"No, it's a statement."

"Can said statement be proven?"

"You'll have to see it for yourself Saturday." Autumn smirked.

"Gladly."

Silence.

"Why are you being so nice to me?" Autumn spoke up, in a soft voice. "You don't even know me."

Elena continued sketching in her notebook. "Because…why shouldn't I?"

"Well, I'm not what you consider 'nice'…" Autumn trailed off.

"You don't say?" Elena smirked, chuckling.

"I didn't say you could agree."

"Watch me agree anyway." Elena taunted. "I'm agreeing. Is it pissing you off?"

"Yes, I'm definitely not giving back your scarf you gave me." Autumn teased.

"I thought you stole it." Elena retorted. "What happened to your daring nature, Castillo?"

"It's in there. You just have to rile me up enough to bring it out of me." She responded.

Elena smiled as she put the finishing touches to her sketch. "Challenge accepted."

"That wasn't a challenge." Autumn couldn't help but grin.

"Well it is now."

"What happened to the awkward girl that stuttered out in pure terror when I first met her?" Autumn teased playfully, laughing.

Elena's heart fluttered at the laugh. "She's in there. You just have to catch me by surprise to bring it out of me."

"Challenge accepted."

"That's not a very fun challenge."

"Then give me one."

Elena thought for a moment before saying. "Bring out the confident side of me."

There was a long, silent pause.

"Challenge accepted."

Elena grinned as she stared at the finishing sketch.

"I have another challenge for you, Elena." Autumn said after another silent pause.

Elena raised an eyebrow. "What is it?"

Autumn pursed her lips. "Make me see again."

"How do I do that?" Elena said, confused. "I can't make you see again."

"Keep it in mind. You'll know what that means soon enough." Autumn replied simply before hanging up without another word.

Elena put her phone to the side before staring at the sketch she drew.

It was of Autumn. And she stared intensely at the drawing before reaching an epiphany. Autumn wanted her to help her see again...in other words...

She wanted Elena to help her see the light.

CHAPTER FIVE

Sixth period rolled around and Elena was in her locker collecting her things to head to the library to study. That was the correct thing to do, however, the piano playing coming from across the hall made it impossible to come to that decision.

Shutting her locker, Elena practically ran to the music room (almost falling on the way there) to stop at the door. She stood there for a moment as she watched Autumn play the notes with such grace. Smiling, she stepped inside and chewed on her lower lip nervously.

Elena leaned against the piano, her hands touching the shiny and glossy grand piano as she felt the vibrations of each key playing. She closed her eyes and felt herself lose herself in the music with Autumn too. She swayed slightly to the music and felt each touch of emotion as Autumn's fingers kissed the black and white keys, because there was such profound love that Autumn had for the instrument. And Elena could feel it, and she wondered for a moment if Autumn could love a person like she loves the piano.

Once Autumn finished, she sighed in content. "That was 'Fin' by Mélanie Laurent." She said aloud, smirking. "I know you're here, Elena."

Elena was taken back, opening her eyes and widening them immediately. "How did you—"

"Ears like a bat." Autumn grinned. "When you're blind, you need to depend on your other senses to get around. My ears are not just my ears, they're my eyes too in a way." She explained. "That, and I heard your shoes squeaking when you nearly tripped." She chuckled.

Elena blushed a deep shade of red and looked away. "Interesting."

"Indeed." The other girl nodded.

"I see you're wearing my scarf." Elena noted, grinning even more. "It looks great on you."

Autumn's cheeks turned pink. "Yeah—you're not getting it back." She chuckled.

"It's fine, it suits you so much more than it suits me anyways." She shrugged, sitting on the piano bench next to Autumn. "So, um, do you have any idea what are you going to do for our assignment for art class?" Elena asked, deciding to initiate a conversation with the girl.

Autumn tapped her fingers against the ivory keys. "I was meaning to talk to you about that actually. See, in case you haven't noticed...I'm blind." Autumn said sarcastically.

"Wow, no way! I had no idea!" Elena exclaimed sarcastically right back.

Autumn chuckled. "Right. So obviously I have no idea what you look like. And other than descriptions, I visualize things in my head by touch. Because like I said, when you lack on one sense you have to depend on the other senses to make up for it." She paused. "Would you mind if I...touched your face?" Autumn asked. "Wow that sounded better in my head..."

Elena stayed quiet for a moment. If Autumn already made her feel like she was going to drop dead any second, if the girl touched her with those delicate hands on her one more time...she'd make it to heaven and back.

"Fuck, I shouldn't have asked. I'm sorry." Autumn immediately apologized, running a hand through her hair and taking of her glasses to rub her eyes.

"Do it." Elena spoke up again, nodding. "It's okay." She whispered.

Autumn quirked an eyebrow. "You sure? I don't want you to do it just because you feel obligated to. I know I'm not exactly the easiest partner—"

"I don't mind, really." Elena insisted. "We're partners so we need to help each other in any way possible. If you can properly do the assignment this way, then why not?" she shrugged.

Autumn nodded. "Okay." She agreed, taking out her sketchbook and sharpened pencil and placing it on top of the piano. She turned her body towards Elena so that she was facing her properly before reaching her hands out.

Elena visibly gulped and thanked that Autumn couldn't see her nervousness. She pushed herself closer to Autumn so that Autumn's hands could reach her face.

Delicately, Autumn's pale hands cupped Elena's face. Her fingers brushed her skin softly as she began tracing the outline of Elena's face and then working her way to her inner features.

Elena's breath hitched as Autumn's eyes looked at her brown ones intensely as she traced Elena's pink lips with her finger. She felt like her heart was about to burst out of her chest and her entire body had chills running down her body. Autumn's touch was so delicate.

Like Elena was a piece of fine china and she couldn't let it break one bit.

If only she knew.

"Can you smile for me?" Autumn asked, running her hand through one of Elena's brown locks.

"How do you know I'm not already smiling?" Elena retorted, breaking out into a smile.

Autumn laughed, smiling herself as her finger traced Elena's smile. She removed her hands from Elena's face and she reached for her sketchbook and pencil. "You're really pretty." She suddenly told Elena.

Elena blushed. "I—you can't possibly know that…" she trailed off, her insecurities getting the best of her.

Autumn looked up as she began on the sketch, tracing the outline of her drawing. "What? Because I'm blind?" she raised an eyebrow.

Elena nodded. "Well…yeah…" she mumbled awkwardly. "You can't see me. And if you did you would—"

"Think you're beautiful." Autumn cut off. "I think you should trust my word more than anyone's when I say you're beautiful."

The younger girl gulped. "Why should I?"

"Because…I don't need eyes to see your beauty. It's there. And I felt it. It felt beautiful. Therefore, you are." Autumn replied. "My eyes may be shit, but my hands function quite well. And either way, blind people are the most honest when it comes to determining beauty." She said matter-of-factly.

If Elena could marry words, she'd marry those. Autumn was surprising her more and more as they continued speaking.

"Why do you say that?" she asked.

"Because we think everyone's beautiful." Autumn replied. "Especially the ones that let us see them. All of them. There's no such thing as ugly, society invented that bullshit. There's only beautiful. And you're by far the most beautiful thing." Autumn blushed at her words and went back to working on her sketch.

Elena stared at Autumn with a stunned expression. No one's ever said something like that to her. Of course, her parents and the people closest to her would call her beautiful. But never in the way had Autumn called her beautiful.

Autumn was seeing right through Elena, was she really that readable. She sadly couldn't say the same about Autumn.

Despite the fact that they were getting along, Autumn hadn't opened up to her the way she would like to. Those walls were built on around her so that they'd be indestructible.

But even the most indestructible walls could be torn down, and Elena had to bring them down somehow. She found it intriguing how nice Autumn was to her.

Compared to how she was with the rest of the world, it made her feel special. Like it was a reserved kindness that Autumn had just for her. However, she wanted everyone else to witness this side of Autumn.

"I think the last question you asked me applies to me more." Elena blurted out.

Autumn looked up and raised an eyebrow. "What?"

"Why do I get the feeling you're about to mess up my entire life?" she recalled.

Autumn smiled. "Because I've already began." She spent the last couple of minutes placing the finishing touches on the drawing before showing it to Elena. "This is what I imagined when I touched your face…is this how you look like?"

Elena studied the drawing closely before her eyes widened, it looked surprisingly similar to her. She looked up at Autumn with a grin. "Wow. That looks a lot like me." She said, stunned.

"Then you're definitely beautiful." Autumn smiled softly.

Elena stared at the girl, a smile on her face. She was falling for her, she knew that more than ever. Autumn's determination to tell her how beautiful she is made her heart swell. No one ever tried so hard to show her that. But Autumn did, Autumn tried harder than anything.

She shook her head off her thoughts and coughed, placing the sketchbook on top of the piano again. "So...I think you should play me something." Elena suggested. "On the piano."

"I technically already did, remember?" Autumn grinned.

"Ah, yes. But this is different." Elena said as she stood up and walked over to the guitars stored in the farthest corner, picking one out and taking out the green guitar pick she carried around with her all the time.

She began tuning the guitar and placed the guitar on top of the piano before lifting herself up on top of the piano too.

Crossing her legs, she placed the piano on top of her leg and continued tuning the guitar. "I'm going to play with you." She finally said when she finished tuning the guitar.

Autumn raised an eyebrow but nodded slowly. "Okay?" she chuckled. "What do you want me to play?" she asked, positioning her hands on the keys.

"Just... follow along." Elena told her, smiling softly.

"Okay." Autumn whispered.

Elena smiled before beginning to fingerpick the strings of the guitar, her fingers knowing where to play next before she even did. Autumn listened intently to the song Elena played and followed along with the piano with a smile. The duo played the song until Elena stopped playing and once they finished the song, Elena was the one to sigh in content.

"That was perfect." She commented.

"Yeah." Autumn breathed out, gulping. Elena suddenly noticed how nervous and tense she seemed and she began to wonder why. Autumn put her glasses back on and pushed them up her nose before collecting her sketchbook and messenger bag. "I-I have to go. I have a...thing."

Elena swung off the piano and raised an eyebrow. "Thing?"

"A-an important thing. And I'm late for it." Autumn muttered before taking her cane out and letting it help her navigate her way. "You were really good. I should go now." Autumn stammered before exiting the music room, leave Elena incredibly confused.

"It's weird." Elena told Maya and Phoenix later on as they sat on the steps of Elena's house. "One moment, she's being freaking perfect and insisting that I'm beautiful. And the next, she's all shaky and nervous and getting out of the room so quickly. Like she'd catch something for being there."

"Oh, she caught something all right." Phoenix snorted. "It's the love bug. Bit her right in the—"

"Phoenix!" Maya exclaimed, and the younger girl only raised her arms in surrender. "I think what Phoenix means is that…maybe you're not the only one catching feelings."

Elena's eyes widened. "Wait—are you saying Autumn might like me back?"

"Exactly what we're saying." Phoenix replied. "I mean, come on. Y'all did a song together and she was touching your face and shit and if that's not indication enough, then what is?"

"Not just that," Maya added. "but Autumn truly acts like a whole different person around you. It's not the Autumn we know and hate. It's…it's like she has a reserved kindness just for you. She's not even that nice to Emma who's her best friend. She's different around you. And how she acts so different around you in the short amount of time you've known each other only indicates one thing…Autumn likes you."

Elena couldn't quite wrap her head around it. How could someone like Autumn fall for someone like her? Elena wasn't as special. She was just another girl who had way too much time on her hands. And with that time, she spent it painting, playing guitar, and playing pretend with her little sister.

Autumn was like the moon and she was a star; Autumn was the biggest and brightest of them all while she was just another one of the many bright-lit stars. How could someone like Autumn like someone as insignificant as her? She couldn't quite comprehend it.

"You're thinking, should that scare us?" Maya asked.

"I don't know…it just seems surreal. How can Autumn like someone like me?" Elena questioned.

"How could she not?" Phoenix retorted. "You're such an amazing person and if anything, the whole world should fall for you." She smirked. "I mean…with that ass…"

"Phoenix!" Maya exclaimed. "This is not the time!"

"God, lighten up!" Phoenix rolled her eyes. "I'm trying to bring light into the situation."

"I'm about to burn that light into your face, don't try me, princess." Maya warned playfully.

They both turned to Elena in hopes that it would crack a smile, but their efforts seemed to fail. "Damn…she's thinking a lot." Phoenix whispered to Maya as they watched Elena place her elbows on her thighs to support her head resting on her hands. She seemed deep in thought, thinking of none other than the girl who was definitely messing her up.

"One minute she's telling me that I'm beautiful and the next, she freaks out and runs. I fear that I'll fall in deeper than I expect, but she won't be falling with me. I mean, how do I even know if she's into girls in the slightest? It could just be some hopeless fantasy I have…because a girl like Autumn cannot fall for a girl like me." Elena sighed in frustration.

"I hate this, because she sees right through me and yet I can't see right through her. She's got perfectly kept walls that I am not even sure are capable of breaking. What if all of this just isn't worth the hard work?"

"But what if it is?" Maya placed a comforting hand on Elena's shoulder. "Look, Autumn has never rubbed me the right way—"

"Yowza!" Phoenix smirked, causing Maya to glare at her. "Sorry."

"But from what I've gathered, you two have something there. And whether you choose to ignore it or not is up to you, but sometimes the greatest risks come with the greatest rewards. You don't get to choose who you fall for, you just have to deal with it correctly. Take it slow, because from what I see Autumn is just as terrified as you are over this feeling. There's a connection, you can't deny it."

"And also, Autumn would be a total idiot for letting a catch like you go. She sees something in you, and I know that because Autumn is acting different with you. She is never this nice to someone she just met. If this was any other person, Autumn would've had them running to their mamas so quickly. She's got the hardest of hearts but I think you're softening it up a bit." Phoenix told her, smiling at Elena.

Elena smiled back, unable to resist it. "You think so?"

"Oh heck yes! Go for it, Lena, it's better than sitting here with us thinking of all the 'What ifs'." Phoenix encouraged.

Elena could hear Mrs. Freya's voice in the back of her mind.

"Get out there. Make mistakes and then make 10 more. Smile more. Cry more. Get angry more. Fall in love and then get your heart broken. Make friends and lose friends. Start making adventures for yourself and drag along others with you. You'll never see the greatness in life unless you search for it yourself. So get out there kid, live."

"You're right." She agreed. "I can't live in a shell my entire life, I need to break it. Starting now." She said affirmatively.

Phoenix patted Elena's back with a proud smile while Maya grinned. "Good for you, Lena. Count us in for anything, whatever it is we will help you as best we can."

"Yeah," Phoenix agreed. "Consider us your wing women." She winked.

Elena smiled, enveloping the two in a hug. "You guys are so amazing. We haven't been friends for more than a week and you're already being so supportive and trustworthy. I owe you guys so much!"

"Get me some hot wings and you won't owe me a thing." Maya joked.

"You and your hot wings, gosh." Phoenix rolled her eyes playfully. "But Lena...you can repay me with Beyoncé tickets..."

"I only have a green guitar pick in my pocket, try again." Elena teased, suddenly finding herself in a much improved mood than before.

Autumn, on the other hand, was suffering an inner turmoil. "Breathe, Autumn!" Emma instructed as they sat in Autumn's bed. "What is up with you? Talk to me."

Autumn was so unlike herself, she was fidgeting nervously and stuttering and she had a look of terror on her face. She pushed up her glasses with shaky hands. "N-nothing." She muttered. "I'll get over it." She hoped she would at least.

She didn't know when or how really, but the time spent with Elena in that music room gave her a feeling she couldn't quite describe yet.

But it was a nice feeling because for the first time in so long, Autumn was so close to just letting her guard down in front of Elena. She made it so damn easy.

Elena was so nice to her even if Autumn could give her a billion reasons not to be. But that wasn't what struck her most about Elena, what struck her the most was that Elena didn't acknowledge the fact that Autumn was blind as much. Or revolve everything around her disability. She was treated like a regular person and Autumn felt relieved that finally someone saw something more in her.

"You've been acting like this since sixth period ended. It's like you've seen a ghost, and you're already pale enough as it is so this is a new shade of white." Emma teased.

Autumn chewed on her lower lip. "It's complicated."

"Oh come on Autumn, you know that I know complicated left and right. Shoot, I live complicated. Throw it at me, I'm your best friend. You know you can tell me anything, right?" Emma insisted, secretly hoping Autumn would finally open up to her about something.

Autumn let out a shaky breath. "Do you think it's possible to live again? Metaphorically speaking. "she asked. "I mean, do you think that even in the lowest point of your life, you can still find one thing that makes that lowest point...less low? Does this make sense?"

Emma thought for a moment. "Yes. Of course. Life sucks sometimes, but there's always going to be something good. Nothing can suck forever, there's always going to come a time where you suddenly start to feel like you're alive again." She shrugged, looking at Autumn curiously.

"Are you feeling this way? Do you feel more content with yourself?" Emma asked.

"But what if you're scared to live again? What if you feel like there's a less chance of getting hurt if you just choose to live under the radar? Isn't that better? Not getting hurt. Emotional pain is worse than physical pain." Autumn continued.

Emma lied down next to Autumn and looked up at the ceiling. "There's always fear in living again. But when you finally feel and taste and experience what if feels like to live again, you'll wonder why you were so afraid in the first place. Don't let anything stop you from living. You're capable of living, I know you are." She smiled softly.

"Have you ever thought that maybe you're already dealing with pain? That it's just so much you're enduring that you don't even feel it anymore? Like you're numbed by pain?" Emma questioned.

"Still...living is hard." She argues weakly. "I...I never thought about it that way." Autumn lifted up her head and both girls were staring straight up at the ceiling. "Do you think I've numbed my pain?"

"Everything's hard, but at the same time nothing is hard. It's all about perspective and how you deal with it." Emma replied.

"Yes." Emma whispered in answer to Autumn's question. "You've numbed your pain so much, you pushed everyone and everything away and let your numbness create a wall. A hard, indestructible wall I've spent years trying to break..."

"Emma..." Autumn whispered. "Do you think my walls could break? Do you think someone can break them?"

"Yes, everything is destructible. Including your perfectly kept walls. If you let your walls break, you'll start living. And the numbness will go away and the Autumn I know will come back." Emma paused. "Do you think someone's breaking your walls, Autumn?"

"I..." Autumn trailed off. "I think there's a tiny crack. But I'm trying to cover it up again."

"Why?"

"Because I can't possibly…"

"Can't possibly what?" Emma insisted.

"I can't possibly…fall for someone." Autumn confessed.

Emma turned to her, wide eyes. "You like someone?"

"I don't know…I'm not sure what to make of it yet. It terrifies me." Autumn chewed on her lip.

"Well…what do you feel when you're around that person?" Emma asked, resting her head on her hand.

Autumn thought for a moment before answering. "I feel like they woke up my body and soul. And…they make me feel like I can tell them anything. Sometimes, like I don't even need words to tell them. Because I feel like they're capable of seeing me—*really* seeing me. And there's these little sparks of electricity when I touch that person, and those little sparks makes me want to touch them more. I'm also different. They make me want to be different. I can't be this angry person to them, so I show them a different side of myself I hadn't brought out in so long. They make me smile and laugh and it feels nice. They also make me want to prove to them heavily how amazing they are even if they can't see it for themselves. I feel different, like a woken up Autumn you could say…"

Emma smiled. "That, Autumn, isn't something you're getting rid of anytime soon." She chuckled. "You're experiencing the possibility of being in love. But for now, it's just a crush. And I think you should go for it."

Autumn shook her head. "I can't."

"Why not?"

"They're not ready—I'm not ready."

"Ready for what?" Emma questioned.

Autumn played with the special scarf that hung around her neck, sighing. "To get my entire life messed up."

CHAPTER SIX

"Invite them to sit with us." Maya told Elena as the trio glanced over at Emma and Autumn who were sitting in their regular table.

Elena turned red and her eyes widened. "Do you want to kill me?" she gulped.

"What's the worst that can happen?" Phoenix asked. "I mean, you *can* fuck up horribly…" Elena turned to her with a terrified look. "But there's always the possibility that you'll be fine!"

"I can't. I can't do it. I'll become this stuttering mess that can barely say one coherent sentence and I'll just embarrass myself." The Latina declared, putting her hands on her face.

Maya and Phoenix shared a knowing look before Maya began waving her arms to Emma. "Emma!"

Elena removed her hands from her face immediately and turned to her friend. "What. Are. You. *Doing*?" she squeaked, her face turning to a darker shade of red.

"Being a great wing woman." Maya smirked as Emma walked up to them.

"Hey girls, what's up?" Emma asked with a grin.

"Come sit with us! You and Autumn." Phoenix exclaimed.

Emma looked taken back. "Yeah? You want us to sit with you...are you sure? You know what happened last time we sat with you..." she trailed off, throwing an apologetic look.

Phoenix shrugged. "We're over it, consider it thrown under the rug! I'm sure it can't be as bad!" Phoenix assured.

Elena casted a look to Phoenix. There were a variety things that could go wrong at this point.

"Come sit with us, Emma! It'll be fun, we won't take anything Autumn says to heart. Get your ass here, short stack." Phoenix teased.

Emma laughed, biting her lower lip as she pondered for a moment before nodding. "Fine. I'll be right back." She told the girls before walking back to the table where Autumn was and they watched the two girls talking, Autumn looking unsure.

Elena groaned. "I hate you guys so much right now."

"That's a lie." Maya argued. "Come on, Elena, what's the difference of you talking to Autumn now as opposed to when you two are alone?"

"That's the thing, I *don't* know how she is when she's with me and other people. There are a million things that could happen right now when they come over here and I don't think my lungs are supplied with enough air!" Elena exclaimed, a look of panic on her face.

Phoenix snapped her fingers in front of Elena's face. "Lena, *breathe.* It's just us girls having lunch together. Just think of it as something as casual as that." She told her.

"*Just* casual?" Elena exclaimed. "It's not *just* casual when one of the girls I'm having lunch with I have a huge cru--

"Hey girls! Thanks for inviting us over to sit with you guys." Emma greeted with Autumn beside her.

"Even if some of us were brought here against our own will…" Autumn muttered, causing Emma to elbow her ribs as discretely as possible. "Ow!" she exclaimed through gritted teeth, rubbing her side as the two girls sat down.

Maya and Phoenix gave a feign laugh as they glanced at Elena who wouldn't stop blushing with Autumn sitting right in front of her. "So, Autumn and Elena, you guys take AP Art together, right?" Phoenix asked, starting up a conversation. "That's pretty cool."

Elena glanced over at Autumn, her eyes lingering a little too long. Emma noticed this quickly and quirked up an eyebrow in curiosity.

There was staring, but then there was *staring*…and the way Elena was staring indicated it wasn't a platonic stare. She smirked slightly and looked away, resting her head on her hand.

Elena shook her head as her eyes looked away from Autumn. "Um—yeah, we're taking the same class. We're partners for an assignment." She replied awkwardly. Autumn wasn't saying anything, just fiddling with the sleeves of her grey jumper.

"Oh really? Do tell." Emma asked interestedly.

"Um," Elena stammered. "we have to create an art piece involving our partner and what we've learned about them." She explained. "So we've been getting to know each other since then."

Emma looked amused. "What have you learned?" Autumn looked up interestedly to hear what Emma would say.

Elena gulped. "Well, Autumn's a sea shell collector." She smiled softly. "They're pretty cool sea shells, actually, and she says she really likes collecting them because they remind her of the beach—which she's never gone to. So now every time she has a sea shell she always feels the texture of it to know whether it's a sea shell she has or doesn't have." She paused to think of something else. "She loves fireflies, too. She told me that they have a really special meaning to her."

Autumn had shared that fireflies had a special meaning to her because her grandmother had died of cancer when she was nine years old. Her grandmother was diagnosed with cancer a year after she was diagnosed with Retinoblastoma. So her grandmother told her: "Yo vivo si tú vives". Translating to, "I'll live if you live".

Autumn lived by those words religiously until she was declared cancer-free when she was 10. Her grandma was still suffering from the fatal disease and Autumn told her, "I'm so close to living again, so you need to live with me now too." Unfortunately, her grandmother wasn't able to promise her that and passed away.

It's another reason Autumn had so much anger in her, because not only was Autumn losing her vision but she also lost someone she loved dearly at the same time.

After her grandmother passed away, Autumn's vision grew continuously worse. But before she lost it completely, Autumn saw a fireflies. Billions of them, she described with a dreamy look in her eye.

Her grandmother loved fireflies, so she found those fireflies to be her grandmother giving her a sign that she was still here for Autumn.

Autumn also shared to Elena that she wanted to get a tattoo of a firefly and the words her deceased grandmother constantly repeated to her: "Yo vivo si tú vives".

Elena was taken back when Autumn shared something so personal to her, but she felt special knowing she trusted her enough to tell her.

Autumn gave a small smile and Elena continued. "She's also got an unhealthy obsession with classical music and the piano. I think she needs help." She teased, causing Autumn to chuckle quietly. "But I'm sure she's got a bomb ass taste in music that I'd love to listen to one day."

The other three girls watched the small interaction with amused expressions, the three looking at each other with smirks.

Elena grinned, staring at Autumn. "She's also good with words, even if she rarely shares them. But she's incredibly eloquent when she speaks, it's awesome. Autumn's also amazing at drawing, she draws what she sees in her mind and if that's not incredible I honestly don't know what is." Autumn felt a blush creep onto her cheeks and bowed her head down so no one would notice it.

Emma hummed, smirking. "Looks like you two have really gotten to know each other, huh?"

Elena had still not taken her eyes off Autumn and smiled, nodding. "Yeah…we have."

"Fascinating." Emma commented. She was definitely going to talk to Autumn about this little interaction later.

The five girls spent the rest of lunch talking animatedly about everything their minds would come up with. Autumn was quiet, and surprisingly had no snarky words to throw to any of the other girls.

"I think Autumn and Emma should sit with us permanently." Maya commented as the lunch period ended. "You make a nice addition here."

Phoenix nodded in agreement. "I think so too. Join our trio and make it a five…o?" she furrowed her eyebrows in confusion. "But seriously, we should plan a day for us to hang out. Like a movie night." She suggested. She whispered to Elena. "And it gives you more leisure to stare at Autumn." Elena turned red and glared at her friend who smirked.

"I like that idea." Emma smiled. "What do you think, A?" she asked, turning to her friend.

Autumn shrugged. "Sure, I guess. Just don't expect me to be very into the movies I can't see at all." she said in a monotone voice.

"Oh shit, right." Phoenix mumbled. "Well, we could always do something else."

"There's not much you can do with a blind girl." Autumn told her. "There's really not *anything* you can do with a blind girl. So don't try to accommodate me. Emma can join your group, she'll be much happier."

"Autumn—"Emma began but Autumn raised her hand to her to indicate she wasn't done.

"I get it, you felt bad for the poor blind girl and her caretaker." Autumn spat. "But let's cut the bullshit and fully admit to ourselves that you guys would rather slit your throats than become besties with me. Emma can happily join your little group and become a cheery and annoyingly loud little foursome. Don't burden yourselves and add me in the group out of pity." She said before letting herself out of the table.

Emma sighed and called after Autumn who ignored her completely, exiting the lunchroom. She turned to the other speechless girls. "I am *so* sorry. I know you guys aren't doing it out of pity and I'm sure she doesn't think so either—"

"Don't apologize, Emma." Maya cut off, smiling sympathetically. "It's okay.

Emma nodded hesitantly. "I should go look for her—"

"I'll go." Elena spoke up, making eye contact with Emma. "I'll go." She said affirmatively, nodding.

"You sure?" the tiny girl asked, unsure. "You don't have to. "

"I want to." Elena insisted, standing up.

The other girl nodded slowly. "Okay, good luck." She told Elena before she went after Autumn.

Once Elena left, Phoenix turned to the other two girls. "Okay, so here's what's going on," Phoenix began. "Elena has a thing for Autumn, she *really* likes her."

Emma nodded. "I figured as much. The way she looks at her it's not how I look at a friend." She told them.

"Right." Maya nodded. "So do you think there's a chance Autumn might feel the same way? You know...does she dig girls?"

Emma thought for a moment. "Honestly? I don't know. Autumn's never displayed an interest in anyone." She paused. "Well, until now. She told me the other day how she had a crush on someone. But she never told me who." Her eyes suddenly widened. "Holy crap, do you think her crush might be Elena?"

"That's what we're trying to find out." Phoenix clarified. "But from what I see, I think it might be true. Autumn's different with Elena, she's kinder to her. Like a reserved kindness just for her. So maybe we're right and Autumn might be crushing on Elena too."

Maya chewed on her lower lip and spoke out her thoughts. "If that's the case, it's going to get *really* complicated for them two." Emma and Phoenix looked at her expectantly for her to continue. "Think about it: Autumn already made an outburst because she thinks we want to be friends with her out of pity. So what if she thinks it's the same case for Elena? That it's only out of pity?"

"You are right there…" Phoenix agreed.

"Not just that, but can they handle it?" Maya questioned. "We can deny it all we want, but we know that Autumn's disability is going to cause complications. They can never be a normal couple if they do try dating. Because they can't just go out and see a movie like any other couple, or go to an art museum or any of that." The dark-skinned girl shrugged. "I don't know, but I'm just saying…it's going to be hard."

"You're right…but at the same time you're not." Emma argued. "If there's enough spark and enough love, they can handle anything." She paused. "I'm not saying it's going to be easy, because it's clearly not. But I don't think we should try to stop anything that could be developing there. "she told them. "You don't know how long I've wanted Autumn to finally be happy again," she confessed. "and I know I'm not the person that can fully bring her back." She said sadly.

"But if Elena is that person instead, then that's fine. I just want my best friend back."

"Even if they get hurt in the process?" Phoenix questioned.

Emma shrugged, looking at the two girls. "Sometimes you need a little pain in your life." She paused. "But all Autumn's known for most of her life *is* pain. Physical, emotional…you name it, she's had it." She told them. "A little more won't hurt, right?"

Elena walked down the hallways and walked to the music room to see Autumn sitting on the floor beside the piano and wiping her cheek with her sleeve, she had been crying.

"Hey." Elena spoke up, approaching the other girl cautiously.

Autumn immediately straightened up and tried to appear like she hadn't been a crying mess. "That was some dramatic exit you pulled there." She joked lightly, but Autumn wasn't laughing. "Bad joke, sorry. "She apologized.

"You're full of them." Autumn murmured.

Elena chuckled. "Indeed." She agreed.

They stayed quiet for a moment before Elena spoke up again, leaning against the piano and looking down at Autumn. "Do you really feel that way?"

"Feel what way?"

"Like people just want to be friends with you out of pity?" Elena questioned. "Because I have a lot of arguments to that notion."

"Please don't act like my fucking therapist right now."

"I'm not." Elena argued. "I'm acting like a friend."

"Don't." Autumn said quietly. "Just go back to your friends and leave me alone."

Elena plopped down next to her. "I have a friend right here that needs me. And if I go back there to *our* friends, then it's with you right next to me." She insisted.

"Stubborn ass." Autumn muttered.

Elena shrugged. "I could say the same thing." She retorted, looking at Autumn. "Talk to me."

"How about no?" Autumn bit back. "There's nothing *to* talk about and there's nothing that I want to *willingly* talk about."

"Why not?"

Autumn sighed frustratingly. "Because I don't want to fucking talk about how I'm a fucking burden to everyone!" she snapped. "For most of my life, everything's been fucking accommodated to me and I'm just treated like a sick little puppy that can't do anything. That's because I *can't* do anything, I'm fucking blind. I'm just a pity case. I can't live properly because everything I do, I have to do cautiously. I can't just let it be. I can't…I fucking can't." she banged her fists against her thighs and sighed.

Elena stared at her for a moment. "You're not a burden."

"You don't fucking know me, Díaz."

"I don't need to." Elena replied. "Because no one's a burden. You're still here for a reason. You could've died, Autumn, at any moment the little shit known as Cancer could've taken your life…but it didn't. And there's a reason for that, because you still have a purpose here." She told her. "And you'll never know what you're purpose is unless you break out of that hard ass shell you've pushed yourself in. You *are* capable of living, you just don't know how." She paused, intertwining her hand with Autumn's and feeling her heart flutter and her stomach tighten. "So let me teach you."

Autumn stayed quiet for a while, the two just sitting on the floor with their hands intertwined. Elena pursed her lips before speaking up again. "Yo vivo si tú vives."

Autumn's head darted up and she felt her throat tighten, a sob wanting to escape but she swallowed it like every other emotion that threatened to come out. What struck her the most was that Elena remembered and that Elena *meant* what she said. And Autumn wanted to believe it, she *really* did.

But she was afraid she'd lose Elena just like she had lost her grandmother. She'd known Elena for a such a short time, but already she felt a connection with her. She couldn't pinpoint how or when they connected, but they did. And she didn't want it to end.

"You can't promise me that." She whispered.

"Why not?"

"Because I've had that promise broken before."

Elena squeezed her hand. "I won't break that promise. Trust me."

"I want to, but I can't." Autumn told her.

"Why not?"

"Because it's hard for me to trust people."

Elena licked her lips. "You know how you said you wanted to live?" Autumn nodded. "Consider the first step towards living is trusting me."

"I want to but—"

"Then do it." Elena insisted. "Let me teach you something." She paused, letting go of Autumn's hand. "Say whatever." She commanded.

"What?" Autumn asked, confused.

"Say whatever." she repeated.

"Why?"

"Because…you need to learn to just not give a shit sometimes." Elena replied. "Contrary to popular belief, when people say 'Whatever', they really don't mean it. Because a part of them still think, 'Wait no, it's not whatever…it's something!'" Elena said dramatically. "Most people don't grasp the concept of not giving a single fuck. But I do. I learned to not give a fuck about some things because they're just not worth giving a fuck about." She shrugged. "When you let everything become your problem you're just bitter and miserable. So say it. Say, 'Whatever'."

Autumn was still confused but said it anyway. "Whatever?"

"It's not a question, it's a statement." Elena corrected. "Allow me to demonstrate…" she smirked, coughing. "Whatever." Elena said casually, throwing her arms out. She turned to Autumn. "Now you say it."

"Okay…" Autumn trailed off before exhaling and preparing herself to say the word. "Whatever." She said again, crossing her arms.

Elena nodded approvingly. "Good. Now say it again."

"Whatever." Autumn said again, a small smile appearing.

Elena smiled as well. "Yeah! There you go!" she praised. "Say it louder."

"Whatever." Autumn said, raising her voice slightly.

"Louder!" Elena exclaimed.

"Whatever!" Autumn grinned, saying it louder than before.

"Louderrrr!"

"Whatever!" Autumn said, an octave more louder.

Elena grinned. "Yeah! Now shout it!" she told her. "Come on!"

"WHATEVER!"

"WHATEVER!" Elena shouted too.

"WHATEVER!" Autumn threw her hands up.

"WHATEVER!"

"WHAT. EV. ER." Autumn shouted, enunciating each word.

"Yes! There you go!" Elena praised.

The two girls continued shouting the word back at each other and Autumn had never felt so free. And all she was doing was screaming "Whatever" like a complete maniac.

It wasn't until a teacher came in to the room to nag at the girls to tune it down and not shout because they were interrupting other students who were trying to learn. The two girls nodded and once he left, a warning look plastered on his face as he walked away.

Once he was gone, Autumn and Elena burst out laughing. Autumn couldn't stop laughing and even had to wipe some tears away from her eyes because she was laughing so much.

Elena could safely say that Autumn had the best laugh in the universe, it could cure anything. She'd work hard to make sure she'd hear it way more often.

Once their laughing died down, Elena decided to speak again. "How did that feel?"

"Whatever." Autumn shrugged, smirking.

Elena chuckled, rolling her eyes playfully. "Okay, I think you're grasping the concept of 'Whatever' a little *too much* now."

"Whatever." Autumn grinned, giggling.

"Seriously, stop it."

"Whatever."

"Autumn Castillo…" she warned, but her smile still intact.

"What. Ev. Er." She teased.

"I have created a monster." Elena said dramatically and Autumn laughed again.

"No, but seriously…" Autumn said, her playfulness toning down. "Thank you, I needed that."

"What are friends for?" Elena shrugged, feeling slightly disappointed to say 'friend'. But she'd rather be friends with Autumn than nothing at all.

Autumn nodded slowly. "I'm glad you moved here."

Elena blushed, breaking into a grin. "Me too." She whispered.

The two stayed quiet for a moment, simply appreciating each other's presence. Suddenly, Autumn leaned in to kiss Elena's cheek. Elena felt her heart stop for a moment and her lungs lose oxygen when she felt Autumn's soft and warm lips touch her cheek.

"Wha—what was that for?" Elena stuttered, her cheeks turning red.

Autumn shrugged, standing up and taking her cane out in front of her. "Just…a little token of gratitude."

"Okay." Elena breathed out.

"Okay." Autumn smiled. "I actually do have an important thing this period to go to. Guidance counselor." She explained. "I'll catch you later." She said as she walked out of the music room.

"Are we still on for Saturday?" Elena asked quickly.

Autumn stopped and grinned. "Only if you are."

"Then Saturday's a go." Elena smiled cheekily.

"It's a go." Autumn confirmed as she stopped for a moment by the door. "Bye Ellie."

Elena blushed at the nickname that she quickly took a liking to. "Bye Autumn." And the girl slowly left, the Miami native hearing the faint sounds of a cane tapping as Autumn guided herself down the hallway. And Elena spent the rest of the period sitting there on the floor beside the piano, a goofy grin on her face. She faintly touched the cheek Autumn's lips had kissed and exhaled. "You're fucked."

CHAPTER SEVEN

Elena spent the next two days memorizing New York City's streets and attractions to make sure the day spent with Autumn was a day well spent. It really wasn't as hard to memorize, being that New York City was laid out like a gridline.

Plus, New York was divided into five boroughs: Brooklyn, Queens, Staten Island, the Bronx, and Manhattan. So memorizing it wasn't the most complicated thing in the world. And she had to learn her way around the grand city sooner or later.

She even had Phoenix and Maya quiz her constantly and teach her the ways to get around involving the bus, the subway, and her own two feet.

"Avoid hauling a taxi cab as much as you can." Maya had advised. "That shit's expensive and not to mention that the cab drivers are rude as fuck—even ruder than Phoenix!"

"Who?" Phoenix questioned.

"I said you—"

"*The fuck asked you?*" Phoenix cut off midway through Maya's response, and the two went at it with their notorious bickering.

Regardless, they had helped Elena out when it came to planning out the day-long adventure around New York City.

"You do realize that this is technically a date, right?" Phoenix smirked as they helped Elena pick out an outfit in the girl's spacious room.

Phoenix was the most shocked one at how big her room was. *"In my house, we'd have 10 of us sharing this room!"* she had exclaimed as she looked around.

Elena blushed and tried to suppress the large grin on her face, but in no way working out in her favor. "We're just friends." She clarified, even though the three girls knew that it wasn't something Elena planned to keep that way for long.

Maya snickered as Phoenix rolled her eyes. "Lena, what rhymes with horseshit?" Phoenix asked as she looked through Elena's closet to pick out an outfit whilst Maya helped with Elena's hair and make-up.

"I'm afraid to answer." Elena asked as she and Maya shared a confused look.

"Smart choice." Maya agreed.

Phoenix shrugged, continuing anyway. "It rhymes with *bullshit*." She clarified. "Why? Because it's such bullshiterry that you and Autumn are spending the *whole* day together as 'just friends'!" Phoenix said, using her hands as quotation marks. "If Jacob had asked *me* to spend a whole day with him, it definitely wouldn't be just as friends. Not just that, but you don't see her as just a friend. You see her as something else."

"You and Jacob were never friends to begin with." Maya retorted.

"*Not* the point!" Phoenix exclaimed. "The point *is*...I think you should take advantage of this day."

"To do what?" Elena asked obliviously as Maya brushed her long hair.

Phoenix turned to her with a raised eyebrow as if she was stating the obvious. "To make your move!" Elena still stared at her friend with a lost expression on her face. "Are you serious?" Phoenix questioned. "Have you ever even dated anyone before?"

Elena turned red and shook her head. "No..." she muttered.

Phoenix's mouth gaped. "You mean to tell me you haven't let *anyone* get a piece of *that ass* yet?" she exclaimed dramatically.

"Your weird fetish for my butt is getting out of hand." Elena said seriously. "But no, I've never dated anyone before. I mean, I *have* been kissed before, but never dated anyone. I've gone on a couple dates but they never went farther than that because I never felt anything for them." She explained.

"But you do with this date." Maya stated, looking at Elena with an expectant look.

"It's not a date!" Elena exclaimed.

"Do we need to go back to what rhymes with horseshit?" Phoenix questioned. "Call it what you want, but we both know this isn't just two friends hanging out. What *you* feel is in *no* way platonic. You don't see Autumn as a friend or sister, you see her as the girl you want to take to your bed to—"

"Phoenix!" Maya looked at her with wide eyes. "Hold back on the details please! I don't want to know!"

"Neither do I." Elena said with wide eyes.

Phoenix shrugged. "Okay, sorry." She apologized, but not meaning it. "But let's be real, just friends don't spend two days memorizing New York front and back and going out of her way to make this day extra special. *Just friends* don't do that."

Elena stayed quiet, knowing very well that Phoenix was right. "I'm going to agree with Phoenix here." Maya agreed. "You and Autumn will never be *just friends*. As hard as you try to make things seem otherwise…it's just not going to happen." She paused, neatly placing Elena's hair into a loose, but still perfectly in place, side ponytail. "We were talking to Emma after Autumn's outburst and she knows you have a thing for Autumn. And she told us Autumn has a crush on someone, but Autumn wouldn't tell her who." She told Elena.

Elena suddenly frowned and looked down. "Oh. That's...good for her, right?" she said, disappointment evident in her voice. She was completely oblivious to the fact that Phoenix and Maya were referencing that Elena was more than likely to be Autumn's mystery crush.

Phoenix face palmed as she took out a red daisy skater dress and placed it on Elena's bed. "We're talking about *you,* fool!" she laughed. "We think *you're* Autumn's mystery crush."

Elena's eyes widened. "M-me?" she stuttered out. "But Autumn hasn't...she—"

"You two are the most oblivious people I've ever met." Maya commented, chuckling. "The way you act around each other...it's in no way platonic. So let's stop fooling ourselves."

Elena blushed. "Okay...so what if she does? That doesn't mean Autumn's going to confess she likes me anytime soon."

"That's what we're getting at..." Maya trailed off. "She won't do it, so you should."

Elena's eyes widened even more as she sputtered out. "W-what? Y-y-you want me t-to w-what?"

"Tell her how you feel. You guys have gotten pretty close in the short amount of the time you've known each other, you're closer than Autumn and Emma are." Maya smiled sadly, imagining how hard that must be for Emma. "It's sad to say, but it's true."

Elena shook her head. "It's not that easy. I need time." She sighed. "The feelings are recent and I need to figure out everything. I told you guys, I want to take this slow. I can't ruin what we have going on right now. I rather be her friend if I don't have the chance to be anything else, because I care about her and I think she needs a friend more than anything."

Maya shrugged. "I guess we can understand that. Just don't take *too* much time. Because if you do she's going to think you don't have an interest in her and she'll move on."

Elena nodded. "I won't." she told her, looking at the outfit Phoenix had picked out. "I like it." She smiled.

"If only Autumn could see it, she'd probably want your body faster than I can say yowza." Phoenix smirked.

Elena rolled her eyes as she stepped into her bathroom to quickly change into her outfit. She came out of the bathroom and Maya told her to sit down on her bed so she can put on some make-up, which wasn't over-the-top. They ended the outfit by putting on a white scarf around her neck.

"You look...*amazing*." Maya gushed.

"Makes your ass—"Phoenix began with a playful smirk.

"Say one more thing about my butt, Phoenix..." Elena threatened with a chuckle, playfully glaring. "But thank you." Elena said, chewing her lip and looking at the full-length mirror in front of her. "I look...really nice." She smiled softly, still not fully capable of calling herself pretty or beautiful.

"You do look amazing." Maya grinned. "We should probably get going. Phoenix and I are heading to the dance studio later on today, dance classes and all that jazz." She told Elena. "But we will be awaiting your call to tell us how your date went."

This time Elena didn't even try to argue and say it wasn't a date because as hard as she tried, her friends were stubborn and would continue to insist it was a date. She nodded. "Of course." She grinned. "I'll go all out on the details."

"Not *too* much though." Phoenix teased, winking.

Elena rolled her eyes. "I'll try to refrain how I shoved my tongue down Autumn's throat."

"Or other places…" Phoenix trailed off innocently.

Elena whacked Phoenix's arm and shook her head, her cheeks red. "Phoenix!" she scorned, laughing. "You're such a little perv. Are you 100% sure you're even straight?"

"Why? Are you offering a little experimenting?" Phoenix winked, laughing. "I'm kidding, Lena, I'm kidding. Sorry to break it to you."

Elena rolled her eyes, shaking her head. "My heart will live." She giggled. "It'll ache for you…but it'll live."

Maya shook her head, laughing. "You guys are ridiculous."

"Ridiculously in love!" Phoenix exclaimed, pulling Elena in for a hug. Elena only laughed, hugging Phoenix back.

"Okay, Hale." Maya rolled her eyes, pulling the taller girl away from Elena. "We should get going, Elena has to go pick up Autumn soon so we need to get her to it."

Phoenix pretended to struggle as she held her hand out to Elena as Maya pulled her out of Elena's room. "Write me, my love! Don't forget me!" she called out dramatically.

Elena laughed as she placed her hand over her heart. "I will, I promise! I'll write you 365 letters, one for every day that I'll miss you!" she played along.

Phoenix laughed. "Have fun, Lena." She told her as they said their goodbyes and Maya and Phoenix finally left.

Elena couldn't wipe the grin off her face as she grabbed her bag and headed downstairs, walking to the living room where her mother was.

"I'm going to Autumn's to pick her up. I probably won't be back until much later, it's a whole-day kind of thing." She spoke up, causing her mother to look up from her book.

Elena had talked to her mother all about Autumn —maybe a little too much. But her mother found it wonderful how quickly Elena was adjusting to the move.

Ana nodded and waved for Elena to walk over to her. Elena walked over to her mom, sitting next to her. "Let me talk to you quickly before you go." Ana instructed.

Elena nodded slowly. "Sure, what's up?" she asked.

"Be careful." She advised. "New York isn't the safest of places and it's a big city, remember what I told you."

"That if I get lost, I get in a car with the kind man offering?" Elena joked.

Ana chuckled. "Yes, that is *exactly* what I told you. That, and accept drugs from strangers."

Elena shrugged. "Your words, not mine." She teased.

Ana shook her head, chuckling again. "Anyways, I'm being serious. Be *careful*. I also want you to be extremely watchful of Autumn." She told her daughter, being told by Elena of Autumn's disability. "I'm sure Autumn is use to handling her disability, but you need to make sure she's okay. But have fun regardless, I'm glad you're making friends." She smiled warmly.

Elena nodded firmly. "I know, I know. I will be watchful of her, I wouldn't want anything to happen to her either. I really care about her."

Ana raised an eyebrow, nodding. "I'm sure you do…"

"What's that supposed to mean?"

"You can't talk so much about this Autumn girl and think you can get away with it." Her mother chuckled. "I know you, Elena. You like her, don't you?"

Elena blushed, hesitantly nodding. "Yes." She replied quietly.

"Be careful with that too." Ana smiled softly. "Being with someone with difficulties such as blindness can come with complications."

"I'll be careful." Elena promised. "I know what I'm getting into, and I'm going to be her friend before anything else. Because she needs a friend. And if that's all I'll ever have with her…that's okay."

"That's very admirable of you, honey." Ana told her, kissing her daughter's forehead. "Have fun, okay? I love you."

Elena hugged her mother before standing up and heading to the door. "I will, I love you too! I'll be back later!" she called out as she opened the door and stepped outside, closing the door behind her.

Elena walked down the steps and placed her headphone buds in her ears and humming the words to herself as she listened to music. She could feel her heart beating quickly out of excitement. A whole day with Autumn Castillo, how better could it get?

―――――――――――――――

Autumn rolled her eyes as her mother worriedly advised her to be careful for the eight time (Autumn was counting, it was *eight* times). "Be careful, okay? And do not steer away from Elena for *one second*." Cora said as she tucked a piece of hair behind her daughter's hair. "Gabe's a great dog, but people can be cruel here. So be―"

"Careful." Autumn finished. "I know, mom, I've lived in New York my whole life. I know how it is. I'll be fine, I promise." She assured. "I appreciate you caring, but care a little less?"

Cora chuckled. "Not possible. If I ever start caring less, I will personally send someone to punch me in the face." She replied, adjusting Gabe's harness.

"Fair enough." Autumn agreed.

"I'm surprised you even agreed to this." Cora said honestly. "It takes Emma an hour to convince you to go out with her. What's the difference here?"

"What? I am not allowed to make friends?" Autumn replied, not answering the question.

"I didn't say that. I'm incredibly happy to know you're making friends, I'm just wondering what's so different about this Elena girl that you'd agree to spend the day with her?" Cora asked.

Autumn pondered for a moment before answering. "She's teaching me the concept of whatever." She paused. "And she's looking past my blindness. She's…something else. I don't know what that 'something else' is, but I'll figure it out soon enough."

Cora seemed to accept the answer and nodded. "Very well then."

The doorbell rang and Autumn immediately tensed up, clutching onto Gabe's harness with one hand. "How do I look?" she asked quickly. Her 14 year old sister, Olivia, had helped her pick out her outfit and get her ready.

Her brother, Dylan, snickered as he walked by. "Horrible." He teased.

Autumn scoffed. "I asked mom, not you dweeb." She replied.

"Both of you, hush." Cora scorned, fixing her daughter's shirt. "You look beautiful honey." She assured as she opened the door with Elena waiting by the other side of it.

Elena smiled immediately and waved awkwardly. "Hi. I'm Elena." She introduced herself to Autumn's mother. "I'm here for Autumn?"

Cora smiled warmly. "Hello, I'm Autumn's mother. It's nice to meet you."

The younger girl nodded. "The feeling's mutual Mrs. Castillo. You're a teacher, right? My sister, Lily, loves you."

Cora nodded. "Yes, I teach 2nd grade. I know who Lily is, she's very sweet. I'm sure she gets it from her sister." She grinned.

Elena chuckled. "That must be it." She agreed.

Cora opened the door further so Autumn could step out with Gabe. The golden retriever led Autumn out of the door and Elena's breath hitched. Autumn looked *gorgeous* and Elena had to resist the urge of letting her mouth gape at the beauty in front of her.

"All right, you two be careful and have fun." Cora told them as the two girls walked down the steps.

"We will, I'll watch Autumn, Mrs. Castillo." Elena promised her.

Cora nodded before shutting the door, but still watching from the window.

"Or how about Autumn watches herself?" Autumn retorted as they began walking.

Elena turned to her with a raised eyebrow. "Considering how your eyes kind of suck at being eyes, we're not taking any chances." She giggled.

"Fair point." Autumn shrugged. "So…what does the day consist of for us?"

"Adventure." Elena said simply.

"Care to elaborate?" Autumn raised an eyebrow curiously.

Elena shook her head, grinning. "Just trust me that it will be a fun adventure."

Autumn couldn't help but break out into a grin. "Fine. Lead the way and Gabe and I will follow."

Elena quickly intertwined her hand with Autumn's without thought and their adventure began. Elena began by taking them to Times Square.

"Where are we going?" Elena exclaimed loudly.

"Times Square." Autumn replied, no enthusiasm in your voice.

"You are not allowed to be a Debbie Downer on such a marvelous day!" Elena told her.

"A marvelous day I can't see." Autumn muttered to herself, but Elena still hearing it.

Elena frowned, pursing her lips. "Then I'll see for you." She offered, a small smile appearing on her lips.

Autumn couldn't stay sad for long, it was impossible to stay sad with a girl like Elena. She wondered how Elena could stay so happy, and secretly hoped it was another concept Elena would teach her.

A small smile appeared on Autumn's face and she exhaled before exclaiming loudly. "Where are we going?!?"

Elena grinned, jumping up in the air. "TIMES SQUARE!" she shouted, not caring of the quizzical looks sent her way.

Once they made it to Times Square, Elena immediately began describing the scene to Autumn. "Okay, so it probably would look way better here when it's nighttime…" she told Autumn. "However, it still looks awesome. The buildings are tall and eye-catching. It'd probably take a billion Emma's just so it could cover one building alone." She chuckled. "And it's incredibly busy—"a random person bumped shoulders with Elena and continued walking without apologizing and Elena nodded. "With people. *Rude* people!" Elena said loudly, emphasizing the person that bumped into her. "But New York's always busy, regardless of the time. It's always moving, so you can *always* hear the sound of footsteps of different kinds of shoes." She took Autumn's hand again and squeezed it. "Listen close and tell me what kind of shoes you hear."

Autumn listened intently and heard the clicking of heels from a woman walking by her. "Heels." She listened again and heard old sneakers squeaking. "Sneakers—old ones." She paused to hear again and heard the sound of flip-flops stomping. "And flip-flops."

Elena smiled. "Awesome." She continued. "There's also a lot of traffic here." The loud honk of a taxi cab proved her point exactly.

"And angry taxi cab drivers." She chuckled. "Regardless, the place is quite colorful. And big, it makes me feel small compared to this place." she paused. "I don't know, it makes me think how I'm honestly just a speck of dirt compared to the giganticness that is the world. There's so many people in this world, so many things…it's hard to make your mark on the world."

"Is that what you want to do?" Autumn spoke up. "Make your mark on the world?"

Elena nodded. "Yes. I do." She replied. "I fear being forgotten." She confessed. "I fear that as hard as I try, I'll leave this world without any recognition that I was here—that I lived. I don't want to leave this Earth without knowing that I made some kind of impact…there's more purpose to me than that." She paused. "It's crazy though, so many people have roamed this Earth and only a handful of that many have been remembered. It's tragic really, because I'm sure no one wants to be forgotten."

Autumn listened intently to what Elena had to say, and Autumn had to admit, Elena wasn't what she expected. She was so insightful and curious about the world—about everything. It was as if Elena wanted to soak up all of the world's knowledge like a sponge, the knowledge seeping into her brain and staying there forever.

"Everyone will be forgotten eventually." Autumn said simply. "I think you should focus less on impacting the world and more on impacting your world." She shrugged. "If you can impact some people's lives, then you've done your part."

Elena nodded. "Do you want to be remembered?"

"No."

"Why not?"

"I don't want to be remembered this way." Autumn shared. "I don't want to be remembered as the girl with the tragic story."

"Your story's only tragic if you let it be." Elena told her. "You're the author and main protagonist of your story, and you have control of how it develops."

"If I had control over my story, I wouldn't be blind. And I wouldn't be angry."

"You're angry because you choose to be." Elena retorted. "You also have the choice of being happy."

"How do I do that?" Autumn asked curiously.

"I'll teach you." Elena smiled softly. "But for now, let's keep this adventure going." She grinned, before dragging along Autumn around New York City and everything it had to offer. She took Autumn to the top of the Rock observation deck, feeling the cool wind hit their faces and Elena described what she saw from the top of the Empire State building, the breathtaking view leave her in awe.

She then took Elena to Prospect Park and also described the scenery to her as well. Elena felt like they went to every place possible, with the help of the subway (which wasn't as fun as she'd seen in movies, nearly missing their stop) and their own two feet. But in reality, she was sure there was more to discover because New York was gigantic. But if she were to discover more of New York, she'd like to discover it with Autumn. Autumn definitely had her share of thoughts of the world around them and it fascinated her. Elena could listen to Autumn talk for hours.

And not once did they ever stop talking, they just bounced off each other. If one topic died down, they'd bring up another one. They never lost interest in each other's words.

By the time they made it to a nearby coffee shop, both of them (including Gabe) were tired from all the walking.

Autumn and Elena stood in line to place their orders in and Elena groaned. "Holy shit, I'm pretty sure we walked all over the city." She said, exhaling.

Autumn laughed. "The side effects of adventure."

"It's worth it though. I've had a great time with you." Elena told her, blushing.

Autumn blushed in return, her head tilting down. "So have I." she mumbled shyly.

Elena smiled. "Really?"

"Really." Autumn confirmed. "Thank you for an amazing day. I never thought someone would ever work so hard to let me have a taste of adventure too. But you, you always seem to defy the norm. I like that."

"Thank you too." Elena told her. "You agreed to join me. And I wouldn't have wanted anyone else to have joined me in on this lovely adventure."

Autumn smiled to her before they placed their orders and went to sit down in a small table in the farthest corner of the coffee shop.

"Do you think everything happens for a reason?" Autumn spoke up suddenly. "Like, do you think certain events happen in your life because there is a greater plan for you—a life-changing one?"

Elena pondered for a moment for an answer. "I think so. But I also think some events happen to shape your character, to help you either grow or lessen as a person." She paused. "Why do you ask?"

"Because I've always thought about the vast amount of reasons as to why the universe decided to make me get sick and ultimately lead me to this state of blindness." Autumn answered.

"Why do you think the universe made you blind?" Elena asked curiously.

"To punish me." Autumn straightened up. "I have this theory that the universe shapes your next life based on the way you lived your previous one." She explained. "Like, if you were a shitty person in your past life, the life you're going to live next is going to be shitty. Like karma, only in reincarnation form. Because I believe in reincarnation and that you live a million lives. So you have a million chances to live the way you always wanted to."

Autumn licked her lips, running a hand through her hair. "So, I think that the universe is punishing my previous life for being a bad person, thus making me suffer in this life like I made others suffer. My past self was a fucking dick then."

Elena thought over on what Autumn explained to her. And in some weird way, it made sense to Elena. "Interesting."

"Do you believe in reincarnation?"

Elena shook her head. "No. But I do believe that when our physical forms die, our souls continue to live on forever. They're in search for something."

"What do they go searching for?" Autumn asked curiously, her head resting on her hand.

"Their soul mate." Elena replied. "Whether they found it when they were alive or not, I think after death you go search for the one person that the universe matched for them. Some find them, some don't. And I think the ones that don't become angry and miserable, and spread misery to others who are still alive. And those are the bad spirits, the ones that never found their soul mate."

"So believe in love?"

"Don't you?"

"No, I don't."

"Why not?"

"Because I don't think everyone has the chance to experience it." Autumn answered. "I'm sure a thing such as love exists, but I don't think everyone will get it."

"Do you think you'll ever find love?" Elena asked.

Autumn shook her head. "No." she whispered. "Like I said, the universe is punishing me."

"I think the universe can be a little lenient sometimes." Elena countered. "Maybe you think the universe is punishing you, but in reality…you're punishing yourself."

Autumn didn't say anything after that and the two received their orders and ate in silence for the first time since their adventure began.

Once they finished, Elena paid for the two (even after Autumn's protests) and they walked out of the coffee shop and began walking down the darkening streets. Elena decided to end the adventure in the simplest way, and led Autumn to the nearest park.

"Lay down." Elena instructed her as she herself laid down on green grass. Autumn raised an eyebrow but lay down regardless next to Elena. "Take off your glasses." Autumn hesitantly took off her glasses and laid them beside her where Gabe was sitting obediently.

"What are we doing?" Autumn questioned.

"Closing our eyes." Elena answered as she took out her iPod and placed an ear bud in Autumn's ear before placing the other one in her own ear.

Autumn closed her eyes. "I do not understand the point of this."

"There is none." Elena scrolled through her songs before clicking on one and placing the iPod between the two and Elena closed her eyes. "We're just going to lay here and listen to this one song with our eyes closed and pretend there's stars up in the sky."

"Why?"

"Because you listen with your ears and you imagine with your heart. You don't need eyes for that."

Autumn didn't question any further and the two lay silently as music played.

The tips of Autumn's fingers touched Elena's and she intertwined her hand with Elena's own. Elena didn't say anything of it and simply continued to enjoy the moment in silence, her heart beating faster and goosebumps invading her skin.

But one thing did happen that Elena no longer had control over.

She had fallen in love with Autumn.

CHAPTER EIGHT

"You seem to be in a great mood today." Mrs. Freya noticed when Elena arrived in the classroom, practically glowing as she clutched onto the canvas— where her painting was— for the project that was due.

Elena grinned even more if it was possible. "It's just a beautiful day to be living, is all." She explained simply as she took a seat, noticing Autumn hadn't arrived yet.

"Every day is a beautiful day to be living." Mrs. Freya agreed. "But I'm not as old as you think, I know when a girl your age walks in practically glowing with happiness is because she's gotten her heart reeled in by someone." She smirked when she noticed Elena blush. "But it's okay, I won't push you to tell me. Good luck with it though." Mrs. Freya winked.

"Thank you." Elena said sheepishly, looking down at her canvas and biting her lip to suppress her smile from grinning. Ever since Saturday, when Autumn held her hand while Ed Sheeran played as they laid on the grass…Elena knew she was in love with Autumn.

The mere thought of Autumn made Elena's heart flutter and her stomach tighten. Her throat would forget for a couple seconds what it was like to exhale and inhale oxygen. Autumn was like oxygen Elena didn't even realize she needed.

More students piled into the classroom, taking their respective seats and mindlessly chatting with their friends while Elena anxiously waited for Autumn to enter, her right leg bouncing in anticipation.

Finally, Autumn walked in and Elena grinned.

Autumn sat down quietly and Elena turned to her. "Hey."

Autumn smiled softly, nodding. "Hi." She said quietly.

"Did you finish your project?" Elena asked curiously, glancing over at the covered work that she assumed was the art piece Autumn had created.

"Yup." Autumn replied simply. "You?"

"Yeah." Elena nodded.

The other girl pursed her lips. "It's a shame I won't be able to see it." She sighed quietly.

"I'll describe it for you." Elena offered, never minding being Autumn's eyes when hers failed at being eyes.

"I had a feeling you'd say that." Autumn smiled. "Thanks."

"Well it's our thing, it's kind of a second nature to me now."
Elena chewed on her lower lip. Autumn hummed in agreement and
Elena turned to her. "So are you and Emma going to sit with us at lunch
today?" she asked tentatively, knowing the last time the two girls sat
with them Autumn had an outburst.

Autumn shrugged. "I'm not sure, I'd have to ask Emma. Since
last time...you know." She muttered, referring to her outburst.

"We've already forgotten about that. You two are more than
welcome to sit with us." Elena replied.

"Thanks."

Elena nodded and before she could say anything else, Mrs.
Freya stood in the front of the class with an excited grin.

"So, I see a lot of great works sitting in your desks." She
observed. "Therefore, we will all share our works to the class!" she
declared, seeing some faces plastered with a look of terror of having to
present in front of others.

"The fear I have instilled in some of your faces is priceless."
The art teacher chuckled. "But do not worry! This isn't a full-blown
presentation." Mrs. Freya assured. "We are simply going to present
what we have created and what we've learned from our partners." She
explained. "So relax and just present your work, work you should be

proud of!" she exclaimed before sitting in an empty seat and calling out names one by one.

Students presented their art works, some appearing more nervous than others. Elena attempted to pay attention to all the presentations, but she spent most of her time staring at Autumn. It wasn't staring in a creepy way, or Elena hoped it wasn't.

"Elena." Mrs. Freya called to her, smiling to her. The girl broke of her thoughts and her eyes directed from Autumn to the teacher. "It's your turn." She told Elena.

Elena nodded, feeling a wave of nerves appear. She stood up, her bar stool making a loud, scratching noise as she took her canvas and walked to the front of the classroom, licking her lips before chewing her lip nervously.

She placed her finished canvas on the wooden easel placed in front of the classroom so she wouldn't have to be holding the finished painting.

Turning to the front of the classroom she let out a breath she didn't even realize she was holding in. "Okay, so—um." She stammered. "My partner was Autumn." Her eyes directed to the girl who was paying attention to what Elena was saying, making her even more nervous than before. "And as you can see, I painted her…but at the same time I didn't." she explained. "See, she's wearing her sunglasses because that's her go-to accessory I'm not particularly fond of because she has the most gorgeous eyes on the planet. They're green and it's like looking into a green forest and not minding for one second if you happen to get lost." She blushed and chuckled.

"Despite the fact that Autumn is blind, that doesn't mean she is incapable of seeing—metaphorically speaking." Elena told them. "See, Autumn is good at reading people and seeing right through them—trust me, she did that with me and it was scary but so freaking awesome."

Elena gave a goofy smile and stared at Autumn as she explained her art work. "Autumn doesn't need eyes to see you because she sees you in the most genuine part…her heart. She sees through her heart and I think that's beautiful because that means she is the most open minded one out of us all. She won't judge you by your appearance, but rather your personality. She sees you. And although she says she's incapable of seeing, I think otherwise."

Elena noticed Autumn smile softly and her cheeks turn pink, her head bowing down so nobody would notice. "But anyways," she continued, looking at her painting and explaining everything else that she had painted and why.

Autumn was in the middle of the canvas and Elena painted her with as much detail as she could, wearing her sunglasses and her eyes over her heart, symbolizing what Elena had explained beforehand how Autumn sees with her heart.

Autumn was wearing a black t-shirt in her painting and wearing a black beanie over her long, dark locks. Elena had painted an assortment of fireflies around the painting of different colors, making the painting bright and colorful. She also had piano keys encircling Autumn in the painting with musical notes all around.

There were band logos of certain bands Autumn was fond of including Paramore, The 1975, Nirvana, Van Halen, and other bands. She had a black raven painted in one corner and a stack of books beside it, showing her love for Edgar Allan Poe and reading in general. She added other small things like a paw print of a dog to represent Gabe, Buddha (with Autumn's fascination with reincarnation), and the quote painted neatly in cursive "Yo vivo si tú vives" in the bottom of the painting.

Elena let out a content sigh when she finished. "And yeah, this is Autumn Castillo in all her greatness." She finished with a smile.

The classroom clapped as they had for everyone else who had presented thus far and Mrs. Freya nodded in approval with a smile.

"Great job Elena." The teacher praised. "It's clear to see you really learned a lot about Autumn, so great job."

"Thank you." Elena nodded as she took her canvas painting and went back to her seat.

Autumn turned to her with a touched expression on her face. "That was…beautiful." She smiled softly. "You did amazing."

Elena blushed, grinning and nodding. "Thank you, I'm sure you're going to do great too."

Right on cue, Mrs. Freya called Autumn to go next and Autumn right away stiffened, nerves taking over. Elena placed a reassuring hand on top of Autumn's. "You're going to do fantastic, I know it." She assured.

Autumn smiled genuinely at the comment and nodded before standing up with her canvas in one hand and her white cane in the other as she led herself to the front of the classroom, feeling other eyes staring at her. They must be curious what a blind girl can create and Autumn gulped nervously at the thought of creating something that would ultimately be ridiculed.

She stood in front of the classroom and nearly ran into the wooden easel, causing some students to snicker and for Elena to glare at them for laughing.

Autumn turned red in embarrassment and placed her canvas on the wooden easel so she wouldn't have to hold it and nervously played with her cane before speaking up.

"So, my partner was Elena." She stated. "And I didn't know what to possibly create off someone I couldn't see physically." She told them, "So I did this…" she revealed the canvas with black paper covering the canvas, causing people to raise questioning looks.

"Now, I know what you're thinking…" Autumn began. "No duh Autumn, you can't see anything when you're blind. Way to try to be deep and poetic." Autumn joked, causing some people to laugh.

"However, as Elena said, I don't need eyes to see." Autumn recalled. "So," she reached for the canvas and as soon as her hands touched the canvas, she ripped the black sheet off completely, revealing the actual drawing.

"I drew what my mind and my heart too—I guess—saw." The drawing was of Elena, surprisingly looking nearly identical to Elena. The drawing was in black in white, with Autumn using charcoal for the most part.

The drawing had Elena lying on her stomach as she sketched something in her sketchbook like she tended to do with headphones in her ears. She was in a beach kind of setting with things revolving around her that involved things Elena liked and felt passionate about, some things surprising the girl herself, never realizing Autumn even remembered some of the details she shared.

"Elena is…cute and goofy combined." Autumn explained. "Honestly, she has no shame and is a total goofball. I'm pretty sure she always has a smile on her face and if I could see that smile, I'm sure it's beautiful and it could cure depression." She shared. "She's so quirky and hates odd numbers with a passion except for the numbers 3, 5, and 63—which is pretty weird, but it's Elena so it doesn't surprise me very much." Autumn shrugged. "She's a total fangirl and freaks out over singers and art and fictional characters and food." She chuckled.

"But she's also incredibly loyal. I haven't known her for very long, but she's already proven to me that she's a friend I can trust." Autumn smiled softly. "I can give her a million reasons to hate my guts but she'd still stick to my side regardless. She also describes everything to me, pretending to be my eyes since my eyes suck at being eyes. And I don't know many people willing to work so hard to accommodate someone and make them happy, but Elena is one of those few people I'm happy to know." Autumn said genuinely.

"I drew in black and white because while I have learned so many things about Elena, there are still things about her I don't know yet. And I'm not sure whether or not she'll ever share those things to me…but if she does, I'm all ears." She nodded. "So

yeah...that's...Elena Díaz. The most fantastic soul I've ever met."
Students clapped again and Mrs. Freya looked impressed as well.

Elena couldn't stop grinning at the kind and genuine words
Autumn shared about her, finding herself falling even more in love for
the girl.

"That was wonderful, Autumn. You've done a great job as
well. You two have really grasped the concept of the assignment." Mrs.
Freya praised.

Autumn nodded and went back to her seat quietly. Elena
turned to her. "That was...that was amazing. I told you that you'd do
great." She smiled, a blush creeping onto her cheeks.

"Thanks." Autumn replied simply.

"Did you mean all of that?" Elena asked, staring at Autumn.
"Do you actually feel that way about me?"

Autumn nodded. "Yes. I know I can be rude and an asshole
sometimes, but I am honest. And I meant every word I said up there."
She said honestly.

"I...thank you. No one ever says things like that about me."
Elena blushed.

"Well they should. And they do, well, I do." Autumn smiled softly. "You're fantastic, Díaz." She chuckled. "Now I'm going to stop showering you with compliments. It's making me seem nice."

Elena laughed and shook her head. "Well, gosh, did you ever consider that maybe you *are* nice?" she grinned.

"Do you know what that'd do to my reputation, Ellie? I can't risk my badassery going away because I gave you some compliments." Autumn teased, playing along.

"It's hard not to compliment me." Elena said cockily, giggling.

"Is that a challenge?"

"You already have your challenge, hush."

"Another one won't hurt, now will it?" Autumn smirked.

Elena chuckled. "You're such an idiot." She shook her head.

"Wonderful." Autumn commented, a grin on her face.

They spent the rest of the period with their playful banter and Elena enjoyed seeing this side of Autumn. It was almost as if Autumn was sharing a tiny part of the real Autumn, the Autumn inside the walls.

Once the bell rang, the two girls walked to lunch together. Autumn was holding onto Elena's arm like she tended to do a lot now. And Elena didn't mind, enjoying feeling Autumn's soft touch.

"So, are we going to have lunch together?" Elena asked. "You, me, Maya, Phoenix, and Emma?"

Autumn thought for a moment and eventually sighed. "There's no getting out of it...right?"

"Such a genius, Castillo." Elena teased. "You've guessed correctly. It'll be fun, I promise." She encouraged as they walked inside the lunchroom.

"Last time we all sat together—"Autumn began.

"What have I been teaching you, Autumn?" Elena cut off. "The concept of whatever." She answered. "Therefore, we will 'Whatever' this and move on. What happened last time, happened last time. This time, it's going to be different."

Autumn raised an eyebrow. "Different how?"

"Don't question it. It's just going to be different." Elena shrugged. "It's a new day, so just..." Elena trailed off, expecting Autumn to answer.

"Whatever it." Autumn finished with a soft smile. "Fine."

Elena grinned and quickly led her to where Maya, Phoenix, and Emma were sitting.

Emma was standing there, not expecting to stay long once Autumn arrived and headed to their usual table.

"Hey guys, we're all going to sit together. That's fine, right?" Elena spoke up as the two girls sat down.

Emma raised an eyebrow. "We are?"

"We are." Autumn confirmed. "I'm sorry about last time, I'll try to not be—"

"Consider it forgotten Autumn, it's okay." Maya assured her. "We all have our days. Trust me, Phoenix has them every day." She smirked.

Autumn chuckled and Phoenix playfully glared at Maya. "Rude." She stuck her tongue out to Maya who returned it.

Emma sat down beside Autumn and smiled at Autumn and then Elena. "So are you sure you want to sit here?" Emma asked quietly to Autumn.

Autumn nodded. "100% sure." She confirmed. "They're...*special* individuals I wouldn't mind interacting with once in a while."

"Some more than others, right?" Emma whispered to Autumn with a smirk.

"What?"

"I'm short in size, not in mind." Emma laughed. "I see the way you act with Elena…"

Autumn blushed. "We're just friends." She whispered immediately.

"That's what they all say." Emma kinked an eyebrow. "You know you can tell me. It's not like I'm going to go off and tell anyone. Who else will I go to? You're my only friend." She retorted.

The younger girl chewed on her bottom lip as she contemplated for a moment. "You can't tell them, okay?" she muttered, her cheeks turning even redder.

Emma suppressed a squeal. "Oh my go—"she was about to exclaim.

"Emma." Autumn interrupted, a small smile creeping onto her lips.

The smaller girl sighed, a smile on her face. "Okay, okay." She relented. "I will keep my mouth shut." She zipped her lips. "My lips are sealed. But we'll have to talk more later."

"Thanks." Autumn smiled. "We will talk more later, I promise."

Emma broke into a grin. For a moment there, it was as if she and Autumn were back to the amazing friendship they once had. It was as if she caught a glimpse of the old Autumn again. "That sounds awesome."

"Talking shit you two?" Phoenix called them out with a playful smirk. "Say it to my face instead of being so secretive!" she teased.

The two girls laughed. "It was nothing." Autumn said, blushing still.

The other three girls quirked up an eyebrow, Maya and Phoenix casting a look to Elena who felt her own cheeks grow red.

"So many red faces I'm seeing…" Maya trailed off, smirking.

"Screw you, Maya." Elena mumbled.

Maya shrugged. "I'm flattered, but not into that." She laughed.

"Can we move on?" Autumn spoke up, regaining her composure.

"I second that." Elena agreed.

"Lames. Both of you." Phoenix chuckled. "But sure, Maya and I actually were talking and we were thinking that the five of us should head over to this karaoke place that's over in the East Village. " She suggested to the group.

Elena was the first one to agree, slamming her hand on the table due to excitement. "All you needed to say was karaoke because fuck yeah I'm in!" she grinned. "What's this place called?"

Phoenix laughed. "Of course you'd be excited." She commented. "But it's called Cooper's Karaoke Bar." Phoenix answered. "Now before you all begin to freak out because the word 'bar' scares you," she began. "On Friday nights it's strictly only those under 18 so, sadly, we won't be getting any alcohol."

"I'm in." Elena shrugged. "Karaoke is the best thing ever next to knitted scarves."

Maya turned to Emma and Autumn. "So three of the five have agreed,…what about you two?" she asked. "It'll be fun!"

"I'd love to." Emma told her. "But I'll only go if Autumn agrees to go." She said, turning to look at Autumn expectantly.

Autumn chewed on her lower lip. "I don't know. I mean, what can I possibly do at a karaoke bar? I'm pretty sure I'd fall off the stage."

"Girl!" Phoenix exclaimed. "There are a lot of things you can do! Just because you can't see for shit, doesn't mean that you should spend a Friday night confined in your room. Live a little!"

"Yeah, but..." Autumn argued weakly. "I don't want to hold you guys back. I mean, I don't want to be extra baggage."

"You're not." Elena immediately said. "You're plenty of fun and you won't hold us back. You and I have hung out before and went all over New York City basically, what's the difference with going out to this karaoke bar?" she questioned. "Besides, I think us five hanging out is long overdue."

Autumn pondered for a moment. "Just don't expect me to get up and sing anything." She half-heartedly agreed.

Emma squealed excitingly while Phoenix scoffed. "Oh Castillo, you're absolutely hilarious for thinking you won't get up on that stage and sing. You're singing, we're all singing." She said matter-of-factly.

"Good luck with that." Autumn retorted, smirking.

Phoenix raised an eyebrow at the reply. "Okay, how about this..." Phoenix trailed off, reflecting Autumn's smirk. "If I can manage to get you to get up and sing on stage, you have to complete a dare of my choice." The girl suggested. "How about it?"

Autumn pondered for a moment before grinning. "Whatever."

Elena broke into a smile, biting her lip as she found herself growing fonder of the girl. Phoenix chuckled. "So is that a yes?"

Autumn nodded. "It's a yes." She confirmed. "Good luck."

"I don't need luck, because it's going to happen." Phoenix assured.

"Do you have evidence to back that up?" Autumn countered.

"I'm Phoenix Hale," Phoenix declared, flipping her hair. "that's evidence enough."

Autumn pursed her lips to stifle a laugh and rubbed her forehead. "No comment."

"I won this argument, ha!" Phoenix teased.

"What will I ever do?" Autumn retorted sarcastically. "I didn't beat Phoenix Hale in an argument. My life cannot possibly go on."

Phoenix laughed as the other three girls watched the interaction in amusement. The girl waved her finger at Autumn. "I like you, Castillo." She grinned. "I mean, I still think you're a bitch but hey, you can't always get what you want."

Autumn shrugged, indifferent. "Whatever."

Elena stared at Autumn, a smile on her face.

You're not whatever, not to me. Elena thought as she watched Autumn and Phoenix continue to bicker playfully, the whole table laughing.

She rested her chin on her hand and bit her lip. Definitely not whatever.

CHAPTER NINE

"What is it like to have a panic attack?" Autumn asked suddenly as Emma drove over to Maya's house to pick up the other three girls for their karaoke get-together.

Emma was applying a coat of lip gloss when they stopped at the red light. She turned to Autumn with a confused look. "I don't know I've never had one before." She replied. "Wait—are you okay?" she asked suddenly, looking at Autumn with an alarmed expression. "Does anything hurt? Do you feel like you're going to pass out? Castillo, don't you dare pull any shit on me right now or so God help m—"

"I'm fine." Autumn assured, fumbling with her cane. "I'm just…" the younger girl chewed on her bottom lip nervously.

The light turned green and Emma's small foot hit the car pedal to start driving again. "Just what, A?" she questioned, taking a quick glance at Autumn.

Autumn hesitated for a couple minutes, an awkward silence consuming them.

Emma frowned, looking at Autumn with sad eyes and wishing her best friend could see her hurt expression. "You don't trust me, do you?"

Just when she thought she and Autumn were getting somewhere, when they were finally beginning to rekindle their friendship, Autumn just out-of-nowhere shuts her out again. She really didn't know why. At first, she didn't think much of it because Autumn tended to shut out everyone and enclose a hard wall around her.

But now Emma was confused.

Elena suddenly comes in and Autumn's sharing more with her and becoming closer with her than Emma ever could be with Autumn.

Did it anger her?

Yes, *so* much.

Because while Elena was a nice girl, Emma's been there for Autumn in more ways than Elena has. From Autumn getting diagnosed with cancer, to losing her eyesight…Emma was the only friend that ever stuck to Autumn's side.

And to this day, she *still* was there for her in any way Autumn let her—*if* she ever let her. She's proven to be a worthy friend, heck, Autumn doesn't know the things Emma has done for her—the things *she* has sacrificed to be a friend to Autumn.

Emma can give a million things she's done for Autumn, but Autumn will never appreciate or acknowledge a single one. And it hurt, because it made it seem like Emma was just another person to her when to Emma, Autumn was like a sister.

God she needed a drink now, she thought as she rubbed her forehead when Autumn didn't answer her question.

Emma scoffed as they drove in silence. "That is indication enough to what I asked, thanks." She mumbled, gripping onto the steering wheel.

Autumn didn't say anything. She continued fumbling with her cane, feeling guilt for what she's just done—what she's *been* doing since the longest to Emma. It wasn't that she didn't trust Emma, because heaven knew that Autumn trusted the smaller girl with her life, it was Autumn's stubborn need to not dump her problems to people.

Being blind was already a big enough problem, why did she need to add more? She didn't know why, but lately she's felt like Emma had things going on that Autumn couldn't help her with. She couldn't pinpoint what the problem might be, but she couldn't approach Emma about it.

God she was such a bad friend.

And then there were her feelings for Elena. Autumn rubbed her forehead at the thought because the Miami native was *all* she could think about lately. It surprised her just how much of an effect Elena had on her, because she made it so easy for Autumn to open up to her. She had this presence about her that made it easy for Autumn to trust her.

She hated the fact that Elena was slowly seeping into her perfectly kept walls but at the same time, she didn't mind. Because since the longest, Autumn couldn't recall a time she felt truly happy. And all Elena had to do was simply be there for Autumn to feel this overwhelming joy she hadn't felt in so long.

But she knew. She knew she couldn't get her hopes up that anything other than a friendship could surface between the two. They were just friends and Elena would be absolutely insane to be in a relationship with a blind basket case like Autumn. It would be too hard, too complicated. And besides that, who could fall for a girl like Autumn? Elena was too good for her.

Elena was like a beautiful, blooming rose in a garden and Autumn was the asshole that picked them out and ripped off the petals. She couldn't hurt her like that. She had to avoid as many casualties as she could because if she hurt a rose like Elena, she'd never forgive herself.

The car stopped in front of Maya's house and Emma didn't say anything, only sending a text to Maya that they were outside waiting for them.

Autumn pursed her lips before hesitantly speaking up. "I'm sorry." She whispered, just loud enough for Emma to hear her.

Emma turned to her and only nodded. "It's fine." She said quietly, smiling weakly. How many times would she forgive Autumn until she couldn't forgive anymore?

Pushing her shades up the bridge of her nose, Autumn exhaled. "I want you to have fun tonight." She ordered Emma. It wasn't a request, it was a demand. "For one night, don't worry about being my bodyguard or anything. Be a teenager and have fun for once." Her head lifted up to await Emma's reply. "Okay?"

Emma stared at her with a surprised look, not expecting Autumn to say those words. The tiny girl nodded slowly. "Okay." She relented. "But...you should have fun too."

"Emma," Autumn began. "you and I both know I'm only doing this out of commitment. There's not a lot a blind girl can do at a karaoke bar." She shrugged. "But it's fine, as long as you're having fun, that'll be enough for me." She corners of her mouth lifted slightly. "Don't worry about me."

Emma knew for a fact that regardless of what Autumn was saying, she'd try her best to make this night as fun as possible for her best friend. "Thank you." She whispered softly, smiling.

Autumn didn't say anything else after that and they waited in silence until their silence disappeared with Maya, Phoenix, and Elena's loud voices entering the car.

"Hey girls!" Maya greeted as they got inside the car.

Emma grinned and nodded to her. "Hey! Are you guys ready to go?"

"Hell yeah! I'm ready to bless the club with my beautiful vocals." Phoenix said cockily with a smirk.

Maya bowed her head and pretended to pray. "God, Jesus, Buddha, *anyone.*" She began. "If you care about the human race *just a little bit*, you'll prevent Phoenix Hale from singing on stage tonight. My ears would like to stay with ability to hear, please." She smirked.

Phoenix whacked Maya's arm and playfully glared at her. "I'll whack you into another nationality, Andrews!" she threatened, chuckling.

"I'm kidding, Nix." Maya rolled her eyes playfully. "We all know you've fucked with my hearing a long time ago." She smirked playfully, causing Phoenix to gasp dramatically.

"Lena, you better hold me back right now because I'm about to start a beat down!" Phoenix exclaimed to Elena. Though Elena was too busy staring a little too long at Autumn who was quiet but clearly listening to the interaction since she had a soft smile on her lips.

The girl broke from her thoughts and looked at Phoenix. "What?" she asked, dazed.

"*Clearly* being a bodyguard isn't nowhere near your future profession." Maya replied, chuckling.

"But staring at Autumn is a skill she's a professional at." Phoenix muttered for only Maya to hear who laughed.

Elena heard Phoenix and glared at her. She sometimes hated her friends for teasing her so much.

"I will burn *all* your Beyoncé memorabilia." She threatened Maya. "*Both* of you."

"You wouldn't dare!" Phoenix exclaimed, putting her hand over her heart.

"Arson can be considered art." Elena smirked, wiggling her eyebrows.

Maya raised her hands in surrender. "I don't know about you, Phoenix, but I love Beyoncé too much to risk it." She said in defeat.

Phoenix crossed her arms and nodded. "You win this round, Díaz, but we'll be back." She threatened. "We will come back *hard.*"

Maya nodded in agreement and mouthed the word, 'Hard', with a smirk.

Elena laughed and shook her head. "I question why I became friends with you two."

"You love us, shut up." Maya argued.

"I won't confirm nor deny that." Elena said simply.

"Are you guys done now?" Autumn spoke up, sounding irritated.

"*Now* we are." Maya mumbled. "Such a kill joy, Autumn." She pouted. Autumn only shrugged, indifferent to the accusation.

Emma drove off and they headed to the karaoke club.

Phoenix spoke up suddenly. "I hope you remember our bet, *Autumn.*" She addressed.

Autumn raised an eyebrow. "I have no idea what you are talking about." She said sarcastically.

Phoenix smirked. "You *know* what I'm talking about." She told her. "And you *know* you're going to lose."

"Good luck with that, Hale." Autumn scoffed. "You will not drag me into that stage even if my life depended on it."

"I like to consider myself a pretty strong individual." Phoenix retorted. "Your ass is going up that stage. I hope you have songs picked out in your head, Castillo."

Autumn hummed. "Okay." She said uninterestedly.

"I wonder what the dare should be…" Phoenix continued, finding a weird pleasure in pushing the other girl's buttons.

"If it's to stay away from you for a whole week, I wouldn't mind that dare." Autumn bit back, a smirk plastered on her face. Phoenix wanted to play? Autumn would join in on the game.

Phoenix crossed her arms as she reflected Autumn's smirk. "Very funny," she said amusedly. "But I think I have a *much* better dare in store for you."

"You act like you've won already—which you won't." Autumn retorted, scoffing. "But please, spare me the details of whatever dare your twisted mind came up with."

The other girl only hummed. "Fine." She grinned to Elena. "But I will say one thing," she said. "The dare will be *very* entertaining—for some people at least." She wiggled her eyebrows to Elena who glared at her friend.

Elena was going to murder Phoenix in her sleep the next time she had the chance, she thought. She loved the girl to death, but if she could just not embarrass her for one second or meddle into her non-existent love life, it'd be great.

The rest of the car ride was nowhere near quiet; Maya and Phoenix insisted they listen to Beyoncé on the ride to *Cooper's Karaoke Club*. So through the whole car ride, pop music blasted in the car while Phoenix, Maya, and even Emma sang loudly along to it.

Elena giggled when she watched Autumn acting annoyed and rubbing her forehead, throwing out comments like "I'm already blind, do I really need to be deaf too?" or "Let Beyoncé sing solo, she doesn't need the accompaniment of screeching crows."

But Elena knew Autumn was only faking her annoyance; because she caught a small smile appear on the girl's face when Emma began singing and laughing along to an 80's classic. Autumn didn't show it, but Elena knew that she deeply cared for the short girl driving.

Finally, they arrived to the karaoke club and once Emma parked the car in the parking lot, Elena, Phoenix, and Maya practically jumped out of the car in excitement.

"Quick question," Autumn spoke up as she opened the car door and placed the cane out in front of her. "Are we hanging out with teenage girls or children?"

Emma laughed and playfully pushed Autumn. "Shush, you know you find it amusing."

Autumn stepped out of the car and her cane guided the dark-haired mystery. "I don't know how that—"she referred to Phoenix, Elena, and Maya's voices singing loudly. "Is amusing." She finished.

Emma walked next to her, locking the car. "It's *fun*." She insisted. "You're no fun at all, Castillo." She teased. "All you do is read depressing poetry and listen to Lana Del Rey."

"Hey now," Autumn defended. "Edgar Allan Poe is a genius." She exclaimed. "And I like a tortured soul." She shrugged. "And Lana Del Rey has the sexiest voice on Earth." She chuckled as she linked her arm with Emma's.

Emma suddenly smirked. "I'm sure there are many things you find sexy."

Autumn quirked up an eyebrow. "Explain."

"You're smart, right?" Emma smirked even more as they entered the busy karaoke bar. "Figure it out."

Autumn protested. "That is downright cruel, Emma!" she exclaimed with a grin on her face.

Emma laughed, enjoying seeing the playful side of Autumn resurface. For how long? She didn't know. But she'd enjoy it for as long as it would last. "I love you too, Autumn." Was all she said as she led Autumn to the table Elena, Phoenix, and Maya had occupied, the three girls laughing their butts off.

"You *do not* want to know what Elena just did to get us this table." Maya said through fits of laughter.

Autumn sat down in front of Elena, putting cane away. Emma watched amusedly the three girls laugh. "Well, color me curious." She chuckled. "What did you do Elena?"

Elena's laughter died down. "I—um," her cheeks turned red. "I *kind of* tried to flirt with the host since most of the tables are occupied." She paused. "The host is a male." She explained. "I am the gayest to ever gay." Phoenix and Maya burst out laughing again. "So in my terrible attempt to flirt, I offered him a blow job."

Emma joined in on the booming laughter coming from Phoenix and Maya. Autumn was the only one with a raised eyebrow, but her face threatening to break the façade and burst into laughter herself.

"You...did...*what?*" Emma exclaimed in between laughter fits.

"I offered him a blow job." Elena said innocently. "Isn't that what guys like? They're raging hormones." She shrugged.

"Stick to girls Elena, stick to girls." Phoenix snickered.

"What did he say after that?" Emma asked curiously.

"He was in so much shock, he just sent us to the table most far away from him." Maya answered, recovering from her laughter fit and wiping away the tears that came out due to the laughter. "She scared him away!"

Emma shook her head. "At least we got a table and not kicked out because I'm sure that's sexual harassment." She said optimistically.

"We could've still gotten a table." Phoenix argued.

"How?" Emma raised an eyebrow.

She smirked playfully. "We just show them Autumn — automatic table."

Autumn, although wearing sunglasses, glared. "Bitch."

"Hey!" Phoenix exclaimed. "You are my friend with benefits, I'm relishing it!"

Elena face palmed. "Phoenix, you are such an idiot."

"And you *just* noticed this *now*?" Autumn finally addressed Elena.

The other girl giggled. "I just tried being straight five minutes ago, what do you think?" she joked.

Autumn chuckled, shaking her head. "You're crazy, you know that?"

"Artists tend to be crazy." Elena agreed. "I mean, Van Gogh chopped his ear off…"

"Are you implying that you are going to chop your ear off, Díaz?" Autumn teased. "If so, I will personally take you to seek professional help."

Elena chuckled and before she could say anything else, Maya decided to shout. "WE SHOULD GET SOME HOT WINGS GUYS!" Elena pouted that she couldn't say anything else to Autumn but got over it quickly.

"Only if we can get pizza too." Elena grinned.

"How about you guys order that stuff while I go get drinks?" Emma suggested. "I figure once we eat, we can talk who's performing."

Everyone agreed and told Emma what they wanted for drinks. Emma nodded and took her bag, walking to the bar where they were serving drinks. She turned to see if the girls were looking at her, but Maya and Phoenix were ordering the food while Elena and Autumn were just sitting there. So she reached into her bag and took out a water bottle—only the water bottle didn't have water. She took a swing of it and felt the vodka warm up her throat and sighed in content.

She just needed a little bit to loosen up.

"Okay," Elena turned to Autumn with a grin. "Let's say, hypothetically, you were to perform tonight. What song would you pick?" she asked Autumn.

Autumn lifted her head up, assuming Elena was talking to her. "Why are you asking?"

Elena shrugged. "What? I can't spark up a conversation with you?" she giggled.

"No, but how do I know you're not conspiring with Phoenix to get me to sing?" Autumn retorted, a smile forming on her lips.

Elena chuckled. "You're smart." She observed. "But I was just asking for the heck of it. Though I wouldn't mind hearing you sing. You must sing beautifully." She said honestly.

Autumn blushed. "I've...never sang in front of people. I've just played the piano." She mumbled.

"Well," Elena bit her lower lip. "Maybe we should change that. Tonight."

Autumn shook her head. "Nah, maybe another time."

Elena pouted. "I wish you could see my pout right now."

Autumn chuckled. "I'm glad I can't. I'd probably fall for it and you'd get me to do whatever you wanted."

Elena suddenly wondered if Autumn had the ability to see, would she have a chance with her? She shook her head; she had to stop thinking this way. Autumn would never be interested in her in that way. And the sooner she admitted that, the less heartbreak she'd suffer.

"Probably." Elena said softly.

Their conversation grew silent and the two didn't say anything, awkwardly shifting in their seats.

"Heroes." Autumn suddenly spoke up. Elena stared at her with a bewildered expression. "Heroes by David Bowie would probably be the song I'd pick to sing." She clarified with a soft smile.

Elena broke out into a grin. "Nice choice."

"Thanks." Autumn smiled softly. "Big fan of him."

Elena chewed on her lower lip nervously before reaching over the table separating the two girls and gently removing Autumn's sunshades. Autumn's eyes fluttered, feeling weird without sunglasses covering her face.

Elena smiled, still chewing on her lower lip. Autumn's gorgeous green eyes always captivated her and she would stare at those emerald orbs all day if she could.

"Why did you take them off?" Autumn asked, rubbing her eyes gently.

The other girl placed the glasses on the table. "Because your eyes are beautiful." Elena smiled even wider. "And I can't go another day with you covering them." She said simply. "Besides, covering your beautiful eyes is a crime against nature."

Autumn blushed and grinned, bowing her head sheepishly. "You think my eyes are beautiful?" she mumbled, not hiding the grin on her face.

"More than that." Elena argued. "I think *you're* beautiful." She confessed, her own cheeks turning red.

Autumn played with her hands and licked her lips in an attempt to suppress her grin from growing even wider. She titled her head up and locked eyes with Elena without even knowing it.

But she felt it, she felt Elena's eyes bore into her own. And in that moment, she wished more than anything that whoever was up there granting wished would grant the one she had now. She wanted to be able to look, *really look*, into Elena's eyes and tell her she was beautiful too. Elena didn't believe when she said it, but *God*, Elena was beautiful. She didn't need to see to know that.

Elena's eyes locked with Autumn and immediately felt her stomach tighten and her throat close up. Autumn was looking at her, but at the same time she wasn't. Autumn didn't see her physically, but she saw her in all the parts that mattered.

"What's your song?" Autumn asked, her eyes no longer on Elena's.

Elena frowned slightly at the broken eye contact. "You'll see." She smiled again.

Autumn pouted. "That's no fun. I told you mine!" she argued.

"Doesn't matter." She shrugged. "You'll hear soon enough." Elena teased, she giggled.

Autumn couldn't protest any further because Emma had arrived with their drinks and the food came soon after, so Autumn silently ate her food but listening to the rest of the girls talking and joking around. Autumn snickered and smiled at the lame jokes Elena would come up with and even joined in on the laughter when Maya and Phoenix's bickering returned again.

"Okay," Phoenix spoke up. "I don't know about you guys, but I want to get my karaoke on!"

"I surprisingly agree with Phoenix here, I want to get up there and sing." Maya agreed, suddenly smirk. "Who's up for some Destiny's Child?" Phoenix loudly agreed to that.

Emma squealed. "Me! Me! I am!" she exclaimed. Emma had loosened up a lot since her impromptu vodka session, but not drunk enough for the rest of the girls to notice.

Maya turned to Elena and Autumn. "Destiny's Child *is* a trio but we can always make exceptions…" she suggested.

Elena shook her head. "I'm fine for now. But I will be up there later though." She winked at Maya.

Maya chuckled and looked at Autumn. "What about you Autumn?"

Autumn shook her head. "I'm good."

Phoenix smirked. "You won't be later."

Autumn glared at her and this time Phoenix was able to see it since Autumn hadn't put her sunglasses back on since Elena took them off.

Maya rolled her eyes. "We're going to go sign up." she told the two girls. "Don't have too much fun now." She winked. "I heard sitting in a table can get pretty chaotic." She teased as she dragged Emma and Phoenix along with her to sign up for a song and leave the other two girls alone.

Elena turned to Autumn. "I bet you five dollars right now they're singing 'Bootylicious'."

Autumn laughed. "I honestly wouldn't be surprised if they do. I mean…it's them we're talking about. But I'll bet they're singing 'Survivor'. That's one of their most popular songs."

Elena nodded, taking Autumn's hand and shaking it. "It's a deal then."

Autumn chuckled. "It's a deal." She paused. "So are you going to sing?"

"Yeah, soon." Elena smirked. "Why? Is the curiosity of what I'm going to sing eating you alive?" she teased.

The other girl rolled her eyes. "No."

"Of course it's not." Elena said sarcastically. "I definitely believe you."

Autumn raised an eyebrow. "I can wait." She couldn't suppress the smile. "Try not to hurt yourself up there."

"Aw, you worry about my own safety?"

"No, I worry about everyone else's." Autumn smirked.

Elena feigned hurt. "Ouch, right in the heart Autumn."

Autumn only laughed, her eyes squinting from the laughter. Elena grinned, feeling satisfied with herself knowing she made Autumn laugh.

Phoenix, Maya, and Emma took the stage and broke out into Destiny Child's "Bootylicious", making Elena smirk while Autumn rolled her eyes.

Autumn burst out laughing. "Oh my god…"

Elena banged her hand on the table with excitement and pointed at Autumn. "You owe me five bucks! Ha!"

Autumn grumbled and playfully glared at Elena, reaching into her pocket and pulling out a five dollar bill. "Whatever."

Elena smirked, taking the bill and stuffing it in her pocket. "You weren't ready for this jelly."

"You are such a dork, you know that?"

"A dork that's five dollars richer." Elena countered.

Autumn rolled her eyes, bobbing her head while Phoenix, Emma, and Maya slayed the Destiny's Child song. The crowd was definitely enjoying it, dancing along to the song.

"They're really good." Elena commented through the loud song.

Autumn nodded in agreement. "I know, right? Emma's been singing since I can remember. She's always loved to sing." She smiled as Emma right on cue took over a verse. The tiny girl was shaking her hips, a grin on her face.

"She's really good. " Elena agreed. "Maya and Phoenix are great too. Phoenix wants to be a singer when she's older; she's really passionate about music."

"We have talented friends." Autumn said.

"We do. We should have them start a trio, become a super famous girl group." Elena joked.

Autumn chuckled. "And then we demand for 12% of their total earnings."

"I like the way you think." Elena waved her index finger to Autumn. "It should be 12% *each*."

"Even better." Autumn mused.

Elena laughed and clapped when the three girls finished the song with fierce poses. She cheered loudly for them and surprisingly so did Autumn. She smiled and bit her lip as she stared at Autumn, but it didn't take long for Phoenix, Maya, and Emma to come back with a rush of adrenaline still present from the performance.

"That was so much fun!" Emma exclaimed, giggling.

"You guys were great! Autumn and I were thinking about both of us taking 12% of your profit if you decide to start a girl group." Elena joked.

The other three girls laughed and sat back down. "So when are you going to go up, Lena?" Phoenix asked.

"Soon." Elena smirked at Autumn. "Although Autumn is dying over there because I won't tell her what song I'm singing so I should hold it up a little longer." She teased.

Autumn rolled her eyes. "You're terrible."

"No," Phoenix argued. "*I'm* terrible."

"Why?" Autumn raised an eyebrow.

Phoenix smirked. "Because I signed you up to sing."

Autumn's eyes widened and her mouth gapes. "You did *what?*" she squeaked out. "Why would you do that?" she exclaimed.

Phoenix shrugged. "Autumn, you cannot just expect me to just let you sit there all night and do nothing."

"Yes you can. I am perfectly content sitting in this spot! My butt is enjoying sitting here listening to you guys sing." Autumn argued. "I don't want my ass sitting on the floor after I fall off the stage because in case you need a reminder Phoenix: I'M BLIND."

"Exactly." Phoenix agreed. "You're blind, but your vocal chords work, don't they?" she argued, crossing her arms. "I'm not asking you to twerk on the stage Autumn, I just want you to sing a song and loosen up a little. God knows you of all people need it!"

Emma nodded in agreement. "She's right, A, just let go for today. You're young just like the rest of us."

"Phoenix just wants to win the bet." Autumn scoffed.

"It's not even about the bet anymore, Autumn, I just want you to have fun like all of us are." Phoenix said sincerely. "You cannot tell me sitting here and watching the rest of us enjoy the night is enjoyable to you."

Autumn sighed. "Whatever. You're not going to get me up there."

Elena suddenly stood up. "What if I make a total fool of myself right now?" she spoke up.

Everyone turned to her with a confused look. "What are you talking about?" Maya questioned.

Elena slid out of the table and put her hands on her hips. "You'll see—or in Autumn's case—*hear* soon enough." She said before making her way over to sign herself up.

"What is this idiot going to do?" Phoenix asked, chuckling and taking a sip of her soda.

"Didn't you hear her? She's going to make a fool of herself." Maya recalled. "And she's doing it for you Autumn so feel very special right now."

Autumn blushed and looked down. "It's not going to convince me to get up there and sing."

"Never say never!" Emma sang in a very Julie Andrews-esque voice.

"You just did!" Autumn sang back. "Twice!"

Emma laughed, a little *too* much and everyone gave her a baffled look. "What?" she asked innocently, still giggling. "It was funny!"

Elena suddenly got up on stage and tapped on the microphone, making a loud, screeching noise echo through the club. "Shit, my bad." She muttered, her eyes widening. Some people snickered and her cheeks turned red. What was she getting into?

"So—um," she stuttered into the microphone. "I decided to get up here and sing to you all, but I'm specifically singing and embarrassing myself completely because my friend Autumn Castillo over there doesn't want to get up on here and sing which is pretty sucky to be honest." Elena explained, pointing over to Autumn who sunk in her seat slightly and blushed. "So, I'm going to show her that having fun and embarrassing yourself while doing it is completely okay." She smiled when some people cheered encouragingly. "Right now." She nodded to the DJ to play the song and she exhaled. "Okay, game face." She muttered to herself.

Elena began singing a cheesy 80's pop song, awkwardly swaying as she tried to get rid of the nerves.

Maya and Phoenix cheered. "Go Lena!" both girls exclaimed.

Elena grinned at the cheering and winked at them. Autumn listened interestedly with a raised eyebrow. Elena sang with more confidence, flipping her hair and beginning to dance around with no care in the world.

People began to cheer for her and join in on the dancing too. Elena continued her embarrassing karaoke session and brought out some embarrassing dance moves like the sprinkler.

Maya put her hands on her face and laughed. "This girl..." she trailed off.

Phoenix was laughing loudly, banging her fist on the table. "She's such an idiot!" she exclaimed in between laughs.

But the cutest idiot, Autumn thought as she had a wide grin on her face as she heard Elena sing, wishing she could see the performance for herself. But she could only imagine what Elena must be doing, and it made her giggle.

Elena began feeling daring and stage dived into the small crowd that caught the small girl and cheered. Elena threw her fist in the air and sang confidently to the song. She hoped that it would make Autumn want to get on stage herself.

Elena was brought back to the stage and finished the chorus jumping around and singing with a dorky grin on her face.

Everyone in the club cheered loudly and whistled. Elena laughed and had the cheesiest smile on her face as she felt her face turn red. "Thank you!" she exclaimed before getting off the stage and walking back to her friends out of breath.

"You were so great, Lena!" Emma exclaimed, clapping her hands together. "It was pretty hilarious. Maybe we should consider you for our imaginary girl group." She winked.

Elena smiled cheekily. "Thank you, I'll consider it." She winked back.

Some people walked up to the girls' table to tell the four girls minus Autumn what amazing performances they gave.

"It was an entertaining performance." Autumn spoke up. "Really embarrassing," she added, chuckling. "But it was good." She smiled softly.

Elena blushed profusely. "Thanks." She chewed on her lower lip. "Does that mean you're going to go up there to sing?" she asked with a hopeful voice.

Autumn opened her mouth to say something but suddenly a voice spoke up. "That was quite the performance you gave Elena."

Elena turned around and her eyes widened at the person she saw. "Valerie?" her mouth gaped.

The tanned, doe-eyed girl flashed a grin. "Missed me?"

Elena immediately embraced the small girl in a tight hug. "What kind of question is that?" she retorted with a small laugh.

Valerie chuckled, breaking the hug. "A pretty stupid one." She blushed. "It's been two years."

Elena nodded. "Two years since you graduated and headed off to L.A. to make your dreams come true. How's that going by the way?" Phoenix, Emma, and Maya watched the interaction curiously while Autumn listened in.

"You never texted me or called me like you said you would." Valerie pouted. "But it's going great, I actually got signed." She grinned proudly.

Elena turned red. "Yeah, sorry about that." She muttered sheepishly. But she quickly shook it off when Valerie gave the big news. "No way! That's amazing Valerie! Congrats!" she exclaimed, hugging the girl again.

"It's fine. You're here now...looking quite great actually." Valerie chewed on her lower lip as she eyed Elena up and down shamelessly, making the other girl blush. "Thank you! I'm working on my album right now, and they said New York City was great for inspiration. So my label flew me down here to work on it." She explained.

Valerie looked over and noticed Elena was with other people. "I'm sorry, I completely forgot to introduce myself!" she exclaimed to them. "I'm Valerie, a...*special* friend of Elena's."

"It's cool, I'm Phoenix." Phoenix smiled softly to Valerie and sending a suggestive look to Elena.

Emma smiled at Valerie. "Hi, I'm Emma. It's really nice to meet you."

"I'm Maya, Elena has never told us about her special friend. So she has a lot of explaining to do later." Maya said, raising an eyebrow at Elena who turned even redder.

Valerie laughed. "Well that hurts." She pouted to Elena. "And all I could ever do is talk about you." She winked.

Autumn's jaw clenched when this Valerie girl began flirting with Elena. There was no way she was going to bite her tongue if Valerie tried to talk to her.

Elena blushed even more and couldn't hold back the grin. "Oh god..." she muttered.

"What?" Valerie feigned innocence. "It's true! I even annoyed my producers because I'd talk so much about you." She chewed on her lower lip. "And now I'm going to have much more to talk about…" she trailed off as she eyed Elena up and down again, clearly checking her out. "But I think I'll have to keep those thoughts to myself."

Emma glanced over at Autumn and noticed her jaw clenching and her fists tightening in obvious jealousy. She nudged Phoenix and Maya who smirked when they noticed Autumn.

Elena bit her lip and chuckled nervously. "You don't change, do you?" she questioned.

Valerie shook her head. "Nope. But you clearly have, I mean, look at you!" she exclaimed. "You have definitely evolved to become even more beautiful since I last saw you."

Elena blushed even more and began to wonder how red she must look at the moment. She hadn't seen Valerie in two years when the then senior graduated and ventured off to L.A. to get discovered.

Elena was a freshman then when Valerie left, and they had met through drama club which Valerie dominated. Elena was helping with the set design when Valerie caught her eye. She had a crush on Valerie since the longest at the time and Valerie noticed quickly.

The two got to know each other and became quite close. Valerie was Elena's first kiss and they went on a couple dates, but never went beyond that since Valerie told her she couldn't have Elena fall too hard only for her to leave soon after.

It broke Elena's heart, but she eventually got over it. Seeing the girl again definitely brought back memories that made Elena's stomach tighten.

"I could say the same thing." Elena smiled.

Valerie smirked and then noticed Autumn sitting at the table too. "Oh shoot, I'm sorry. I didn't see you there!" she addressed Autumn.

Autumn turned red with anger and said through gritted teeth. "Neither did I. " Phoenix snickered and Maya glared at her.

"Nice to meet you. I'm Valerie in case you didn't hear me introduce myself." Valerie extended her hand for Autumn to shake, completely oblivious that Autumn was blind.

Autumn didn't move and obviously couldn't see Valerie offering her hand. Elena coughed awkwardly. "Um, Autumn can't see…" she told Valerie.

Valerie's eyes widened and she turned red in embarrassment. "God, I'm so sorry." She apologized immediately. "I didn't know—"

"Of course you didn't." Autumn said venomously.

"Autumn." Emma warned, knowing very well this wouldn't end well if Autumn continued talking.

Valerie looked taken back by the harsh reply. "Whoa, hey look, I'm really sorry if I offended you. I didn't know."

"Clearly." Autumn spat. "If you did indeed know *anything*, you wouldn't be this annoying and perky."

"Autumn!" Emma scolded, looking at Valerie apologetically.

"What?" Autumn questioned. "You can't possibly tell me this isn't sleazy, she's practically throwing herself to Elena." She pointed out. "But please, don't let me interrupt. I'm sure there's a janitor's closet here somewhere where you two can be in private." She growled. Valerie turned red and looked down at the floor, not saying anything.

"What the hell is wrong with you, Autumn?" Elena glared at Autumn, completely shocked by Autumn's unexpected behavior.

"Me? Nothing." Autumn said sarcastically. "You? Well, I could practically smell your hormones raging. You might as well hold up a flashing sign that says 'Desperate lesbian seeking sexual partner'."

Elena looked hurt and shook her head at Autumn in disappointment. "Fuck you, Autumn." She spat angrily before storming out of the club.

Maya, Phoenix, and Valerie immediately ran after Elena while Emma stayed behind with Autumn.

"What the hell was that, Autumn?" Emma exclaimed, disappointment evident in her voice.

Autumn ignored her question and crossed her arms. "I want to go home." Was all she said.

"No! We're not going *anywhere* until we talk about this." Emma insisted. "Talk. Now."

Autumn scoffed. "What *is* there to talk about Emma?" she retorted,

"How about we start with your clear jealousy over Elena talking to Valerie?"

"Jealousy?" Autumn rolled her eyes. "I'm not jealous." She told Emma. "Elena could marry that Valerie bimbo for all I fucking care." She growled, tightening her fists.

Emma sat next to Autumn. "You're a terrible liar, you know that?" she put her hand on top of one of Autumn's tightened fists. "Talk to me."

Autumn let out a frustrated breath. "I am jealous." She confessed. "I am fucking jealous, because Valerie can see Elena. She can flirt with her and tell her she's beautiful and watch Elena blush and smile at the floor because her flirting is working." She gulped. "Me? I can't do that. No matter what, *anyone* is a better match for Elena than I could ever be. So yeah, I really like Elena but she's never going to feel the same way. Because there's always going to be someone better."

Emma frowned and rubbed Autumn's back. "Autumn …"

"I don't want to talk about this anymore." Autumn muttered before reaching her hand out for her glasses and cane, putting on her sunglasses. "Take me home."

Emma sighed. "Fine. Let me just text Phoenix and Maya, because I am going to have to come back to get them." She relented.

Autumn didn't say anything while Emma sent a text to Phoenix and Maya. The two girls replied and told Emma it was fine, Valerie was giving them a ride home.

Emma drove Autumn home in silence, Autumn consumed by her own thoughts. She didn't know what went over her, but she was just so *angry*. Angry at life, angry at her eyes for being shitty, and angry at herself for believing she had a chance with Elena.

She was blind, and now she thought she was pretty stupid too.

"Autumn," Emma spoke up as she parked in front of Autumn's house. "do you love her?"

Autumn stayed silent, wincing. She opened the car door and stepped out, her cane in front of her. But before closing the door, she croaked out as if she was about to burst into tears:

"Yes."

CHAPTER TEN

"I have a right to be pissed, don't I?"

Elena ranted once again to Valerie, running her hands furiously through her hair.

Two weeks.

Two weeks since she had last talked to Autumn. At first, she avoided the girl like a plague and Autumn did the same, she was angry at Autumn for her sudden outburst at the karaoke bar.

But now, she was just hurt.

Hurt that Autumn would think of Elena in that way. She was also hurt because she thought she was different to Autumn, but Autumn treated her like she treated everyone else, with pure venom in her words.

"I mean, *she* insulted *me*." Elena continued as she walked back and forth in Valerie's small apartment. "She spit out her words like venom and now I'm infected. But as much as I want to stop having her venom rushing through my veins, it's there anyway. "She sighed.

Valerie listened to Elena's rant from her spot on the couch. "You do have a right to be angry with her, but I don't think you should hold on to that anger. It's not worth it, Lena." She told the younger girl.

"I'm not even angry anymore…" Elena trailed off with another sigh as she sat down next to Valerie. "Just hurt." She frowned. "I felt like I was the only exception with her. I was the only person she confided in, the only person she treated kindly, the only person she ever exposed her true side to…now I'm just everyone else. I'm ordinary, you can even say." Elena exhaled frustratingly. "She's just so…" she tightened her fists and groaned in frustration. "I can never know what she's thinking or what she's going through because she doesn't say *anything*. But she can read me so easily. It's frustrating."

Valerie frowned slightly and embraced Elena into a hug. "We always think we can change people until we realize the hard way that they can't be changed at all. Not easily, anyways." She advised. "You can't always be the person that picks up the pieces, Elena, you're going to have to let Autumn clean up this mess herself." She told her. "If she values your friendship with her, she'll make the attempt to keep it intact."

Elena cuddled into the hug and nodded. "You're right." She agreed, breaking the hug and nodding affirmatively. "You're right." She repeated. "If she wants to talk to me, she can. If she doesn't, well…whatever."

Valerie nodded and high-fived the younger girl. "Right on." She chuckled.

Elena smiled softly and looked at her phone for a second before dramatically throwing herself on the couch and whining. "I want to call her."

"You sound like a clingy ex-girlfriend."

"Am I at least a vengeful one?"

"Not even close." Valerie laughed.

Elena only pouted playfully and leaned her head back and stared up at the ceiling. Instinctively, she began to guess what specific color the white ceiling was. Eggshell white? No. Lime white. Definitely lime white.

"Can I ask you a question?" Valerie spoke up suddenly.

Elena turned her head to face Valerie and nodded. "Sure, lay it on me."

Valerie's doe eyes stared intently at Elena's own. "Autumn's not just a friend to you, is she?" she whispered.

Elena blushed and felt guilty at the faint nod she gave to Valerie, knowing very well the other girl wasn't over her. "No." She whispered back.

The other girl nodded. "I see…" she trailed off. "I knew it the moment I saw you again." She told Elena, not hiding her heartbreak. "You look at her like she's the only person in the room. It actually makes my heart ache less because it's cute." She smiled softly. "I just want you to be careful." She advised. "Regardless what happens between you and I, I am always going to care about you, Lena. And if I'm being honest…Autumn makes me worry."

"Why does it worry you?" Elena asked. "Autumn's never going to have any interest in me—"

"Exactly." Valerie cut off. "Even if she never does, I don't want you to do what I did." She paused. "I don't know why, but I waited for you. I guess a part of me hoped that if we were to see each other again, you'd still like me." She confessed, running her hand over her straightened hair. "Of course, that isn't the case anymore." She laughed awkwardly. "But I don't want you to get hurt, Autumn's the worst person you could fall for—not because she's a terrible person."

Valerie quickly added. "Because I'm sure she isn't. It's just…Autumn's the mess you want to fix." She told her. "Elena, you've always had this weird thing for wanting to help the entire world. If you see someone with even a *hint* of being broken, you automatically have this need to want to fix anything broken." Valerie observed. "I mean…remember—"

"I get it." Elena cut off, not wanting Valerie to mention the person that meant so much to her. "But Autumn's so much more than a story or a person to fix to me." She argued. "Autumn's almost...my dream girl. I know she's not perfect—she's far from it, really. But the feeling she gives me, it's like no other. She's my muse, my dream..." she trailed off, pursing her lips. "And I love her."

Valerie pursed her lips, nodding. "Regardless Elena, I want you to be careful. The last thing I want is for you to get hurt. Girls like Autumn are—"

"Worth getting hurt." Elena finished, even though she knew Valerie wasn't thinking that.

Valerie forced a small smile, worrying how deep in love the girl beside her had gotten. Regardless that Elena didn't reciprocate the feelings she felt still, she cared about Elena. And if the girl got hurt, she'd never forgive herself. "Does that mean you're going to call her?"

"No." Elena replied. "Like you said, let her pick up the pieces."

Just don't let her pick up any broken pieces of your heart when she hurts you. Valerie thought.

_____

Like the proper, rebellious, and angsty teenager Autumn was, she blasted Nirvana and wrote hastily in a cluttered journal that had post-it notes and slips of paper sticking out. It was the literal definition of word vomit so to speak. Even though she could never go back to reading what she wrote, it was nice to know that she spilled the words she needed to spill.

Everyone in the Castillo household was fully aware that when Autumn was in one of *those* moods, she was *not* to be disturbed. So when she heard the faint creak of the door opening, she sighed in frustration and angrily closed her journal.

"Olivia, what the hell did I say?" she shouted through the loud music. "I want to be freaking alone!" she growled, pushing her glasses up.

Ignoring her protests, the person walked up to her speakers and turned them off. "Well it's a good thing I'm not Olivia then." The voice spoke up.

Autumn furrowed her eyebrows in confusion. "Maya?" She was taken back by the sudden visit, she and Maya were civil enough with each other, but not enough to visit each other's homes and talk like they were connected to the hip.

"Your ears still work even after listening to this loud music, impressive." Maya sat down in front of Autumn, arms crossed.

"What are you doing here?" Autumn asked.

"I was casually strolling through the neighborhood and then I realized something—an epiphany, if you will." Maya replied. "You and I have more in common than you think." She told her. "And so I came here to address them."

"Oh really?"

"Really." Maya agreed. "You and I are basically polar opposites."

"Clearly."

"But there are a couple things we share in common."

"Please do enlighten me, Andrews." Autumn muttered uninterestedly, opening her journal again and scribbling back to where she last left off.

"For starters, we both care about Elena deeply." Maya began. "Of course, it's clear you care about her more profoundly." Autumn flinched at the mention of Elena. She had been trying to forget about the name and the person for the past two weeks, hoping that avoiding her would make her fall out of love.

Unfortunately, it wasn't a proven case. Maya noticed Autumn's change of behavior and took it as a sign to continue. "So being as you care about her so much, you must know that this fight is killing her. She misses you and you can't possibly tell me you don't miss her." Autumn shifted uncomfortably but still refused to say anything.

"I'll take that as a yes." Maya continued. "Look, this not talking to each other is getting ridiculous. I think you two should kiss and make up or whatever." She smirked when Autumn blushed and gulped when Maya mentioned kissing. "It's obvious you two miss each other."

"It's better off this way." Autumn replied, pursing her lips.

"No, it's not." Maya disagreed. "You can't leave things like this because you're always going to have that regret biting you relentlessly for letting go of possibly one of the greatest things to ever happen to you." Maya paused. "You and I both know she's not just another person to you. She's more than that. You have never treated someone the way you treat Elena. I see it, Autumn, you cannot deny me your feelings for her."

Autumn gulped, shaking her head. "I-I don't know what you're talking about." She stuttered nervously. Maya was right in everything she said, but she couldn't talk about it. If she talked about it, her feelings would worsen.

Maya pursed her lips and sat down beside Autumn. "You don't have to lie to me, I know. No one had to tell me because I see it." She smiled softly. "You're happier, even if you don't show it. She makes you happy. And you make her happy." She paused. "Which is why you can't let things stay how they are, talk to her. Make the first move."

"I can't."

"Why not?"

"I can't tell you." Autumn whispered, closing her journal.

Maya nodded in understanding. "I get it." She replied, shifting uncomfortably before speaking up again. "Can I tell you something and swear not to tell anyone? I'm trusting you on this."

Autumn nodded slowly. "Okay."

Maya chewed on her lower lip before saying what she needed to say. "My mom has breast cancer." She confessed. "She has been fighting since I was 11 and some days she's better, but other days there's the possibility I might have to say goodbye to her—*if* I even can." Maya gulped, feeling a knot in her throat. "That's why I have this weird obsession with never letting things stay unsaid or unsolved. Actually, it's more like a fear." She explained. "Because I'm afraid that like the situation with my mother, I'll spend the rest of my life with regrets—haunting regrets." She turned to Autumn.

"Look Autumn, I know about your struggle with cancer and how it contributed to your blindness…but I'm begging you, don't let those two things stop you from going after what you want." Maya advised. "My mom always says, 'Don't ever hesitate adding more sugar to your black coffee because if you're not content with the flavor, then keep sweetening it until it's perfect.'" Maya shrugged. "I never knew what she meant by that until recently, when I thought about you and Elena." She told her.

"Right now, you only taste black and bitter coffee because you're afraid of adding sugar into it—into your life. Elena is your sweetener and you're afraid of adding it because you're afraid it might not taste great, but what if it does? Don't be afraid of making your life sweeter, Autumn, because eventually you're going to grow tired of your black coffee and, by then, there'll be no sugar around to add."

Autumn didn't say anything because she was so stunned yet moved by Maya's words. Who knew Maya could be deep? But she knew Maya was right, her life was bitter and when something sweet like Elena arrived, she was afraid to go on and taste something different. She wanted to get out there and live and be happy but there was always one foot out the door and the other still glued onto the other side of it, forbidding her from fully exiting.

She was a coward, she knew that. She was afraid of what would happen after her walls were fully broken and everyone could see Autumn for who she truly was. She was also afraid of falling in love and ultimately getting her heart broken. For a girl who had endured pain for most of her life, she was afraid of the most painful thing. She was afraid of a pain not even *she* could numb out: love.

Maya patted Autumn's back and nodded. "I'm going to go and let the words sink in. I have to go see my mom right now anyways." She said to Autumn as she stood up. "If you do decide to taste a different coffee flavor," Maya stopped at the door and looked at Autumn again. "let me know how it tastes." She said before exiting the room.

———————————

Elena stuck her tongue out in concentration as she painted on the canvas in front of her. She had decided to skip lunch to work on her painting in Mrs. Freya's room instead. Although the true reason was to avoid Autumn again. As much as she wanted to mend their friendship, she was too stubborn to go talk to her. Besides, she was going to have Autumn pick up the pieces this time. And if Autumn truly cared about rescuing their friendship, she'd come to her.

She did miss Autumn, though.

She missed her tremendously.

She missed making her laugh and being the reason for the smile on Autumn's face. And she missed looking at Autumn's eyes. The girl had not *once* taken off her glasses, hiding not only her eyes from the rest of the world, but herself too. She sighed, as much as she loved the company of Phoenix and Maya and even Valerie, she felt lonely.

Putting her paintbrush down, she stared at the painting of the solemn girl in solitude in a room. She connected with the painting heavily right now.

"Solitude and loneliness, two of the worst feelings a person can experience." Mrs. Freya spoke up behind her. "But are portrayed *wonderfully* in art."

Elena nodded, putting on a small smile. "Yeah…" she trailed off.

"You want to talk about it?"

"The painting?"

"You know what I'm talking about." Mrs. Freya offered a warm smile.

Elena sighed. "It's just…someone is avoiding me since we had a disagreement—well, she did. I don't even know why to be honest, one minute we were fine and the next she was angry at me and lashing out." She explained. "I would normally approach to her about it, but I don't want to always pick up the pieces, you know?" she sighed again. "It's stupid."

Mrs. Freya thought for a moment. "I'm going to go out on a limb here and assume it's Autumn?" she guessed.

Elena blushed and nodded. "How—"

"You've been avoiding each other during class. I know I'm old, but I'm not *that* old yet. I still like to think I can detect teen angst."

The younger artist chuckled. "Right." She agreed.

"Well," Mrs. Freya began. "Autumn's a very guarded girl, I think you are aware of that." She paused. "So you can never know what's going on in that mind of hers, and that gets frustrating. You want to be there for her, and just when you think you're getting somewhere, she puts up another barrier for you to go through. It gets tiring, and it's easier to give up and leave. Autumn's use to people leave, so you need to show her you're not one of those people. Show her you're a permanent addition to her life, whether she likes it or not."

"I want to, but I don't want our relationship to be one-sided. I don't want to be the only one putting in the work while the other doesn't do anything." Elena told her, biting her lip. "I don't want to lose her, and I want to keep being there, but she doesn't put any effort either."

"Give her a reason to put effort then."

"How do I do that?"

"That," Mrs. Freya smiled. "Is for you to determine."

In Emma's car, the shorter girl was listening to what Autumn had to say, it was shocking how easily Autumn was speaking about her feelings and what she wanted to do about the Elena situation.

"So what do you think?" Autumn asked, chewing on her lower lip. "Should I talk to her?"

Emma nodded. "Definitely talk to her, Autumn," she agreed. "this whole not talking thing has gone on for long enough. And I don't know, maybe you could tell her how you feel about her…"

Autumn gulped, immediately shaking her head. "I don't want to ruin anything between us. I already tampered with our friendship, I don't want to ruin anything else." She paused. "And I want to make things easy for her, you know? Because being friends with me is hard enough, she couldn't possibly handle a relationship with me. I'm complicated in every sense of the word."

Maya's words still lingered in the back of her mind, but Autumn was afraid. If she confessed her feelings, things could either go well…or go completely wrong.

Emma placed her hand on top of Autumn's and offered a small smile. "You got to start taking chances, Autumn; you never know…maybe she feels the same way." Although Emma was fully aware that the feelings Autumn felt would be reciprocated. "But I'm not going to force you to jump into something you're not ready yet." She removed her hand from Autumn's and pursed her lips. "But talk to her regardless. Whether she's your friend or girlfriend, I know for a fact you want her in your life."

Autumn remained silent for a while, chewing on her lip so hard Emma could see her lips beginning to draw blood. She knew she was contemplating what her next move would be, but she sure was surprised what she said next.

"Start the car."

Emma placed the keys in the ignition and started the car with no hesitation. "Where to?"

"Elena's house."

_____

"What's a word for missing someone?" Ana asked Elena as she did a crossword in the kitchen.

"Saudade." Elena deadpanned, reading a book assigned from her English.

Ana raised an eyebrow. "*English* words, mija." She chuckled.

"Longing. Absence. Void."

"How cheery of you." Ana said sarcastically as she filled in the crossword with the word that fit the designated boxes. "Longing fits." She looked up at her daughter. "What's wrong?"

"Nothing." Elena lied. "It's the…color of the kitchen walls." She paused. "They bother me."

"The color mint bothers you?"

"Yeah," she nodded. "I mean, if the color made everyone's breath refreshing…then it would be a much better color."

Ana gave her daughter a quizzical look. "That makes no sense mija…" she chuckled.

"You're not an artist so you don't see it from *my* perspective."

"I think we need to check what paints we're buying you."

"The fumes give me a psychedelic feel, you can't take away what gives me inspiration." Elena joked.

Ana shook her head at her daughter, chuckling. "You're crazy."

"It's the paint, I can't help it."

The doorbell rang and Ana stood up, playfully whacking the back of Elena's head. "We'll talk about your issues with paint fumes later missy." She teased as she walked to the door, opening it.

Elena laughed and went back to her book, her eyes looking over the words. She could barely hear who her mother was talking to and soon after her mother came back.

"Elena, someone's here to see you."

"Who is it?" Elena closed her book.

"Go look." Ana grinned, patting her daughter's shoulder before she sat back down to work on her crossword puzzle.

Elena raised an eyebrow but walked to the living room, stopping when she immediately saw the person standing there awkwardly. "Autumn?"

Autumn gulped. "Hi." She whispered.

Elena stepped closer to her. "What are you doing here?"

"I want to talk." Autumn replied nervously, fumbling with her glasses. "But if you don't want to, I can leave. Emma's waiting anyways so—"

"We can talk." Elena smiled softly, feeling incredibly happy that Autumn was here. "Let's go to my room." She suggested, taking Autumn's hand and leading her up the stairs.

The two sat down on Elena's bed and sat there in awkward silence. Elena cleared her throat and turned to Autumn. "So...I think I have an idea what you want to talk about." She spoke up. "And I really want to know what I did to get you so mad and whatever it is I did, I really am sorry for making you feel that way. But this whole not talking thing *really* frustrates me because it's hard enough getting you to open up to me so then I'm just here thinking the worst and..." Elena rambled nervously.

"I don't want to lose you over something like this. You mean so much to me, but god damn it Autumn you frustrate me so much." She huffed. "Just...talk to me. It's as simple and as difficult as that." She pursed her lips. "And another thing—"

"I'll start talking as soon as you shut up." Autumn cut off.

Elena's face flushed. "Sorry." She muttered. "Go on. I'm all ears."

Autumn rubbed her sweaty hands together anxiously. "Well," she began. "I was…"Autumn chewed on her lip, nearly drawing blood again. "I was mad that Valerie was flirting with you." She confessed, bowing her head. "I didn't like that she was flirting with you and you were getting all flustered and giggly and…it angered me because…" she gulped.

Elena stared at her intently at Autumn, trying to decipher what the other girl was trying to say. But yet again, Autumn only opened up a small part of herself. Her hands reached Autumn's sunshades and gingerly removed them, noticing the other girl's green eyes full of fear and moving frantically back and forth.

"Because what Autumn?" Elena asked softly, urging the girl to continue talking.

Autumn's mouth was dry and she could feel panic settle in with ease at the thought of confessing feelings—a concept entirely new to her. "I can't do this." She said in a whisper, standing up immediately. "I'm sorry…but I just can't." she stammered, her white cane placed in front of her to make her way out.

Autumn had hit the nerve that was itching Elena for the past two weeks and she stood up, standing by the door in front of Autumn so she couldn't leave.

"*This* is what frustrates the fuck out of me!" Elena exclaimed in frustration, running her fingers through her hair hastily. "Just when I think I'm going to get through to you, you just shut yourself out again and build an even taller and stronger wall in front of you. I can't do this much longer Autumn," she sighed. "If you still want me to be involved in your life, then you need to pick up the pieces you broke recently." She told her, poking Autumn's chest. "*You*, not me."

Autumn lifted her head slowly, licking her cracked lips and gulping visibly. "I…" she began, knowing Elena was waiting for what she had to say. "I don't want to be your friend."

"What—"Elena said, her voice full of hurt. This was going in a direction she was hoping wouldn't happen.

"Let me finish." Autumn interrupted Elena. "I don't want to be your friend." She repeated again, her voice shaky. "Because friends don't want to kiss their friends." She paused. "But I do." She whispered, just loud enough for Elena to hear.

Elena's eyes widened in shock, unable to put together in words at what she was feeling at the moment with the unexpected confession. Autumn had feelings for her? Not platonic feelings, *romantic.* That hit her hard, she never expected Autumn to say that. She had a mixture of feelings; from fear to joy to anxiety to love. But at that moment, she couldn't express those completely to Autumn because she was just... shocked.

Autumn's eyes were full of panic and regret. "I shouldn't have said anything." She muttered, attempting to move past Elena.

Elena broke out of her thoughts and refocused back on Autumn. "Do you mean it?"

Autumn wet her lips again and nodded subtly. "Yes."

The two of them stood in silence, both their heads bowed down. Elena looked back up and stared at Autumn. "I want to kiss my friend too." She said quietly, watching Autumn's head lift up in surprise.

"What?"

"I like you Autumn. And it's nowhere near platonic." Elena clarified.

This time, it was Autumn's turn to be shocked. "Oh." She said stupidly.

Elena smiled at her response. "That sums up my thoughts exactly." She giggled. Autumn's cheeks flushed and turned her head away sheepishly, making Elena smile even more. "Now what?" she asked, biting her lip nervously.

"Now?" Autumn repeated. "Now, I want to lay in bed with you and listen to music and talk about nothing."

Elena broke out into a grin, stepping away from the door entry and grabbing Autumn's wrist. "I can arrange that."

She smelled like peaches.

That was all Autumn could think about, quite frankly, as Elena eventually leaned her head on Autumn's shoulder by the fifth song they listened to through Elena's headphones.

She was also warm.

Elena tentatively bundled closer next to Autumn, feeling Elena's warmth against her and the smell of peaches become a stronger scent. Autumn's hands could never stay warm, for the most part, they were always ice cold. But the moment Elena's warm hand met hers, her hands automatically became warm too.

Classical music (upon Autumn's request) filled the two girls' ear and Autumn smiled, feeling her heart flutter and she felt genuinely happy.

"I love this song." Elena spoke up with a smile, squeezing Autumn's hand.

"Me too." Autumn smiled.

She wasn't sure what to label her and Elena at the moment, because they hadn't discussed what would become of them. But right now, all of that didn't matter to her. She was next to a girl she had fallen in love with completely all at once.

Autumn turned to Elena, her fingers reaching out to trace the outline of Elena's soft lips. She licked her lips and wished for the millionth time since Elena came into her life that she could see her.

For once, she wanted her eyes to be able to look into hers. For once, she wanted things to be easy for them.

For once, she wanted to be brave and tell Elena just how much she meant to her. But Autumn wasn't there yet, and she didn't know when she'd get there. But in this moment, Autumn didn't think of all the things she needed to do. Right now, Elena was right in front of her. And she couldn't see her, but she was so beautiful. She didn't need to eyes to see just how much she loved Elena, because her heart felt it and that's all that mattered.

"Can I kiss you?" Elena whispered.

Autumn nodded, feeling touched that Elena didn't just go for the kiss. She asked for Autumn's permission. She wanted to make sure their kiss wasn't out of impulse. She wanted their kiss to be something they both wanted. And Autumn wanted it.

She suddenly felt Elena's soft lips against her own, and Autumn closed her eyes as she melted into the kiss, cupping Elena's face with her hands and sighing in content into the kiss.

Her coffee wasn't bitter anymore.

It was sweet and warm.

It was Elena.

CHAPTER ELEVEN

Autumn flinched when the inexperienced medical student jabbed the needle in her arm clumsily. Why did she give permission to these poor coordinated interns to stab needles in her and play doctor? She could never give you a proper answer to that question.

A part of her hoped one of these Doogie Howser wannabes somehow had enough oxygen coming into their brain to give them the full ability to *think*, and maybe—*just maybe*—they'd cure her of the dark world she lived in.

"Um, looks like I didn't find the vein." The med student laughed nervously. "Let me try again."

Definitely not this one, Autumn thought as she sighed in frustration. The medical student placed the alcohol wipe over Autumn's forearm again and cleaned the surface. Autumn felt the coldness of the sticky iodine being rubbed over her disinfected skin and decided to distract herself by opening her cluttered journal and scribbling some lyrics that were stuck in her head for the past couple of days.

The medical student glanced over curiously over Autumn's messy writing, managing to read some of the lyrics jotted down in the journal. On top of the written lyrics was what he assumed the instrumental arrangement for the song.

"Those are some good lyrics you've written down there." he complimented before sticking the needle in Autumn's arm again. "You're a musician?" he asked curiously.

Autumn didn't flinch this time when the medical student stabbed the needle in her arm. She wished looks could kill in that moment because *no one* was allowed to look or touch—let alone *read* her journal. He was lucky she had on sunglasses and he couldn't see her death glare.

"You're not supposed to read them." She scowled, quickly closing her journal and placing her needleless hand over it protectively. "And that's none of your business."

"Oh. My bad." The med student stammered, feeling intimidated by the younger girl. "But—um—that song...is it for someone?" he asked tentatively, despite the girl's harshness.

Autumn huffed. "Why don't you stick to minding your own business and sucking at being a medical student since you can't even find a freaking *vein* on my arm?" she spat harshly. "This isn't an episode of *Grey's Anatomy*, just find my vein and take my blood samples, tell me I'm still blind as a bat, jab some experimental drug on me that *just might* restore my vision—when we *all* know it won't, and

I'll be on my way waiting for the doctor's call of whether or not my body's being shitty…*again*."

The older boy gulped and nodded. "Okay." He agreed quietly, going back to his expedition of finding Autumn's vein for the third try.

Was that too harsh? Autumn thought to herself, suddenly feeling a twinge of guilt for snapping at the medical student. *Oh please, I once told a nurse her hands were too manly and they felt like burnt sausages. This is the nicest I'll be.*

In the back of her mind, she swore she could hear Elena's voice telling her to apologize. Autumn was in no way going to do that, so she settled for the next best thing. She sighed, she hated how much power Elena had over her. Here she was, feeling a change of heart for being unpleasant to the potential doctor.

After minutes of silence and the shaky med student *still* exploring the depths of her skin to find a vein, she spoke up again.

"Her name's Elena." Autumn mumbled.

The boy looked back to her and a small smile formed. "She sounds nice." He finally found the vein and began extracting blood from the vein and to small cylinders for testing. "How long have you been together?" he asked.

Autumn blushed. "We're not—I mean—there's something—but then again we haven't made much progress since—"she stammered.

"So it's complicated?" the older boy chuckled.

Autumn nodded. "Sort of—yeah. I mean, I want her to be my girlfriend, it's just...I'm more than just a girl she could potentially date, you know?" she paused. "I come with so much...work." she didn't understand why she was suddenly telling all of this to a guy she had yet to ask his name.

The med student placed two samples of blood on the tray beside him and continued taking the second to last sample. He hummed, indicating he was listening. "Well," he began. "I think if Elena really cares about you, she'll put in the work needed to be with you. Just as long as you put in your part too." He advised. "No relationship, regardless of what barriers they face, will *always* need to have effort put in. In the case of you and Elena, it's your health and...personality that's a barrier. But if you really want to make it work, you'll find a way."

Autumn listened intently and nodded slowly. "I just..." she trailed off. "Nothing." She shook her head, thinking she had shared enough already.

What she wanted to tell him was that a part of her was afraid to experience falling in love and ultimately getting her heart broken—because ultimately she would. It was hard to believe, but when Autumn loved someone—family, friend, or lover—she loved hard. She just showed it in small ways no one else would notice.

Emma didn't know it, but Autumn would purposely not hang out with Emma or cancel on plans so Emma could go out with other friends or do things she wanted instead of babysitting Autumn like she usually did. She wanted Emma to be a teenager, so she'd sacrifice her friendship for Emma's happiness in a heartbeat. She knew she's hurt the girl in many ways, but ultimately, Emma was like a sister to her.

Then came her parents. Every treatment, every surgery, every experimental drug that coursed through Autumn's body, was for them. If it was up to Autumn, she'd be dead already. Because she didn't want to live a life of darkness, no one ever does. But she kept her strength up for them, because she knew how hard it is for them to see Autumn in the position she's in.

And then…Elena.

Elena was someone Autumn loved profusely. If she was honest, Elena is the first person in a long time where she expresses her love for her. Granted, it was when the two were alone. But she opened up for Elena, she let her walls crack subtly, and part of her heart Elena was currently carrying. It was a big step for Autumn, because she still feared the repercussions that came with giving yourself to someone. She feared that Elena would eventually see how hard it is to be with Autumn and would ultimately give up, because soon come to see how much easier it would be for her to be with someone else than be with her. And by the time Elena would realize that, Autumn would be in too deep. Was it worth it? She'd come to find out if she tried.

The medical student didn't want to press any further, not wanting to overstep his boundaries. "I'm Toby by the way." He introduced himself. "Toby Sinclair He gave a small smile.

Autumn was thankful he didn't force an answer out of her and nodded to him with a soft smile. "You probably know my name already. But see, I'm trying out this thing called 'being polite' and so I think this is one of those things." She chuckled. "Autumn Castillo. 17." She introduced herself, reaching her hand out for Toby to take. "Nice to meet you Toby. But can I ask you a question?"

Toby chuckled, taking Autumn's hand and shaking it with his gloved one. "Sure, go for it." He nodded.

"How are you in medical school when you're 20 years old? Are you not as stupid as I thought you to be?" she half-questioned, half-teased.

"I skipped a couple of grades, yes. This noggin ain't empty." Toby tapped his head with his gloved finger with a laugh. "I'm in my third year of medical school; I was graduating high school when I should've been starting my first year of high school." He shrugged.

Autumn appeared impressed and nodded. "I don't think that was 'a couple' of years, but that's interesting. You actually are a real-life Doogie Howser…"

Toby furrowed his eyebrows together as he picked up the tray with the blood samples. "Who?"

"No." Autumn shook her head and groaned. "*Do not* tell me you've never heard of the show!"

"Am I supposed to?"

"How do you expect yourself to be a doctor if you've never seen it?" Autumn exclaimed.

Toby laughed. "I'll add it to my list of shows I need to watch." He told her. "I'll have your dad come back in the room; I got to take your blood for the vampires I hide in my apartment that feast on the blood of girls who have a severe case of the love bug." He joked, opening the door.

Autumn scoffed, a small smirk on her face. "*Goodbye,* Toby." She chuckled as he walked out the door. "And don't talk to me until you've watched Doogie Howser!"

Elena was mindlessly strumming random chords in her guitar and humming along when Phoenix barged into her room, uninvited, with an excited grin.

"What's cooler than cool?" Phoenix exclaimed.

Elena turned to look at Phoenix. "Ice cold?"

Phoenix winked at her. "I knew there was a reason our friendship exists." She quipped with a laugh.

"Wait," Elena furrowed her eyebrows. "We're friends?" she questioned. "I thought our friendship was based off of me supplying your hunger and weird fetish for Beyoncé memorabilia?"

"It is." Phoenix played along. "Which by the way, you need to go grocery shopping. Tell your parents." She teased. Elena giggled and Phoenix jumped onto the bed and propped up her elbow so that her head rested on her palm. "So I came here with a very important question that needs to be answered or I just wasted my energy and time getting you laid."

"What?"

Phoenix revealed two tickets to a show that had the New York Philharmonic label neatly printed on.

"I was not aware you had an appreciation for classical music." Elena raised an eyebrow in confusion.

The girl rolled her eyes. "I *don't*." she clarified. "But Autumn does."

"So you're taking her?" Elena questioned. "That's really sweet of you, Nix, I'm sure she'll be really excited."

Phoenix face-palmed and exhaled. "Have you been inhaling too many paint fumes that you're acting this naïve?" she retorted. "They're for *you* and *Autumn* to go!" she exclaimed.

Elena's mouth formed an 'o' shape in realization. "Oh." She said stupidly, taking a closer look at the tickets and her eyes widening. "HOLY SHIT YOU GOT TICKETS TO SEE YO-YO MA AND EMANUEL AX?" she shouted. "AUTUMN'S OBSESSED WITH THEM." She watched Phoenix's eyebrow raise in amusement and Elena blushed. "I mean—so I heard." She tried to play off nonchalantly.

Phoenix rolled her eyes playfully with a chuckle. "So will you take Autumn?"

Elena nodded without a second thought. "What kind of question is that?" she retorted with a laugh. "How'd you manage to get these tickets Phoenix? They're not the cheapest tickets to buy."

"I know a little person." Phoenix shrugged.

"Well how much were they? I'll pay you back—"

"Don't worry about it." Phoenix smiled.

"But—"Elena tried to object.

"Don't." Phoenix warned with a playful grin. "Focus on your potential date with Autumn." She wiggled her eyebrows. "Who knows? You guys might become an item after that." She winked.

Were her cheeks red? They probably were. A smile formed on her face and she bit her lip, her stomach tightening at the mention of Autumn. They've been more than better since the two confessed their poorly hidden feelings to each other.

Of course, they weren't exclusive or anything, but she could feel like that would happen any minute now. The perfect timing hadn't arrived yet.

Phoenix immediately noticed her cheesy behavior and raised an eyebrow. "Talk. *Now.*" She demanded, leaning closer in curiosity. Neither Elena nor Autumn had said anything about the two what happened between the two.

Elena blushed and looked down at her guitar before mumbling. "Autumn and I kissed."

The girl let out a loud scream of excitement that Elena was sure that her hearing had decreased at least 65%.

"Was that necessary?" Elena said as she rubbed her ears with a pout.

"Um, you just told me you and Autumn kissed..." Phoenix trailed off. "How else do I react?" she squealed, whacking Elena's arm instinctively.

"More humane?"

Phoenix glared teasingly. "Don't make me burn these tickets in front of you. All your chances of Autumn throwing her panties at you will quickly disappear." She waved the two tickets in front of Elena.

Elena rolled her eyes. "Does your mind think of anything else other than sex, Beyoncé, and food?"

"It also thinks about Alena."

Phoenix grinned cheekily at a blushing Elena who rolled her eyes again. "You're so terrible."

"So what happened after you two kissed?" Phoenix asked.

Elena blushed a deeper shade of red and couldn't suppress the wide grin. "We were just lying on my bed listening to music and talking about nothing." She smirked. "And kissing. A lot. The kissing was really, *really* good." She chewed on her lower lip.

"So are you guys dating now? Is my ship sailing?" Phoenix questioned with a smirk.

"Not yet." Elena frowned slightly. "But soon." She assured. She wasn't sure who she was assuring more—Phoenix or her.

Phoenix didn't say anything and handed the tickets to Elena. "So the show's at 8 p.m. on Friday, dress like uptight and spiffy old rich people." Phoenix gave a small smile. "I do hope you and Autumn become something more soon—whenever that soon may be." She said genuinely.

Elena returned the smile. "Thanks."

Phoenix nodded. "No problem." She sat up on the bed. "So I would be cautious on Friday. I heard it gets pretty wild at a symphony. There's panties' being thrown and intense head banging." She teased. "Don't let things get out of control, Díaz." She winked before the two said their goodbyes and Phoenix left.

Elena immediately grabbed her phone that was sitting on her nightstand and scrolled through her contacts and pressed on Autumn's name, dialing her number and waiting for the call to connect.

"Hello?" the other end of the line answered groggily—
Autumn must've been sleeping.

"You have a cute sleepy voice." Elena blushed, sitting on the
edge of her bed.

Autumn stretched on her bed and her eyes were fixated on the
ceiling. "Is that why you called me? Because I have a cute sleepy
voice?" she grinned with a blush on her cheeks as well.

Elena chewed on her lower lip and grinned. "It is now." She
said smoothly. "I actually called you for another reason." The Miami
native reached for the tickets on her desk and lied back down on her
bed, lying on her stomach. "What are you doing Friday night at 8?"

"Convincing my parents that I'm not depressed because I
refuse to come out of my room and listen to angsty music. Why?"
Autumn asked. "Are you asking me out on a date?" she grinned.

She giggled and shook her head at Autumn's dark humor but
then blushed. "I was, actually. But it looks like you're far too busy
being a teenager raging with angst to come with me to the New York
Philharmonic and witness a grand performance by Yo-Yo Ma and
Emanuel Ax…"

The other line went quiet for a while and Elena feared for a moment that Autumn was going to reject their potential date. She sat up a little and coughed. "Autumn?"

"You're fucking with me." Autumn said suddenly. "You are not currently in possession of tickets to heaven."

Elena chuckled, waving the tickets in front of her. "Alas, I am not messing with you. I am currently holding two tickets to see two of your favorite composers." She replied. "I can hear Emanuel Ax now…" Elena trailed off. "Autumn Castillo, come play a duet with me on the piano. I want to see your fingers dance on the black and white keys." She mocked in an exaggerated deep voice.

"Do not insult Emanuel Ax in that fashion!" Autumn scorned, hint of playfulness evident in her voice. "He is a Grammy-award winning classical pianist!" she informed.

"So you've told me a million other times." Elena teased, finding it incredibly cute how geeky Autumn could be when music came into the conversation. "I take it by the clear excitement you say yes to Friday?"

Autumn couldn't hide her grin filled with excitement. "I'd be a big idiot if I said no."

Elena fist pumped and was really glad no one was around to witness that. "You would. Dress in fancy clothes—or so I've been told. The more snobby, the better." she chuckled.

Autumn laughed. "How did you even manage to get those tickets? I heard they were really expensive *and* almost sold-out."

"A captain gave them to me." Elena pursed her lips to suppress herself from bursting into laughter. "She owns a ship."

Autumn's eyebrow rose. "Do I even need to ask?"

"Not really." Elena giggled.

Autumn joined in on her giggling. "You're so weird." She grinned. "I like it."

"Thanks." Elena smiled, placing the tickets back on her desk.

"Are you sure you're going to want to endure two hours of classical music? *Incredible* classical music, of course, but not everyone's into it. So don't force yourself to do something just because I want to." Autumn told her.

"I want to." Elena insisted. "Life's about making new experiences, right? I'm sure going to a classical music concert will be a refreshing experience." She smiled softly. "And besides," she paused. "There's nowhere else I'd rather be than right there next to you."

Autumn felt her cheeks grow hot and her smile grew even bigger. "Friday then."

"Friday." Elena confirmed. "I can't wait."

"Me neither." Autumn agreed. "I should go, I'm kind of drained of energy from my doctor's appointment."

Elena's eyes widened. "Doctor's appointment?" she repeated. "For what? What happened? Are you okay?" she asked worriedly.

Autumn giggled. "I'm fine, it's just a check-up to see how I'm doing. Everything's fine, Ellie, my body hasn't failed me yet."

Elena couldn't help but feel uneasy when Autumn said "*yet*". She couldn't possibly believe that she would get sick again eventually. Elena couldn't stand the idea of Autumn getting sick again, but decided to keep the thought to herself.

"Good. That's good." Elena sighed in relief. "I should let you go then, get some rest."

"Okay." Autumn yawned. "Bye, Elena."

"Bye." Elena said softly.

Before Elena could hang up, Autumn spoke up again. "Oh, and Elena?"

"Yeah?"

"Tell the captain of the ship I said thanks." Autumn smirked.

"So they're set for Friday?" Emma asked Phoenix as she, Phoenix, and Maya sat in her room talking about their little plan.

Phoenix nodded, showing the other two girls Elena's texts. "I think this gives enough proof."

Lena: *ASDFGHJKL AUTUMN SAID YES NO BIG DEAL.*

Lena: *PHOENIX SHE SAID YES AND I CAN'T COME UP WITH COHERENT SENTENCES NOW.*

Lena: *PHOENIX I'M GOING ON A DATE WITH AUTUMN HOLY SHIT.*

Lena: *PHOENIX. PHOENIX. PHOENIX. PHOENIX HALE ANSWER ME. PHOENIXHHHH!*

Lena: *MAYA WON'T REPLY TO MY TEXTS EITHER COME ONNNNN.*

Maya smirked. "She's *still* sending me messages." She waved the phone that kept vibrating.

Emma laughed. "Okay, well we got that over with." She grinned. "Do you think things will go well for them?" she asked nervously. She had been the one to propose to Maya and Phoenix that they give Elena and Autumn a little push so that they could grow some lady balls and start dating. Emma wanted to see Autumn happy, and she came to see that Elena had been making her happy since she first crept into Autumn's life.

"I'm sure they will." Maya assured. "Nothing brings people together like old men playing classical music." She teased.

Emma smacked her and laughed. "Shut up! I spent a lot of allowance money I had saved up on those tickets. Autumn loves those composers—especially Emanuel Ax. It's going to be a magical night!" she sighed dreamily. "I just want to see Autumn happy, and Elena makes her happy. Even if she doesn't full-on admit it, but I see potential in them. I know it will be hard for them, but I know they can do it."

"You're a good friend, Emma." Maya smiled. "I think they'll be just fine. There's only so much we can do, so let's let them take over now. And whatever happens, well, happens."

Emma nodded. "You're right. They'll be fine." She sighed. "I just hope things end well for the two of them. If Autumn says or does anything that hurts Elena, it'd be my fault." She said dejectedly. "When Autumn gets scared, or fears that she's going to get hurt, she shuts everyone out and builds harder and stronger walls to get into. Trust me, she's done that to me countless times. I just don't want her to do it to Elena. Elena's a great girl and I don't want her to give up on Autumn like other people have. There are only a handful of people that still believe in Autumn." She smiled sadly.

"Hey," Phoenix spoke up. "If there's anything I know about Elena, it's that she doesn't give up." She told them. "Seriously, Autumn could throw Elena a pile of bricks at her face and Elena would still think Autumn is a good person." Maya and Emma laughed at Phoenix who shrugged and continued. "Elena cares about Autumn, and she knows what she's getting herself into. We've told her since the moment her and Autumn met that Autumn comes with hard work, but she still went for it anyway. She sees something in Autumn that none of us see yet, so we shouldn't underestimate Elena's power. I mean, have you seen how much more talkative Autumn is with us. She's laughing more and smiling more and even joking around more since Elena appeared. Heck—she's *actually* being nice to Maya and I! I never thought that'd happen!" Phoenix exclaimed. "Point is, they're going to make it. I know that because I'm captain of the S.S Alena." She saluted.

"Um, and who told you that you were captain?" Emma teased, crossing her arms. "In case you don't remember, *I* bought the tickets for their date. *I'm* bringing the world Alena."

Phoenix raised an eyebrow. "Okay, *yeah*…but who delivered those tickets?" she retorted. Phoenix smirked and pointed to herself. "I did."

Emma pouted. "Not fair!"

Phoenix rolled her eyes playfully. "Okay, *fine* you can be co-captain I guess…" she mumbled.

Emma clapped her hands and together. "Yay!" she squealed. "We should totally get sailor hats and have them stitched with 'Co-Captain of the Alena ship'! We'll wear them whenever Elena and Autumn are around!"

Maya laughed and shook her head. "They're not even together and you two are basically planning their wedding now."

Phoenix smirked. "Guess you don't want to be a bridesmaid then."

Friday came sooner than Elena hoped and as soon as the bell of her last period rang, she ran out the door and tripped twice getting to her locker to collect to her belongings and once while walking home. An excited Elena came an extra clumsy Elena.

When she made it home (thankfully all in one piece), she almost ran into her mother as she dashed into the kitchen to grab a banana.

"Whoa! What's with the rush, speedy?" Her mother questioned.

Elena grinned and squealed, enveloping her mom in a hug. "I have a date with Autumn!"

Ana had a surprised look at first but then turned into a grin. "That's so great mija! I'm happy for you! I hope your date with Autumn goes amazing, where are you going?"

"We're going to the New York Philharmonic to see some composers Autumn likes. She's really into classical music and is actually classically trained in the piano." She replied.

"Well," Ana smiled. "whenever the chance comes, I'd love to meet Autumn properly. If she's making you this happy, then by all means, go for it." She squeezed Elena's cheeks affectionately. Elena grinned at her mother. "Now, go get ready for your date." She kissed her daughter's forehead. "I can't have my daughter looking like a homeless person." She joked.

Elena pouted. "Are you saying I look like a homeless person *now*?"

Ana only smirked. "Is that the phone ringing?" she questioned obliviously with a chuckle. "I should go answer it."

"Mom!" Elena exclaimed with a laugh. "You're so mean!" Ana only laughed as she waved her eldest daughter off to go get ready.

Elena did and wound up burning her forehead and hand with the curling iron twice and changing her outfit a dozen times—literally. She applied a small amount of make-up while jamming out to music. She smoothed her navy blue dress and adjusted her white scarf, approving of what she was wearing before grabbing the tickets and her purse. She gave a quick goodbye to her mother and Lily before heading to Autumn's with a fluttery feeling in her stomach.

The walk was short (mostly because Elena nearly ran to Autumn's house), and Elena let out a short, nervous breath as she slowly walked up the steps and rang the doorbell.

Elena smiled politely at the person who opened the door. She recognized the person as Autumn's little sister, Olivia, and nodded to her. "Hey. I came to—"

"Pick up Autumn?" Olivia finished with a grin. "I'm aware." She chuckled, moving aside for Elena to enter. Elena thanked her and stepped inside the cozy home. Olivia shut the door and turned to Elena. "Autumn's in her room with Emma getting ready." The younger girl explained. "I'm usually the one that helps Autumn get ready but Emma insisted on helping." She shrugged. "You can wait in the living room or go to Autumn's room or...whatever you want." Olivia smiled softly. "I'll be upstairs in my room if you need anything."

"Ow! Fuck, Emma!" the two girls could hear Autumn curse at Emma who was apologizing profusely.

Olivia laughed awkwardly. "Should I...?"

"I'll go." Elena offered. Olivia thanked her and ran up the stairs to her room while Elena chewed on her lower lip and walked over to Autumn's room, debating whether to barge into the room or knock.

"I'm sorry for hurting you, but you won't stay still, Autumn!" she could hear Emma scold.

"Well *maybe* if you were gentler, I wouldn't be in so much pain!" Autumn bit back.

"I *am* being gentle!" Emma argued. "You just squirm so much! It's not like this is your first time!"

Elena raised an eyebrow, wondering what was going on the other side of the door. Either her mind needed to get out of the gutter, or she was hearing exactly what she was thinking.

"It *is* my first time with an idiot like you!"

The Miami native suddenly opened the door and watched Emma curling Autumn's hair with a curling iron while Autumn looked frustrated and pissed off.

She needed to get her mind out of the gutter.

Emma turned to her and grinned. "Hey Elena!" she chirped.

Autumn immediately turned towards the door. "Ellie?" she called out and the hot curling iron burned her forehead again. She hissed and instinctively placed her hand on the burnt area. "Fucking shit!"

"That was not my fault..." Emma muttered as she took another long strand of Autumn's dark hair and rolled it on the curling iron.

Elena suppressed the urge to laugh and walked closer to the two girls. "You look beautiful..." she tilted her head. "Burns and all." She giggled.

Autumn blushed. "Thanks." She gestured Elena to walk closer to her and Elena hesitantly walked closer to her. Autumn's eyes weren't looking at her, but nevertheless, her hands reached out to softly touch Elena's face and then the fabric of her dress. Whenever Autumn touched Elena, she always felt her stomach flutter because Autumn was so gentle when she touched her.

"Yeah," Autumn smiled. "you look beautiful too."

It was Elena's turn to blush and she looked down at her hands to hide the wide smile. "Thanks." She mumbled.

Emma was watching the two girls interact with a wide grin on her face and suppressed the urge to squeal loudly. She couldn't suppress it, especially because the curling iron burned her hand. "Jesus! Ow!" she hissed. "That burns!"

Autumn smirked. "Serves you right after burning me 50 times."

"I'd say screw you…" Emma trailed off. "But I'll leave that up to Elena." She smirked.

Elena's eyes widened and Autumn coughed awkwardly. "What?" Autumn asked, attempting to feign innocence.

"Nothing…" Emma shrugged with her smirk intact. "nothing at all." She turned off the demonic curling iron and grabbed the can of hairspray and sprayed it all around Autumn's hair so that the soft curls would stay.

Autumn coughed. "Shit, Emma, are you trying to fuck up my lungs?" she breathed out. "I already have shitty eyes."

"So I've been told…" Emma chuckled.

"I think the ozone layer is even more fucked up now that you used that entire can of hairspray."

"You know, a 'Oh! Thank you Emma!' would be nice."

Autumn raised an eyebrow before sighing dramatically. "Thank you...*Emma*." She paused. "Nice enough for you?"

"Absolutely." Emma nodded as she put on some lip gloss on Autumn's lips. "My heart just swelled at your kind gesture."

Autumn grinned. "Aw, my sarcasm is rubbing off on you."

The tiny girl rolled her eyes playfully. "I didn't have much of a choice. I needed to adapt in order to survive."

"You make it sound like it's such a bad thing."

Emma snickered. "No comment." She stepped back and closed her lip gloss. "Your date is officially ready, Elena." She turned to her. "Try to ignore the burns, just like I ignore 97% of the bullshit that comes out of her mouth."

"See, I'm trying to be mad..." Autumn replied. "But the amount of sass you incorporated right now has me feeling like a proud mother."

Elena and Emma laughed at Autumn's comment and Elena couldn't help but feel joyful that Emma and Autumn were getting along so well. Compared to their relationship back when she first met Autumn, she'd like to say its improved drastically.

"Can one of you pass me my cane?" Autumn asked as she stood up and smoothed her maroon colored dress. Emma reached for the white cane that was beside Autumn's nightstand and placed it on her friend's hand. "Thanks…" She smiled softly. "Emma?"

Emma chuckled and nodded. "Yup. And you're welcome."

"Do you have any plans for tonight?" Autumn inquired. "Maybe with any of your other friends or Ethan?"

Emma shrugged. "Um, not really. I was planning on hanging around here for a little while. Your mom did promise to teach me how to make one of her delicious desserts." She replied. "*Or get drunk out of my mind.*" Emma thought to herself.

"That," Autumn stated. "is the saddest thing I've ever heard. And that's coming from a blind person." She said bluntly. "Seriously, how is hanging out with my mom more fun than going to screw your boyfriend?" she questioned. "Or going out to eat and *then* screwing your boyfriend."

Elena laughed but nodded in agreement, turning to Emma. "Yeah, Emma, you should go out tonight and have some fun. I'll take care of Autumn with my life." She told her. "You're a teenager too.

And hanging out with Autumn's mom on a Friday night isn't such a bad thing....but you should probably be doing teenager-y things. Like Autumn said—not saying you have to have sex with your boyfriend...but...yeah."

Emma raised an eyebrow. "So you're encouraging me to have sex with my boyfriend?"

Autumn shrugged. "I said you could eat before that too, don't limit your options. Except protection, don't limit your options there."

Emma rolled her eyes. "I need to recite you some passages from the bible, missy." She teased.

Autumn scoffed. "Been there, done that, and never going back." She retorted.

"Oh right...that exorcism never did work out, did it?" Emma smirked, pouring some of the water from a nearby water bottle on her hand and flicking some of it to Autumn's face. "THE POWER OF CHRIST COMPELS YOU!"

Autumn flinched at the contact with the water. Glaring, she tried her best to hold back from laughing. "Screw you, Emma!"

Elena was laughing hard while clutching onto her side. Watching Emma and Autumn interact was priceless when you saw it.

"I said the power of Christ compels you!" Emma continued, flicking water to Autumn's face again. "DEMON, FREE YOURSELF FROM THE POOR GIRL'S SPIRIT!"

This time, Autumn couldn't help but start laughing. She fell back on the bed and giggled maniacally. "Emma...you're...so..." she muttered in between laughs.

Autumn's laugh could solve the mystery of what happiness is. Because her laugh made Elena become the happiest girl in the world. Watching the two girls interact made Elena realize how happy Autumn made her without truly trying, and she knew in this moment that this was it. These were the moments to cherish. Because once in a blue moon did she get to witness the more youthful and happier side of Autumn, and she had to celebrate the moments when this side was here.

Emma and Autumn's laughter soon died down and Emma turned to Elena. "Well, I think my work is done here. I should get going, I will be calling Ethan up actually. Not for sex, for food." She smiled. "Have fun." She squeezed Elena's arm as she made her way out, collecting her things.

"Don't I get a goodbye?" Autumn asked, feigning hurt.

The shorter girl rolled her eyes playfully. "*Goodbye, Autumn.*" Emma said, faking annoyance.

Autumn only giggled and stood up with her trusty white cane in her hands. Emma left and the two girls were left by themselves.

"So that's Emma and I's friendship in a nutshell…on a good day." Autumn spoke up with a chuckle. "Sorry you had to witness that."

Elena snickered, shrugging. "It's fine. I found it rather entertaining, actually."

Autumn blushed. "I'm glad you did." She paused. "Should we go now?" she tilted her head to the side and Elena couldn't help but find it incredibly adorable.

"Can't contain your excitement quite longer, can you?" she smirked.

Autumn shook her head. "Not really, I'm five seconds away from having a screaming session."

"Well, let's not have *that* happen." She chuckled, squeezing Autumn's hand. "I rather have your breath taken away by something else."

"Like what?" Autumn asked.

"Me." Elena smirked.

Autumn laughed, her cheeks turning red. "Smooth, Díaz, very smooth."

"I try." Elena shrugged, chuckling. "Let's go, I wouldn't want you to miss out on one of the most monumental moments of your life besides meeting me."

Autumn rolled her eyes, snickering. "Let me just get my glasses."

"You don't need them." Elena assured.

Autumn fidgeted for a moment. "I just feel more comfortable with them on."

"I'll be your sunglasses then."

Autumn smiled. "Okay." She said softly.

"Although thinking about it now, I don't know how I'll be able to be your sunglasses…" Elena said worriedly.

"Why?" Autumn raised an eyebrow.

"I shine too bright and I'm too hot for my own good."

––––––––––––––

Elena wasn't the biggest fan of classical music, but she was the biggest fan of Autumn. Throughout the entire symphony, she spent more time watching Autumn deeply immersed with the music than the actual symphony itself. She found it endearing how her fingers pretended to be playing along with Emmanuel Ax himself and Autumn looked like she felt the music more than she heard it. Music was a passion for Autumn and she could clearly see it now.

Once the symphony was over, the two exited the building and walked the swarmed streets together. Autumn hadn't stopped talking *once* since the show finished and Elena only listened, a grin on her face.

"The way Mr. Ax played literally clenches the soul—at least mine." Autumn rambled for the thousandth time. She blushed, shaking her head. "Sorry," she chuckled awkwardly. "I must be boring you with my rants. I'm not crazy I swear, just passionate."

Elena shrugged, shaking her head. "I don't mind your rants. I like them." She assured.

Autumn nodded. "Did you like it? The show? I know two hours of that couldn't have been the most fun for you…"

"I liked it." Elena replied. "I mean, I spent most of the two hours staring at you…" she trailed off, watching Autumn blush. "But the music was enjoyable. I think you're way better, though." She grinned.

Autumn grinned. "You think I'm good?"

"I think you're incredible."

"You make it really hard not to like you." Autumn chuckled, blushing. "I could almost hate you for it."

"But you don't because you like me." Elena teased.

"Shush." Autumn giggled. "You're awfully humble today, aren't you?"

Elena flipped her hair dramatically. "Well," she said in a very elegant tone. "what can I say? I'm adored heavily…by *me*." She laughed, grinning cheekily.

Autumn snickered. "Dork." She mumbled.

The two walked in silence for a while, suddenly stopping when Elena saw a man playing the keyboard and a female cellist playing in a corner of a street. Elena always loved to watch street performers.

The duo was playing Beethoven and Elena watched as Autumn closed her eyes and let the music flow freely through her entire being.

"Can I hold your hand?" Elena whispered to her.

Autumn opened her eyes and nodded, reaching her hand out for Elena to take. Elena smiled, intertwining Autumn's cold hand with her warm one. They listened to the rest of the performance, Autumn's head resting on Elena's shoulder.

These were also the moments, Elena thought. These were the moments she had to cherish too. The moments of pure bliss. The moments where neither of them had a care in the world. The moments where Elena felt she could stay in this position forever.

Once the performance ended, Elena placed money in the cello case and never once let go of Autumn's hand.

"I had a great time tonight." Elena spoke up as they eventually reached Autumn's home.

"So did I, I can't thank you enough for doing that for me." Autumn said genuinely. "I always have the best time with you."

Elena blushed, looking down at the floor. "I do too." They walked up the steps and stood there, both unwilling to say goodbye just yet. "I'd like to do this again sometime with you—if you want to, of course." Elena said awkwardly. "Because, you know, I don't want to pressure you into, like, hanging out with me again or anything because I know I can get annoying since I tend to ramble a lot and say the dorkiest things and—"

Autumn interrupted her with a soft kiss on the lips, cupping Elena's face. Elena melted into the kiss and her hands reached to caress Autumn's face.

Once they broke the kiss, Autumn blushed. "You do ramble a lot."

"Y-yeah…I-I do." Elena said, flustered.

"But I love it." Autumn grinned, ringing the doorbell.

"I love you too." Elena blurted out, her eyes widening as Autumn raised an eyebrow. "I-I mean it…I love it too…my—uh—rambling. Yeah…rambling and…words." She stammered awkwardly, feeling her cheeks grow hot.

Autumn chuckled. "Even after that I still would love to do this again."

"Yeah?"

"Yeah."

The door opened and Dylan was on the other side. "All right ladies, cease the making out. You are in a family home for God sakes." Autumn rolled her eyes, recognizing Dylan's sarcastic voice.

"For a moment there, I thought I was in a zoo since you're here." Autumn replied.

"Ouch, sis…" Dylan said, pretending to be hurt by her words. "Hold off the venom there." He chuckled.

Autumn scoffed and turned to Elena. "I'll call you later." She smiled softly, squeezing Elena's arm. "Bye, Ellie."

Elena smiled back, nodding. "Yeah, bye Autumn."

Autumn walked inside her house and Dylan nodded to Elena and Elena returned the gesture before he closed the door.

Elena turned to walk down the steps when the door opened again and she turned back around. Autumn surprised her again by reaching out to her and giving her a small kiss.

"What was that for?" Elena whispered when they broke away.

"It was an 'I'll call you later' kiss."

Elena grinned and stared at Autumn's green eyes; they weren't looking at her but instead gazed at whatever was behind Elena. She kissed Autumn this time, feeling her stomach explode with butterflies once more at the contact. She leaned her forehead against Autumn's. "That was a 'You're driving me crazy' kiss."

Autumn chuckled, taking a small step back and grinning. "Bye, Ellie." She said, cupping Elena's face and softly kissing her cheek.

"Bye, Autumn." Elena said softly.

Autumn went back inside and closed the door, leave Elena alone again. She couldn't wipe the grin off her face as she walked back home and thought of all the types of kisses she could give Autumn.

She thought of 33.

CHAPTER TWELVE

Maya walked in the familiar hospital, having visited the same one every day for the past six years already.

Clutching onto the laminated folder filled with papers of research she had done the night before; call her obsessive but she knew everything there was to know about cancer.

When her mother was first diagnosed when she was 11, she was still oblivious of the potentially fatal condition. She only knew her mother was sick at the time. She just didn't know the degree of it. But by the time Maya was 13, and she nearly lost her mother to the killer disease, that's when she sprung into action.

She spent countless days on her laptop and at the library filling her brain up with every single piece of information there was to know about breast cancer. She even wrote research papers, she was *that* obsessed with it. Pretty soon, she expanded her knowledge and learned more about other types of cancers and tumors.

She did it for one reason: to have her mother stay alive. Maya loved her mother—*worshipped* her even. The idea of her mother possibly not being around for much sooner *terrified* her, she's spent nights crying herself to sleep because the idea of never getting the chance to say goodbye to her mother left her paranoid. Every time she went somewhere that wasn't the hospital near her mother, she feared she'd lose her mother and wouldn't get the chance to say goodbye.

While she did love dancing, singing, acting, and worshipping Beyoncé, her life revolved around her mother. Maybe a little *too* much. She'd often spend her day researching potential treatments for her mother and consulting with her doctor rather than hanging out with her friends or attending dance class. But if it meant getting more time with her mother, she'd make the sacrifice. Because time was something Maya cherished deeply.

She knocked on her mother's door from outside her hospital room. Her mom hasn't been home in two years, and needless to say it killed her. Maya's head peeked into the room and her mother was sleeping, a nurse checking her vitals. She smiled softly at the sight; even though her mother looked sick, with her thin body, heavy bags under her eyes, and no hair on her head, she still looked beautiful in Maya's eyes. Like her wise mother says, "When someone shows heart and soul to you, they're even more beautiful than anyone else in the world." And her mother always showed that to Maya.

Stepping inside the room, she heard the beeping of the heart monitor that kept her sane. It meant there was still life in her mother, and that sound was the most comforting sound she's ever heard.

The nurse turned to Maya and smiled politely. "Hello."

Maya returned the gesture, turning to look at her mother again. "How is she?" she asked softly.

"Better than most days I suppose." The nurse sighed quietly. "She's eaten a little today, surprisingly, since she had chemo this morning."

Maya placed her warm hand on top of her mother's and kneeled beside her, her fingertips cold as always. "It's better than nothing, I guess." She shrugged.

The nurse smiled sadly, nodding to the laminated folder in Maya's hands. "Got a new batch to show Dr. Rivera?"

Maya looked down at the folder and nodded. "Yeah, it's a clinical treatment I read in this study I found online. I think it could help my mom since the chemo isn't being as successful this time around..." she explained briefly.

The nurse patted Maya's shoulder. "Well I'm sure that Dr. Rivera will be fascinated with what you have to show her." She assured the younger girl. "She's always talking about you and how she sees so much potential in you."

Maya smiled. "Thanks." She said softly. The nurse nodded to her and made her way out, off to assist other patients.

Once Maya was left alone with just her mother, she turned back to her mother a smile on her face. She spent almost an hour just kneeling next to her mother while she slept, watching her tenderness in her eyes.

Her mother's eyes fluttered opened and looked around the room before her eyes landed on her daughter with a grin on her face. "Hey there May bear." She greeted warmly.

Maya grinned as well, kissing her mother's cheek. "Hi mom."

"Don't you have dance class today?" Grace queried. "Unless the day's gone by quickly again and you already went."

"I skipped it." Maya replied. "I have this possible treatment I found that I want to show Dr. Rivera."

Her mother smiled proudly, lifting herself up so that she was in a sitting position. "As proud as I am that my baby is one smart cookie, you shouldn't be wasting your time with all this research. You worry about being a teenager and I'll worry about this. I'm the adult and you're the child."

"I don't mind, mom." Maya insisted. "If it means you getting better, I'll spend all my time doing this for you."

Grace smiled at her daughter again, caressing her daughter's cheek. "I really hit the jackpot, didn't I?"

Maya grinned cheekily, shrugging. "A little, yeah." She agreed, making the two laugh. The two dived into a different conversation, talking about anything but cancer. "So I've been thinking about changing up my hair." Maya told her mom, running her hands through her straightened, brown hair.

Her mother stared at Maya for a couple moments, running her hand through her hair. "Why don't you leave your hair in curls? I love your curls." She suggested.

Maya smiled wide. "See, this is why I only trust you when it comes to things like this. You have exquisite taste, mom." She praised.

The older woman shrugged. "I try." She chuckled.

Maya's stomach suddenly growled and her mother raised an eyebrow. "Have you eaten anything baby?"

"I ate this morning." She defended weakly. "I'll just go get something from the cafeteria really quick." She stood up. "I won't take long." She assured.

"Take all the time you need. I'll still be here." Her mother reassured.

Maya's smile faltered. Time. What a bitch it could be, sometimes. "Okay then."

Maya walked out of her mother's room and opened up the folder again, looking over the papers and making sure everything was credible enough to show Dr. Rivera later. Too preoccupied in the contents in her folder, she didn't notice the person coming the opposite direction.

All her sheets scattered everywhere on the floor and the taller body instinctively grabbed Maya from falling backwards. The girl squealed and was about to tell off the person that dropped her papers (which she thankfully numbered) but suddenly was met with a pair of striking blue eyes.

Oh.

"I-I am so, *so* sorry miss!" the boy exclaimed, an apologetic look on his face. A very *cute* face, Maya would like to clarify. His eyes were *so* blue; it was like looking into an ocean. He had pale skin, clear of blemishes, making his blue eyes stand out even more. He wasn't muscular, he was more on the lankier side, but Maya still thought his face was carved by the gods.

For a second, Maya forgot how to talk and just let out a noise she couldn't quite make out as anything other than *embarrassing*. She turned red and chuckled awkwardly. "It's—um, it's okay. You're okay." She stammered nervously.

The boy chuckled and his eyes locked with Maya's and she was sure she would melt on the spot. Realizing he was still holding her, he let go of her and laughed awkwardly, rubbing the back of his neck. "Uh—let me help you with your papers." He mumbled, kneeling down to pick up the scattered papers.

"Oh—no—you don't have to…" Maya trailed off, kneeling on the floor to pick up some sheets of paper herself.

They picked up the sheets in silence, looking up at each other every couple of seconds and smiling at each other and looking back down with a blush creeping onto their faces.

Finally picking up all the sheets, they stood back up and the boy's eyes scanned over some of the papers, reading what Maya had on it curiously.

He looked back up and handed the papers back to Maya. "You wrote this?" he asked.

Maya nodded shyly. "Yeah. It's a research paper I wrote for one of the doctors here—"

"Which doctor?" he tilted his head.

"Dr. Rivera. She helps my family and me with…a close relative's condition." Maya replied, tucking a strand of hair behind her ear, biting her lip.

The boy nodded slowly. "Impressive. This is incredibly well-written." He praised. "I've heard of this clinical treatment. It's for breast cancer, right?"

"Yeah, it's a type of vaccine for breast cancer. It's currently being tested and it's worked in some cases." Maya explained. "It attacks the cancer cells with the boosted immune system with the vaccines given. And it could really help my—a special person to me." She smiled softly.

The boy stared at Maya for a while that made her feel flustered until he spoke up again. "How old are you?"

"17." Maya answered.

The boy nodded. "Given your age, the amount of knowledge you possess is quite fascinating. From what you just told me, and from what I briefly read, I can tell you know a lot about the topic of breast cancer. *Very* well, actually. Have you considered going into medicine?"

Maya looked down at her stacked sheets and shrugged. "I have considered it." She replied sheepishly. "But I also have Julliard eyeing me. I'm a dancer." She told him. "So I don't know. Cancer hits close to home, and if there's a chance that I could stop another family from feeling the pain I have felt alongside my family by pursuing being a doctor…I would do it in a heartbeat."

He broke out into a grin and *God* he had a gorgeous grin. "You'd make a great doctor." He extended his hand. "Toby Sinclair. 20."

Maya blushed. "Maya Andrews." She took his warm hand and shook it. She suddenly noticed the white lab coat he was wearing and tilted her head in curiosity. "You're a doctor?"

"Doctor in training." Toby shrugged. "I'm in my third year of medical school."

"Impressive. Given your age." She teased him, using the words he had used on her earlier.

He chuckled. "I see what you did there." He grinned.

The two remained silent for a while before Maya remembered she had to go get something to eat and then head straight back to her mother. "I should—um—I should go." She spoke up, smiling apologetically. "It was nice meeting you." She mumbled, about to keep walking until Toby grabbed her arm.

"Wait!" he exclaimed. Maya turned to him, eyebrow raised. He turned red again. "I—uh. I'd like to see you again." He told her. "Do you think we can do that?" he smiled softly.

Maya grinned, nodding. "Yeah…I think we can do that."

At the unexpected break-up between Jacob and Phoenix, the girls immediately decided to host a sleepover at Emma's place.

With all the necessities on dealing with a break-up (dancey music—sad, break-up music is a no-no, movies with lots of violence and gore, carb and sugar loaded junk food, and lots of laughing), the girls were huddled around Emma's kitchen, Emma bringing out her incredible baking skills and making an enormous amount of cookies.

"Emma, these cookies smell *so* good." Phoenix hummed, practically drooling over the chocolate chip cookies and snickerdoodles. "You should totally become a baker. I'd be your loyal customer if you opened up your own bakery."

Emma chuckled as she took out another batch from the oven. "Thank you, Phoenix." She smiled. "I have considered it, actually."

"You'd make a fortune with Phoenix and her family." Autumn smirked. "Since 75% of New York's population *is* Phoenix's family."

Phoenix rolled her eyes playfully. "*So* funny, Loser." She replied.

Autumn shrugged. "It's my attempt of making you feel better for getting dumped." Phoenix snickered while Emma whacked

Autumn's arm with a wooden spoon, giving her a look. "Ow!" Autumn rubbed her arm. "Emma! Haven't you heard of dark humor?"

"I've known you since birth, of course I do." Emma retorted, placing the newest batch of cookies on a plate. "Now someone help me bring up all of this food to my room, we have a broken heart to mend."

"And bones to break." Elena chimed in, helping Emma with some of the vast amounts of junk food.

Maya finished replying to the text she received before putting her phone away and helping out as well. "That's for later, Lena." She joked. "Arson might be included too." She winked.

"This is why you're the one that comes up with the genius ideas, May Poodle." Elena grinned cheekily, ruffling Maya's newly curly hair.

Maya glared at her playfully while fixing her curls. "After we burn the douchebag, I'm burning your scarf collection." She grinned sweetly. Elena gasped dramatically.

Phoenix snorted. "He's not even worth potentially going to juvy." Phoenix shrugged and faked a smile, carrying bags of chips and two liters of soda. "He can go die in a ditch for all I care."

The worst part was that Phoenix did care, she always would. Jacob was one of her closest friends before they became a couple, so she didn't just lose a boyfriend, but also a best friend. But he did her wrong, he told her things that made a gunshot to the stomach sound like a better idea than listening to him say those things to her again.

When you come from a big family like Phoenix's, it's pretty much expected that money would be a little tight.

Well for Phoenix it wasn't a little, it was a lot. Her dad had lost his job a while back and so that was one less paycheck coming in the large household. Eventually, the bills came in like a tidal wave and they couldn't pay for them all. Especially the rent for the apartment they lived in back then. They were eventually evicted and had to move in with other family members, making it a household of 22 people.

It had been eight months since they had to leave their home and their situation was worse than ever. With a bigger household came even more demand for food, clothes, and other necessities to live comfortably. Well, it was far from comfortable.

And she thought Jacob understood that she couldn't go out like she use to with him because she had her cousins and siblings to watch. He did, at first. But he grew frustrated and Phoenix to go on dates and football games, but Phoenix couldn't keep up.

So today, after spewing out a series of insults to her and even making her cry, he ended things.

"That's the spirit." Autumn butted in, walking up to them with her trusty white cane.

Phoenix laughed. "Thanks, Loser."

"I'm sure he's going to regret dumping you. Because who wouldn't want someone who loves Beyoncé more than them?"

To Autumn's standards, that was her being at her nicest. Phoenix gave Autumn some credit for that. "Was that you trying to be somewhat nice?" Phoenix teased. "Don't tell me the Castillo ice heart is melting."

"Oh please," Autumn scoffed. "There will always be a cold spot in my heart." She smirked. "Just for you."

"Enough with the kind words Autumn, *please*." Phoenix chuckled. "People are going to think I'm a big softie or something." Autumn only snickered. Phoenix offered her arm to Autumn which the girl happily took as they slowly walked up the stairs.

"So…" Phoenix smirked. "You and Elena, huh?"

Autumn blushed, thanking the heavens above that she was wearing sunglasses so Phoenix couldn't see the distress in her eyes. "Wha-what about us?" she stammered.

"It's *almost* cute when you're flustered." Phoenix provoked with a grin.

"Shut up." Autumn muttered, feeling her face grow hotter.

Phoenix's grin only stretched more. "You know, here's a thought." She began. "If you like Elena, you should…I don't know…maybe make it official?" she suggested, kinking an eyebrow.

"We're taking things slow." Autumn told her.

Phoenix hummed. "Well, don't be *too* slow now." She advised the shorter girl. "Lena can only wait so long."

"I know." Autumn said quietly.

Phoenix didn't say anything else as they walked in Emma's spacious room. Autumn let go of Phoenix's arm, having Emma's room memorized from the billion of times she's come here. She sat on Emma's bed, leaning against the headboard as she heard the girls setting up their sleepover, hearing the laughter, teasing, and jokes being exchanged.

She sometimes she wished it was simple enough for her to just join in on that. They tried their best to include her, but sometimes it was just hard for a blind person to do something that is so simple to a person who could see.

"What have I told you?" Elena approached her, taking off her sunglasses. "I like seeing your eyes."

Autumn smiled. "So you've told me." She replied.

Elena stared at her for a couple moments, biting her lip. She broke herself out of the trance and coughed. "Well anyways, I hope you don't think you're going to be here all by yourself tonight." She told her. "You're about to join in on the crazy too." She laughed.

"Why does that suddenly scare me?"

"Because it should…" Elena trailed off mysteriously before bursting into a fit of giggles that made Autumn's stomach flutter.

Autumn snorted. "I never took you as a mysterious girl."

"Oh yeah, I'm full of mystery." Elena bluffed, flipping her hair. "For example, right now the biggest mystery about me is how many of Emma's cookies can I eat in a sitting." She winked.

Autumn giggled, rolling her eyes. "Knowing you, I'm sure you're capable of eating all of them."

Elena shook her finger at Autumn. "Guess you do know me."

"It's kind of impossible not to."

"Why's that?"

"Because…" Autumn smiled softly. "You're worth learning everything about."

God she wanted to kiss Autumn right now. Could she be even more amazing? When Autumn said things like that, it reassured her that it was going to happen. Soon, they would be together as a couple. It assured her that Autumn was worth the wait.

Elena kissed Autumn's cheek, taking her hand. "Get ready to be stupid with us." She grinned.

Autumn squeezed her hand. "I've been mentally preparing myself." She smiled as Elena led her to the middle of Emma's room where the rest of the girls were already eating from the variety of junk food and trying to pick out a movie to watch.

"I'm not sure I want to watch *Machete* or *Texas Chainsaw Massacre* while eating food…" Emma trailed off, popping some gummy worms in her mouth. "I want to keep my room vomit-free."

Phoenix shrugged. "You're probably right." She agreed. "Plus, you shouldn't give a crazy ex-girlfriend like me any ideas on how to murder my boy—*ex*-boyfriend." Her face grimaced.

"But *Texas Chainsaw Massacre* is awesome!" Autumn whined as she sat down on the carpet floor.

"That movie traumatized me for life." Emma turned to Autumn. "Remember when we watched a crazy amount of movies because you said you wanted to see every movie possible before…you know…"

Autumn smiled fondly. "That was fun."

"It was. When we weren't watching horror movies, at least." Emma chuckled, briefly reminiscing memories from their childhood and feeling nostalgic.

"You've always been such a wuss." Autumn teased with a smirk.

Emma rolled her eyes. "And you've always been such a…Autumn." She chuckled.

"Ooh, burn. I think I need someone to apply some ice to that monumental burn."

"Shut up." Emma laughed.

Everyone else had amused expressions on their faces at Emma and Autumn's witty banter. "I honestly could watch you two go at it all day, it's *that* hilarious." Maya spoke up with a laugh. Her phone vibrated again, indicating a text and her eyes quickly darted to her phone. She and Toby had exchanged numbers and hadn't stopped texting since.

Elena smirked. "You see that guys?" she chuckled. "Well, Autumn can't but that's not the point."

"That's a bad joke, Ellie." Autumn laughed.

Elena shrugged. "I'm full of them, remember?" she grinned. Autumn grinned as well and shook her head. "But anyways…who you texting there, May?" Elena addressed.

Maya was smiling at the text Toby had sent and looked up with the smile still intact. "What?"

"Phoenix, take her phone." Elena smirked playfully.

Phoenix quickly tackled Maya and snatched her phone out of her hands, throwing it to Elena who caught it. "No! Give me back my phone you jerks!" Maya exclaimed, suppressing the urge to laugh.

Elena only glanced at the contact name. "Toby Sinclair…" she trailed off with a grin. "Ooh, sounds sophisticated." She teased to a blushing Maya who was struggling to break free of Phoenix's grasp. "And Maya's *blushing*!"

"I hate you guys so much!" Maya glared at Phoenix and Elena.

"Doogie Howser." Autumn said, surprised at hearing the name. "I know that guy. He couldn't find my vein while collecting blood samples from a doctor's appointment. He's a stuttering mess."

"It's cute!" Maya argued as Phoenix freed her, she quickly walked to Elena and yanked the phone from her hands.

Phoenix pointed at Maya accusingly. "Aha! So you admit that he's cute!" causing Maya to blush even harder.

"How do you know him?" Autumn continued.

Maya's eyes widened. "Um, I…I was…" she thought up of an excuse. "One of the guys from my dance class broke their leg and I was visiting him. I ran into Toby there." She lied, sitting back down on her spot.

"So this Toby guy is a doctor?" Emma asked with a grin. "Ooh, how interesting. You *have* to tell us about him!"

"I…" Maya looked down sheepishly. "I don't know…"

"Please, May!" Phoenix pleaded. "I'd love to get my mind off Jacob and if you talk about this Toby guy, it'd help."

Maya pursed her lips and sat down on the floor again. "I guess I can say a little…" she mumbled sheepishly.

Phoenix, Elena, and Emma squealed and sat back down to listen to what Maya would tell them. "Speak, now!" Elena exclaimed, moving closer to Autumn.

Maya ran her hand through her curls before speaking. "Well, he's got the bluest eyes I've ever seen. It's like looking at the sky, almost. They're so amazing and that's all I could stare at—minus his really cute face." She blushed and looked at the girls to make sure they were still listening while she rambled. "He's really sweet too and so adorable. He was probably as much of a nervous wreck as I was."

"You're meant to be then, if that's the case." Emma teased with a wink.

Maya rolled her eyes playfully. "*Anyway*, we ran into each other—*literally*—and he helped me pick up my things and we talked a little and he told me he wanted to see me again." She couldn't suppress the smile on her face. "And we haven't stopped talking since then."

"I think I'm about to puke glitter and cupcakes." Autumn spoke up. Everyone turned to look at her. "In a good way. That was...kind of cute. Almost heartwarming."

Maya chuckled. "Thanks, Autumn." The girl only smiled softly and nodded and Maya happily returned it, even if she knew Autumn couldn't see it.

"So is Moby a go yet? Is this another ship I must embark in?" Phoenix grinned.

"We just met—"

"Your point?" Phoenix cut off. "I think if there's a connection there, you should go for it. You've only been in one other relationship before and that didn't last long. And most of your dates always end in disaster. I think this Toby guy might be what you've been looking for."

Maya shrugged. "I don't know, I don't really have time for a boyfriend…"

"Love doesn't have a schedule." Elena shared. "If it did, then it's really late with me." She laughed.

"I agree with Lena." Emma nodded. "Just go with the flow. If it happens, it happens. But don't put too much thought into it. Keep it casual with him. But if something does start and your feelings grow stronger, don't push them away." Emma glanced at Elena and Autumn before her eyes directed back to Maya. "Every girl deserves a love story."

Maya smiled softly. "I'll do that. Just keep things calm. We just met anyways and—"

"You guys are crazy for each other." Phoenix teased. "You text him like crazy and blush at whatever he writes. If that's not feelings surfacing from the get go, I don't know what is…"

Maya rolled her eyes. "Change of subject before Phoenix starts planning my wedding."

"What makes you think I haven't already?" Phoenix winked. "Beyoncé's been booked already in…15 years time."

"Wonderful."

"I also bought you lingerie for when you and your lover…" Phoenix whistled.

Maya laughed awkwardly and threw a pillow at Phoenix. "I can't deal with you sometimes."

"But you still do anyways." Phoenix retorted.

"Because if I didn't, you'd be in a juvenile correctional facility right now." Maya smirked.

Phoenix stared at her for a couple moments before nodding. "Okay, *true*."

"I don't know what bickering is better, Phoenix and Maya's or you and Emma's…" Elena told Autumn with a laugh while Phoenix and Maya argued.

"Both. Both are good." Autumn smiled.

Elena smiled and leaned over to her ear. "Can I hold your hand?" she asked softly.

Autumn nodded. "I'd like that."

"Your hands are always freezing cold, of course you would." Elena giggled, placing her hand on top of Autumn's and squeezing it.

"I like your hands. They're so warm and soft." Autumn squeezed back.

"And yours are clammy and freezing."

"I think that's the perfect combination, don't you think?" Autumn asked.

"Are you saying we're perfect for each other?" Elena grinned.

"Maybe." Autumn shrugged. "But I know for a fact our hands are."

And that was good enough for Elena at the moment.

"Hey, lovebirds! The party is over here!" Emma laughed.

The two girls blushed. "Right. Of course." Autumn replied awkwardly, letting go of Elena's hand. Elena pouted slightly at the loss of the cold and clammy hand.

"So, how about we take a break from the love lives you all seem to have and I don't and we…dance?" Phoenix suggested.

"Oh yes, let's have a blind girl dance." Autumn agreed sarcastically. "She won't fall or break several bones at all. Perfect suggestion, Phoenix Hale."

Phoenix rolled her eyes. "It's not so hard. Just live a little and try, Castillo."

"I haven't danced since I was 10 years old." Autumn told her. "That was before I became blind and Emma and I had a five hour long dance party."

"Well in my defense, I was running on a liter of Dr. Pepper and a bag of skittles." Emma butted in with a laugh.

"Yes, and I with sour patch kids and Sprite—surprisingly a good combination." Autumn replied before turning back to Phoenix. "Point is, I don't dance and I'm not even sure I *can* dance anyway." She shrugged.

"That is why we're going to try right now." Phoenix stood up and walked over to Autumn, taking her hands and pulling her up. "We'll make sure you don't fall." She assured.

Autumn still looked hesitant. "I don't know…"

"Be a teenager girl for once Autumn." Phoenix insisted, smiling softly and turning to the rest of the girls. "Let's *all* be a teenagers for at least one night. We'll forget any problems we're dealing with and just focus on right now and dancing our asses off."

"I'm with Phoenix on this one." Maya grinned, standing up and walking over to Emma's speakers, plugging in her phone and putting a song.

"Yeah, and we'll even move the furniture to the sides so Autumn doesn't run into anything and fall." Emma turned to Autumn. "Come on Autumn, let's be crazy for one night." She told her while moving some furniture to the corners of the room to give them more space.

Elena helped Emma rearrange the furniture and turned to Autumn. "Remember the concept of whatever." She simply said before picking up a chair and putting on a corner of the room.

Autumn ran her hand through her hair, sweeping it to the side before sighing. "Whatever." Elena grinned. "If I hurt myself, you guys are paying for my hospital bill."

The rest of the girls cheered and finished rearranging the room. "I'm glad you agreed to this, because with your fine Latina ass, I'm sure you can dance." Phoenix smirked.

Autumn raised an eyebrow. "I wasn't aware my ass was fine."

"It is. I think it's a Latina thing." Phoenix shrugged. "Because
Elena's ass is so fine, it should have insurance." Autumn only laughed
awkwardly.

"That's J-Lo's butt!" Emma butted in.

Elena passed by them, holding a beanbag chair. "And you
need to stop talking about my butt, it's getting to an obsessive point."
Phoenix only slapped her butt and Elena glared at her.

"Maya! Will you hurry up? I want to get my dancing on!"
Phoenix walked over to Maya and the two began arguing about what
songs would be perfect to dance to.

Elena ran up to them with her phone in her hands. "Use my
music!"

"Hell no! I want to have fun, not cry!" Phoenix exclaimed.

Elena pouted. "No! Phoenix! I have a playlist specifically for
dancing and jamming out! Please!" she begged, tiptoeing up to her
friend's face, pouting even more.

Phoenix sighed, rolling her eyes. "*Fine.*" She agreed, a smile
on her face. She took Elena's phone and plugged it in with the
speakers. "Work your magic, Díaz." She teased, handing Elena her

phone. The girl stuck her tongue out and tapped on her phone before putting her iPod on shuffle.

A Demi Lovato song began playing and everyone minus Autumn cheered at the song choice. Autumn simply crossed her arms and raised an eyebrow.

Emma pulled Autumn into the middle of the room with a giggle. "Come on, Debbie Downer! Dance!" she exclaimed to Autumn as the rest of the girls screamed out lyrics—Phoenix, especially.

"What do I even do?" Autumn questioned as she swayed awkwardly to the song.

Emma was moving Autumn's arm and jumping her tiny body. "Not what you're doing right now!" she laughed. Autumn glared at her and Emma stopped laughing. "Just go with it. Don't think about it too much." She advised.

Autumn nodded and slowly began swaying her hips and Emma nodded in approval. "Yes! You're getting it! Come on! Get pumped up! Pretend you're running only on sour patch kids and soda again!" she giggled.

The other girl laughed and shrugged. "Fuck it." She breathed out before she began dancing a little more, shaking her hips and spinning around. She laughed when she almost stumbled on her feet.

Emma laughed and danced with Autumn, the two joining the other three who cheered when Autumn let loose and danced with them.

They all let loose and just danced because they could. There was no stress and no thoughts about any problems they were going through. They were just five teenage girls dancing like they didn't care and singing their heart outs to a dance-y song.

They were all out of breath and were laughing. "Well damn, Autumn, you do got some moves in you." Maya teased as Autumn blushed.

"And here she was saying a blind girl can't dance." Phoenix added with a smirk.

Autumn rolled her eyes. "Whatever." She chuckled. "Shut up and dance, Phoenix Hale."

"Gladly!" she exclaimed over the music.

An hour later, the girls all crashed down on Emma's bed. "I think I just lost a billion calories because of all this dancing." Emma laughed, wiping some sweat off her forehead.

"I hope I get abs off this workout." Phoenix joked.

"Where they at though?" Elena teased, sticking her tongue out.

Autumn laughed as she tried to catch her breath. "That was fun, though. I haven't done something like that in years."

"I agree with Autumn. I mean, I dance and stuff. But never like this, never with the intent of just being so carefree." Maya agreed, ruffling her curls.

"You were a little too carefree May, you jumped on my bed with Elena and nearly pushed her off the bed." Emma laughed.

"Yeah, *Maya.*" Elena added, glaring at her playfully. "I almost *died.*"

"You were in my spotlight." Maya argued, chuckling.

Elena playfully pushed her. "And I almost got a concussion. Who's the real winner here?"

"Still not you." Maya smirked.

"Whatever, I'm going to get some water." Elena chuckled, jumping off the bed.

"I'll go with you." Autumn stood up, grabbing her white cane and standing alongside Elena.

The other three smirked. "Don't take too long now." Emma told them. "Or I'll take my secret stash of holy water and go pour it on y'all." She joked.

Autumn rolled her eyes. "Shut up, Emma." She laughed.

Elena glared at them and flicked them off before she walked downstairs with Autumn and to the empty kitchen, grabbing a water bottle and taking a gulp of it.

"So are you having fun?" Elena asked her.

Autumn nodded. "I am, actually. I actually felt like for a moment I wasn't a sick teenager..."

"That's because you are." Elena retorted.

Autumn shook her head. "I'm not." She insisted. "And that's okay. Because you guys make me feel normal and—"

"You're not normal either." Elena smiled. "You're special. The most special person I know."

Autumn blushed. "And you're the oddest." She giggled.

Elena stared at her for a couple moments. "Dance with me." She said suddenly.

Autumn raised an eyebrow. "We just did..."

"Just with me though. Let's slow dance in this kitchen. It'll be romantic." Elena grinned.

Autumn blinked. "But...there's no music."

"I know." Elena smiled. "So we'll pretend there is." She took Autumn's cane and put it to the side, pulling Autumn by the refrigerator where there was more space to dance.

"I've never done a slow dance before." Autumn confessed, flushed.

"And I've never danced with a beautiful girl before." Elena said smoothly. "We're both experiencing something new."

Autumn broke out into a grin. "Okay then, Ms. Díaz. I'll slow dance to no music with you. All while wearing pajamas." She giggled.

"I know, it's perfect." Elena breathed out.

She guided Autumn's arms to place them around her neck and then placed her own hands on her waist. Elena laughed when they almost fell from slow dancing, there was no stopping her clumsiness. They probably weren't the best dancers, but the moment was perfect.

"God, you're unreal sometimes." Autumn spoke up, smiling. "You're just...so amazing and magical and I sometimes wonder if you're a figment of my imagination. You're too good to be true."

Elena kissed her cheek. "I'm real. I promise." She assured.

The two stood in silence for a while, their arms still wrapped around each other before Autumn spoke up again. "I want to be with you."

Elena tilted her head. "You're already with me right now."

The other girl laughed and shook her head. "No…like…I want us to be together…like a couple." She said sheepishly.

Elena stared at her for a couple moments. "Are you…are you asking me to be your girlfriend?" she grinned from ear to ear. She couldn't believe she was hearing this right now.

"Yeah…I am." Autumn smiled, flustered. "You know—if you want to of course. I know this isn't the most romantic way to ask you. I mean, I'm asking you in Emma's kitchen for god sakes…if you totally reject me right now we can just forget I ever asked and—"

Elena cut off her rambling. "Can I kiss you?"

Autumn nodded. "Yeah."

Elena immediately leaned in and placed a soft kiss on Autumn's lips, her lips tingling at the feeling of Autumn's lips on hers. "I would love to be your girlfriend, Autumn." She grinned.

"Are you sure?" Autumn asked. "Because I'm not the easiest person to be around with—let alone *date*. I'm not perfect. I probably will make mistakes and fuck up—"

"And that's okay. I'll accept you any way you are. I fell for you, Autumn Castillo, just the way you are." Elena assured.

Autumn broke out into a smile. "No matter what happens, just know my feelings won't change for you. Even if I'm a mess or a being a bitch, I'll still feel this way about you."

And that was enough for Elena.

CHAPTER THIRTEEN

"She's going to hurt you."

"Stop it." Elena snapped, sighing as she threw her sketchbook on the coffee table. "She's not *doing* anything. If anything, *you* keep bringing her up and pointing out her flaws. We all have them, Valerie, and I'm learning to accept hers."

Valerie crossed her arms. "Girls like her—"she began again.

"Want to be loved too." Elena finished, rubbing her temple. "I'm fully aware of the baggage Autumn comes with, and I'm willing to carry it. I love her, Valerie. It's going to be hard, and some days won't be the best with her, but that's okay. I'll cherish those alongside the good days too. Because *that*, is love." She proclaimed. "I'm taking the good days and the bad days and everything else in between on my back and reminding Autumn that I don't mind the weight. "She frowned, crossing her arms. "Why do you constantly keep reminding me that Autumn is no good for me? We've been together for over a month now and all you do is be this pessimistic person instead of being happy for me."

The other girl exhaled. "Autumn has other stuff going on in her life. Do you really think she can balance a relationship too? You're going to be carrying all the weight Elena and you say you don't mind now, but what about later? What about when it becomes overwhelming being the only one putting an effort? Autumn doesn't know what she wants right now."

Girls like Autumn always kept their walls up. Even when they have some cracks, they still manage to keep their walls sturdy. They'd never truly let someone in.

Elena stared at her. "I do know what she wants." She said quietly. "She wants to see. And not in the way you think."

"Autumn doesn't know how to express love, Elena." Valerie continued. "She can barely love herself, what makes you think she's capable of loving another person?"

Elena tried not to let what Valerie was telling her seep into her mind and make her question her new relationship with Autumn. "She will." She argued weakly.

"She will…or do you *hope* she will?" Valerie questioned. "I'm trying to protect you from getting hurt." She said softly. "You deserve to be with someone who can properly express her feelings and show you how much she loves you."

Elena scoffed. "Someone like who? *You?*" She crossed her arms. "We never even *had* something, Valerie. You never let it become something. And that's fine, I'm over it. But *you* won't let it go." She accused. "You had your chance, and you didn't take it. I'm with Autumn now, and I'm happy. You may not think she can love me, but I know she can. She won't show it the way other people do, but I know she's going to love me."

Elena picked up her sketchbook and put on her scarf and jacket, the November chill becoming increasingly colder.

Valerie sighed. "Lena..." she trailed off. "Yes, I'm not over you. But I'm telling you this as a friend." She tried. "How long are you going to wait for her to love you the way you want to be loved? Months? Years? You're going to hate her when she doesn't express her love for you like you want her to." Valerie told her. "She can't love you, Elena. She can't love anyone."

Elena glared at her, flaring her nostrils. "You know," she began. "A lot of people have said that Autumn and I aren't going to last. People say I'm only with her out of pity, or any other kind of bullshit reasons. They say I won't be able to handle the pressure of being with a person who has a disability." She zipped up her hoodie. "But I look at her, and she's just Autumn. She's the Autumn that calls me beautiful and tells me I have sweetened up her coffee or whatever. I make her smile. I make her laugh. And I make her happy. And she makes me feel the exact same way. People can say whatever they want, but I'm with Autumn for as long as she'll have me. And not you, or anyone, are going to prevent me from being with her." She finished before walking over to the door.

"Fine." Valerie sighed. "I'll be here with tissues when she breaks your heart."

Elena opened the door and stepped out. "Fuck you." And she angrily slammed the door.

She stomped to the elevator and pressed the button to go down. No one *knew* Autumn the way she did, no one *saw* Autumn the way she did. All Elena saw is a gorgeous girl with a heart of gold only few were fortunate to witness. Autumn did care about her, she did.

That's what she's been telling herself since they started dating.

Elena shook her head as the elevator doors opened and she quickly stepped inside. She couldn't think this way, she couldn't let Valerie's words seep into her brain. Simply because Autumn didn't proclaim how much she loved her (*if* she loved her), didn't mean she didn't feel it. She wouldn't be dating Elena in the first place if that was the case.

The elevator doors closed and began descending down to the front lobby. Elena leaned her head back and sighed. Why did she suddenly doubt her relationship with Autumn? Was it because there was the possibility that Valerie did hold some truth in what she said to her? Could Autumn ever love her?

The doors opened and Elena stepped out and walked out the apartment building, hugging herself as the cold air hit her and she walked to a nearby subway station.

No, Autumn was human. She had emotions. Of course she could reciprocate the feelings. She told Elena she liked her, and Autumn was the one that asked her to be her girlfriend. She would've never asked if she didn't feel the same way.

But why was Autumn always so hesitant to show Elena any sort of affection? Was it because she was questioning her feelings for her? Was she second-guessing their relationship?

Elena hated herself for thinking this way. She was being like everyone else, doubting Autumn. She wasn't like everyone else. Because everyone else didn't know Autumn, but she did. And she knew Autumn cared.

She had to care.

Because Elena cared.

Elena cared a lot.

Maybe too much.

But she didn't mind.

Or did she?

Elena sighed in frustration as she walked down the steps towards the subway station to catch her train. Since the moment she met Autumn, she knew Autumn wasn't easy to talk to. She kept those tight walls around her and Elena could barely manage to slip into the cracks. Autumn told her she wasn't going to be the easiest person to be with. But Elena didn't mind the hard work, if it meant being with Autumn.

But would she grow to mind? Would she grow frustrated that Autumn wasn't at the same level as her? Would she grow frustrated that Autumn wasn't showing affection the way she did? What if Autumn took too long to open up to her? What if Autumn *never* opened up to her?

All these thoughts racing gave her a headache, maybe even heartache too. Elena ran to her train, barely making it on time as she slid into a seat beside a woman wearing scrubs. The woman smiled politely at a distraught Elena and Elena returned the smile weakly. The train began moving and Elena's leg was shaking anxiously and chewed on her lip as her thoughts consumed her.

"Are you okay?" the woman who had smiled at her minutes ago asked, a concerned look on her face.

Elena looked at her, was talking to a stranger a wise choice? Then again, this *was* New York City. She'd seen stranger things happen. This woman only wanted to talk, and if anything, she could just scream for help.

"Not really." She answered truthfully.

The woman hummed. "I know I'm a stranger to you, but do you want to talk about it?" she offered. "You'll probably never see me again after this."

Elena sighed. "I've been with my girlfriend for about a month now, and we're fine...I think so anyways." She told her. "She's blind, and that's not really the problem. It's her being so...covered. Like, she struggles with expressing how she feels and keep these extremely tight walls that I have a hard time getting into. I know this is all new to her, her being in a relationship...but it is for me too. And I'm afraid she won't put any effort into our relationship. I'm afraid she's not going to love me like I love her. "Elena explained. "I just don't want our relationship to spiral down, especially since it's still so new. I don't want to lose her after I've worked so hard to get her, you know?"

The train stopped and the doors slid open, the woman in scrubs stood up and looked at her. "Everything you've just told me?" Elena nodded. "Tell that to her." She said simply before exiting the train.

Elena made a mental note to talk to strangers more often on the subway.

Autumn was playing a song on the piano, pausing every once in a while to scribble song lyrics into her journal. She suddenly heard footsteps entering the room and Autumn smiled to herself.

"Hey Ellie." She greeted, assuming her girlfriend was coming.

"I'm not Elena." Phoenix chuckled as she walked up to her. "I saw you coming in here and I figured I'd follow you in here to see what Autumn Castillo did here. I figured you just made out with Lena here since I see you two coming inside here often." She shrugged. "Guess I was wrong."

Autumn rolled her eyes, pushing her shades up. "Well, you've seen. Now you can leave."

Phoenix scoffed. "Now why would I leave my little Auttie alone?" she cooed, squeezing her cheek and Autumn smacked her hand away.

"Don't call me that."

Phoenix shrugged, indifferent, and sat down beside Autumn. "What are you working on?"

"Stuff."

"Stuff?"

"Stuff."

Phoenix raised an eyebrow. "Care to elaborate on the 'stuff' you're doing?" she chuckled. "Unless it's drugs, then please spare me the details before I become your accomplice." She joked.

Autumn snorted. "It's a song. I'm writing a song."

"Ooh, can I hear it?" Phoenix asked, intrigued.

She blushed, peering down. "I—um, I don't know…it's a song I wrote for…Elena—still writing." She confessed as she turned redder. "But I wasn't planning on showing her." She mumbled.

"Why not? I'm sure she'd love it. She'd love anything from you. Especially your panties." Autumn's eyes widened and coughed awkwardly. Phoenix laughed, knowing she made her uncomfortable. "I'm kidding—sort of. But I'm 69% kidding." She smirked at her clever little innuendo.

"You're something else, Phoenix Hale." Autumn scoffed, shaking her head.

Phoenix shrugged. "I rather be something else than everything else."

Autumn pondered for a moment and hummed. "Insightful."

Phoenix nodded. "So how about that song?" she tried again with a smile.

"Well, you're going to insist until I do it and I rather spare myself the bickering." Autumn relented with a sigh. "Please tell me what you think, for some reason you seem like the only other person that really *gets* music."

"Did you just say something nice to me?"

"I did." Autumn gasped dramatically. "Hold on, let me come up with an insult…"

Phoenix playfully pushed her, chuckling. "Shut up and sing the damn song, Castillo."

Autumn smiled softly, surprising herself when she tentatively slid the journal towards Phoenix. "The lyrics are right there. You can follow along or give suggestions if you want." She said shyly. Phoenix nodded, taking the journal and glancing over the lyrics. She waited for Autumn to start singing patiently, turning to her.

The girl positioned her shaky fingers on the keys, playing the first notes on the piano. In her mind, she heard a guitar accompanying her.

Autumn's smooth voice rang in the music room. It was shaky at first, but the song spoke to Autumn in so many ways, that she quickly blended in with the song. Hearing Elena's voice…her soft, raspy voice…it made Autumn absolutely blissful. She felt an instant serenity whenever Elena talked to her.

Elena's voice assured Autumn one thing: this was real. *She* was real. The younger girl turned Autumn's world upside down, but Autumn wasn't minding the mess. Because she made Autumn happy. Happier than she's been in years.

Autumn broke out into a grin. Elena was getting better as they spent more time together. The more Elena dived into her world, the more Autumn slowly (*very* slowly) let her in. It was a work in progress, but she was letting Elena into her world, through her eyes, slowly.

Autumn's raspy voice intoned. She was a work in progress. Actually, Autumn was more like a fucked up mess. She was so use to shutting out everyone else and completely disregarding everyone else's feelings but her own.

But now, she had Elena. And she didn't want to hurt Elena. That's the last thing she wanted to do. But old habits die hard, it was hard for her to suddenly open up the walls she kept up and express herself. Autumn was so use to keeping everything in, she couldn't let anything out.

Phoenix knew right then that Autumn wasn't faking any feelings for Elena. She assumed because of Autumn's closed off behavior, she didn't truly have any feelings for the other girl who was completely infatuated with Autumn. But she was wrong. Autumn may not show it to Elena, but *God*, this girl loved Elena. Yes, *loved.* The lyrics were beautifully written, they presented the feelings Autumn had difficulty expressing. This song expressed the love Autumn had for Elena. And Phoenix found that absolutely beautiful. Autumn wasn't an emotionless robot, not at all. She had feelings. True, genuine feelings.

Autumn could feel Elena's warm hands intertwine with her constantly freezing ones right now. They were the perfect combination, they fit so well together. She always felt instant sparks at feeling Elena intertwining her hand with hers. The most wonderful part of it all was that Elena always asked. She never did anything spontaneously, not unless she wanted to. She was considerate of Autumn, she cared. Little things like that assured Autumn that Elena cared.

Autumn stopped playing and smiled sheepishly.

"That's all I have…" she mumbled shyly, her cheeks turning a tint of red.

Phoenix smiled. "That was beautiful, Autumn." She told her honestly.

The other girl shrugged. "I didn't think it was all that good."

The girl scoffed. "Well of course it wasn't good." Autumn furrowed her eyebrows and Phoenix grinned. "It was *amazing*." She finished.

"You think so?" Autumn asked, a soft smile forming on her face.

Phoenix nodded. "It is. It's *really* amazing." She paused. "I actually have some ideas on how you can finish the song. Like, I have some ideas for the bridge." She grabbed the pen on top of the piano. "Do you mind if I write in your journal?" Autumn shook her head and Phoenix immediately began scribbling lyrics on the journal, playing some piano notes and humming to herself. Phoenix played the piano, but not as trained as Autumn was. She was taught by her grandfather by ear.

After about 20 minutes of silence, Phoenix turned to Autumn. "Okay so I finished the song. I'll read you the lyrics and tell me what you think?"

Autumn shook her head. "No, sing it. You wrote it." She told her. "I'll accompany you on the piano."

"Are you sure?"

"Positive." Autumn affirmed.

"Okay, well, this is what I wrote thinking about your relationship with Elena. In my perspective, anyway. Please give me any feedback." Phoenix replied.

Autumn nodded and Phoenix instructed her to increase the piano playing to a more dramatic approach. Autumn did so and Phoenix looked at the lyrics again before opening her mouth to sing.

Phoenix sang the remainder of the song, shocking Autumn with her impressive voice. When Phoenix finished, she turned to Autumn.

The two remained silent for a couple moments before Autumns spoke up.

"Well damn."

"Is that good or bad?" Phoenix asked, biting her lip.

"Good—*great*." Autumn answered. "I love it."

"So do I." another voice spoke up. The rather short woman, who didn't look past her mid 20's, slowly walked closer to the two younger girls. "That was really good." She praised.

"Ms. Kate." Phoenix addressed, feeling awkward in front of her former chorus teacher.

"Phoenix." The shorter woman nodded to her with a smile. She turned to Autumn. "And Autumn Castillo, right? You're quite infamous at this school. I know you by your impeccable piano skills. Actually, your piano playing is phenomenal. I wasn't aware you were a singer, too, however."

"Thanks." Autumn mumbled timidly.

"Well you two have written quite the beautiful song." Ms. Kate acclaimed, crossing her arms. "I always took Phoenix as an outstanding singer," the older woman turned to Phoenix. "but I wasn't aware you were a songwriter too. It makes me miss you being in choir more, actually."

Phoenix looked down. "I miss it too." She confessed.

"Then you should consider coming back, we miss you." Ms. Kate encouraged, her brown eyes darted to Autumn. "You should consider joining too. If not, you should definitely consider joining the all-teen musical orchestra Julliard runs." Autumn's ears perked up at that. "I think you'd have a good shot."

Autumn only nodded, smiling softly. Phoenix was chewing her lip nervously and shrugged. "I want to, but I can't." she replied to the young teacher.

Ms. Kate had been practically stalking her since she shockingly quit choir. Phoenix had been a dedicated member of the group since her freshman year. And when she quit, the woman was shocked to say the least.

If there was one thing about Ms. Kate, it was that she was stubborn. She would not rest until Phoenix rejoined choir, because not only was she incredibly talented that she needed her in the group, but she was also aware that Phoenix loved it. She loved singing and choir, Ms. Kate knew it because she'd lose herself while performing.

Ms. Kate turned to Autumn. "Do you mind if I borrow Phoenix for a second?" Phoenix sighed, running a hand through her hair.

Autumn shrugged. "You can do whatever you want."

The older woman didn't hesitate a second to grab Phoenix's arm and drag her outside the empty hallways. The woman looked up at Phoenix, with her short stature and Phoenix's taller one. But you could still know who the one with the upper hand was.

"Okay, Phoenix, what's going on? You quit choir a month ago and I heard you quit dance too. That's not normal. You'd never in a million years quit two things you love." Ms. Kate approached. She gave Phoenix a concerned look. "You can talk to me, you know that right? I've known you since you were a freshman, I like to think we're close enough to be considered even friends." She crossed her arms.

Phoenix looked down on the floor. "I don't want to talk about it." She muttered.

The choir teacher placed a comforting hand on Phoenix's shoulder. "I don't know what you're going through, but quitting things you're passionate about will not better the situation. You need something to turn to when things aren't going your way. And I know singing, above all, is one of those things."

Phoenix wanted to just tell her right then why she quit.

She wanted to tell her why her life was going in ruins. She wanted to tell her she had to quit because she had to take care of her siblings and cousins at home because she was the oldest and no one else could watch the young children.

Her mother had begun taking earlier shifts at her new job and her father worked the night shift so he would be too tired to watch the kids for very long or pick up the ones that went to school. She had to take on responsibilities that her parents didn't want to give her, but had no choice but to. They couldn't afford babysitters. She wanted to tell her that her uncle and aunt were having difficulty sustaining more than 20 people in their household, and had begun telling her parents that they had to find somewhere to live quickly because then they'd lose their home too.

She didn't want to be homeless again. She didn't want this life she was currently living. Everything was so hard to handle. Life was getting hard to handle.

Phoenix didn't say any of this to her. Instead, she said. "You should have Emma do the solo for the upcoming competition. She's really good at doing high notes." She smiled sadly before walking back inside with Autumn, leaving the teacher with an even more concerned look on her face.

"Phoenix?" Autumn called out as she heard footsteps approaching her.

Phoenix nodded. "Yup."

"Okay." Autumn said softly.

"So, about our song." Phoenix continued, wanting to think about anything else but her own problems. "I think you should sing it for Lena. She'd love it." She thought for a moment. "Actually, how many songs have you written about her?"

"Like…" Autumn paused. "about three. Including this one." She guessed.

"What if you record the songs and make it into a mix tape and give it to her? Elena loves mix tapes. I'm sure she'd love that." Phoenix suggested.

"Do you think she'd like it?"

"Why not?" Phoenix shrugged. "Look, I'm telling you, Lena needs some kind of romantic gesture. This is probably the most beautiful thing you could do for her. Shoot, if I wasn't straighter than an arrow and you made me a mix tape of songs *you* wrote about *me,* I'd automatically marry you...and bang you."

"I'm going to ignore what you just said minus the romantic gesture." Autumn rolled her eyes. "But, I agree. I don't want to make her think I don't care about her. Because...I do." She mumbled.

"I know you do." Phoenix agreed. "You just have a very subtle way of showing it."

"Yeah." Autumn frowned. "And she's so sweet and amazing to me. She's always doing all these things for me and I'm just the worst girlfriend in existence." She sighed.

Phoenix smiled kindly. "You're not a bad girlfriend, Autumn." She assured. "You just need a little help learning how to love and give love back. Everyone is capable of it."

"Even me?"

"Even you."

Emma Charlotte Brooks hardly wore a frown.

On the rare occasion would you catch her with a frown on her face. Emma was basically a ray of sunshine, that's what she displayed to the world. That's what she wanted everyone to think of her. She had to show everyone she was okay. Life was great. Everything was okay.

If she was ever found in a vulnerable position, it usually involved Autumn.

Or Riley.

Riley was her little big brother (he was very tall, taller than Emma. Then again, *anyone* could be taller than Emma). He was a year younger than her but was only a freshman due to him missing out a year in school.

Riley had always been a rather shy and quiet person, that's what she and her parents assumed it was. But Riley was more than just shy and quiet. He would literally freak out when he had to interact with people or have to do any kind of social situation. It *terrified* him. He would have panic attacks that only Emma knew how to control.

But Riley was also a rather thorough and organized boy. He couldn't help but feel the need to constantly organize things like books in his shelf, arrange his clothes based on color, or his guitar picks too. It wasn't that he liked to do these things, but his anxiety led him to perform these compulsions. Emma couldn't blame him, it wasn't Riley's fault.

He liked counting. He counted everything and anything. He'd count his steps, he'd count Emma's steps, and he'd count his parents steps. He'd count how long it took Emma to get to her room. He'd count the number of times Emma would laugh and for how many seconds. He'd count his food and his vinyl record collection. Counting comforted him.

So was repeating. He'd flick the light switch exactly 26 times whenever he entered a room with one, and he locked and unlocked the door 53 times to make sure intruders wouldn't come inside their home. Riley does it every morning before they go to school and every night before they go to bed. He also repeated words, certain words. He tended to repeat every 14th word three times, because he'd count his words.

Social anxiety and obsessive-compulsive disorder as a result of his anxiety. That's what the psychiatrists and therapists had diagnosed him with once they took him to see someone when he was 12 years old.

Riley was bullied heavily once word got around, it was to the point where he missed school practically a whole year. His classmates gave him panic attacks. They wouldn't let him count, they wouldn't let him do his habitual routines, and it scared him.

Emma helped him though. She loved her little brother too much not to. She counted with him and helped make things comfortable for him. Their parents were often busy with work and depended on Emma when they couldn't be there to make sure he'd go to therapy, he'd take his medication, and that he was okay.

It was stressful because Emma had to not only help Autumn, but she had to help Riley.

But nobody ever thought to help her.

Nobody helped Emma.

She didn't need help. She was fine.

She didn't have it as bad as Riley or Autumn. They needed her.

She couldn't be selfish.

So she kept it in.

She kept it all in until it was hard to keep all her feelings in. But she'd hold it together for them.

Emma rubbed her temples as she felt an agonizing headache. She sneaked in a bottle or two to her room and…kind of finished them. The hangover she woke up wasn't the best end result.

She was trying to pay attention to what her teacher, Mr. Martin, was lecturing. But, *God,* she had such an intense headache…

Suddenly a teacher knocked and entered the room, interrupting Mr. Martin mid-lecture. She taught 9th grade algebra, she was so *old.* She had to be past her 50's. Emma couldn't remember her name, but she knew she was one of Riley's teachers.

Riley. She quickly lifted her head up a little higher as the teacher and Mr. Martin were talking quietly to themselves, feeling panicky about whether this involved Riley or not.

"Emma?" Mr. Martin called her, and all eyes turned to her.

"Y-yeah?" she stuttered nervously.

"Mrs. Johnson needs your assistance at the moment." He told her, motioning for her to go. "Don't rush to come back to class." He gave her a knowing look. This was a routine now.

Emma nodded, forgetting the painful headache and collecting her belongings and following Mrs. Johnson out.

"What happened?" she asked, trying to not appear as worried.

The older woman sighed. "I just called on him to answer a simple question I know he knew the answer to and he got *very* nervous and, well, you know. He started panicking and some of his classmates began laughing at him and it didn't help the cause."

"You're supposed to warm him beforehand that you're going to call on him during class." Emma snapped, maybe a little too harshly but she didn't care. "He needs to prepare himself so he knows what's coming. If not, he freaks out. You should *know* this."

The woman looked taken back and decided to rebuttal Emma. "It was *just* answering a question—"

"Not to him. It's *so* much more than that. It's not just answering a question to him, it's pushing aside all of his fears and worries to do *just that*. Do you realize how much work that is? A lot. It's tiring. You can't push him to work so hard. It's a work in progress that must be taken one step at a time." Emma told her. "You're a teacher, how is it that I know how to handle situations better than you?" she huffed.

The woman was stunned to say anything else and simply guided Emma to the classroom that was being supervised by a teacher while Mrs. Johnson collected Emma.

Emma immediately barged into the classroom. Her eyes darted around for Riley and found her brother sitting in the corner in his desk, trembling and his chocolate brown eyes darting around in fear and hyperventilating. His lips were moving as he counted to himself while running his right hand through his hair a certain number of times.

All eyes in the room were on him, not easing his panic attack. Emma wished she could glare at every person in the room for not helping her brother in any way. She walked over to him, and crouched down slightly beside him.

"Hey ducky…" She whispered to him, using the nickname she had given him when the two of them were little kids. "I need you to breathe. "She said soothingly, rubbing his back.

"Everyone was…looking at me." He said in between panicky breaths. "I…couldn't…handle it. She…she didn't warn me." He tapped his fingers on the desk eight times. "Warn me—warn me—warm *me.* " He repeated, his mind never stopping count even in midst of a panic attack.

"I know she didn't." Emma empathized. "That was such a bitchy thing for her to do and trust me, I gave her a lot of shit for it." She saw a small smile form on Riley's face and she couldn't help but smile too. "There's that smile I love seeing. Now breathe and smile at the same time, yeah?" she rubbed small circles on his back gently. "Deep breaths."

Riley stared at Emma as he began breathing in and out slowly. His breathing was still shaky, but he wasn't hyperventilating anymore.

"There we go, ducky." She smiled. "How about you and I get out of here?" she suggested.

"But school…I can't let you miss class…" Riley stammered. He already felt bad enough taking his sister out of class and having her here, he didn't want her to miss school every time he couldn't keep it together.

Emma scoffed. "Does it look like I care?" she disregarded. "Besides, your health comes first to me. I could care less about school right now if you're not okay."

"It's not fair to you." He sighed. "To you—to you—to…*you*." Riley repeated.

"You're getting me out of class, *everything* is fair." Emma laughed lightly, causing Riley to smile.

"You laughed for three seconds." Riley pointed out.

"Really? Well I'd like to laugh some more." She grinned. "I'll tell you what, you agree to leave and I'll take you to the record store and buy you *four* vinyl records." She bribed.

Riley smiled even more. "Deal." He agreed. "But what about Autumn?" he tapped his fingers another eight times.

"Her girlfriend can handle her." Emma chuckled. "I'll make sure to tell Lena to take her home. Now," Emma stood back up, extending her hand for Riley to take. "are you joining your sister or what?"

The younger sibling only grinned and took her hand, being led by his little big sister out towards the hallways. Emma didn't even bother letting the teachers know of her plans when they couldn't even bother helping her brother adequately, so she wouldn't give them a heads up adequately.

Once they were situated in Emma's car, Riley turned to her.

"X equals 40." He told her randomly.

"What?" Emma raised an eyebrow.

"I knew—I knew—"he sighed. "I *knew* the answer. I just couldn't get it out of my throat and formulate words—words—*words*." He repeated.

Emma smiled sadly, squeezing his hand twice. "You'll get there, ducky, don't worry." She assured.

"Thanks ladybug." Riley returned the smile, using the nickname he used for her when they were younger.

Emma ruffled his hair. "Anything for my ducky."

Anything for them, yet nothing for her.

Elena and Maya were in their 7th period English class together. They were supposed to be discussing themes in *Pride and Prejudice,* but Maya was secretly texting Toby while they were working.

Elena placed a finger by her mouth and fake gagged as she watched Maya giggling at reading one of Toby's messages from under her desk to go unnoticed by Mr. Martin. Maya looked up mid-giggle and glared at Elena.

"Just kiss and date already is all I have to say." Elena shrugged as she played with the sleeves of her knitted sweater.

"Maybe…" Maya trailed off.

"Do you not like him?" Elena asked with an eyebrow raised.

Maya straightened up in her seat and shrugged, biting her lower lip. "Well…yeah…"

"But…" Elena urged her to continue.

"I'm afraid it's not going to work out."

"Why wouldn't it?"

Maya sighed. "Because…I wouldn't be able to fully commit myself to our relationship—if we ever have one." She told her friend. "I have other things going on that are bigger priorities to me. I don't think he'd want a girlfriend that doesn't fully commit to him."

"Well," Elena began, turning her body to have her full attention on Maya. "I don't know Toby very well. All I know is that you're into him and he's the one that works with Autumn when she has doctor appointments. But he makes you happy, and I *may* have sneaked glances at the texts he sends you when you think I'm not looking." Maya glared at her at the confession. "*And*," Elena continued. "he seems to be sweet. And a total dork. But that's okay because you're one too!" she teased, causing Maya to roll her eyes playfully. "But anyway, what I'm trying to say is that he seems to be into you, and he will understand if you have other priorities, as long as he knows you care about him like cares about you. Don't give him the vibe that you're not into him when you are, it'll only cause a huge mess." Elena advised, using her own dilemma at the moment.

"I—"Maya began before deciding not to say anything else and nodded. "you're right, you're right." She agreed.

Elena stared at her for a couple moments. "It seems to me like you're looking for any excuse for you and Toby not to work out…am I right?" she assumed.

"No I'm not!" Maya protested and Elena raised an eyebrow at her. The girl sighed and mumbled. "Okay…maybe."

"Why?"

"I don't want to get hurt or hurt him." She told her. "I have *so much* going on…and I don't want to be more hurt than I already am. Especially by a boy."

"Well, whatever you have going on, you can always talk to me about it." Elena offered with a small smile. "Pain is a part of life unfortunately, May, you just have to know how to handle it." She shrugged. "Or you can 'whatever' it. But I doubt that's how you want to handle the situation right now." Maya only smiled softly, glancing down at her book.

The bell rang, signaling the end of class. The two girls collected their things and walked out of the classroom together. "Only one more class and we're out for the day." Maya breathed a sigh of relief.

"I know." Elena beamed. "Emma had to leave school, so she told me to make sure Autumn gets home and we're going to hang out at her house later." She smiled.

Maya fake gagged, doing what Elena had done earlier. Elena playfully glared at the girl. "You guys make me sick. I seriously puke glitter and sunshine because of you two." Maya teased as they walked down the hallways to Elena's locker.

"You should see someone for that. I think you might be turning into one of us." Elena's eyes widened. "Toby better make sex change if that's the case."

Maya slapped Elena's arm and snorted. "You're such a dumbass sometimes."

"Sometimes?"

"You're right," she agreed. "More like all the time." Maya smirked.

Elena put in her combination on her lock and opened her locker. "Rude."

"I have to get to AP Bio, I'll text you later." Maya told her. "Have fun with Autumn. Use protection." She winked.

"The beauty of being a lesbian is that we don't need protection!" Elena exclaimed.

Maya rolled her eyes. "You act like you're actually getting some when we know Autumn's got her legs duct taped."

"You act like I base my relationship off of sex when I don't." Elena retorted with a laugh.

"I have Biology to get to." Maya chuckled.

"Right." Elena nodded as Maya walked down the hallways. "Get your chromosome party on May bear!" she shouted after her, receiving weird looks from students walking by. Elena shut her locker and walked to U.S History class dreadfully. And she found herself wondering how things would be like if Autumn wasn't blind.

"Why do you have stars painted up?" Elena asked Autumn as they were lying on Autumn's bed. Her head was leaning against the headboard of Autumn's bed while Autumn's head was resting on Elena's thighs, Elena playing with Autumn's long, dark locks. Her sunglasses were off and Autumn's eyes were staring up at the ceiling, as if she could actually see the stars painted up on her ceiling.

"I like stars." Autumn answered. "Astronomy is one of the geeky topics I'm really informed about. "She clarified. "When I was younger, you know, before I went blind." She frowned slightly. "My parents would take me, Dylan, and Olivia camping. It was nice to leave the city and go somewhere isolated—quieter." Autumn broke out into a small smile before continuing. "My dad would take Dylan and I to a special spot he said had the best view of the sky. We would lie on the open space with the green grass staining our clothes—my mom would be so pissed." Elena chuckled as she listened intently to the story; Autumn joined in and laughed lightly. "But Dylan and I would listen to him as he explained the constellations to us. And the stars would be shining so bright." Autumn smiled. "It was so nice—beautiful, actually." She reminisced. "So I had my dad paint the stars on the ceiling for me, so I could pretend there were stars up there, and it'd be like being back in the woods with that open space and the staining clothes and looking up at the luminous stars."

Elena smiled sadly. "You miss your sight, don't you?"

Autumn sighed. "Yeah…I do. But there's nothing I can do. I only rely on the miracles of science at this point. I'm lucky if I make it another 10 years without any signs of cancer."

"You shouldn't think like that."

"Think like what?"

"Like you're going to die. Because you're not going to." Elena insisted. The two staying quiet for a while. "I have another concept to teach you."

"I thought we weren't done with the concept with whatever." Autumn teased.

"Well, no." Elena laughed. "But I think you need another concept to be taught."

The paler one nodded. "Okay, what is it?"

"Faith."

"Oh no, you're not going to try to convince me to enter Jesus in my life are you?" Autumn groaned, burying her face in Elena's sweater by where her abdomen was.

Elena giggled. "No, silly, there are many different types of faith. Not necessarily the religious one. I'm not very religious myself, so there's no point in teaching you the word of God when I don't know it myself."

"Okay, so what type of faith are we talking about here?" she raised an eyebrow.

Elena twirled her finger, wrapping some of Autumn's hair on her finger. "Believing that there is good in this world, and that the universe is going to return what they took away. I have a theory, actually."

"You are quite notorious for theories, continue."

Elena stuck her tongue out playfully, wishing Autumn was able to see it. "Well," she began. "I think that the universe gives you a test, see." She paused. "They take away something from you, something that you desperately need. However, I think they do it for a reason. It's to see if you're capable of living without it. I think the universe is trying to see what you do with this thing taken away from you. They want to see what you'll do and how you'll handle it. And if you handle it with the positivity and strength with the belief that it'll come back to you, it will. But if you choose to handle it filled with negativity and bitterness, believing it'll never come back to you…then it won't."

Autumn stayed quiet for a moment, removing her face from Elena's sweater. "I don't think I'll be able to do this concept correctly." She mumbled.

"I think you can." Elena told her. "I think you can do anything."

Autumn smiled, a blush creeping onto her cheeks. "I want to add something to your theory."

"Okay." Elena nodded. "What is it?"

"I think…" Autumn trailed off. "I think the universe took away my blindness, yeah, but the universe gave me something better in return." She smiled. "You." Elena broke out into a grin. "Even if I never get my sight back, the universe has compensated for it with giving me you." She paused. "I know I don't show it much, but I really care about you, Elena. You matter to me a lot. And I'm trying. I'm trying to be better for you, and I'll keep trying to be better for you until I am."

Elena leaned down and whispered. "Can I kiss you?" Autumn nodded and Elena kissed Autumn, the other girl's soft lips giving Elena a tingling sensation on her lips when she pulled away. "I love you." Autumn's eyes widened at the confession. "You don't have to say it back, say it when you mean it. Because right now, I truly mean it."

"Okay." Autumn smiled.

Elena realized in that moment that Autumn did care, she didn't need to second-guess it. She cared. There was still that voice in the back of her mind telling the opposite, but she tried to hold the firm belief that Autumn cared. In her own way, yes, but she still cared.

"I'm so glad the universe gave me you too." Elena whispered.

"Did it take anything away from you?"

That was a story for another day Elena would have to tell.

CHAPTER FOURTEEN

"Elena…" Elena heard a husky voice call out to her.

She groaned and hid underneath the covers of her bed. A giggle escaped from the husky voice and shook Elena. "Ellie! Wake up!"

Elena peeked her head out of the blankets and furrowed her eyebrows. Autumn was hovering over her, a smile on her face. But what struck her the most was that there were no sunglasses covering her eyes, there was not a cane in her hand, and there was no opaque gloss over her green eyes.

In fact, she was *looking* at Elena.

Literally looking at her.

What was going *on*?

Autumn ripped the blankets away from Elena and crawled next to her. "Good morning, Elena." She grinned.

Elena stared at her with a confused expression on her face. "What's going on?"

"I'm waking you up, like I have to every day because your lazy butt doesn't know what an alarm clock is." Autumn teased, kissing her cheek.

"No," Elena reached to touch her hands and they were warm. *Warm*, not cold. "I...you can see?"

Autumn raised an eyebrow and laughed. "Of course I can see, Elena!" she tilted her head. "Are you okay?"

Elena continued staring at her. "I don't know...you're not...you're not blind." She thought aloud. "And you don't...you're not sick."

Autumn stared at her weirdly. "Blind? Sight-wise, no. But I am in love with you. A blind fool in love perhaps." She grinned cheekily, making Elena blush. "And I did have a cold last week, but I don't know if you count *that* as sick." She shrugged. "Are you sure you're okay?" she touched Elena's forehead. "Maybe I passed the cold on to you." She pouted.

Elena had never been more confused in her life. Autumn was here, a *completely* different person. A person full of life, full of sight, and fully open to the world. It wasn't the Autumn she knew, and she was puzzled.

"Is this real life?" Elena wondered.

Autumn chuckled. "Pretty sure it is, Ellie…" she trailed off. "Now hurry up and get dressed!" she gave Elena a quick peck on the lips and hopped off the bed. "Emma and Riley are waiting outside for us!" she called to her as she walked out of the room.

Elena felt her heart flutter at the quick peck. They still felt like Autumn's lips. At least something still felt normal.

Elena slowly rolled herself out of bed and looked through her closet, picking out a knitted sweater and some old jeans and quickly put them on. She put her hair in a messy ponytail and grabbed a red ribbon, tying her ponytail into a bow.

She slipped on some red ballet flats, grabbing her backpack and sketchbook on her way out. Elena rushed to brush her teeth and walked down the stairs to see Autumn leaning against the doorframe, a smirk playing on her lips.

"Took you long enough." Autumn teased.

Elena rolled her eyes. "Shut up." She laughed.

Why did it feel so right? She should be baffled by all of this sudden change. But a part of her felt like this was the Autumn that she was meant to know. This was supposed to be the true Autumn if she hadn't gotten sick and gone blind.

Autumn pushed herself off the doorframe and kissed Elena's cheek. "You won't need the backpack by the way." She paused. "But definitely take your guitar."

"Aren't we going to school?"

"How about we go on an adventure?" Autumn suggested. "I like it when we go on our adventures."

"But Emma and Riley are—"

"Heading to school right now." Autumn grinned cheekily. "Without us."

Elena raised an eyebrow. "You sneaky little devil." Elena dropped her backpack to the floor.

Autumn shrugged, pulling Elena close to her. "My parents call me their little Diablita for a reason." She winked.

Elena laughed, shaking her head. "You are something else, I like it." She smiled. Seeing this side of Autumn made her feel like this was the Autumn she wanted to be with, it all felt so...*easy*.

"You love it." She retorted.

"Mmmm...that's debatable."

Autumn pouted. "Ouch, that hurts." She placed her arms around Elena's neck. "A kiss will make me feel better." She grinned.

Elena blushed and gave her a quick peck on the lips. Autumn shook her head. "No, more." Elena laughed, kissing her again. "Mmm...I feel like I need another one."

Kiss.

"No, still doesn't feel enough."

Kiss.

"Just one more."

Elena giggled and kissed Autumn again.

"Okay, last one I swear."

Elena cupped Autumn's face and kissed her deeply, licking Autumn's lower lip. She pulled away and Autumn let out a sigh and grinned.

"Yeah, that's enough...for now." She winked before intertwining her hand with Elena's. "Shall we go on our adventure?"

"Where are we going?"

"Just hold my hand and I'll lead you." Autumn smiled.

Elena smiled. "So you'll be my eyes?"

"I'll be your eyes." Autumn reciprocated the smile and kissed Elena softly before pulling away. "Go get your guitar, I'll be waiting." Elena nodded and turned around, Autumn smacking her butt with a smirk.

Elena turned around and playfully glared at her. "Can you not?"

"It's big. And beautiful." She reasoned with a shrug. "I can't help it."

Elena walked upstairs. "Self-control isn't your forte, clearly."

"I'm glad it's not." Autumn grinned. "Because who could resist you?"

Elena only laughed, walking in her room and grabbing her guitar and placing the strap over her head so that it was hanging off her back. She walked back downstairs and leaped into Autumn's arms, kissing her. "Hi again." She whispered as she clung onto her girlfriend.

Autumn held onto her easily and smiled. "Hi." She whispered back.

Elena hopped off Autumn and took her hand. "Be my eyes and lead me." She ordered.

Autumn was more than happy to oblige and leaded Elena down the busy streets of New York, the two never losing conversation. It all felt so comfortable and relaxing for Elena, *so easy*. They walked into Central Park and Elena turned to her with a raised eyebrow.

"Central Park?"

"Yup." Autumn smiled as she pulled Elena to a tree that provided them with shade and enough isolation from the people walking by. She had Elena sit beside her and rested her head on Elena's lap, looking up at Elena with a cheesy grin.

"So we're just going to spend all day here?"

"Yup."

"This is your idea of an adventure?"

"Just because it isn't grand doesn't mean it isn't adventurous. There's adventure in simplicity, babe." Autumn told her, plucking out pieces of grass.

Autumn's choice of words weren't any different either, Elena noticed. She smiled at Autumn. "You are something else, Autumn Castillo."

"Do you like it?"

Elena laughed, leaning down to kiss her lips. "I love it." She whispered.

Autumn's cheeks turned pink and she grinned. "Good." She quipped.

The two remained silent for a couple minutes, it was a comfortable silence that both enjoyed as they took in their surroundings. It was colder now, fall soon turning to winter. But that didn't stop the amount of people that passed by them as they walked through the large park.

Autumn looked up to her girlfriend. "Teach me a song." She spoke. "On your guitar."

"What song?"

"Any song."

Elena nodded with a smile. "Okay." She whispered.

Autumn lifted her upper body up and sat beside Elena as her girlfriend adjusted the guitar on her lap. She pondered for a moment a song to teach Autumn, a simple enough one where she wouldn't be confused.

"I got one!" Elena announced after a pause. Autumn leaned closer to her girlfriend so she could closely see the chords she'd teach her. "Let's see if Ms. Piano Prodigy can keep up on the guitar." She teased.

Autumn laughed, having mentioned to Elena on their walk to Central Park that practice for the all-teen orchestra at Julliard was gruesome, practicing for hours on end. Elena was glad that she was playing the piano, and that she was still as amazing at it.

"Challenge accepted." Autumn smirked.

Elena giggled before looking back down on the guitar. "Okay, so there are only four chords you need to know." Elena demonstrated the four chords to Autumn, positioning her fingers and then strumming each chord. "Do you get the chords?" Elena asked after demonstrating each chord.

Autumn pursed her lips and furrowed her eyebrows in concentration. "Can you play the first two chords again?" Elena nodded and played the two chords slowly so Autumn could see it. "Okay, I think I got the chords."

"Such a fast learner. I might need to find a way to reward you." Elena smirked, winking at her girlfriend.

Autumn quirked an eyebrow. "I'm sure you can think of something…" she mimicked Elena's smirk.

Elena laughed, shaking her head and going back to the guitar lesson. "Okay, so basically you play the chords in the same order for most of the song—which is Journey, by the way." Elena explained, playing the said chords while explaining the chords. Autumn was staring at the way she was playing the chords intently. "Do you get that?"

Autumn nodded. "Yeah, I think so. I might fuck up a little bit, but I get the concept."

"How about you play the chords and I do the strumming patterns? I'll tell you when to switch the chord to the next one." Elena suggested.

Autumn nodded at the suggestion. "That seems like an easy enough task. " She chuckled. "How about you sit on my lap and hold the guitar, I can reach the chords a lot more easily and it gives me a good reason to be close to you." She smiled cheekily.

Elena blushed but nodded, she lifted herself up with her guitar and plopped down in between Autumn's legs, looking back at her and smiling. "Is that fine?"

"Perfect." Autumn returned the smile.

"Okay," Elena breathed out. "Ready?"

Autumn nodded. "Ready."

Elena smiled softly at her before turning back to the guitar and beginning to strum the guitar. She instructed Autumn when to switch chords and Autumn wasn't half bad, only making a couple mistakes while switching chords. They kept playing the song until it finished and Elena kissed Autumn softly.

"I love you." Elena whispered as she pulled away.

Autumn's gaze dropped. "It's easier this way, isn't it?"

Elena tilted her head, confused. "What are you talking about?"

"It's easier to be with me in your dreams." Autumn continued. "But not in real life."

Elena's heart sank at the realization that this was all a dream. She wasn't really living this. There was a reality outside this world, and the sad part is she didn't want to leave it.

"I—"

"Try to see me without sight. Look at me without seeing me. Then you'll realize you don't need dreams to make things easier." Dream Autumn told her. "The Autumn you see now is not the true Autumn, it's the Autumn *you* want. Don't try to change someone because it's easier, change someone because they need it."

Elena suddenly opened her eyes and she was in her bedroom, no one hovering over her. Just alone in her large bedroom. She quickly hopped off her bed and changed into a knitted sweater with jeans and converse, her hair up in a ponytail with a ribbon tied in her hair. She brushed her teeth quickly and grabbed her backpack and ran downstairs, grabbing a banana and saying goodbye to her parents and Lily as she made a dash out the door.

By the time she arrived inside the building, Elena wished she took gym class more seriously. Her breathing was heavy and her chest rising and falling, the rest of her fellow alumni must assume that she was dying. But nonetheless she speed-walked her way to the music room, hoping the girl was there. And there was the beautiful Autumn, the *real* and in-no-way-a dream Autumn. She walked up to her and while panting she asked. "Can I kiss you?"

Autumn looked up from her journal and smiled. "No hello?"

"Hello… can I kiss… you?" Elena asked in between breaths.

"Are you okay? You sound like you're having an asthma attack…you don't happen to have asthma, right?"

"I ran…here."

Autumn raised an eyebrow, taking off her sunglasses. "Why would you run here?" she rubbed her eyes that looked swollen to Elena. Had she been crying?

"Because you're… real." Elena breathed out. "You're so real and amazing and so, so, *so*... beautiful." She continued. "And I don't want you to ever think I think otherwise of you. I wouldn't want any other Autumn. I don't want an Autumn that doesn't give me a challenge, and I don't want an Autumn that makes life easier. Because I don't want you to be easy, I want you to be complicated and moody and…and…messy. Please be messy. And keep being messy. I want to keep cleaning you up. And I never want to stop. "

Autumn remained quiet before scooting over so that Elena could sit on the bench with her. She reached out her hands. "Sit with me." She whispered, she looked tired and feverish.

Elena sat down beside Autumn. "You look tired, and a little sick. Are you okay?"

Autumn nodded. "I'm fine. It's probably just allergies, no biggie."

"Are you sure?" Elena asked, still feeling wary.

"Positive. And besides, you're here now and I feel automatically better." Autumn smiled softly. Elena felt a chill rush down her spine as Autumn traced her lips with her fingertips. "Can I kiss you?"

"Please kiss me, my beautiful mess."

Autumn broke out into a grin and traced her girlfriend's lips once again before her own lips connected with Elena's. Butterflies burst in Autumn's stomach and she pulled away, blushing at the realization that she kissed Elena this time instead of the other way around.

"So…what's with this sudden need to tell me I'm a beautiful mess?" Autumn asked curiously, trying to push past the clear exhaustion she felt.

Elena looked down and pursed her lips. "I had a dream." She told her. "And you were in it. And you were…different."

"How so?"

"You were never sick or blind. And you had this…brightness about you. You weren't quiet or mysterious, in fact, you were the opposite. It was easier, this side of you. I didn't have to try so hard to keep you happy and you were so easy to talk to." Elena saw Autumn's eyes grow insecure and shifted down.

"But then dream Autumn said some things and made me realize that the easy way isn't always the best way. I don't want to change you unless you need it. I don't want that Autumn, I want this Autumn. And I know I complain about how closed off and quiet you are. But you've been messy for so long, no one ever cleaned you up. But I will, I promise." Elena lifted Autumn's head up with her hand, staring at those green eyes with the opaque gloss. "And I won't pressure you to tell me anything you're not ready to tell me. I love you Autumn, especially when you're this big, complicated mess. I want you to be messy. I want you to show me your flawed side. I don't want perfect Autumn, I want real Autumn. The real Autumn is the perfect Autumn, so show me that side. You don't have to hide that side from me. You don't have to put a front with me, you never do."

"I'm trying—"Autumn told her softly.

"I know you are." Elena smiled softly. "I know you're trying. That's all I want from you." She kissed Autumn's hand softly.

Autumn smiled lazily. "You're my beautiful mess too. Literally." She giggled, and Elena joined in. "You're a mess too though, like me. We're the biggest of messes, I think. But we'll clean each other up, right?"

Elena nodded. "Always."

"You'll tell me why you're a mess too, right? One day?" Autumn questioned.

Elena smiled sadly. "One day."

Maya snuck out of her mother's room while she rested after an aggressive chemo session. She had gone to the hospital instead of school to support her mother and her aggressive treatments. She would head to school after her fourth period, but for now she'd focus on her mother's health. She fixed up her curly hair and pleated invisible wrinkles from her clothes as she walked to the hospital's cafeteria to see Toby sitting alone in a table. A wrinkled book in his hands and chewing on a granola bar, his eyebrows furrowed in concentration as he read.

Maya couldn't help but grin at the sight. It terrified her, but her feelings for Toby only grew stronger as she talked to him more. She still kept a respectable distance from Toby, afraid of growing attached to the boy. But Toby was the kind of boy you couldn't help but grow attached to. He was so caring, so sweet, so dorky, and so genuine. He made Maya feel okay. And she hadn't felt okay in so long.

"That doesn't look like a patient chart to me." Maya teased as she sat down in front of him. "I just might tell on you, Dr. Sinclair."

Toby looked away from the book and to Maya with a blush on his cheeks and a grin on his face. "You make it seem like I spend my life in this hospital."

"You do." She laughed.

Toby blushed even more. "Okay…I kind of do." He relented with a laugh. "But you're no better, Ms. Andrews." He winked, handing her the extra granola bar he had gotten for her.

Maya blushed, shaking her head. "What were you reading?" she took the granola bar and smiled thankfully at him, opening it and taking a bite.

"Only my favorite author in the world…" Toby grinned, tapping the book with his hand. "Mr. Stephen King. It's probably the second time I've read this one. It's called *Lisey's Story*."

Maya tilted her head. "What's it about?"

Toby ruffled his hair, making messier than it was. "It's about this widow who's clearing out her dead husband's office—he was a famous author—and finds out a bunch of stuff about him basically. It's very morbid, emotional, but still carrying a touch of romance." He explained. "Oh and she has a crazy, dangerous stalker who's after her husband's unpublished works and leaves a dead cat in her mailbox."

Maya couldn't help but laugh. "Morbid love stories with creepy stalkers who leave dead cats in mail boxes…Stephen King sounds like my kind of guy."

Toby laughed. "He's a great writer, I love him. I use to read his scarier books at night when I was 11 and scare the shit out of myself."

"Why would you do that?" Maya asked.

"Because there's nothing more frightening than the words of another person. "Toby replied. "Especially when horror turns out to be a reality."

"How deep." Maya commented. "I think reality itself is a horror genre."

"Why?" he asked, his blue eyes staring intently at her brown ones.

"Because there's nothing more frightening than losing the things you care about most."

"What are you afraid of losing?" he asked her softly.

Maya looked away, looking down at her granola bar. "That's a story for another day."

Toby nodded understandingly. "Um, \well..." he licked his lips as he stammered. "How...how about we share our stories outside of...of the... the hospital cafeteria or hallways?" he chewed down on his lower lip nervously.

Maya stared at him. "Like, hang out? We already do that here, what would be the diff—"

"No…like, like a…" he rubbed his clammy hands together. "like a date."

"You want to go on a date with me?" she asked softly.

"I want nothing more, really." Toby said sincerely. "But if you don't want to, I understand." He stuttered. "Forget I even said anything…" he muttered.

In her head, she could hear her mother's voice exclaiming to accept the date. She had told Autumn to sweeten her black coffee if she didn't like the taste, because she might not ever get the chance to…would it be hypocritical of her if she refused herself the right to do the same?

So Maya Andrews did the boldest thing she's done in years. She pushed aside the novel and took Toby's sweaty hands and looked at him. "I'd want nothing more than to tell you my story and hear yours. And…I'd want nothing more than to talk about why you love Stephen King so much and I'd want nothing more than to spend more time with you." She smiled. "Yes." She whispered.

Toby stared at her with disbelief that the most beautiful girl he'd ever laid eyes on said yes to his stammering and nerve-wracking form of asking her out on a date. He squeezed her warm hands and smiled. "How's Saturday night at six?" he smiled.

Maya chewed on her lower lip and nodded. "I'll be ready and waiting for you."

Toby stared at her for a couple moments. "Magical." He whispered.

"What?"

"You are magical." He said, louder this time.

Maya blushed. "I'm not."

"You are." He smiled. "You just haven't taken the chance to see it yet."

"Well maybe you can show me."

"Maybe." He smiled. "I think you should see it for yourself, though. It's quite amazing."

"Well what if I can't?"

"You will." He paused. "I promise."

Promises were another thing that terrified Maya. Because promises were the hardest thing a person could keep. And she didn't want Toby to be another person to break a promise, she really didn't.

"Just come back to choir, I can make something work Phoenix." Ms. Kate insisted once more as she approached Phoenix at her locker.

Phoenix refused to lock eyes with her former choir teacher and placed a textbook in her locker in exchange for another one. "I can't." she said softly.

"You *can*." The small woman told her. "Just tell me what's keeping you from being a part of it." She looked at Phoenix intently. "I know how much you miss it, I see it in your eyes. And I've caught you sneakily trying to observe choir practice for a couple minutes after school." Phoenix slowly turned to look at her, and the woman offered a small smile. "Don't put your passion on hold, Phoenix, please."

Phoenix closed her locker, and turned her body to Ms. Kate. "I want to tell you, but I can't. It's too personal. And you'll look at me differently."

"I can *never* look at you any differently." Ms. Kate replied. "I see you, Phoenix. You're an incredible person I've had the honor of getting to know. Nothing you tell me will make me view you anything less than that." The teacher looked through her messenger bag and took out three pieces of paper and handed them to Phoenix. "These are the songs we're practicing for this week. It might become part of our set list." She said softly. "Take them." Phoenix stared at the papers. "I wanted you to sing the solo song." Phoenix's eyes shifted back to the woman.

"You wanted me to have it?"

Ms. Kate nodded. "You have one of the most versatile voices besides Emma in the group. I originally planned on giving it to you, but the offer still stands if you come back."

Phoenix wanted to scream that she couldn't. No matter how badly she wanted to come back to choir, she couldn't. She had to take care of the little ones and keep the overcrowded household running while the adults scrounged up money with the jobs that barely paid them enough. She didn't have time for it anymore. She barely had time to even do homework and she'd be doing it in between classes and lunch. Some people saw it as her being an overachiever, Phoenix saw it as barely achieving.

Phoenix locked eyes with Ms. Kate and gulped. "Give it to Emma." She tried to muster up enough strength so she wouldn't break down into tears right then and there. "I'm sure she'll do great." She smiled weakly. Phoenix attempted to move past her teacher but Ms. Kate grabbed onto her arm.

"Phoenix—"

"Just leave me *alone!*" she snapped, causing students passing by to stare at them. "Stop pretending like you care! The only reason you're even a freaking teacher is because *you* weren't talented enough to be anything more than that! So quit pretending like you actually *give* a shit about what happens to me. Because you care about my *voice*, not me!" she growled, a part of her feeling guilty for snapping at Ms. Kate who only wanted to help her.

Ms. Kate stared at her, her eyes hurt and nodded. "If that's what you think…then okay. But I'm not giving up on you."

"Whatever." Phoenix mumbled, ripping her arm away from the teacher's grip as she practically ran to her third period class, tears streaming down her face the moment she was from a far enough distance from everyone else.

She made sure to wipe the tears from her cheeks and act like she wasn't crying a couple moments ago. Phoenix had class with Elena this period and she couldn't have the girl know she was crying.

"Hey Lena." Phoenix greeted with a smile. Nothing happened, she wasn't crying. She was okay. Phoenix kept repeating that to herself.

Elena looked up from a sketch of an old woman that she was working on and smiled back. "Hey Nix."

Phoenix sat on the desk next to Elena's and peered over to see the drawing Elena was working on. "Whatcha working on there, Lena?"

Elena put her pencil down and turned to Phoenix, an excited gleam in her eyes. "Okay, so I was riding the subway the other day because I wanted to buy some new paints for this project I'm working on. And the paints I want are sold in this place about 25 minutes from here, and that's if I take the subway, if not it'd take 50 minutes by car." She rambled. "But anyway, so this old woman was sitting in front of me and she was watching me observing everyone riding the train because I do that all the time. I found myself staring at her for little bit and we made eye contact and she tells me in a heavy Polish accent, 'What are you looking at, young lady?'" Elena impersonated a terrible Polish accent and Phoenix chuckled.

"And I was staring at her eyes that were a striking gray color. It reminded me of smoke that comes out from a cigarette, so I told her that I was staring at her eyes because they were beautiful and that she was a very beautiful woman." Elena paused. "She started crying out of *nowhere* because she explained to me that no one has called her beautiful since her husband and he died five years ago." She pouted.

"So then that got me thinking about how people depict the meaning of a beautiful person until they reach a certain age, then they're just...people. But not *beautiful* people, which is bullshit because I think age doesn't determine beauty. I mean, Meryl Streep…Julie Andrews…Jessica Lange…Tony Bennet…I could go on about beautiful old people. So then she talked to be about her life and her late husband and I asked her if she would give me permission to draw her because I thought she was beautiful. She agreed and even let me take a picture of her so I could get her perfectly. Her name is Joanna. She was such a nice woman."

Phoenix had listened to Elena the entire time; the girl had a knack for talking for a *long* time about her art and the inspiration behind it. She had grown use to it, it helped distract her from her troubles. "You meet the most random people ever. I mean, didn't you last week meet a mime that was in prison for four years for attempting to rob a bank?"

"He robbed three convenience stores. God, Phoenix, do you ever pay attention?" Elena teased, laughing.

Phoenix joined in. "*Excuse* me I wasn't aware you were so passionate about theft."

"Only when it involves mimes!"

Their chemistry teacher walked in, signaling class starting and both girls paid attention to her instructions. They had to work on some textbook assignment in pairs, so naturally Phoenix and Elena paired up together to continue with their conversation.

"So I've been meaning to ask you," Elena spoke up as they worked on the assignment. Phoenix looked up, her heart pounding at the possibilities. "I was looking through past yearbooks since they're assigning me as head photographer for the yearbook, and I want to get a good idea of what kind of pictures to take. And I noticed you were in choir from your freshman year to sophomore year. So I assume you're still in it." Phoenix cringed. "So I was wondering if you'd think you can let me sneak in a rehearsal so I can invade everyone's personal space and take pictures."

Phoenix stared down at her textbook. "I'm not in choir anymore. I quit this year." She mumbled. "You can ask Emma, she's in it too."

Elena tilted her head. "Why would you quit? You look like you love it." She observed. "I took the liberty of looking up videos of the choir and you're...wow. You're an incredible singer and you were *on fire* up on stage. You're the Beyoncé of that choir, why would you quit something you seemed so passionate about?"

Phoenix looked up from her textbook. "So what'd you get for the third question?"

"Why are you avoiding my question?"

"Why are you avoiding this assignment? I'm trying to pass this class, Elena, not fail it." Phoenix retorted, looking back down at her textbook and working on her assignment.

"I'm sorry…I just don't like seeing my friends unhappy. That's the last thing I want, really." Elena apologized, biting her lower lip.

"I'm not unhappy, stop assuming things." Phoenix huffed.

Elena looked at her worriedly. "You just look—"

"*What?*" Phoenix snapped, glaring at Elena. "I look broken to you or something? We're not all your fucking girlfriend, Elena, stop trying to fix every single fucking person like you're some kind of therapist!" she exclaimed. Surrounding classmates turned to the two girls in interest of a potential fight while their teacher observed them carefully.

"Phoenix!" Elena exclaimed, shocked at the words Phoenix replied to her with. "I'm not trying—"

"Oh cut the crap, Elena, ever since you came here the first person you truly gained an interest in was Autumn. Why? Because she's possibly the most fucked up person at this school. She's blind, she's got the emotional appeal of a scarecrow, and she's challenging. You just seem to have this thing for fucked up people; this incessant need to fix *every* person in the world like you actually give a shit. Well wanna know a fun fact, Elena? You can't fix everyone. So why don't you get down from your pedestal and stop acting like you're some kind of saint doing everyone a favor by making everyone your charity case?" Phoenix slammed her book shut and stood up. "And do *me* a favor and don't make me *your* charity case. Nobody helps me anyway, and I don't freaking need it." Elena could've sworn she saw Phoenix's brown eyes well up as she made a beeline for the door, not even excusing herself as she left.

Elena simply stared at the door that Phoenix had left in, what Phoenix said had stung. It stung a lot. But she knew Phoenix didn't mean it, she couldn't have. Something was probably going on that made Phoenix snap at her. But she did wonder if she truly was the kind of person who wanted to fix every person going through something. She had her reasons for it, she just couldn't find the heart to tell anyone about it. There were people with bigger and more serious problems than her own, she couldn't be selfish.

She suddenly felt her phone vibrate in her pocket and it was a text from Emma.

Emma: *Something's happened.*

Elena felt her pulse rise as she quickly replied.

What happened? –Elena

Seconds later, her phone vibrated again, this time it was a phone call from Emma. She looked up at the teacher and asked to be excused, quickly collecting her things and dashing out the door and answering the call. "Emma?"

She could hear Emma sniffling from the other end. "Lena...Autumn." Elena's breath hitched. "Her nose started gushing out blood and...and then she passed out suddenly during class and she's not...she's not waking up." Emma choked back a sob. "They called an ambulance and they took her to the hospital. They didn't let me go with her. I'm in the girl's bathroom on the first floor." Emma sighed. "I want to go to the hospital, but I can't leave my brother here."

"Take him with you. I'll go with you, too." Elena said nervously, rubbing the back of her neck.

"I'll text Riley and we'll go in my car." Emma wiped tears from her eyes and her voice cracked. "I'm so scared, Elena..." She whispered.

Elena felt a tear escape her own eye and she quickly wiped it away. "Me too. I knew there was something wrong, she looked so tired and sick and her eyes were swollen...God, I'm so stupid." She cursed herself.

"You couldn't have known." Emma chewed on her lip. "Meet me in the school parking lot, you know where I park my car."

"Okay." Elena hung up the phone quickly and choked back a sob as she ran down the hallways and down the stairs, to the exit. The only name running through her mind being Autumn's.

CHAPTER FIFTEEN

The last thing Autumn could remember is Emma telling her that her nose was bleeding in a panicked voice. She reached to touch her nose and then she felt it: a warm liquid dripping down her fingers. And it didn't take long for her entire hand to be covered with the warm blood.

The rest was a blur.

Now Autumn could feel thin, cold hospital sheets covering from her abdomen all the way down to her icy feet (her hands and feet were never at warm temperatures, she knew that now). The steady beeping of her heart rate irritated her, as did the unnecessary needles piercing her arms. Her hand instinctively reached for the IV needle, but a warm hand grabbed it before she could yank anything out of her.

"I wouldn't do that, you kind of need that." Her mother's soft voice spoke. Autumn could hear the hoarseness in her voice; she assumed her mother must've been crying. Her mother was a rather emotional person, but what parent wouldn't when their kid wasn't exactly the poster child for exceptional health.

"W...wha...what happ—"

"You've been unconscious for a couple hours—three. It wasn't just an ordinary nosebleed ..." Cora sniffed, squeezing Autumn's hand. "I...they ran some tests..." her mother's voice croaked again. "I'm going to get Dr. Richards. She's going to explain everything."

Autumn felt the loss of her mother's warm hand. "Elena? Where is she?" she asked.

Cora smiled sadly. "In the waiting room with Emma. They haven't left since you got here."

"I want them to—"

"I know. And they will later. I promise." Her mother assured. "I'm going to get Dr. Richards now, hold tight."

Autumn heard the faint footsteps of her mother leave and waited in dread for the doctor to come. She respected her doctor, but she lived for the day she would never have to visit the woman ever again. And she was sure Dr. Richards returned those sentiments herself.

Her mind kept drifting back to Elena and how she must be feeling with the news. And Emma. Emma always put a strong front, but she knew seeing Autumn in this state always hurt her.

She didn't have a very long time to think about them, because Dr. Richards entered with both her parents. Her father was less subtle in his crying, hearing his sniffling every couple seconds.

"Autumn." Dr. Richards addressed. "I see you're awake."

"And here I thought for a second I was lucidly dreaming."

The doctor hummed. "It's nice to know your sarcasm hasn't left in your time away from us." The blonde doctor tucked a strand of her hair behind her ear and let out a sigh, unsure how to tell her patient.

"Just say it. Rip it like a Band-Aid. Whatever you say is going to get a reaction anyway." Autumn told her. "You've always been upfront with me, don't stop now."

Dr. Richards nodded. "Very well." She looked at Autumn. "The injections we've been placing on your eyes did not work."

Autumn gave a faint nod. "You said they would this time…"

"I know I did. And once the treatment worked we were going to perform surgery on your eyes." Dr. Richards agreed. "But we can't do that anymore."

"Why?"

Autumn felt a warm hand squeezing her hand while the other squeezed her shoulder. Dr. Richards gulped. "We did an MRI scan."

Autumn gulped, nodding. "Okay…" she whispered.

"We found tumors in your eyes, Autumn."

Autumn felt her heart stop for a moment and she gulped down the knot in her throat. "Oh." The room was silent, except for the sniffling from her father. There was more to share and she knew it. "Well…we can just do chemo again, right? And surgery? I'll be okay."

The doctor pursed her lips. "Before I tell you anything, answer me these questions."

"Okay."

"Have you experienced easy bruising?"

"I…a little…" she mumbled.

"Fatigue and flu-like symptoms?"

Autumn played with her hands and nodded faintly. "Yes."

"Have your eyes been hurting? So much you consistently rub them?"

"Yes." She said almost inaudibly.

"Did you experience nose bleeds before this one?"

"A couple times. But they weren't as bad as this one."

Autumn heard the scribbling coming from Dr. Richards. She stopped writing down everything Autumn told her. "Autumn," she spoke again. "While you should've consulted me or your parents about this sooner, because you know any suspicious symptoms cannot go ignored, you're going to have to take seriously what I tell you now." Dr. Richards paused. "I wish I could say that you only had tumors in your eyes again. The treatment would be much easier to handle…but…"

"But what?"

Her parents squeezed her tighter. "You have cancer spreading to other parts of your body. The most significant traces were in your bones—your spine especially."

The world stopped for Autumn at the words. The wretched disease spread to other parts of her body and the likelihood of surviving reduced by so much in the blink of an eye. Just when she thought she'd escaped death, it came back. Just when she thought she'd get to experience actual happiness with Elena, her friends, and her family, it came back. Anger spread just like cancer did, and frustration, and sadness, especially sadness.

"Autumn?" Dr. Richards spoke cautiously.

Autumn didn't respond.

"Autumn, honey." Joseph spoke up, squeezing her shoulder.

Nothing.

Her arms reached the needles piercing her skin, but Dr. Richards grabbed her hand before she could do anything.

"Autumn." The woman spoke more sternly.

Autumn only shook her head, trying to release the grip from her doctor. She wanted to run, run far away from here. She couldn't deal with this now, or later. She wanted to run, because soon she wouldn't be able to do that.

"*Autumn*, talk to me." Dr. Richards spoke again, the sternness still present in her voice.

Autumn still didn't say anything.

"Come on, talk to Dr. Richards." Cora encouraged, wiping tears away from her own eyes.

The room was deathly silent. No one spoke for a couple minutes until Autumn finally spoke up.

"Am I going to die?"

"We don't know that yet. We need to start a treatment plan for you. The cancer has spread significantly fast. I'm going to consult with oncologists on how to proceed with treatments." She placed her hand on Autumn's leg and patted it. "Just know I'm not giving up on you regardless. I will not rest until I find any method to give you more time."

Time. That word had become the biggest blessing and the biggest curse since the word cancer came into her life.

––––––––––––––––––

It was seven pm and Elena had managed to make a bed out of the uncomfortable chairs in the waiting room without having to be incredibly flexible. She was curled up in two chairs and closing her eyes, but not feeling herself drift off to sleep. Autumn was constantly on her mind and leave her worried.

Emma was no better; she was pacing around the waiting room while rubbing her forehead. She desperately needed some alcohol in her system to drown out reality as much as possible. She couldn't help but think the worst, because that's the bad feeling that was eating away her chest. Riley was counting Emma's steps, observing his sister worriedly. He was supposed to be the "nervous one" of the two.

Suddenly, Cora appeared in the waiting room. Her eyes were red and puffy, indicating she had been crying. Emma immediately ran up to her.

"How is she?"

Elena opened her eyes and quickly followed, crossing her arms. "Is she awake?"

Cora nodded faintly. "She's awake." She replied softly. "I need you two to sit down, please. Autumn wanted me to tell you both because she isn't in the right mindset to tell you."

Emma and Lena casted each other worried looks but sat down on the uncomfortable seats. Cora bit down on a nail nervously and looked at both girls.

"Cora...what's wrong?" Emma asked tentatively.

Cora wiped another tear from her eyes. "Autumn...she...she has..." her voice cracked as she choked back a sob. "She has tumors in both her eyes again." She paused. "And she has cancer spreading all over her body." Cora couldn't stifle her sobbing any longer and broke down crying.

Emma gulped and felt tears streaming down her face. "No...you...you...you can't be serious?"

"There's a chance she'll be cancer free again. But...it's spreading so fast and..." Cora continued crying, embracing Emma when the tiny girl hugged her, sobbing in her chest.

She couldn't lose her best friend. Not like this. The idea that Autumn really could die this time…she couldn't imagine a world without Autumn and didn't want to imagine one ever.

Elena stared at the floor, she wasn't crying. But she sure as hell wanted to. She stood up and glanced at Cora.

"Can I see her?"

"I don't think she wants to see anyone—"

"Please?" Elena begged.

Cora pursed her lips. "Room 315."

"Thank you." She placed a comforting hand on Cora's shoulder. "And I'm so sorry." Cora only nodded as she rubbed Emma's back, attempting to console the sobbing girl in her arms.

Elena's legs couldn't have run faster to the elevator and up to Autumn's room. She walked through Autumn's floor and noticed Joseph talking with a blonde woman, his eyes puffy, red, and welling up with more tears.

She nodded to them, giving a soft smile as she stepped slowly into Autumn's room. The girl was lying on her side, her eyes fixated on the window that was illuminated by the New York streets and buildings.

Simply looking at Autumn made her eyes well up in tears as reality truly hit her, Autumn had cancer. And it was bad this time, and there wasn't a good prognosis.

"I heard you started a lights show in the MRI room when they found all that cancer in your body." Elena spoke up as she leaned against the doorway. Autumn's ears perked up and she shifted her body so that she was sitting up. "It's a shame I wasn't there, I have a lovely song to accompany it." She gulped down the knot in her throat to prevent herself from crying.

Autumn stretched her lips forcibly and patted the hard mattress, indicating she wanted Elena to lie down with her. Elena didn't deny this request for one second and climbed onto the hospital bed and quickly wrapped her arms around Autumn, careful not to entangle herself in any of the needles and tubes.

"I really want to kick cancer's ass right now." Elena confessed. "You don't deserve this."

"Remember my theory?" Autumn asked. "Your past life indicates your current life, and my past life was a shitty person so I'm going to have a shitty life." She said, muttering the next lines. "Or whatever is left of it."

Elena managed to overhear shook her head, breaking the hug. "Don't say that." She said sternly. "Don't start giving up. You are going to fight this and you will not give up for one freaking second, understand? I want you to stay here for as long as possible with me." Elena's voice cracked.

Autumn remained silent and Elena embraced Autumn again, the girl lying back down on her side and Elena wrapping her arms over her. Autumn always liked to be the little spoon.

They remained silent, Autumn's eyes fixated on the wall this time and Elena staring at the same wall while tracing patterns on Autumn's arms.

"You haven't cried yet." Autumn spoke up.

"I know."

Autumn turned over so that her front body was facing Elena. "It's all right to cry."

"I know." Elena bit down on her lip as she suppressed the urge to cry.

"You're not weak if you cry." Autumn continued.

"I know." Elena whispered, feeling her eyes well up.

Autumn reached a hand out to touch Elena's face. She cupped a side of Elena's face with her hand and rubbed Elena's cheek with her thumb. "Let me be the strong one for once." She said softly. "It's okay to let your guard down, I've been doing that with you a lot. So do it with me."

"I can't." Elena replied almost inaudibly.

"Why?"

Elena gulped. "Because if I start crying…I won't ever stop."

"Then I'll wipe your tears forever." Autumn whispered softly.

Elena remained silent and placed her hand over Autumn's cold one that cupped her cheek. She stared at Autumn's green eyes and began to think of all the pain Autumn had endured and all the pain she was going to continue enduring.

She began to wonder what pain looked like.

Was it the 8th beer that left you without inhibitions? Was it the isolation, when all your faults poured onto your skin through a razor blade? Was it the second or third anti-depressant you popped into your mouth because you wanted to paint a picture of a happier world? A world without you in it? Was it the text message that only said "I'm sorry." and you poured apologies out of your mouth like a waterfall?

Or did pain simply look like tears? Salty tears that drown your eyes and stain your cheeks and wet your clothes.

Because Elena was tasting pain right now, it was salty and it was wet and it stained her cheeks.

Autumn wiped the tears escaping Elena's eyes slowly and pulled her girlfriend closer to her as Elena released a gut-wrenching sob into her chest. Autumn wasn't the best candidate for comforting, but she did her best. She rubbed Elena's back and continued kissing the top of her head, hoping the kisses could take away the sadness. If only it was that easy.

Autumn felt her hospital gown stain with Elena's tears, the wetness from the tears rubbing against her skin and Autumn could swear she could even feel the Elena's pain through her tears.

"Please don't die, Autumn…" Elena sobbed. "Please don't leave me too." She muffled as her face was buried in Autumn's chest.

Autumn's heart sank and she only hugged Elena tighter. "I'm sorry…" she whispered.

Elena hiccupped as she removed her face from Autumn's chest, her eyes red and puffy from crying. "Yo vivo si tu vives."

Autumn closed her eyes. "I wish I could promise you that, Ellie, I want to say I'm going to live. But that's not for certain, nothing with me is ever for certain. And I warned you that."

"Then promise me that whatever time there is left…it could 20 minutes, 20 months, or 20 years…but promise you'll spend that time with me. Please? Promise me time?" Elena begged, sounding like a young child begging their parent for a toy on a shelf.

Autumn licked her chapped lips and nodded. "I promise. Whatever time I have, I'll make sure you're a part of it. A huge part of it."

Elena sniffed. "Can I kiss you?"

"I always love it when you do." Autumn smiled softly.

Elena chuckled, rubbing her eye. "I'm such a mess right now." Elena leaned in to give Autumn a small kiss.

"It's okay, I love seeing the messy side of you. It makes it easier for me to show you mine." Autumn took hold of Elena's hand, tracing the outline of Elena's hand, her touch delicate.

"Emma's here too, you know." Elena told her. "I'm sure she'd love to see you."

"And she will," Autumn nodded. "Once I'm done being here with you." She smiled. "Now tell me about this song you say accompanies my cancer lights show."

Emma had decided to leave the hospital instead of seeing Autumn. Elena was already there, and the girl wouldn't leave and Autumn wouldn't let her leave. Autumn clearly had deep feelings for Elena, and Emma was happy for them. Elena was good for Autumn, Autumn was much happier now. But Autumn never opened up to Emma the way she did for Elena. And that, that angered Emma.

So now she was at Ethan's, having raided his parent's liquor cabinet and grabbed a bottle of vodka. Ethan was eyeing her suspiciously as she gulped down the bottle more than he had. They were in his basement, his parents out of town for the week, and Emma had been quiet. She was just drinking and getting drunker by the second.

"You're drinking way too much, Emma. You should calm down a little." He observed, attempting to take the bottle away but Emma pushed him off, taking another swig.

"Right, keep telling me what to do. Everyone does anyway." She snapped, her words slurred. "Watch Autumn, take care of your brother, and make sure they're safe. They're not okay so you have to help them be…" Emma mimicked the words she had heard for years. "But do they ever check if I'm okay?" her eyes watered. "No. No one checks if *I'm* okay. And that's okay. That's fucking fine…"

Ethan moved closer to his girlfriend, concern in his face. "Are you okay, Emma?" he asked softly.

Emma took another large gulp, the vodka burning her throat. "I have to respond yes." She spoke, turning to her boyfriend with a look he wasn't accustomed to seeing; an empty look in her usually gleaming brown eyes.

"You don't have to respond yes if that's not the right answer. Not to me. You know that, right?" he told her, squeezing her shoulder. "You can talk to me."

"There's no point in it." Emma whispered. "No point…"

"Yes there is, your feelings matter Emma. They matter as much as Riley's and as much as Autumn's. You don't have to hide your feelings with me. Because *I'm* here to listen to *your* feelings and understand them. I love you, and I want to know if you're okay." Ethan said sincerely, attempting to take the bottle from Emma and failing again.

Emma stared at him and looked away after a couple of seconds, taking another swig from her nearly empty bottle. "Just let me drink."

Ethan sighed. "That's all you ever tell me. To let you drink." He told her. "I think…I think I've been letting you drink way too much and way too often…it's getting to a point—"

Emma groaned in frustration. "If I can't drink in peace here, with my fucking boyfriend, then I'm going to leave. I will find somewhere else to forget everything." Emma stood up, coordination lost and the tiny girl nearly falling but Ethan managed to catch her in time.

"I'm not letting you leave." Ethan said firmly, taking the bottle from Emma.

"Let me go, Ethan!" Emma shouted, attempting to break free of his grasp but Ethan wasn't budging for a second. "Just leave me alone!"

Ethan shook his head. "I'm not letting you go like this, you're drunk out of your mind!"

"Well it's better than being sober!" Emma shouted angrily, tears forming in her eyes. "It's better than being sober…" she whispered, tears streaming down her face.

Ethan frowned, a concerned look on his face. "Emma…" he placed the bottle on the table and wrapped his arms around the tiny girl.

Emma cried softly in his chest. "It's easier being drunk. I don't feel anything. It's better. Nothing hurts." She slurred.

Ethan sat back down on the couch, Emma still in his arms. "I…I don't know how to help you." He confessed, feeling guilty of being unable to help his girlfriend.

Emma wiped the tears from her eyes. "Just…just let me drink. Please. Just…just…let me drink." She begged.

And Ethan did.

Elena did eventually have to go home. Visiting hours were over, and she had to part way with Autumn for now. She'd visit in the morning before school.

The day itself had been long and tiring. From Autumn's recent diagnosis to Phoenix's outburst. She had tried throughout the day to send texts to Phoenix and even calling her a couple of times, but not answer in both attempts.

*"You just seem to have this thing for fucked up people; this incessant need to fix **every** person in the world like you actually give a shit. Well wanna know a fun fact Elena? You can't fix everyone. So why don't you get down from your pedestal and stop acting like you're some kind of saint doing everyone a favor by making everyone your charity case?"*

Phoenix wasn't exactly lying at the accusation. If Elena had magical healing powers to fix everyone, however they needed to be fixed, she would use it on every single person. She had too much guilt gnawing at her skin to let something remain unfixed. The last thing she let stay unfixed wound up becoming just another stone in an empty field.

Elena sighed, running her hands through her hair as she walked up the steps of her home. She had to fix things with Phoenix soon. Phoenix was becoming one of her closest friends. The idea of losing her, or anyone, terrified her. Because loss was another thing Elena both loathed and feared.

She took out her keys to open the door and shuffled a key around, eventually opening the door and stepping inside.

"I'm home!" Elena exclaimed.

Ana appeared from the living room. "Good. I've been worried sick about you Elena. But at least you called earlier." She looked at her daughter. "How are you? How's Autumn?"

Elena sighed, looking down at the ground. "Well, it wasn't just a nosebleed. She…" her voice cracked. Ana immediately embraced her daughter, leading her to the living room and sitting her down on the couch.

"Qué paso, mi linda?" Ana whispered, kissing her forehead.

Elena wiped a stray tear away. "She's got cancer…just…spreading all over her body. I…she might not have much time left mami…"

Ana frowned, immediately hugging her daughter. And for the second time, Elena cried. Even worse than when she cried in Autumn's arms, but Ana held onto her daughter tightly and attempted to soothe the crying girl in her arms as best she could.

"I…love…her." Elena said in between sobs.

"I know you do, Elena, I know you do." Ana said softly. "Which is why you can't leave her now. And you're not going to let her fall apart right in front of you. She may appear strong and tough, but she's vulnerable. And you know that, she just has a hard time expressing it." She wiped Elena's tears away. "Whatever time she has left, make it count." She smiled sadly. "I'm sorry your first love turned out this way, but she's still here. And she had a miracle happen once, it can happen again. I can't promise you miracles always happen, but you have to keep faith that they still exist and that they still work."

Elena sniffed. "I wasn't intending on leaving her side." She said, determined. "Autumn needs me and I need her just as much. I don't want to lose her…" she trailed off. "I don't want her to leave this earth with her still not fixed from the damage done by this sometimes cruel world—"

"Autumn doesn't need a guardian, Elena. She needs her girlfriend. By all means, support her and help her. But don't let that become you're only objective. She needs more than just helping, she needs love too." Ana advised.

Elena nodded in response. "I've been told I have an obsession with fixing things."

Ana smiled sympathetically, squeezing her shoulder. "You've been through a lot these past months, I can understand why you have a desire to fix things." She paused. "Which is why I'm hesitant in giving you the box that came in today...I think I'll give it to you tomorrow. You've had a long day today."

"No, what came in for me? I can take it upstairs to my room. I'm fine." Elena insisted.

"It's from Miami." Ana gave her daughter a worried look.

"Okay...did grandma send me a care package or something?" Elena asked obliviously.

"It's from Hailey's parents."

Elena gulped. "Oh." She looked down. "Haven't heard that name in a while…" she trailed off.

"You can take a look at the package whenever you're ready—
"

"I'll take it now." Elena cut off, chewing her lower lip nervously. "Where is it?"

"Elena…are you sure?"

"*Yes*, mami I'm sure." Elena paused. "I can handle it. I've handled a ton of things today, one more won't hurt."

Ana sighed. "It's in the kitchen counter." She nodded towards the direction of the kitchen and Elena immediately walked to the kitchen. "Let me know if you need anything." Ana called after her.

Elena took a deep breath as she grabbed the huge, heavy box in her skinny arms and silently went upstairs without another word to her mother. She stepped inside her room and put the box down on her unmade bed, staring at the box for a couple minutes as she debated whether to open the box or not.

Once she reached for a pair of scissors, she knew her answer was to open it. Ripping open the box, she gulped as she slowly unloaded the items from the box.

Old photographs in albums, mix tapes (Hailey's specialty) labeled with sharpie pen based on moods or genres, Hailey's cassette player, stuffed animals that belonged to Hailey, Hailey's journals that even Elena never read…

Elena's eyes watered as she took out Hailey's black leather jacket that the girl wore often. She hugged the jacket close to her, inhaling the fading scent that once belonged to Hailey. Lavender.

She took out a jean jacket that was Hailey's favorite. Elena use to love wearing that jacket and would steal it all the time (Hailey would always pretend to be mad about it, even though she never was).

Other personal belongings came out of the box that once belonged to Hailey: beanies, necklaces, books, sweaters…

Hailey's ukulele.

Elena grinned as she held the small wooden instrument in her hands. She strummed the ukulele, clearly out of tune after not being used for months.

"Oscar Meyers." She whispered to herself. Ridiculous name. Hailey had gotten the ukulele when they were 13 years old, and both had a fascination with eating hot dogs from a vendor by the park they'd frequently visit.

When thinking of a name for the ukulele, Elena had suggested a hot dog theme name after Hailey dropped her hot dog on her ukulele when it was resting on her lap. There, the nameless ukulele was baptized with the name Oscar Meyers.

Elena put on the jean jacket that still smelled like Hailey as she tuned the ukulele. After she tuned it, she placed it aside as she kept taking out belongings that belonged to Hailey.

Her eyes widened as she took out Hailey's favorite thing in the world wrapped neatly in bubble wrap: her camera (a very expensive one) that she used to film her short movies. Hailey wanted to be a film director.

"Pearl." She whispered as she unwrapped the camera. Hailey had named the camera after her crazy fascination with pearls.

"All the crazy things we filmed with you…" she said to the camera, tracing the outline of the camera with her finger.

She turned back to the box to see what else to take out, but there was nothing left. She threw the box off her bed as she continued looking through all the objects she had taken out.

She sighed, her heart aching at how much looking at all this hurt. All the memories, all the laughter and tears…

She placed her hands inside the pockets of the jean jacket only to feel her hands crumpling a paper in one pocket and feeling a small, tangible object in the other.

She took out the crumpled and folded piece of paper written in Hailey's writing after she opened the folded paper.

Elena,

Always stealing my fucking jacket, right? I'm sure you didn't steal it this time. I gave it to you. Well—I sent it to you—actually, my parents sent it to you.

I didn't.

I can't. I assume you got the box. I packed everything in there. My parents probably found it in my closet. That's where I left it for them to send to you.

Hopefully you're not, like, 35 or something when they sent it... I wouldn't blame them for taking all that time until they finally came inside my room. It must hurt to.

This must hurt you too.

But anyway, I wanted you to keep everything that mattered to me because I trust only you to cherish these items (unless our 11 year friendship meant nothing to you and you throw all this shit out). I do hope you decide to keep them, but I'd understand if you didn't.

Check the other pocket Elliebellie, there's a USB in there. It's really important you take a look at it. There are some videos that will help answer the questions I know you want the answers to. And the other videos are videos to watch now that I'm not there with you anymore. Watch the video labeled #1. It's important you see that one first before you see anything else.

I hope things are doing great for you. I know you're moving to New York, so if you're already there by the time you get this...I hope the experience is great.

This is probably the most awkward letter I've written, I'm sorry. I really don't know what else to tell you other than I'm sorry and I love you.

Take care,

Hailey.

Elena reached into the other pocket, taking out a blue USB and quickly hopping off the bed and walking to fetch her laptop. She opened the laptop and plugged in the USB, waiting for the item to load.

Her breath hitched when the USB said, *For Elena.* Elena closed her eyes, taking a deep breath before clicking on the item and watching a vast amount of videos appear on her screen.

#1.

That was the first video on top and Elena knew she had to click on that one. But was she ready to click on it? Was she ready to see what was in it? What was even *in it*?

Elena gulped, as her pointer moved to the video. She plugged in her headphones and placed the ear buds in her ears. Double clicking on the video, she waited for the video to play.

Hailey Gorman in all her glory appeared on the screen with a sad smile on her face. Tears fell down Elena's cheeks at the sight of her best friend, not being able to hold back the sob.

"*Hey, Elena.*" Hailey greeted softly, rubbing her hands together. "*If you're watching this, then I'm dead already. And I'm not sorry for what I did, I'm only sorry for leaving you.*" Hailey looked down at her hands. "*I wish things were easier for me that I didn't have to. But…you're moving to New York and…and…you'll forget me soon enough.*"

Elena scoffed. Hailey was wrong in that statement. There wasn't a day she didn't think about her.

Hailey looked back up at the camera. "*I'm assuming you're wondering why I did what I did, and why did it get so bad that I had to resort to suicide...well...you'll find out with all of these videos.*" Hailey chewed on her lower lip. "*But just know that there are other things on here. Like, I made videos for you for all the experiences you'll have that I won't be there for. I won't be there for those times, but hopefully this kind of makes up for it.*" She shrugged. "*I doubt it will help much, but it's something.*" Hailey sighed, leaning back on her chair. "*I'm so sorry it had to come to this, Lena...you told me to get help and I never listened, I let myself turn like this...*" Hailey continued talking.

Elena sniffed as she watched the rest of the video. "But I let you..."

CHAPTER SIXTEEN

"You know, life can be the trickiest thing sometimes," Elena listened as Hailey spoke in another video, having watched a couple in the past couple weeks since she received the package. *"Some people are the luckiest fuckers to roam the earth because they have no troubles financially, medically, socially, mentally, emotionally, romantically...they're just...lucky. And then others, like me, fall on the opposite side..."* Hailey stared at the wall in deep thought.

"It's like, no matter how hard I try, Elena, I can't be happy. And I should, right? I'm fine in most aspects. I'm healthy...ish. Mentally, not really. But in all other medical areas, I'm perfectly healthy. My parents aren't the richest, but we're good. I don't have to worry about anything like that." Hailey paused.

"I have you...and you're the most amazing person I've ever known. And I wish you were a stronger reason to my happiness. But you're not—nothing is." She sighed, running a hand through her hair. *"I...I can't help being sad, Lena...I can't explain why out of nowhere I'm miserable or why out of nowhere I'm not. It's like trying to explain why some people have diabetes. They just...do. And telling me to just stop being sad or to just start eating again or to stop cutting myself is like telling one of those people with diabetes to just stop having diabetes, you know? It's not something I can help."*

But Elena could've helped her, she thought. She would've helped Hailey in anything she needed. She'd do anything for her best friend. Elena swallowed a sob rising to her throat, she'd cried enough these past few weeks.

The door knocked and Elena quickly paused the video and took out her headphones from her ears before her mother peeked her head in her room. Elena smiled softly. "Hey mom, what's up?"

Ana glanced at the laptop. "Are you still watching those videos?"

"Is that what you came in here for?"

"No, it's for something else…" Ana sighed. "I'm worried about you, mija…"

Elena looked at the screen. "What was that something else?"

Ana frowned when Elena ignored her comment. "Autumn's mother called me. She said Autumn has another chemo session today if you were interested in going." She told her.

Elena immediately nodded. "Of course. What time?"

"Two o' clock." Ana answered.

"I'll be there."

Ana nodded slowly before glancing at her again. "You know, Elena, you don't have to hide that all of this hurts, at least not to me. This is a lot to handle. With Hailey and Autumn... it's okay if you need to take a breather, Autumn would understand."

Elena stared at her. "I'll be there." She repeated.

"Okay." Ana whispered, not taking Elena's distant approach to heart. Her daughter would open up when she was ready. "Two o' clock." She repeated.

Elena nodded. "Okay, thank you." Ana left and Elena pressed play on the video again, inserting he headphones in her ears.

"I don't know Elena, it's so difficult to understand everything—to understand ME. I wish things were easier. I wish I was one of the luckiest ones, you know? The ones that can easily find happiness and joy and everything I don't have. Those are the luckiest ones. The ones that can easily smile and easily speak their feelings and easily find a reason to keep going. They're the lucky ones because they remain intact despite all the reasons not to be. But me? I'm not the lucky one. But you? You're the lucky one." Hailey looked up and stared at the camera. "You've *always been the lucky one with that. You're happy, and you smile so easily...you laugh and you love and you help and you understand and you're just...you're lucky."*

Elena paused the video and sighed, closing her eyes. Was she really lucky? Right now she felt like her world was crashing down. She's lost too much in the course of the year that was near ending as the holidays were just around the corner, and Elena wasn't sure how much more she could endure.

With Autumn's diagnosis, losing Hailey, and Phoenix *still* not speaking to her, she wasn't sure whether lucky was the proper term for her.

She wasn't one of the luckiest ones.

———————————

Phoenix was cramped up in her bed that she shared with three other people. The room was small and six people managed to cramp up in here. She was trying to do homework while the younger kids ran around playing, distracting her every couple of minutes when she'd hear crying.

She was babysitting again, like she did every day. And being on winter vacation only meant bigger responsibilities in watching the kids all while trying to complete homework she was left over break.

As she heard another cry emerge from the other room, she sighed and closed her textbook. Phoenix stood up and walked to the other room, her baby brother, Noah, crying on the floor. She scooped up the one year old in her arms and bounced him on her hip as she rubbed his back. She turned to the other little ones with a raised eyebrow.

"What happened?" she asked sternly as Noah still cried in her arms.

"He fell." One of her cousins shrugged.

"I understand that, but *how*?" Phoenix urged.

The three little boys looked down guiltily.

Phoenix hummed. "Someone pushed Noah, right?"

She heard some muttered agreements and Phoenix still looked down on them sternly. "What have I said about playing rough?" she scorned. "Especially when you're playing with someone as little as Noah!" she told them. "You have to be careful, he's only a baby. He can barely walk guys, so bring it down a few notches. I'm not mad, okay?" Noah sniffed as his crying calmed down and Phoenix rubbed his back, kissing his chubby cheek.

The three boys nodded obediently and took off running again. Phoenix sighed, rubbing her temple with one hand as she turned to Noah. "And *you,* Noah, are staying with me now, okay?" she cooed, bouncing him on one hip. Noah only babbled with a toothy grin and Phoenix chuckled.

It didn't take a couple seconds until the other kids needed her assistance in some way or another. From helping with homework, resolving a fight, or giving a snack, Phoenix literally didn't have a second to breathe.

So much for completing homework, Phoenix thought. She took a seat at the small table in the tiny kitchen apartment with Noah on her lap.

Things weren't getting better.

Her mother had taken more shifts, her father still hadn't found a job, and time was running short. They'd need to pack their bags soon since her aunt and uncle couldn't maintain the household afloat with them here.

It was getting harder. And Phoenix put up a strong front, but how long would that last? She had so much responsibility thrown at her that she wasn't sure she was even a teenager anymore. She had to mature too quickly, too suddenly that she was on the verge of breaking down.

She couldn't tell a soul though, they'd only pity her. Pity her that her family used food stamps, that her family bought their clothes at the Salvation Army or a thrift shop (they could barely even afford *that*), that she shared a small room with six people, and that she was a couple weeks short to being homeless.

Phoenix wiped a tear that escaped and took a deep breath, watching as Noah banged a plastic cup on the table.

She heard the door open and heard children squealing and greeting happily her mother, Hope. Phoenix stood up and walked toward where the kids had gathered around her mother, the tired woman laughing as they talked all at once.

"Hey mama." Phoenix smiled softly.

Hope looked up and smiled big for her daughter, walking over to her and kissing her cheek. "Hi baby, did these brats bother you too much? So I can *beat their asses*!" Hope made sure to project the last sentence louder, laughing.

Phoenix laughed as little eyes bulged out in fear, thinking Hope was being serious. The younger girl shook her head. "No, they were good. As good as they can be." She replied simply with a shrug.

Hope raised an eyebrow, noticing Phoenix's demeanor. "You okay, love?"

Phoenix nodded, forcing a smile. "Of course, just a little tired but everyone is." She assured.

Her mother eyed her suspiciously, not believing Phoenix for one second. "Okay, so when exactly were you planning on telling me you're lying?"

"It's nothing mom—"

"Phoenix, I know you." Her mother cut off. "You're more than just tired…" she sighed as she took Noah away from Phoenix's arms, the toddler immediately resting his head on his mother's shoulder. "This whole situation is hard on you, I know it. You shouldn't be tackling so much responsibility, and trust me if I could handle everything on my own, I would." Her eyes watered. "I hate the fact that I had to take away so much from you just to get by. Like hanging out with your friends…or choir. I know how much you loved it. And when things get better, you sign right back up, understand? This is only temporary, things are going to get better. Your father's going to get a job real soon and we'll make good enough money to find a new place and things will be good again. I promise."

Phoenix only nodded, hugging her mother. "I know, mom." She whispered to her.

Phoenix didn't believe it though. Things *weren't* getting better, but she kept that fighting spirit for her family. Because that's all she had at to this point.

"Actually," Hope began. "call up one of your friend and hang out. I can give you some money and you can get something to eat or—"

"No, it's okay mom. I don't need to go out. They're all probably busy anyway." Phoenix assured.

"Baby, it's fine. I can handle these kids, go out. Do something. Call up Maya…or that other friend you got…Elena?"

Phoenix looked down at the mention of Elena. She still wasn't talking to the girl. And maybe she had exaggerated a little and the fight was stupid, but she was still so angry, so dejected. It wasn't Elena's fault, it was her own pent up frustrations that caused her to lash out on Elena.

"I don't talk to Elena anymore." Phoenix said quietly.

Hope tilted her head. "Why?"

"We had an argument."

"About what?"

Phoenix hesitated but her mother's look made it hard to stay quiet. "She was asking me about choir and if I had anything going on because I was so distracted and distant and…I snapped at her. I didn't mean to but it's just," she sighed. "I have so much going on and she kept persisting that I talk to her about it and Ms. Kate kept persisting too and I just…I don't want people knowing about our…situation."

Hope nodded slowly. "Do you care about Elena?"

Phoenix nodded. "Yeah, we've become good friends recently along with Emma and Autumn. I care about them."

"Okay, then fix things. I know things are hard for us, and they don't need to know if you don't want them to, but you're going to need someone there for when I can't be there or your dad. Friends are there for each other, and you're going to need yours just as much as they need you." Hope advised.

Phoenix agreed. "Right. But what if Elena won't forgive me?"

"Something tells me she will. Just talk to her and tell her as much as you want to tell her." Hope told her.

"Okay," Phoenix whispered. "I'll talk to her."

"Good." Her mother smiled. "I'm glad you came to your senses, dumbass." She teased.

Phoenix giggled, shaking her head. "You're so nice, mom."

"I try." Hope shrugged. "Now call up Elena and patch things up with her. Or go to her house and talk face-to-face."

Phoenix nodded. "I will…tomorrow." Hope eyed her daughter. "I have homework to finish up mom." She told her. "Damn, you don't have to give me such dirty look."

Her mother chuckled. "Fine, get your homework done." She motioned her daughter to go and Phoenix walked back to her room.

Could she patch things up with Elena? Phoenix sighed as she plopped down on the bed and opened her textbook up again with her notebook beside her. She had been so harsh with Elena when the girl was only worried.

But it wasn't like Phoenix had exactly lied when she told Elena all of that. The girl did have a knack for fixing the broken. Phoenix didn't know why exactly, but something told her there was a lot she didn't know about Elena. Elena appeared to be an open book, but Phoenix could see now how closed she truly was.

Elena never talked about her *real* feelings and often took on other people's problems rather than her own. Maybe Phoenix would address that soon, but for now she'd settle just getting her best friend back.

"Is she coming?" Autumn asked her mother as her mother parked the car in front of the hospital.

Cora shrugged. "Emma didn't answer, I'm sorry." She said, frowning.

Autumn's face looked dejected for a second but quickly recovered, not wanting to show her disappointment over it. "Oh. Okay. Is Elena coming?" Autumn chewed on her lower lip.

"Ana called me back and said yes, Elena will probably be a little late. I called right before we came here." Cora explained to her.

"Okay." Autumn nodded, a part of her still dejected over Emma avoiding her. It wasn't like Emma to not be here. She always supported Autumn in anything, this just wasn't like her. She thought they were restoring their old friendship again, but Emma's distant behavior said otherwise.

Cora turned to her. "How are you feeling, Autumn?"

"What do you mean?"

"Physically..." her mother trailed off. "Emotionally....mentally..."

Autumn shrugged. "Physically I feel pretty crappy. I mean, it's my second chemo session so I expect it to get gradually worse. Emotionally and mentally." She paused. "I'm okay."

"Okay," Cora said slowly. "But you'd tell me if you weren't?"

"Sure, I guess." Autumn mumbled.

Cora sighed as turned off the ignition and took out the keys. "Autumn, are you aware of the severity of your diagnosis?"

"I have cancer everywhere mom, I think I get it."

Cora closed her eyes for a brief moment. "I know you know that. But do you know what's going to happen?"

"I'm going to slowly die. I know mom." Autumn gulped. "I have cancer spreading in my bones and gradually to other parts. I'm going to lose my ability to walk." She explained. "But the worst part?" she closed her eyes. "I'm going to die in darkness."

Cora's eyes watered. "I'm sorry. I shouldn't have said anything—"

"It's okay mom." Autumn assured. "At least you're not in denial like dad is. He thinks I'm going to magically get better, but you and I both know that probably won't be the case. And even if I do magically go back into remission, I'm going to be strapped onto a wheelchair and possibly worse than that. That's the cold, hard truth. Nothing's going to get better at this point because my body has betrayed me in so many ways now. My body is damaged—"

"But your soul isn't." Cora squeezed Autumn's free hand. "That isn't damaged. You have that fighting spirit Autumn. Despite the fact that you're aware of the consequences of this treatment, you're doing it anyway to have a chance—a slim chance—but you're taking that chance anyway. A part of you still believes in miracles."

Autumn pursed her lips. "Possibly." She half-agreed. "I believe in something much stronger though."

"What is it?"

"Getting what I lost back."

Cora smiled softly, kissing her daughter's forehead. "And you will." She assured. "Let's go fight the good fight?"

Autumn nodded as her mom opened the car door and walked around to Autumn's side, opening the door and helping Autumn out the car. The cool breeze of New York City's wintertime hit her face, and Cora immediately pulled down Autumn's black beanie. Autumn's ears felt warmer, but her hands and feet remained freezing cold. But that was already a given.

"Hey mom?"

"Yeah?"

Autumn reached her arms out to hug her mother and grabbed her mother by her shoulders and pulled her in for a hug. Cora was taken back but quickly reciprocated the hug, her eyes watering again at the affectionate contact with her daughter.

"I love you." Autumn whispered.

Cora choked back a sob, tightening the hug even more. Autumn hadn't said those three words for such a long time up until now. Those words held a tender hope in Cora, because she hoped to hear those three words from Autumn more often.

"I love you too, Autumn, so, so, so, so, soooooo much." Cora whispered back.

"I know." Autumn squeezed the hug tightly before letting go.

The short walk inside the hospital went on in silence. But Autumn held onto to her mother's arm tightly, the vibes given from the hospital never hitting her quite right. The environment was always so depressing. Her surroundings were only of death, or near death. There was no difference in a hospital because everyone wound up in the same place at some point: the grave.

Cora checked in Autumn for her chemo session while mentioning to the nurse that Elena would be arriving soon and to let her enter the Chemotherapy Unit. If it was up to Autumn, she'd have her own room and just get the chemo over with.

But her mother insisted that being surrounded by people in the same situation would help. That only would depress Autumn more, if she was being honest. But Autumn decided not to protest further. Her parents went through enough; she had to make them content somehow.

Once they entered the Chemotherapy Unit, Cora guided Autumn to the empty recliner chair where a nurse was already waiting to assist Autumn. Her mother helped Autumn out of her coat, scarf, and mittens. Autumn opted for having her beanie removed, the beanie keeping her slightly warm.

The nurse rolled up the left sleeve of Autumn's sweatshirt and cleaned the area in Autumn's arm where she'd inject the drip. Even after having billions of needles poked at her, Autumn still hated the feeling. She flinched when the needle was jabbed inside and the nurse left after Autumn assured her she had no other concerns.

"Just two or three hours here and we're done." Cora assured, taking a seat beside Autumn and looking through her bag to take out some assignments to grade for her second grade class.

Autumn only nodded, forcing a small smile. She pushed her sunglasses up and let out a small puff of air, pushing her head back further into the recliner.

Before the two could say anything else, Elena stumbled in with her goofy smile when she caught sight of Autumn. Walking over to her, she greeted Cora with a hug before sitting beside Autumn.

"Hello, gorgeous." Elena did her best to mimic Babra Streisand's accent in *Funny Girl* that she and Autumn had watched (well, Elena watched. Autumn listened) the other day and laughed at her failed attempt.

Autumn chuckled, blushing. "Hey, Ellie."

"I got you something." Elena announced with a proud grin, quickly looking through her messy messenger bag.

Autumn smiled. "What did you get me?" she asked curiously.

Elena took out a king sized Reese's Cup bar and a tiny, stuffed monkey, placing the two items in Autumn's hands. Autumn first felt the stuffed animal, tracing the outline of the monkey before smiling.

"You got me a monkey?"

"Yes, because you drive me bananas." Elena grinned cheekily.

Autumn snorted, shaking her head at her girlfriend's lame joke. "What about this?" Autumn asked, running her hands over the plastic wrapping.

"What's your favorite chocolate?"

Autumn broke out into a grin. "Reese's Cups." She answered, quickly ripping open the candy and breaking the chocolate in half, popping the half into her mouth. "You are amazing." Autumn muffled.

"I try." Elena flipped her hair dramatically.

Autumn only chuckled, offering Elena and her mother a share of her treat. Both declined politely and Autumn kept stuffing her face with chocolate while making small talk with Elena.

An hour into the session, Elena played with Autumn's cold fingers mindlessly while both of them shared headphones and listened to music from Elena's phone.

"Why are your hands always so cold?" Elena asked.

"Why are yours always so warm?" Autumn retorted playfully.

"Because I'm an arctic fox."

Autumn raised an eyebrow. "What are you talking about?"

"An arctic fox has the warmest fur."

"So you're always warm because you're an arctic fox?"

"Yes."

"So I'm dating an arctic fox?"

"Yes. And I'm dating an African bush viper." Elena told her.

"Why am I an African bush viper?" Autumn laughed.

"They're cold blooded animals so they're cold. And you're always really cold. But they also look like dragons. And dragons are cool." Elena explained.

"Are they now?" Autumn asked interestedly.

Elena nodded. "And you're so fierce and you may appear cold on the outside, but you have warmth on the inside—*fire.*" Elena told her with a smile. "People just don't see it because they're so scared of how you appear, but you're the kindest viper to ever exist."

Autumn smiled, reaching her hand out to touch Elena's face. Once she did, she touched Elena's face delicately and moved closer to her to kiss her girlfriend's cheek. "You're the warmest arctic fox alive." She whispered.

"So you'll be the African bush viper to my arctic fox?"

Autumn giggled, nodding. "Yes, I'll be the African bush viper to your arctic fox. Even if they'd never work out because I'd kill you since I'm poisonous."

"But we work, right?" Elena asked, biting her lower lip.

Autumn nodded. "We're the exception, I could never poison you."

"Thanks, I really appreciate it." Elena smiled. "In return for your kindness, I'll keep you warm with my fur." She said, cupping her warm hands with Autumn's.

"Okay." Autumn whispered.

"I promise to always keep you warm." Elena said, a more serious tone this time. "I don't want you to be cold ever again."

"You're too good for me sometimes, I swear." Autumn told her. "I don't deserve you."

"Yes you do. You deserve the world. I'll give you the moon and the stars and the galaxies and put them in a canvas for you. I'll give you everything. Everything, everything, everything!" Elena kissed her still icy hands.

Autumn kissed Elena's cheek again. "So you'll buy me more cute stuffed animals and Reese's Cups?"

"And sunflowers. Lots and lots of sunflowers." Elena smiled.

"Sounds perfect." Autumn sighed in content.

The two were silent for a couple minutes before Elena spoke up, noticing Autumn's constant look of discontent. "Do you feel okay? It's only your second chemo session, but are you okay?"

"Tired." She muttered. "My head hurts."

Elena frowned slightly. "Rest. I'll still be here. I promise." She kissed Autumn's hands again. Elena used her puffy jacket to make it into a pillow for Autumn and took off her hoodie underneath to place over Autumn when she fell asleep. She played with pieces of Autumn's hair while still holding Autumn's free hand with the other.

Autumn quickly rested her head on Elena's puffy jacket and enjoyed the warmth of Elena's hoodie, inhaling Elena's sweet scent. "Can you take off my glasses? They won't let me sleep." she asked shyly, usually not one to ask for favors.

Elena smiled, taking off Autumn's sunglasses and placing them beside her. She went back to playing with Autumn's hair and holding her hand, staring intently at Autumn's beautiful green eyes before her girlfriend closed them. She kissed Autumn's forehead and watched as she slept, smiling softly at Autumn's content face.

"Thank you." Cora spoke up, smiling as she watched the interactions between her daughter and Elena.

Elena turned to her with a confused expression. "For what?"

Cora's eyes shifted from her sleeping daughter to Elena. "For loving my daughter. I've never seen her so happy. You did that. She smiles more and laughs more and has this glow in her since you came into her life. It's magical, really." She paused. "I can never thank you enough for making her happy."

Elena glanced at Autumn before looking at Cora. "There's nothing to thank, she makes me the happiest girl alive too. I love her." She looked at Autumn again. "I didn't think it was possible to love someone so much." Elena said softly, looking back up at Cora.

"Did you know that Vincent Van Gogh use to eat yellow paint because he thought eating a bright color would make him happier? Well, Autumn's kind of like my yellow paint. There was a dark period in my life before I got here, but Autumn showed up and suddenly I felt like the color yellow; bright, happy, and optimistic. Yellow's my favorite color now because of her. And it's going to remain that way, I know it."

Cora's smile only grew at Elena's words. "You're Autumn's yellow paint too." Her voice cracked. "And I do think you'll be her yellow paint for a really long time."

"I'll be her yellow paint for as long as she wants me to be." Elena kissed Autumn's hand. "And I'll paint her everything yellow; the sun, lemonade, bananas, sunflowers, stars…I'll paint her happiness. I promise you that, Mrs. Castillo. I'll never paint her an ounce of blue or black or grey. She'll only know of happy colors as long as she's with me."

Cora nodded, walking to Elena to hug her. "I firmly believe that to be true, Elena. I really do."

"I'm glad you're so supportive of Autumn and I. I was worried you and your husband would be hesitant of the relationship—"

"Elena," Cora butted in, laughing. "Do you realize we live in New York City? Why on earth would we ever be hesitant?"

Elena laughed. "Okay, true." She agreed.

"We were surprised when we found out Autumn was dating a girl, because we just assumed she was only attracted to boys. But after everything my daughter has been through, I don't care who she's with. As long as she's happy." Cora smiled. "As long as someone paints her happy colors."

CHAPTER SEVENTEEN

Autumn Castillo hated many things.

Open doors, Chihuahuas (their incessant barking was annoying to hear), socks (being barefoot was way better), the smell of cheese, being away from Elena, people, socializing, and a gazillion more things.

But one thing she didn't hate was the holidays.

Surprise, surprise, Autumn Castillo was not a Grinch reincarnate! But truth be told, she enjoyed the holidays quite a lot. Her mother's cooking was heavenly, the movies her father and Dylan picked out were bearable, and most Christmas carols didn't make her want to run into a glass door (not that she had any experience with running into glass doors...).

Her parents carried many traditions when the holidays rolled around. Like the 12 grapes on New Year's, the many, many, *many* jam sessions with her father on guitar while she played the piano, and the entire family sang Christmas songs, her mother forcing her and her siblings to write letters to Santa (despite them finding out long ago about Santa's identity), and the stereotypical tacky Christmas sweaters they wore for their Christmas card (Autumn pretended to hate it).

There were other traditions that use to be done, back when Autumn could see.

They'd go ice skating at Rockefeller Center (she'd cling onto her father and laugh when they'd fall down together), seeing the 80-foot Christmas Tree at Rockefeller Plaza (it was so big, Autumn would tell her parents that she wanted a tree like that in their house. Never happened.), see the department store window displays on Fifth Avenue and the decorations at Sixth Avenue (her and Olivia would go crazy over how bright and colorful and shiny everything was), seeing the Christmas lights tour over in Brooklyn (people were freaking creative—and crazy—with decorations), visiting Santa Claus, and so much more.

But she missed seeing the ball drop most on New Year's in Times Square. Her parents use to take them every year when they were younger. But then Autumn got sick, and they couldn't do these things anymore.

Autumn *had* to ruin everything.

And now she was about to ruin another Castillo holiday extravaganza because she couldn't even get out of bed. Her back was killing her, her head felt like she was hit repeatedly with a baseball bat, she was puking as if she was facing the repercussions of a drunken night, her appetite was zero to none, and she was basically Sleeping Beauty with all the sleeping she'd done.

Chemotherapy was a bitch and Autumn hated it. It was getting in the way of her enjoying the holidays. Potentially her *last* holiday.

Autumn groaned into her pillow, wrapping her blanket around herself again. Her hands and feet were cold. That wasn't a surprise, but she really wanted Elena here. She wanted her warmth and for Elena to hold her until her arms grew tired. But she understood that Elena wanted to celebrate Christmas and New Years with her family, so she'd settle with the phone calls she'd get from Elena.

The door knocked and Autumn croaked out a "Come in." before groaning again at the sudden sharp pain on her back.

Joseph entered his daughter's room and smiled sadly. "Hey, kiddo." He greeted softly, kneeling beside her bed. "How are you feeling?"

"Terrible." Autumn replied.

Joseph sighed. "Anything I can do to help?"

"I don't think so." Autumn told him, pausing before hesitantly speaking up again. "Could you hold my hands, dad?" she asked shyly. "My hands are really cold."

Joseph smiled, knowing how hard it was for Autumn to ask for help when she needed it or let herself be vulnerable. He quickly took Autumn's cold hands and placed his warm ones over hers. "Better?"

Autumn nodded. "Better."

The room was silent for a couple minutes before Joseph spoke up again. "Do you think you can get up and have breakfast downstairs with us today? Mom's making her special blueberry pancakes. I know how much you love those."

Before Autumn could answer, she felt vomit rising up to her throat and removed one of her hands from her father and placed it over her mouth. Joseph quickly knew what that meant and grabbed the trashcan nearby and gave it to Autumn who vomited until her chest was rising and falling rapidly and her breathing heavy. Joseph rubbed her back and held her hair as his daughter vomited.

When Autumn finished she wiped her mouth with the back of her hand. "I'll take that as a no. I'll have your mom save you some for later when you're up for eating. But you have to eat something today Autumn, you didn't eat dinner last night."

"That's because if I put any food near my mouth, I puke my guts out." Autumn rasped.

Joseph sighed. "I know." He sympathized. "But hey, Christmas Eve is tomorrow. That's exciting, right? We're planning a movie marathon. And maybe if you're up for it, we can do a little jam session. It'll be great." He said, trying to sound as enthusiastic as possible.

"Yeah…" Autumn trailed off, seeming to be in deep thought. "You should take Dylan and Olivia ice skating at Rockefeller, and take them to see the tree too."

"It wouldn't be fair if they—"

"Yes it would. Because I want them to." Autumn cut off. "It's not fair that they don't get to enjoy Christmas or New Years because of me. I want them to enjoy the holidays as best they can, and I don't mind if I miss out. Do this for me, yeah? Make sure they have a good Christmas and New Years."

"Will it make you happy?"

"It'd make me the happiest."

"Then I will." Joseph smiled, kissing his daughter's forehead. "You're a good sister."

Autumn smiled weakly. "I think I might go to sleep again. I'm really tired."

"Okay." Joseph nodded. "Call us if anything, we'll be right down the hall."

"Thank you and if—"

"I'll wake you up so you can talk to Elena." Joseph laughed.

"Yeah, but if Emma also calls…or visits…let me know. I haven't seen her in weeks. Is she mad at me?" Autumn asked, wrapping her blanket around herself.

Joseph frowned slightly. "I'll let you know. I don't think Emma's mad, maybe she has things going on that she doesn't have time to visit. She'll probably stop by tomorrow." He told her.

"Okay." Autumn said, dejected. "Thanks dad, for everything."

Joseph smiled, picking up the trashcan Autumn had vomited in and nodded. "No problem kiddo, I'll always be here."

But I probably won't be, Autumn thought.

———————————————

The door knocked exactly four times on Emma's bedroom door and Riley's quiet voice called out to his sister. "Emma?"

Inside the room, Emma's curls were all over her pillow in a messy manner and hid underneath the covers. Hearing the knocking immediately made her groan. Last night's drunken event catching up to her in the form of a hangover.

The light peeked in from her window and made Emma squint her eyes and her headache become more intense.

"Fucking hell..." Emma murmured, holding onto her head as if it was going to fall off.

Riley knocked the door again four times. "Emma, you okay?"

Emma sighed, hopping off her bed and noticing she was still wearing clothes from last night and *reeked* of alcohol.

"I'm fine." She croaked out, rubbing her eyes and attempting to ignore the prominent throbbing coming from her head.

"Okay, well, mom and dad are making breakfast...if you—if you—if *you* want to come join us." Riley told her. "I'd like it if you did..." he mumbled, not having been around his sister much in the past couple of weeks since Autumn's diagnosis.

He had noticed his sister not address the news once or even try and go visit Autumn. And he's had to go to therapy on his own because Emma hadn't taken him. He had to take the subway and all the people tightened together made his panic attacks more frequent than normal.

Emma reached for the Advil placed on her dresser and took two, drinking a half empty water bottle afterwards. "Maybe." She replied simply. "We'll see, Riley."

Riley nodded, frowning. "Okay…bye Emma—Emma—Emma." he sighed in frustration at his counting. Always counting.

Riley tried to suppress tears. Emma promised to take him ice-skating today. But that was a couple weeks ago, and a different Emma.

Emma pursed her lips as she heard Riley walking away. Her phone vibrated for a few moments, indicating a phone call from someone. She knew it was from Autumn, but chose to ignore it.

"Your best friend since childhood is suffering right now and could die, so you think the best way to support her is avoiding her? Nice going, Emma." Emma grabbed the nearest object she could get her hands on and threw it against a wall and felt her eyes well up.

Balling up her fists, she fell to the ground and punched her thighs angrily. She would probably form dark bruises, but she didn't care. She was angry and sad right now. The world was cruel and she was just as much.

"Useless, you're so fucking useless." Emma continued punching her thighs aggressively before she broke down to a gut-wrenching sob.

"You're heartless." Emma placed her hands on her face and felt her hands grow wet with her tears.

"*You're abandoning your best friend. You're abandoning your brother. How selfish. You're so selfish Emma, think about them and how they feel. They have it worse than you.*" Emma dug her nails on her forehead, knowing she drew blood from the pressure.

She moved her hands away and punched her thighs again. "Bad. You're a bad person." She said to herself, last night's make-up running down her face. "Bad…" she sobbed.

"*Go do what you do best, Emma, go drink. Drink until you can't think straight.*"

Emma crawled underneath her bed, reaching for a box she had with some bottles of beer, whiskey, scotch, etc. She took out a Jack Daniel's beer bottle and quickly opened it, downing it.

"*Drink and you don't feel anything.*" Emma wiped the tears away and took another gulp of her beer.

"*Drink and you'll be fine.*" But she wasn't fine. She was far from fine.

But she couldn't say that.

She had to be there for Autumn.

And Riley.

They had it worse.

She couldn't be selfish.

"Just drink…" she whispered to herself before finishing her beer. Hiding the empty beer can in the same box and stumbled back up and grabbed her throbbing head.

Emma looked at herself in the mirror and sighed before taking a shower, changing into some fresh clothes, and stepping back into the same mirror with a fresher face.

Putting on some make-up, found herself staring at her reflection. Her eyes said help, but everything else screamed okay.

"So when am I going to meet your boyfriend?" Grace chuckled when Maya blushed furiously.

"He's not…he's not my boyfriend." Maya muttered sheepishly.

Grace laughed. "All right, then soon-to-be boyfriend." She clarified in a playful manner. "But in all seriousness, do you like this boy? Is he someone you'd like to be with?"

Maya suppressed a smile. "I do like Toby, but I don't know… I'm kind of afraid." She confessed.

"What are you afraid of?" Grace asked.

Maya shrugged. "That it won't work out." She paused. "He wouldn't be my main priority. And that might hurt our relationship."

"What are your top priorities?"

"You." Maya answered. "Mostly you. And school…but you for the most part."

Grace's smile faltered. "I shouldn't be, Maya. You don't have to tackle all this responsibility. I'm not forcing you to—"

"I know, but I want to." Maya butted in. "I want to because I don't want to lose you…" her eyes watered.

"Baby…" Grace whispered before enveloping her daughter in a hug. "You can never lose me." She rubbed her daughter's back soothingly. "Even when I die, I'll still be here. You won't see me, but I'll be here. I promise."

Maya was silent for a moment before speaking up again. "*When* you die?" her voice cracked.

Grace sighed. "Maya, no matter how hard I fight to beat this cancer, it keeps beating me. I still hold the faith that I can win this time, but the chances are looking slim. You and I both know that."

"You can't think like that mom!" Maya exclaimed, tears streaming down her face. "You can't just give up!"

"I'm not giving up Maya, I'm just accepting reality."

"Well you have a twisted reality…" Maya wiped tears away.

Grace frowned, staring at her daughter. If there's anything she feared it was how Maya would deal with her death. No matter how much she would advise Maya to go and be a teenager, her daughter was stubborn. She insisted on spending her time researching and finding potential treatments and writing essays for her doctors. She appreciated Maya's dedication, she did. But she didn't want her to take it too far.

The sad part was that she already began. Maya was denying herself the right to love someone, to be a careless teenager, to enjoy life to the fullest. Maya created a bubble for herself. And Grace was the only thing in that bubble whether she liked it or not.

"When was the last time you hung out with your friends?"

Maya was silent and pursed her lips. "I don't know…I've been busy with you—"

"When was the last time you went on a date with Toby? Or anyone?"

"Mom, don't do this—"

"No, Maya, I have to do this. You can't spend your life fearing time and fearing making mistakes. Because wanna know something?

Time's going to keep going and there's nothing you can do to stop it. You have to learn to embrace time. Time is all we have, some people just have it longer than others. And everyone messes up. There's not one person who is perfect. And if you meet a perfect person, then I will go buy you dinner." Grace chuckled. "You have to stop being so hard on yourself Maya, you're a great person. I am proud to have raised you. You are extraordinary, and I don't want you to think otherwise."

Maya hugged her mother tightly and kissed her cheek. "I love you mom."

"I love you too baby."

Maya wiped tears from her eyes again. "I bought Toby a gift, actually." She confessed with a blush.

"Then what are you still doing here? Go give that boy his gift!" Grace playfully scorned.

Maya chuckled. "Are you sure?"

"I've never been surer." Grace nodded to her. "Go. I'll be here. I'm not going anywhere."

Maya smiled, hugging her mother one last time before grabbing her gift from her bag and stepping out of the room.

Walking down the halls of the familiar hospital, Maya smiled when she caught sight of Toby from across the hall. Wearing his typical white coat with an incredibly tacky Christmas sweater (blue sweater with a huge snowman in the middle, really?), Toby looked up from his clipboard and beamed at seeing Maya.

Maya waved at Toby with a giggle and began walking over to him when Toby raised a finger to her, signaling her to wait. Almost falling, he ran behind the desk and took out a messily wrapped gift.

Jogging over to her, he pushed his glasses up and smiled. "Hi." He breathed out.

"Hey."

He nodded, blushing. "So—um—I got you something." Toby stammered. "You know, since tomorrow's Christmas Eve and you're probably going to spend it with your family and I won't see you so I figured I'd—um—give you your gift now and not later because celebrating Christmas late sounds ridiculous to me and—"

Maya laughed, Toby always being the rambling dork. She loved it though. "I got you a gift too." She told him, motioning her perfectly wrapped gift.

Toby smiled. "Cool." he paused. "Should we exchange gifts or…do you want to go get something and then exchange? I'm going on a quick break in about five minutes or—"

"I know a place across the street that makes an amazing cup of hot chocolate if you're interested." Maya blushed at the offer.

"Do they add whipped cream?"

"Loads of it." Maya nodded. "And cinnamon."

"Then I'd love to." Toby smiled. "We'll meet up here? We should get bundled up."

"I'll see you then."

Toby nodded, waving to her as he walked backwards and smiling widely. Maya waved to him and gasped when Toby stumbled back and landed on his bottom. She helped him up and cast him a worried look. "Are you okay?"

Toby's face was red with embarrassment and nodded. "Yeah…I'm just really uncoordinated and fall… a lot." He mumbled nervously.

Maya chuckled, squeezing his arm. "You're cute. I'll see you in a bit Toby."

Toby rubbed the back of his neck and nodded. "Yeah, see you Maya."

Maya walked back to her mother's room with a flustered look on her face. "Back so soon?" her mother questioned.

Maya put on her red coat and black scarf. "Toby and I are getting hot chocolate across the street." She grabbed her white earmuffs, looking up at her mother. "Is that fine?"

"Is that fine?" Grace repeated. "By all means, *leave*. I don't want you here." She chuckled.

Maya pouted playfully. "Well if that's how you feel…" she trailed off dramatically before laughing along with her mother. "I'll see you. I shouldn't be long and if anything, I have the nurses on speed dial and—"

"Just go Maya!" Grace exclaimed, laughing. "I'm in a hospital, I'm fine."

Maya simply nodded and waved goodbye to her mother, walking back to Toby who was standing there with his terribly wrapped gift in hand.

He turned to see her and broke out into a grin. "Hey again."

"Hi."

Toby stood quiet for a moment before speaking up again. "Shall we go?"

Maya nodded with a small smile. "Of course."

Without thinking, Toby took her hand and led her out the hospital. Maya's heart pounded as her hand felt tingly as Toby's warm hand held her own. She hoped he wouldn't let it go anytime soon.

Entering the quaint little café, Toby let go of her hand as they ordered two hot chocolates and sat down in a secluded table.

"Your hands are very warm." Maya blurted out, her eyes widening and her face growing hot in embarrassment.

Toby laughed, smiling at her. "Thanks. Yours are very soft. I like holding your hand." He confessed.

Suddenly Maya remembered their first date from a couple weeks ago. He took her to a nice restaurant and spilled water on himself and stumbled over his words on multiple occasions. But she loved it.

She liked Toby so much, it terrified her. It terrified her because she feared losing him. She was on the verge of losing someone special to her, whether she liked to admit it or not, and the idea of losing someone else becoming special to her was fearful. Loss feared her. And time.

"Me too." Maya blushed.

Toby stared at Maya with an adoring look in his eye and smiled before pushing up his glasses and coughing. "So, I—um—I got you something but I don't know if you'll like it…" he muttered, suddenly feeling self-conscious about his gift as he handed it to her.

"I most likely will, don't even worry about it." Maya assured, taking the gift. She handed her own gift and chewed on her lower lip. "I hope you like mine…"

Toby took the gift and blushed. "If it's coming from you, I will."

The two grew silent until Maya spoke up. "On three?"

Toby nodded. "One…"

"Two…"

"Three." They said in unison, casting glances at each other as they unveiled each other's gifts.

Toby opened the gift to see a book by Stephen King. The first edition of his second book, *Salem's Lot*. He looked up at Maya with an astonished look. "How did you find this?"

"I have my ways." Maya smiled. "Look inside." She nodded to him.

He opened the book and his eyes widened. "Is that..." he paused. "His signature?" he squeaked out.

Maya laughed, nodding. "Yes, yes it is."

"Oh my god!" Toby laughed before looking back at Maya. "This is amazing, thank you. I...I love it." He grinned from ear to ear. "This is probably the best gift I've ever received. Definitely surpasses mine."

"We'll see." Maya smiled, finishing opening her own gift. She came across a box and opened the box to see a white Beyoncé sweatshirt with the singer's face on it. She smiled at Toby who chewed on his lip. "This is really nice, thank you."

"There's more." He told her.

Maya raised an eyebrow and took out the sweatshirt and two tickets fell out and Maya picked them up and turned them. Her eyes widened and looked up at Toby. "Are these—"

"She comes in February." Toby smiled. "I figured you'd want to see her."

"Oh my god!" Maya exclaimed. "You're...oh my god!" she was at a loss for words. "Thank you..."she let out a puff of air. "Wow..." her eyes watered. "It's been a while..."

Toby noticed her watery eyes and quickly stood up, sitting next to Maya and squeezing her hand softly. "Since what? You've gone to a concert?" he guessed.

Maya chuckled, shaking her head. "Since someone put so much effort to make me happy."

Toby stared at her with a sympathetic look, wiping her tears away. "I'll always put a great effort to make you happy." He smiled. "Because your happiness and that gorgeous smile of yours is a sight to see, and I think the whole world should witness that."

Maya looked up to him and broke out into a smile. "You help do that."

Maya isn't sure who initiated it, or who leaned in first. But feeling Toby's lips on hers was the most magical feeling in the world. Her heart fluttered and her mind quickly initiated a small fireworks show in her entire body.

She realized then and there that if anything made her happy, it was the boy with the blue eyes kissing her.

Phoenix awkwardly stepped inside the Díaz home with Ana beside her as she led her to the tiny den that Elena used to create and store her art pieces.

"She's been in there all day." Ana shared as she walked her across the hall of the home. Phoenix could hear music playing faintly in the room across the hall and chewed on her lip nervously. "She supposedly woke up with a great painting in mind, so I hope you don't mind the mess that will most likely be in there."

Phoenix shook her head. "I won't mind, I live with a bunch of young kids. They're a billion times messier." She chuckled.

Ana joined in and smiled softly. "Let me know if you need anything. I'll be heading out soon with Lily, so you two won't be bothered by her."

Phoenix nodded. "Thank you Ana." She returned the smile as Ana walked back to the living room.

Phoenix closed her eyes as she took a deep breath and gathered some courage to open the door.

Elena seemed to be in another world, as she didn't notice the door open and Phoenix step in, her eyes fully concentrated on the painting she was doing. Her hair was in a messy ponytail, pieces of her hair accentuating her face, wearing a blue and purple tie-dyed shirt with black shorts. The clothing and even parts of Elena's skin were covered in paint, especially Elena's bare feet.

Phoenix stood quiet for a moment as she observed Elena's painting. The canvas had a girl with an orange umbrella, an orange raincoat, and orange rain boots. Using purple, blue, and white paints, Elena mixed the colors to create a night sky with stars illuminating it.

"Orange is such an ugly color." Phoenix spoke up.

Elena jumped, startled, and turned around. Her brown eyes widened slightly, not expecting Phoenix's presence at all. She turned back to her painting and continued. "Orange isn't that ugly if you think about it."

Phoenix crossed her arms, interested. "How so?"

Elena stuck her tongue out as she painted another star on her canvas. "It's the color of sunsets, the color of tangerines, the color of Nemo the fish, the color of autumn leaves…so I think there's beauty in all colors. We just don't admire it enough."

Phoenix hummed. "That's a beautiful way to look at it."

Elena nodded, wiping her face but only rubbing purple paint on her cheek. "So did you come here to talk about colors with me?"

Phoenix shook her head, walking closer to Elena. She stood behind the canvas and looked at Elena. "I came to apologize…" she trailed off. "I shouldn't have snapped at you like that, but there's things going on in my life right now…" she paused, thinking of how to explain it well enough to Elena so that she wouldn't reveal too much about her life at home.

"Things that aren't too happy. I'm not comfortable in talking about it right now, but just know I didn't mean to take it out on you. I just didn't like being asked too many questions on things even I have a hard time understanding. I'm really sorry Elena, and I understand if you wouldn't want to talk to me aga—"

"I forgive you." Elena looked at her with a small smile. "I understand life gets messy, but if it gets too messy…then just know I'm here to offer any support you need."

"You're really going to forgive me?" Phoenix asked softly. "Just like that?"

Elena nodded. "Just like that." She confirmed. "I think life is too beautiful to hold grudges. If you're sincere, there's no reason for me not to forgive you."

"Oh."

The two stared at each other in silence before Elena spoke up. "So are you going to hug me or not?" she pouted playfully.

Phoenix laughed, shaking her head. "You're messy with paint, I'm not about to ruin this nice outfit." She smirked playfully.

Elena smirked, putting her paintbrush down before enveloping Phoenix in a hug anyway. "I'm adding a dab of artistic value into your cute outfit!" she giggled.

Phoenix didn't even try to protest as she hugged Elena back. "I missed you Lena."

"Same." Elena mumbled. "Do you want to go up to my room? We can hang out for a bit if you have time."

Phoenix nodded. "I'd love to." She smiled, before looking around the tiny room filled with paintings, sculptures, drawings, sketches, and other art pieces. "I already know you were a great artist, but wow you're a great artist." She commented.

Elena unplugged her iPod from the speaker. "Thank you, I'm glad I have a fan." She smiled.

"You have many fans, shut up." Phoenix chuckled. "You're really good, I see you making art in Europe or something. I don't know." She shrugged.

The two girls stepped out of the den and Elena shut the door behind them. "That'd be great, actually. I'd like to make art all over the world." She said. "I see you dominating the music scene in the future, you're an amazing singer."

"That's the dream." Phoenix smiled softly.

"It'll be a reality, I know it. And you'll be super famous." Elena assured as they walked up the steps and into Elena's room.

"Thanks." Phoenix smiled softly.

"So what are you doing for the holidays?" Elena asked, changing out of her shorts into some clean sweatpants.

"Nothing much, just hanging out with the family and having a small dinner." Phoenix shrugged. It was a very small dinner, with no presents. Her parents couldn't afford presents this Christmas. "You?"

"Same. We don't have family here in New York so it'll just be us four. I'll stop by tomorrow to give Autumn her present and hang out with her for a while. I haven't seen her much. Just phone calls. She's been really sick with chemo sessions and all—"

"Wait, *what*? Chemo sessions?" Phoenix asked, the news of Autumn's diagnosis not having reached to her.

"Oh right, we never told you…" Elena realized, sighing. "Autumn has cancer again, like, all over her body. It's really bad." She gulped.

Phoenix frowned, feeling a knot in her throat. "Wow that sucks. Poor Autumn…"

"Yeah…but she's a fighter. I know she'll get better soon, no matter how bad it is. She did it once, she can do it again." Elena assured. To Phoenix or to her, Elena wasn't very sure who she was trying to assure.

"We can only rely on hope and miracles." Phoenix smiled sadly. "Do Emma and Maya know?"

"Just Emma, but I haven't heard much of her. Or Maya. She's been busy, or that's what she tells me. I don't know. But I miss us hanging out together, we haven't been doing any of that."

"We'll change that soon, we should schedule a sleepover or something soon. I guess we've all been busy with our personal lives that we haven't had time for each other." Phoenix told her, sitting down on the bed.

Elena nodded. "Yeah, but we cannot lose our friendship. I refuse for us to grow apart." *I refuse to lose another friend,* Elena thought.

"Same. I love you guys way too much. Even Loser." Phoenix joked.

Elena snorted. "I love you guys too. Especially Loser." She teased.

Phoenix laughed as they continued chattering about anything they could think of. Phoenix suddenly noticed the ukulele sitting on Elena's dresser.

"Hey, when did you get a ukulele?" Phoenix stood up to grab the ukulele but Elena quickly went to retrieve it.

"It's a friend's." Elena said quickly, placing the ukulele in a box beside her nightstand. Phoenix stared at the box that looked to have a bunch of other belongings.

"Does all of that belong to your friend?" Phoenix asked.

Elena hummed in agreement as she stared at the box as well. "Yeah, it did."

"Did?"

"Well, I have it now so I haven't given it back to her yet." Elena lied, biting her lip.

Phoenix raised an eyebrow. "So it's a girl?"

"Yeah."

"What's her name?"

"Does it matter?" Elena asked defensively.

Phoenix raised her hands in surrender. "I was just asking, chill Lena."

"Sorry, those things mean a lot to her." Elena told her.

"To her... or to you?"

Me. She's dead. She's gone. These things don't matter to her as much as they matter to me. It's all I have left. It's all I have left to remember... Elena wished she could say that, but she couldn't say anything. Phoenix had her own problems going on, everyone did. She couldn't be selfish and share her own.

"To her." Elena answered simply. "To her."

––––––––––––––––

Christmas Eve the Castillo family gathered in the living room. For the sake of the holidays, Autumn put in all the energy she had in her to dress nicely.

But simply showering and changing had drained her energy, thankfully Olivia offered to apply some simple make-up. Only mascara, some light eye shadow, and a coat of lip gloss.

Now she was curled up on the couch, her body shivering despite having a blanket covering her and her head was pounding.

Cora rubbed her back soothingly, sighing quietly. "Do you want me to make you tea or something? I can give you an Advil for the pain." She suggested.

Autumn shook her head. "No I just need a quick nap and my energy will come back. I'm just a little tired." She mumbled.

Olivia walked in and sat on the armrest of the couch. "I can put on a movie or some music if you want, Autumn." She suggested, motioning for her mother to go and finish cooking Christmas dinner.

Cora smiled gratefully at her youngest as she kissed the side of Autumn's head and stepped out of the living room and back in the kitchen to finish dinner.

"If you want you can put some music. Just not too loud, my head hurts." Autumn replied, licking her cold lips.

Olivia nodded as she plugged in her iPod and played some calming music. "Is that fine?"

Autumn nodded. "Perfect, thanks Liv." She smiled softly.

Olivia sat next to Autumn and touched her sister's face delicately, noticing how cold Autumn was. Her lips were even blue. "Shoot…Autumn do you want me to get you some more blankets? I can even have mom make you a quick soup or something else warm. You're *really* cold…" she told Autumn worriedly.

"My stomach can't take in anything right now." Autumn groaned. "But I'll take some more blankets." What she knew would warm her up instantly was Elena. She was the warmest person alive. She was her arctic fox.

Olivia quickly went to fetch some blankets and covered Autumn up with three more blankets, tucking a strand of loose hair behind Autumn's ear. "Better?"

Autumn nodded, smiling softly. "Thanks Olivia. You're a good sister."

"So are you." Olivia smiled, rubbing Autumn's blanket-covered arm.

"I'm not…" Autumn mumbled. "I should be the one helping you with make-up and…boys…and picking out outfits and making sure you're not doing anything stupid like a big sister should and I'm not and—"

"And that's okay." Olivia assured. "Those things don't make you any less of a great big sister. You've taught me better things than applying lipstick or knowing the difference between lace and leather or whatever." She smiled. "You've taught me to be strong and independent and to never let anything come in the way of things I love. You taught me that life doesn't stop when it gets rough. And those are better lessons than anything."

Autumn reached her hand out for Olivia to take and squeezed it. "You're wise beyond your years Liv, and you're the best sister anyone could have." She paused. "I know how hard it can be being sisters with me, I get angry and snappy and say things I don't mean…but I love you, okay? Please don't ever think otherwise, because I don't ever want you to think you're not loved. Because you are loved. You are so, so, *so* loved." Olivia embraced Autumn in a hug, her eyes watery.

Autumn and her weren't very close, so this unexpected gesture took her by surprise. But she didn't mind the kind words from her sister. "This is why you're a great sister, Autumn." She whispered. "And you'll never stop being one." She wiped a tear from her eye.

Autumn simply smiled softly and nodded. "Yeah…"

Suddenly the doorbell rang and Olivia excused herself as she went to see who was at the door. Autumn took the opportunity to close her eyes, hoping sleep would consume her for just a few minutes.

"Oh crap, she's sleeping." Autumn heard a voice speak. "Maybe I should come back later, or maybe tomorrow…"

Autumn's eyes opened immediately and broke out into a smile. "Ellie?" she called out, hoping her voice didn't sound too weak.

Elena broke out into a smile as well when Autumn called out to her. "Hey pretty lady." She placed her gift down on the table and kneeled beside Autumn. "I've missed you."

Autumn blushed. "Me too."

"I'll leave you two alone, don't go too crazy kiddos." Olivia spoke up with a smirk before stepping into the kitchen with her mother.

Elena chuckled before looking at Autumn once more. "Can I kiss you?"

Autumn nodded and Elena quickly captured her lips with Autumn's, feeling the same sparks that haven't vanished since day one. "Why do you always ask for permission?" Autumn asked after they broke from the kiss.

"Because I'm a gentlewoman." Elena smiled. "And because I never want to do anything you don't want to do. I don't ever want to disrespect you in any way."

Autumn reached out to touch Elena's face. "I've always said this: you're too good for me sometimes." She pouted. "Now come cuddle with me." Autumn sat up.

Elena laughed before joining her girlfriend on the couch, wrapping her arms around Autumn. "You're so cold my African bush viper." She mumbled, kissing Autumn's forehead.

"You can thank chemotherapy for that."

Elena frowned. "But it's going to make you better soon."

"Right."

Elena couldn't help but sigh. "Enough about that. I have a present for you."

Autumn smiled. "So do I."

Elena reached out for her wrapped gift and placed it on Autumn's lap. "I want you to open mine first." She grinned.

Autumn placed her hands on the wrapped gift and traced the outline of the box before beginning to unwrap the gift slowly. Elena watched with excitement as Autumn opened the gift and began to trace the object, her eyebrows furrowed in concentration as she tried to figure out the gift.

"This feels like a vinyl record."

"Because it is. It's one of your gifts. I got you a couple of vinyls."

Autumn smiled. "You're freaking amazing. Who are the artists?"

"Who have you been obsessed with lately?"

"James Bay. Mumford and Sons. And…Matt and Kim." Autumn smiled even more. "You got me one of their albums?"

Elena felt her heart swell with happiness seeing Autumn's excitement. "I got you James Bay's debut album. Mumford and Son's newest album since that's the one you're missing. And I got you Matt and Kim's second album and the newest one since those were the only I could find."

"You're incredible." Autumn smiled, turning to Elena and reaching a hand out to find where her lips were and leaned in to give her a kiss. "Absolutely incredible."

"There's one more thing."

"There's more?" Autumn exclaimed.

Elena laughed, nodding. "Yes, there's one more thing." Elena told her as she reached back into the table and grabbed an envelope. "So, sometimes, I have trouble forming my feelings and thoughts into words." Elena confessed as she clutched onto the envelope. Autumn nodded, signaling to Elena she was listening. "And I know you do too." Elena paused.

"But I don't want to do that with you. I want to be able to communicate with you in any way I can. Sometimes, speaking is hard for me. But writing is not." She smiled softly, placing the envelope on her girlfriend's hands. "I spent hours doing this, but I know you read braille and so I wrote you a letter in braille. I probably made some mistakes here and there so bear with me." Elena chuckled. "Everything in there is my thoughts and my feelings, some about you…some isn't."

Autumn smiled and reached to open the letter but Elena stopped her, clutching onto her hand. "I don't want you to open it now." Elena whispered. "I want you to open it when you need it most. Promise me you'll do that?" Autumn nodded, kissing Elena's cheek. "Thank you."

"Your presents are incredible. I love them. They're the best gifts I've ever received." Autumn smiled, cuddling closer to Elena. "It makes my present seem like crap honestly."

"I highly doubt that." Elena argued. "I'll love anything you get me."

"You sure?"

"Surer than sure."

Autumn giggled before getting off of Elena and kissing her cheek before disappearing into her room. Elena waited patiently for Autumn, knowing how tiring it was now for her to be out and about. Autumn came back to the living room and let out a puff of air as she sat back down.

"I didn't wrap it by the way, my mom did. If I wrapped it, it'd look like a scrunched up ball." Autumn giggled before handing Elena the small, wrapped gift with an actual bow to wear on top instead of a regular paper bow.

Elena snorted as she looked at the yellow flower patterned bow. "Thank you for this."

"I picked it out." Autumn smiled proudly. "Well, my mom described each bow for me and I picked out the one that sounded nicest."

Elena smiled, kissing Autumn's forehead before putting the bow on the side of her head. "I'm going to open it now."

"I would hope you do that." Autumn giggled.

Elena blushed before beginning to unwrap the gift, she opened the small box and it revealed a CD with 'For Elena' scribbled on it.

Autumn smiled. "Phoenix gave me this idea a while ago...I...I wrote songs. For you. About you. And Phoenix suggested I record these songs. So about a month or so ago, I asked my dad to take me to buy stuff to record the songs. I recorded them all in my room, so the quality isn't going to be the *best*, but...I wanted to show you how much I care about you, Ellie." Autumn told her. "And all these songs, they come from here." Autumn pointed to her heart. "I know it's nothing extravagant but—"

"Can I kiss you?" Elena asked with watery eyes. "I don't know what else to do besides kissing you."

Autumn laughed before nodding. Elena immediately kissed Autumn deeply, cupping her face with her hands as Autumn wrapped her arms around Elena's neck. They continued like this until both were too out of breath to keep going.

Elena blushed. "You know, anybody could've walked in right now and caught us…"

Autumn chuckled. "Well good thing I can't see that." She joked.

Elena laughed, picking up the CD again. "I'm going to listen to this the minute I get home."

"Do you really like it?" Autumn asked, her voice laced with insecurity.

"Are you kidding me?" Elena questioned, wrapping her arms around Autumn and pulling her closer. "I absolutely love it. It's one of the greatest gifts given to me, besides you of course." She said smoothly.

Autumn blushed, smiling widely. "Merry Christmas."

"Can I kiss you?" Autumn nodded and Elena quickly latched her lips onto Autumn's own. She pulled away and sighed in content. "Merry Christmas...ya filthy animal." Autumn playfully whacked Elena's arm and both girls laughed.

"It's African bush viper to you, my arctic fox." Autumn corrected with a smirk.

"God, you're so perfect. Can I kiss you?" Elena laughed. Autumn nodded again, giggling before Elena captured her lips with Autumn's. The two continued kissing when someone coughed.

Both girls separated and Joseph raised an eyebrow, looking from Elena to Autumn. "Having fun there?" he teased.

"Well, we *were* until you interrupted us." Autumn said bluntly, causing Elena's face to turn red.

"No funny business." Joseph told them. "I watch TV on that couch."

Dylan walked by the living room and smirked, having overheard the conversation. "Dad, it's okay if they do...they can't get pregnant from scissoring."

"DYLAN!" Autumn shouted at him, a glare on her face. Autumn felt her face turn a billion shades darker. Elena's face couldn't have gotten any redder as her eyes widened.

"Oh, sorry Autumn." Dylan shrugged, turning to his father again. "They can do more than scissoring, actually. They can fing—"

"DYLAN! I'M GOING TO KILL YOU!"

"Christmas...I've always had mixed feelings with it." Hailey spoke as she wore a Santa Clause hat with her otherwise summer attire. *"I mean, bless baby Jesus or whatever...but who ever thinks about that? Christmas is so commercialized now...I'm wearing a Santa Clause hat for Christ sakes."* Hailey chuckled. *"But no matter how shitty Christmas can be with its annoying need to buy gifts and make food that can feed an impoverished country, the meaning behind Christmas will never disappear."*

Elena watched attentively and she chuckled. "Get on with it!" she exclaimed to the computer.

Hailey paused for a moment, appearing to be deep in thought. *"I think...I think Christmas is about...memories."*

Elena raised an eyebrow.

"I probably sound stupid, but think about it Lena...most holiday movies revolve around memories. Like Rudolph, his past of being bullied for being different is what helps the plot develop. Or "Elf", it's because of where Buddy comes from...it's because of his past that he decides to find his family and shit. And the most important one: "A Christmas Carol". I mean, Lena! It's because of Scrooge's memories of his childhood and early adulthood that he becomes such a shithead! And it's because of his past too that he changes."

"So Christmas brings back memories. And if it wasn't for those memories, how would we celebrate Christmas? How will we sit down and laugh or cry as we celebrate memories? How will we change? Christmas revolves around change too; because no Christmas is the same...you should know that." Hailey pursed her lips. *"You're celebrating Christmas without me this year...and every year after that."*

Elena felt her eyes water and she looked towards the box that contained so many memories. *"But take a moment this year, and hopefully other years too, to celebrate our memories together, Lena. Like, that time we thought adding maple syrup to smoothies was a good idea. Or when we went to the beach and you got stung by a jellyfish...there are so many memories to celebrate. And whatever other memories you may have...good or bad...remember them this Christmas. Remember them every Christmas if you can."* Hailey spoke, taking off the Santa hat and grabbing a picture from her desk and displaying it to the camera.

"Remember me like this if you can, please."

Elena smiled at the photo. She grabbed the photo resting on top of the box, the exact photo Hailey had shown her. It was of her and Hailey when they were 10 years old and had mud all over themselves after going outside in the rain. They danced and ran around like complete idiots, but they were happy.

Elena looked up at Hailey and smiled. "I'll remember you." She whispered.

"I hope you have a great Christmas, Lena, and I hope that the people you spend it with give you the best memories. Just like you've given me." Hailey said to her with a smile, hugging the photo tightly. *"I am hoping it's a special someone, and if it is, I'm probably cheering you on."*

Hailey smirked. *"And I'm also cheering you on in case you get some scissoring action you sneaky little lesbian."* She winked, causing Elena to blush. What was it with people thinking her and Autumn were having sex?

"Merry Christmas ya filthy animal." Hailey smiled at the camera one more time before the video ended.

Elena smiled softly. "Merry Christmas ya filthy animal."

After listening to Elena's vinyl records non-stop, Autumn had a decent Christmas dinner with her family. Thankfully, her stomach was strong that it kept the food she ate. And she had enough strength to play a couple songs on the piano and have a little jam session with her dad. So Christmas wasn't the worst, despite the back pain and constant headaches.

Now, Christmas morning had passed with gift exchanges and breakfast Autumn unfortunately couldn't keep in for long. But her family understood. They always did, and Autumn wasn't sure whether she should be angered by it or relieved.

Autumn lied on her bed, listening to Mumford and Son's newest album. Thank God for Elena Díaz. Autumn wasn't sure she believed in God, but if he gave her Elena...she would reconsider her beliefs.

The door knocked and Autumn muttered a "come in". To her surprise, she didn't hear her parents or her siblings voice speak.

It was Emma's.

"Merry Christmas!" Emma's cheery voice exclaimed. Autumn could've sworn she slurred a little. Emma was way too cheery for a girl who avoided her for the past weeks.

Autumn only hummed. Emma stumbled onto the bed before giggling, when she nearly tripped on her way there. "How's my best friend doing?"

"I have cancer on my body and dangerous chemicals running through my veins to kill it, what the fuck do you think?" Autumn rolled her eyes.

Emma giggled. "Oh right, you're dying."

"Thank for the reminder." Autumn said sarcastically.

Emma poked Autumn's nose and giggled again. "You're being such a grumpypants."

Autumn could've sworn she smelled a trace of alcohol coming out of Emma's breath. "You're being too happy. But then again, you must've visited happy hour somewhere right?"

"What are you talking about?" Emma asked, her words slurred.

Autumn scoffed. "*That.*" Autumn wrapped her blanket around herself as she sat up, groaning as she did so. "Are you fucking *drunk, Emma?*" she asked, shock laced in her voice.

Emma laughed, a little too obnoxiously. "Drunk? Nooooo!" Emma lied. "You're probably drunk."

"Why would I drink to acquire more cancer? Being stuck in this fucking bed or being stuck *anywhere* in this fucking house sucks, okay? Having cancer *sucks*, but you haven't seemed to care one fucking bit because you haven't even contacted me *once.*" Autumn snapped. "I hope I die pretty fucking soon so I won't have to deal with any more of this bullshit. Don't come see me and don't associate with me if you're doing it out of obligation. I don't need your fucking pity, and I *especially* don't fucking want it when you're *drunk.*" Autumn lied back down on the bed and turned her back on Emma.

Emma stared at her. Her mind quickly had a response to that. "*Some fucking friend you are, Emma. You're a terrible person. Bad. You are a bad person.*" Emma stood up from the bed. "Okay…" she whispered, feeling a tear trickle down her face. "I'm sorry."

"Visit me when you're sober, Emma." Was all Autumn said before she proceeded to ignore Emma's presence in the room.

"*But I'm never sober.*" Emma thought.

CHAPTER EIGHTEEN

Elena, Phoenix, Maya, and Emma were hanging out at Elena's house a couple days before New Year's. New York City was one of the best places to celebrate the holiday, and Elena was determined to go see the ball drop this year. She had only experienced it through a television screen and now, she had the chance to see it through her own eyes.

However, Elena wanted to spend it with her friends. And Autumn. Especially Autumn.

"I think it's a great idea to see the ball drop," Phoenix smiled, wanting to desperately get out of the house for New Year's. "but do you really think Autumn's going to want to go? She's such a hermit crab."

"And Autumn's getting chemo too, I don't know if it'd be good for her to be around such a large crowd." Maya added, still not have given the girls a definite answer on whether or not she was going. She wanted to spend time with her mother this New Year's Eve. Who knew if she'd get another?

Elena thought about it for a second and stuck her bottom lip out. "But it's New Year's! It's honestly one of my favorite holidays. It gives me hope for a better year. And I want to bring in the New Year with you guys and Autumn." She smiled.

"I'm in!" Phoenix exclaimed. "I love going to see the ball drop, it's the best experience ever."

"I'll let you guys know, I might have family commitments." Maya told them.

Elena nodded understandingly and turned to Emma who had been awfully quiet since she arrived. "What about you, Emma?" she asked.

Emma looked up from the floor and nodded, not really sure of what the girls were discussing.

"Awesome, you can bring Ethan too if you want. And Riley." Elena told her.

"To where?" Emma asked, tilting her head.

Elena chuckled. "To see the ball drop at Times Square. We're all planning on going. Maya's going to let us know later."

Emma nodded. "Yeah, yeah…we can go. Riley's not big on crowds so he probably will stay with my parents. But I'll go." She smiled weakly. "Is Autumn going?" she asked tentatively.

Autumn had refused to speak to her after their encounter. So Emma had left, feeling incredibly guilty. It only caused her to drink until she couldn't see her hand in front of her. They hadn't spoken since, but Emma tried to visit only to have Joseph or Cora say that Autumn didn't want to have any visitors.

"We're hoping she'll try to go." Elena shrugged. "But it's uncertain. Autumn's not big on going out much, especially not now with chemo and everything. She's trying to regain as much energy as she can to be able to come back to school when winter vacation is over."

"Shit, is she really going to come back?" Phoenix asked, eyebrow raised.

Elena shrugged. "She's hoping, but if the chemo keeps draining her like it has been…she probably won't." she sighed.

"We can only hope she does." Maya smiled sadly, having been given the news a couple days back.

"Yeah…" Elena trailed off.

Phoenix turned to Maya. "So, what's going on with your lover Tobias?" she smirked.

Maya immediately blushed. "We're…taking things slow."

"Just say it girl!" Phoenix nudged her.

Maya chewed on her lip. "We kissed."

Elena and Phoenix squealed immediately. "Finally!" Phoenix cheered. Emma smiled softly, having not been paying attention.

"How was it?" Elena smiled.

"Magical." Maya blushed. "It felt nice kissing him. Like, *really* nice." She chuckled. "He also got me a gift for Christmas. A Beyoncé sweater…and tickets to see her."

Phoenix jumped up and shook Maya dramatically. "MARRY HIM." Phoenix shouted. "HE'S A KEEPER."

Elena and Maya burst out laughing and Maya playfully pushed off Phoenix. "Okay, I wouldn't go as far as marrying him…" Elena said. "Yet." She smirked. "But he is most definitely a keeper. I mean, not just anyone gets Beyoncé tickets, May."

"It's not even just about that," Maya spoke. "he's just…he genuinely cares about my happiness. And he tries to make me smile when I'm not smiling and makes me laugh when I'm not laughing. He's there when I need him despite his busy schedule with the hospital and school…he really cares about me. And I care about him. Like, a lot. I think…I think I'm actually willing to try being in a relationship with him."

"That's great Maya, I'm so glad it's working out with you and Toby." Phoenix smiled. "You of all people deserve to be in a relationship with someone as caring as him. If he makes you happy, then don't try to push off that potential happiness. You deserve it."

Maya smiled and hugged Phoenix. "Thanks Phoenix."

Elena pouted. "I want to hug her too!" she quickly jumped in and hugged Maya and Phoenix, glancing at Emma. The girls locked eyes and Elena mouthed "Are you okay?" to her. Emma smiled and nodded, putting on her façade of her bubbly and bright self. Elena eyed her for a second before nodding and putting a thumb up.

Emma nodded and gave her a thumb up back. It was so easy to lie.

Dr. Richards entered the room Autumn and Cora were in, smiling softly to them. "Hello, how's my favorite patient?"

Autumn looked worn-out, with heavy bags under her eyes and hunched over from the merciless pain she had been getting from her back and her legs. "Terrible." Autumn muttered from her seat.

The doctor turned to Cora. "What's been going on?"

"She's been getting really bad pain on her back and on her legs. She says they feel numb sometimes." Cora explained, glancing at Autumn. "Her balance isn't very great either, she'll be standing and will nearly fall or she'll stumble easily. And she can't be moving for very long because she'll get tired quickly."

Dr. Richards pursed her lips and nodded at the given news. "Well, it seems that it's happening faster than I expected."

"What is?" Cora asked.

Dr. Richards sighed. "As you know, the cancer is spreading to parts of Autumn's body. And there were significant traces found in her lower spine. The cancer has really affected her spine so…she's losing her mobility." Dr. Richards paused. "In other words, Autumn is slowly becoming paralyzed from the waist down."

Cora gulped and glanced at Autumn who had an unreadable expression on her face. "Is there anything we can do to prevent it from coming so quickly? Any physical therapy or exercises?"

"Ms. Castillo, no matter what we do…she's going to lose her mobility. It's inevitable." The doctor said dejectedly.

"How long?" Autumn spoke up.

"How long what?" Dr. Richards asked.

Autumn played with her fingers. "How much longer until I can't walk anymore?"

The doctor sighed. "I give it two or three months. During that time your mobility will only decrease, and then you'll be fully paralyzed."

"Well good thing I still have a wheelchair somewhere in the house." Autumn mumbled.

"The chemotherapy will hopefully help you Autumn, and then all of this sacrifice will be worth it." Dr. Richards said to her.

"I guess…" Autumn trailed off. "If I go in remission, will I still have a chance of regaining my sight?"

"It's a possibility." Dr. Richards nodded. "But I can't guarantee it. If you go on remission, then we'll discuss those options with your ophthalmologist. For now, focus on remission Autumn."

Autumn pursed her lips. "I have another question."

"Okay, shoot." The doctor nodded.

"If I stopped treatment, could I gain my sight back?"

Elena was fixing up her room, her parents having complained that her room was messy and she needed to clean it. It was a proven fact Elena couldn't do anything productive without music playing while she worked, and she kept playing Autumn's Christmas gift without stopping.

After Autumn finished playing another song, the song changed to another one and Elena grinned, turning to look at her laptop. The one about to play was definitely her favorite. Especially Autumn's little rant before she began playing the song.

"Hey Ellie." Autumn's raspy voice played from her speakers.

Elena couldn't help but blush as she picked up clothes (presumably clean) from the floor and threw them in the hamper.

"So, this next song is probably one of my favorites that I ever wrote about you. I wrote it after you took me to see Emanuel Ax and I kissed you. That was probably one of the most magical nights of my life, because I spent it with you. And...you mean so much to me. More than I expected." Autumn paused.

"And, yes, we have our arguments and our fights and we're not the most perfect couple out there...but there's love radiating from us. Yes...love. It's a word I use to be afraid of, but with you...it only excites me more. Because that's what love should be, love should be exciting because you've spent you're whole life waiting for that one

person. And you're my person, Elena. I know it. Despite everything between us, I...I love you. And I'm not afraid to say it anymore."

Elena felt her heart swell and smiled widely at the words. She loved Autumn and Autumn loved her. That's what made everything worth it. Love.

"Okay, so now I'm going to let Riley inside because I didn't want him to hear me all mushy and romantic because that's not me." Autumn giggled. *"Riley!"* Elena rolled her eyes, of course Autumn wouldn't bother cutting that off. *"He's accompanying me on guitar because he's really good on the guitar."* Autumn explained. Elena heard footsteps approaching that she assumed were Riley's. *"Say hi to Elena, Riley."*

"Hi Elena." Riley's shy and quiet voice spoke.

"Awesome, you ready Riley?" Riley only hummed. *"Are you ready Ellie?"*

Elena laughed. "Just sing the damn song goofball."

"She probably called me a goofball right now, I bet you." Autumn presumably commented to Riley. Elena rolled her eyes playfully, giggling. *"All right, let's begin."*

Riley began fingerpicking his guitar and played a soothing melody while Autumn played the piano and sang softly.

Once the song finished, Autumn took a satisfied sigh. *"That was good, what do you think?"* Autumn asked, probably asking Riley.

"It was good. She'll like it. You're really good at songwriting." Riley replied.

"Thanks. We should go get something to eat, I'm starving. Are you hungry?" Elena giggled, Autumn probably didn't realize she was still recording.

"Yes. Yes. Yes." Riley replied.

"Cool." Autumn replied simply, unfazed by Riley's OCD. *"I'll tell my parents to order us a pizza. In the meantime, play me that melody you were doing before I kicked you out of the room."*

"Okay." Riley paused. *"I think you're still recording Autumn..."*

"How do you know?" Autumn asked.

"The button's still red." Riley replied.

Autumn cursed to herself. *"The perks of being blind. Sorry Ellie!"* Autumn exclaimed. Elena laughed, shaking her head. *"Riley, turn it off!"*

And then a static noise was heard before it turned off. Elena snorted, definitely the best present she had received ever. It wasn't the most perfect mixtape, but Autumn tried. And the songs Autumn wrote for her made up for it. Because they were for her and no one else. Autumn didn't even try too hard to make her feel special because just knowing they belonged to each other made her special enough.

Elena continued tidying up her room, listening to the rest of Autumn's mixtape as she finished. Elena sighed in satisfaction as she finished, she put on a mixtape of Hailey's on the cassette Hailey formerly owned. She was in a jazzy mood and Hailey was always the expert when it came to jazz, she pressed play and music quickly filled her ears.

Elena hummed to the song while sketching a drawing in her sketchbook, putting on her glasses to see a bit clearer.

"Elena." Her father, Oscar, stepped into the room, never being able to grasp the concept of knocking.

Elena looked up, pushing up her glasses. "Yeah papi?"

"There's someone outside looking for you, she says she's a friend. Valerie?" Elena rolled her eyes at the name. Her father noticed Elena's displeasure of the name. "Do you want me to say you're not here?" he asked.

Elena sighed, shaking her head and throwing her sketchbook on the bed. "Nah, it's fine. I'll talk to her." Elena threw on Hailey's jean jacket and Oscar raised an eyebrow at her. "What?"

"It's December."

"I'm aware of the month." Elena chuckled.

"We live in New York City."

Elena nodded. "I'm aware of that too."

"It's 28 degrees outside, Elena…"

"I'll put on a hat." Oscar raised an eyebrow at her again. "A scarf too?"

"Coat. Put on a winter coat, Elena."

Elena rolled her eyes, snorting. "*Fine.*" Elena took off the jean jacket and put on her red winter coat and a scarf. "Approve?"

Oscar nodded. "Godspeed my daughter."

Elena saluted him and the two laughed. "I shouldn't be long. Bye papi!"

Elena walked down the stairs and opened the door to see Valerie in a white coat with black mittens with a matching knitted beanie and scarf adorned on her head and neck respectfully. She let out a puff of air, the cold wind making her breath let out a puff of visible vapor.

"What do you want?" Elena asked, arms crossed.

Valerie looked down at the floor and then back up again to meet Elena's brown eyes. "To be your friend again." She sighed. "I'm sorry for making you mad. I should've kept my opinion to myself…it was—it was jealousy I guess…" the smaller girl trailed off. "I was jealous she had you when I could've, but I didn't take that opportunity. I let it slip and she didn't, and it made me mad. I shouldn't have been selfish and put my feelings first without thinking how it would affect you…I'm sorry." She apologized, sincerity in her voice.

Elena simply stared at her. "Do you still think she's going to hurt me?"

Valerie sighed. "No…yes…I don't know! I just…I don't want you to be hurt. When I heard about Hailey's death, I imagined how that must've felt for you. And I know it hurt losing your best friend…I'm afraid of you hurting when—*if* you lose Autumn…your first love. I— um, I heard about Autumn…"

"I won't lose Autumn like that…Hailey killed herself. Hailey chose to die. Autumn isn't. Autumn doesn't want to die, and she won't. She won't die. Autumn's going to pull through just like she always does. Because she loves me and I love her." Elena responded.

"How do you know Autumn doesn't want to die?" Valerie asked tentatively.

"What do you mean?" Elena asked, her eyebrows furrowed.

"Elena…Autumn has cancer. Do you know how shitty that is? It's so shitty. It's a game of pure chance. You can live…or you can die. You just gotta hope whatever treatment you get cures you. And sometimes it does, other times it doesn't. Even when it does…you're left with the side effects. Do you think Autumn wants to live with more setbacks in her life than she already does? Maybe it's easier for her to—"

"Are you *saying* my girlfriend wants to *die*?" Elena growled.

Valerie crossed her arms. "I'm saying she doesn't want to suffer anymore." She huffed. "I'm just being straight up with you Elena. As your friend…I should be honest with you, right?"

Elena looked away. "If you want to be friends with me again you should watch your words. Think before you speak, get me?" Elena looked at her, sighing.

"I get you." Valerie said softly. "Does this means we're friends again? Like I told you before, I rather be friends with you than nothing else."

Elena nodded. "Yeah, we're friends again." She smiled softly. "I did miss you, you remind me of Miami sometimes. Back when things were…different. Better, maybe."

"You know Hailey loved you, right? She had her reasons for doing what she did and you can't judge her or call her selfish for choosing to die. Some people…they just don't know how to handle their emotions and their mind. But that doesn't mean she didn't love you, you guys were best friends. But she wasn't happy, and it would've been better for her to get help…but sadly this society thinks admitting you're not okay mentally shows signs of weakness. But you tried Elena, okay? Stop feeling guilty over something you had no control of." Valerie told her, squeezing her shoulder.

Elena looked down, trying to suppress tears. "I just…I miss her so much." Elena confessed. "I fell in love and she's not here to experience it with me. She won't experience anything with me anymore…it's just gone."

Elena let a tear slip and wiped it away quickly, not wanting to show weakness to Valerie. "I think that's what sucks about losing what you cherish…not being able to create more memories. What you have is what you get and doesn't that just suck? You can't make new memories. And the last memory you have of them is losing them…how sad is that? Despite every other memory you have with them, the two memories that stick out the most is the day you meet them and the day you lose them." Elena chewed on her lip. "I remember both with Hailey so clearly. Especially losing her. I remember it too well…"

"You don't have to remember those two memories, you know that right?" Valerie replied. "They always say the middle part is the good part of any story, because you're past the beginning but not close to the end. Remember the middle part you shared with Hailey." She smiled softly.

Elena smiled softly, admiring Valerie's attempts to make her feel better. "You're right." She agreed. "So how's the songwriting and album coming along?"

"I have four songs done. We're doing 12 songs in total. I haven't written many songs lately though…I think I might be getting writer's block which is the worst thing to get when you're working on your debut album." Valerie told her, sighing.

Elena thought for a moment. "You should try talking with Autumn. She's really good at songwriting." Valerie's eyes widened. "I know you're not fond of her but she's talented when it comes to music, but disregard what you feel towards her and think about your career…" Elena shrugged. "I can talk to her if you want."

Valerie rubbed her cold hands together. "I guess…" she turned to Elena. "If she's willing to, then I'll be too. Only if you're there."

Elena nodded. "It's a deal." Elena shook her hand. "I really did miss you Valerie, I forgot how nice it is to talk to you. Despite you being an ass sometimes."

Valerie snorted. "The feeling's mutual Díaz." She smiled. "I should get going, but have a good New Year. Are you going to see the ball drop?"

"That's what my friends and I are planning, so hopefully." Elena smiled back.

Valerie nodded. "Well hopefully I see you there then."

"Same." Elena nodded back before the two parted ways and Elena stepped back inside her house.

Elena's cheeks and nose were red and she was absolutely freezing, she took off her snow boots and before she headed back upstairs she heard her father comment "I told you wearing a winter coat was a good idea."

Autumn was scribbling in her tattered journal with Gabe on the bed with her listening to James Bay's album thanks to her lovely girlfriend.

Autumn adjusted her black knitted scarf before continuing to scribble, not even looking down at her journal but straight ahead. At what? She didn't know.

Like she spent every New Year's Eve, Autumn was hidden in her room while her family had a small New Year's Eve party at their house. Autumn wasn't fond of parties or social interaction.

Especially when her annoying family members would say *so* sympathetically "It must be *so* difficult being blind"

Yeah, no shit she couldn't see anything.

Or "How unfortunate you have cancer again"

Again, no shit.

Having cancer wasn't exactly on her agenda, but neither was being blind.

Autumn huffed as began petting Gabe softly, pushing up the sleeves of her gray knitted sweater. She wasn't dressed very extravagant, just a simple knitted sweater, jeans, and converse.

Besides, why would Autumn want to celebrate another shitty year ending when she knew the next would be just as bad? Although Elena coming into her life was the only highlight of the year.

Suddenly the door knocked and Gabe's head lifted up at the knock. Autumn was ready to yell at whatever family member wanted to enter and talk (which were only laments over Autumn's crappy health).

"Knock, knock!" Autumn broke out into a smile when she heard Elena's voice.

"Who's there?" Autumn chuckled.

"Daisy!"

Autumn snorted. "Daisy who?"

Elena barged in and jumped on Autumn's bed. "Daisy me rolling! They hatin'!" Elena shouted, trying to sound like a thug but Elena was anything but thuggish.

Autumn laughed, always finding Elena's joke hilariously bad. "Why am I dating you?"

"Because you think I'm cute?" Elena asked, smiling as she greeted Gabe with a pat on the head.

Autumn giggled, reaching out to touch Elena's face before kissing her cheek. "Yes, you are very cute."

"So, you have a party going on at your house." Elena spoke.

"I know, it's horrible."

Elena laughed. "How about we get out of here then?" she suggested.

"What do you mean?" Autumn tilted her head.

Elena pulled Autumn closer to her, kissing her cheek. "Let's go to Times Square to witness the ball drop."

Autumn frowned immediately. "I can't..."

"Why not?" Elena asked. "A bunch of us are going. Phoenix, Maya, Emma, Ethan, Riley, and Toby are coming, it'll be fun. I even asked your parents and they're totally fine with it."

"I'll only hold you guys back. I can't walk very far and I won't even enjoy it...I can't see the ball drop." Autumn replied.

"Then I'll describe it for you." Elena suggested, tucking a strand of Autumn's hair behind her ear and smiling softly.

"That won't change anything." Autumn snapped, huffing.

Elena took a deep breath. "Come on Autumn, let's do something different. Let's be adventurous and bring on the New Year with an adventurous spirit. It'll be fun babe."

"I don't want to be adventurous and I don't want to go." Autumn told her. "You can go, I'm not stopping you. Bring on the New Year being adventurous or whatever."

"But I want you there with me. I want to bring on the New Year with you…" Elena moved closer to Autumn. "Please?"

Autumn pounded her fists angrily on her mattress. "I said I *don't* want to go Elena!" she growled, making Gabe shift closer to Autumn. The golden retriever licked her hand and whined. Autumn petted him to signal she was fine.

Elena jumped at the sudden outburst, backing away from Autumn. "Okay…" Elena whispered, getting up. "Don't go…" Elena went to the door with her head down, upset that Autumn had snapped at her so harshly. She stood by the door, hoping Autumn would say something.

It was silent for a good 10 minutes, Autumn's head bowed down and playing with her fingers.

Autumn gulped, suppressing the urge to sob. "I can't go to Times Square…" she trailed off. "My back and my legs can't take it, Elena…"

Elena turned around, leaning against the doorframe. "Okay…" Elena nodded. "Why?"

Autumn closed her eyes. "I'm losing my mobility. I'll be paralyzed from the waist down in about two to three months." Autumn confessed, blinking away tears. "So I can't go…I'll be tired. I'm sorry

Ellie…" she whispered, her voice cracking. Gabe whined again, sensing Autumn's sadness. Autumn scratched behind his ear to relax him, assuring him again she was fine.

Elena immediately walked over to Autumn, wrapping her arms around her and kissing the top of her head. "Hey, hey it's okay, I understand. You don't have to go." She whispered in her ear. Elena's heart ached at what was happening to Autumn, it wasn't fair.

She thought back about what Valerie had told her a couple days back. Autumn was suffering so much because of chemo and the cancer attacking her…what if it was too much for Autumn? What if it was easier if she just—

Elena shook her head, not wanting to think about that. "Can I kiss you?" Autumn nodded and Elena softly placed her lips against Autumn's, Autumn immediately reciprocating the kiss. She pulled away and sighed. "I'm sorry this is happening to you."

Autumn shrugged. "What can you do?"

"I can stay here with you. We'll bring in the New Year's cuddling and listening to James Bay…it'll be perfect." Elena offered, smiling softly.

"You don't have to do that. They're probably waiting for you—"

"I'll text them I had other plans." Elena cut in. "I rather be with you."

Autumn bit on her lower lip. "You sure?"

Elena nodded. "Positive, Autumn." She caressed Autumn's cheek.

An hour into cuddling and exchanging kisses (Gabe moving to the floor), Autumn lifted her head from Elena's chest. She gulped, wondering why she even came up with the thought in the first place. But it wasn't fair Elena sacrificed so much for and she never did, she had to sacrifice for Elena too.

"Ellie?"

Elena hummed. "Yeah?"

"I…" Autumn chewed on her lips. "I have a wheelchair in the closet across the hall."

Elena stared at Autumn, confused. "Okay…"

Autumn gulped. "I want to use it…to go to Times Square with you."

Elena lifted her head. "Are you sure? We don't have to—"

"I want to. I want to bring in the New Year with you…there." Autumn smiled.

"Are you positive, Autumn?" Elena asked again.

Autumn nodded. "Yes."

A couple minutes later, both girls were bundled up and headed out the door. Elena lugged the wheelchair with her while Autumn slowly descended down the stairs, Elena keeping a watchful eye.

Once they reached the sidewalk, Elena opened the wheelchair so Autumn could sit. "Are you sure you want to do this?"

"Yes, I want to do this." Autumn assured as Elena guided her and plopped down on the wheelchair. Elena nodded as she placed Autumn's small blanket over her lap.

Elena moved behind Autumn and grabbing the handles of the wheelchair. "If you change your mind and want to go back, we can. Okay?"

"I won't change my mind." Autumn smiled softly. "Where are we going?" Autumn exclaimed, mustering up the perkiest voice ever.

Elena grinned as she began pushing the wheelchair. "Times Square!"

Autumn giggled. "WHERE ARE WE GOING?"

Elena pushed the wheelchair a little bit faster and laughed. "TIMES SQUARE!" She shouted at the top of her lungs. They received weird looks by strangers walking past them and Elena laughed. "People are looking at us like we're insane."

"Let them." Autumn smiled. "We'll be insane together."

"Just how it should be." Elena kissed Autumn's cheek before they headed into the subway station that was packed with people trying to get to Times Square with only a couple hours before countdown. But Elena pushed through them, being overly protective of her girlfriend. She'd kick anyone who so much as *touched* a little hair on Autumn's head.

Finally, they made it out of the subway hecticness and arrived at Times Square. Phoenix had texted her where they were and followed the directions given.

"So...are we going to have a New Year's Kiss? I never had one before." Elena asked lowly in Autumn's ear, smirking.

Autumn felt her face grow red (and it was not by the cold weather) at Elena's question. "Um...yeah...yeah...kiss...yeah..." she stammered.

Elena laughed. "You are too cute."

"I am *not*." Autumn argued. "I am a scary force to be reckoned with."

"Yeah, *okay*." Elena teased.

Before Autumn could argue any further, she was met with a booming voice. "THE LOVEBIRDS HAVE ARRIVED AFTER THEIR SCISSORING SESSION." Phoenix shouted over the noise. Emma, Ethan, Toby, Maya, and Riley were in front of Phoenix who waved them over. They were still far from the ball, but enough to see it drop. They didn't want to be anywhere too crowded due to Riley's social anxiety.

Autumn and Elena turned red. "Shut up Phoenix, we were cuddling." Elena told her.

"Is that code for lesbian love making?" Phoenix smirked.

"Is everything sex to you?" Autumn spoke up.

"No, that's where you have it wrong, Castillo." Phoenix argued. "*Alena* is everything to me." She smirked.

"The captain has spoken." Maya spoke up, chuckling as Toby hugged her from behind.

Phoenix rolled her eyes. "*Anyway*, Autumn, you got to pimp out your ride yo. The fuck is this old piece of shit?"

"Exactly what you said Phoenix, an old piece of shit hidden in the closet." Autumn answered monotonously.

"Aw, like Elena." Phoenix smiled smugly at her friend who gave Phoenix the middle finger. "Ooh girl, you should be putting that finger somewhere else!" Phoenix winked.

Elena blushed. "Fuck you, Phoenix."

"Your girlfriend would love it if you fucked her, actually." Phoenix smirked.

"So…countdown? That's what we were here for, right?" Ethan spoke up, laughing.

Emma stared at Autumn, her eyes displaying sadness. She wasn't there for Autumn when she needed her. She was a terrible friend, a really terrible friend.

"Thank you Ethan, thank you!" Elena exclaimed as she pushed Autumn further into the small group of theirs.

Emma tentatively walked towards Autumn, kneeling in front of her. "Hey Autumn…"

Autumn immediately scowled at hearing Emma's voice. "Oh, so are you sober enough to speak to your dying friend now?" she said in a low voice.

"Yes." Emma said quietly, looking down. "I'm sober, Autumn. I'm not…I'm not an alcoholic. I just had a couple drinks—"

"I don't want your explanation." Autumn cut off. "I just want to bring in the New Year being civil to each other. Do you think we can do that?"

Emma nodded. "Of course."

"And I don't want you to get drunk again, Emma." Autumn said next. "Promise?"

Emma gulped. "I—promise." Emma closed her eyes, knowing in her heart she couldn't keep that promise as hard as she tried. "I won't."

Autumn smiled softly, reaching out her hand for Emma to squeeze. "Okay."

Emma smiled, squeezing her hand. "Okay."

They spent the majority of the time talking and joking around with each other before the countdown began. Everyone kept taking pictures with each other and dancing while Autumn smiled in content at hearing Elena having a good time with their friends.

"All right guys, so I am concerned now." Phoenix spoke up, her voice serious.

"Why?" Elena asked.

"Well Alena, E squared, and Moby are all obviously sharing a New Year's kiss but here I am, alone and single…" Phoenix sighed dramatically. "No New Year's kiss for me…"

"Well you could have cancer." Autumn spoke up. Everyone looked at her and Autumn could feel all eyes on her. "Joking…I was joking guys. Jesus, take a joke."

"You, my friend, have a dark sense of humor." Maya told her, chuckling.

"Perhaps, perhaps." Autumn shrugged.

"Disregarding Loser's terrible sense of humor…" Autumn rolled her eyes. "I say Riley and I take one for the team and kiss when the ball drops." Everyone but Riley laughed, knowing Phoenix was kidding.

Riley's brown eyes went wide as if they'd fall out of his face and his pale face immediately turned red, looking down sheepishly. "What? I-um, I don't know how to kiss and…" he stammered nervously, clearly anxious.

Phoenix chuckled, placing her arm around Riley. "I was kidding, Riley."

"Oh." Riley said stupidly, his ears turning red as well.

Phoenix chuckled again, poking his cheek playfully. "You're too cute."

Riley blushed again. "Thanks. Thanks. Thanks." He mumbled, rubbing the back of his neck nervously.

Phoenix only smiled sweetly before going into a conversation with Ethan and Emma. Riley stared at Phoenix for a couple seconds before blushing and looking back at the huge crowd in front of them.

Elena sat down on Autumn's lap after Autumn offered and assured a couple times that it was okay, making the awful joke of "It's not like I'll feel your weight, I can barely feel my legs"

Elena wrapped her arms around Autumn and kissed her cheek. "Are you glad you came?"

"Maybe…" Autumn smiled.

"Admit it." Elena squeezed Autumn's cheek. "Come on, admit it!" she cooed.

Autumn giggled. "Okay, okay!" she grinned. "Yes, I'm glad I came."

"Sorry to interrupt this adorable Alena moment, but I did not waste my money so you guys won't wear these hats sooo…" Maya spoke up as she walked up to them, placing a gold New Year's party hat on Autumn with 'Happy New Year!' in silver glitter on the hat. Maya put on Elena's head a tiara with gold lettering and a black feather on top of it. "You can continue with your sickenly adorable moment." Maya said as she walked away and held Toby's hand.

"Do I look like a total dork with this hat?" Autumn asked when Maya left.

Elena kissed her cheek. "An incredibly adorable dork wearing an incredibly dorky hat." She giggled. "But it's okay, we're dorks together."

"Just the way I like it." Autumn smiled.

Elena took out her phone and switched it to front camera. "Let's take a picture." Elena told her.

"But I don't take pictures…"

"For me?" Elena pouted.

Autumn sighed. "For you." She smiled. "I probably will not even look at the camera…"

"I don't care. I won't either. I'm going to kiss your cheek." Elena smiled.

"All right, fine. Let's take this." Autumn chuckled.

Elena kissed Autumn's cheek and took a couple pictures while Autumn smiled brightly, not looking at the camera as much but she made her attempt.

Elena looked at the pictures and smiled. "They look so cute."

"I wish I could see them."

"I'll describe it for you."

"I'd love that."

Suddenly there was a booming cheer and Elena looked up to see the ball was descending down, people counting down.

"There's a minute until the ball drops." Elena told her girlfriend.

Autumn simply smiled as everyone began counting down. She heard Elena counting down as well, while she held Autumn.

And in that moment, Autumn couldn't have felt happier. This was all she needed right now. Good friends and an even greater girlfriend holding her while they greeted the new year with open arms. Even Autumn found herself hoping for the New Year to come.

As long as she had Elena, she didn't care what happened. She didn't dwell on the possibility of death, she didn't dwell on the possibility of never gaining her sight back, and she didn't dwell on the fact that she was in a wheelchair right now.

All that mattered was the girl sitting on her lap that was so beautiful.

"10...9...8...7...6..." the crowd shouted at the top of their lungs in anticipation. "5...4...3...2...1!" the crowd erupted in a loud cheer as they brought in the New Year.

"Can I kiss you?" Elena shouted through the noise.

Autumn nodded. "There's nothing else I want right now."

Elena kissed Autumn passionately, cupping her face as her lips moved against Autumn's.

Emma and Ethan shared a kiss too, both smiling as they shared their New Year's kiss.

Toby shyly leaned in to kiss Maya who pulled him in by the collar and kissed him, giggling.

Phoenix giggled as she kissed Riley's cheek unexpectedly. The boy jumped and turned to Phoenix who only smiled. "I said I wanted a New Year's kiss..." she laughed. "This is close enough, right?"

"Yeah…" Riley's entire face grew red. Phoenix only smiled before cheering again, Riley surprisingly joining in with her.

Elena pulled away from the kiss and leaned her forehead against Autumn's, panting. "Happy New Year, Autumn." She whispered.

"I love you."

Elena broke out into a smile. Autumn hadn't said it to her directly yet until now and it made her body radiate with joy at those simple three words.

"I love you too."

Autumn touched Elena's lips before leaning in to kiss them. "I love you." She said again.

And that was enough to Elena. Those three words were enough to bring in the New Year.

"I love you too." Elena said through the kiss.

"I love you."

Elena giggled. "I love you too."

"Happy New Year." Autumn whispered.

Elena smiled. "I love you."

CHAPTER NINETEEN

Autumn let out a puff of air as she slowly walked with her weight on the walker she'd been using for the past couple weeks. Her mobility only got worse; she could barely walk across the hallway without feeling incredibly worn out. So now she had to use a walker so she could kind of get around.

And of course, there were the assholes that called her grandma and made fun of her for using a walker. But she was dying; there were worse things to think about than some douche making fun of her walker.

She stepped inside the music room, guitar playing filling her ears and she immediately recognized who it was.

"Riley." Autumn spoke up as she pushed herself towards the piano bench and sat down, panting.

Riley looked up from the stool he was sitting and smiled softly. "Hey." He greeted, taking the stool and sitting next to her. "Sorry I'm in here, I'm waiting for Emma. She's supposed to take me—me—*me* to therapy." Riley explained as he internally counted every time Autumn breathed heavily.

Autumn shrugged. "It's cool. This isn't my room, you're welcome here." She pushed up her glasses. She always had a soft spot for Riley. He understood her in some sense.

Both of them were trapped. The only difference was that Autumn was trapped in her own body while Riley was trapped in his own mind. "I like that…" Autumn took a deep breath, having been tired from the walk. "… fingerpicking you were doing. Sounds like a potential song."

Riley nodded. "I've been working on something…" he trailed off as he tapped on his guitar exactly 10 times. "It's not done yet though."

Autumn hummed. "Let me know when you finish it." She smiled softly.

"I will—will—"Riley groaned in frustration as he sighed. "*will.*"

"Hey, don't beat yourself up for it." Autumn told him. "I don't mind it, you know that. Just like you don't mind when I'm such an asshole." She said, chuckling.

Riley snorted. "Thanks."

The two were silent for a while and Autumn mindlessly played some notes on the piano before Riley spoke up again.

"I'm worried about Emma." Riley spoke up.

Autumn turned to where she heard him, facing him. "Why? I've been a little worried too if I'm being honest."

Riley sighed. "She's not the same anymore. She's so…distant. I—I—*I* don't know. She barely takes me to therapy and she barely talks to me—me—*me* or takes me to buy vinyl records." Riley paused. "I was having a panic attack the—the—*the* other day and you know what she told me? To get over it. She's—she's—*she's* never told me that. Emma always helps me when I needed her and comforted—comforted—*comforted* me when I had a bad day. Now, she's barely around. And when she—she—*she* is, she's just snapping at me and she's so angry and…sad." Riley looked down. "I don't—don't—*don't* want her to be sad…I want her to be okay again…"

Autumn listened intently before pursing her lips. "Has she seemed…drunk or hung over to you?"

Riley thought for a moment, tapping his fingers against his guitar exactly 10 times before replying. "A few—few—*few* times…like when she'd pick me up from therapy, she'd be wearing sunglasses and—and—*and* groaning saying she had a headache. And sometimes when we'd talk, she'd slur a—a—*a* little." Riley looked at Autumn. "What does this mean? Why are you asking me this?"

Autumn nodded, gulping. "I think Emma may be an alcoholic, Riley…"

"Why are you—you—*you* assuming that? She can't be…she—"

"Look at the signs, Riley," Autumn told him. "She's distant, she's angry, she's agitated constantly, she's stopped doing activities she use to do and stopped taking responsibilities she use to have, she's hung over and drunk constantly, and she's not herself. She's pushing everything in her life away to drink. Emma's an alcoholic…but we can't confirm it yet."

Riley remained quiet for a little before nodding. "You're right…" his eyes watered at the idea of his sister struggling through something like this. "How do we confirm it?"

"When she's not home, which is probably very often right?"

Riley nodded. "Yes—yes—*yes.*"

Autumn licked her lips. "Sneak into her room and snoop around for any clues. If you find anything out of the ordinary, then we'll know."

"I can't…that's her room and—"

"Do you want to help your sister?"

Riley sighed but nodded. "Yes—"

"Okay, then you sneak into her room and see if you find anything suspicious."

Riley nodded. "Okay…then what?"

"Then if our suspicions are true…then we're going to talk to your parents and then we'll talk to her…to help her." Autumn bowed her head. "This is my fault. I've always been such a bitch to her. I pushed her away when she tried to help me and be there for me. I never let her be my friend, I never let myself be hers either." Autumn closed her eyes, feeling guilty. "But I love her, Riley, you have to know I love her. She's like my sister and even if I don't show it…I care about her more than anything. I fucked up…"

"It's not your fault—fault—*fault,* Autumn. Sometimes people find comfort or relief in the wrong things. That's where the—the—*the* demons rise and consume them, making them dependent in the wrong things. But if—if—*if* we help her, we can make them go away."

Autumn nodded slowly. "Okay."

"We're going to help her—her—*her* Autumn…we are."

"I know."

———————————————

"I truly think now that when you go to a Beyoncé concert, you are automatically blessed by the queen." Maya gushed as she talked about in detail to Phoenix during their lunch period about the Beyoncé concert she had gone to as a gift from Toby for Christmas. It was one of the best nights of her life, especially because she got to spend it with Toby who she really liked. "She was…magical. Honestly, you and I have to go see her one of these days."

Phoenix forced a smile, happy for her friend but her mind was preoccupied by other thoughts. She had to pick up two of her siblings from middle school, one from elementary, and the other two from daycare after school so they could head…"home".

Phoenix realized home wasn't a permanent thing for some people. Because now Phoenix and her family lived in a homeless shelter and have been for the past month.

Her aunt and uncle had told them they couldn't stay anymore, so they packed their belongings and now lived in a bedroom that had to somehow fit eight people.

She was in charge of her siblings and made sure they were okay while her parents spent the day working, trying to save up as much money as they could to rent out a small apartment. No luck so far.

No luck at all.

Everything was getting harder for Phoenix, everything was becoming too much and she felt she was going to explode.

Phoenix would prefer to explode more than anything. Exploding meant an end, and Phoenix felt an end would be great.

Maya continued gushing. "Toby held me the entire time after he finally had the courage to ask me. He's still so shy and awkward but I love it. He's just…amazing."

Phoenix snapped out of her thoughts and nodded, forcing a smile. "That's so great, I'm really glad you found Toby. He seems like the one." She told Maya.

Maya grinned. "Thanks." She paused. "What about you Phoenix Hale?" the dark-skinned girl smirked. "Any potential lover coming?"

Phoenix chuckled, shaking her head. "I've got other things in my mind, I don't have time for a guy."

"That's a first." Maya teased. "Usually you'd ask me if Toby had any cute friends that were doctors too."

"They're not ready for Phoenix Hale." Phoenix joked lightly.

"I don't think anyone ever is." Maya retorted, enjoying the banter they hadn't had the chance to do in so long.

"That's because my status is equivalent to Beyoncé's." Phoenix flipped her hair. "I don't need a concert to confirm that." She smirked.

"You're such a dork, Phoenix."

"So is Beyoncé."

"Yeah, but Beyoncé makes it look sexy...you just look stupid." Maya joked.

"Stupid...ly sexy."

"Sure, whatever keeps you sane, honey." Maya smirked.

Phoenix crossed her eyes at Maya playfully before giggling. "Who said I was sane to begin with? I'm friends with you."

"We're friends?" Phoenix smacked Maya who pouted, rubbing her arm. "I was kidding, damn!"

Maya's phone rang suddenly and she looked through her backpack to fetch it. "Is it Tobias?" Phoenix teased.

Maya felt her heart stop. It was her dad. Her dad never called unless it was an emergency. "No...it's my dad." She stammered before getting up. "I need to take this..." Maya muttered before walking away to answer the phone.

Phoenix casted a worried glance at her friend as she walked away, wondering what was going on. She'd ask her about it later when she had the chance. She sat by herself awkwardly, looking down at her phone to pretend she was doing something so she wouldn't look like a total loner.

Suddenly, she was tapped on her shoulder and she turned around to see Ms. Kate *again.* That woman would not leave her alone as hard as she tried to avoid her. A part of her appreciated it. It made her feel like someone cared about her.

"Let's go to my office, yes? I want to talk to you, Phoenix." Ms. Kate smiled softly as she pleated invisible wrinkles off her red pencil skirt.

Phoenix stared at her for a couple moments before nodding hesitantly. She rather follow Ms. Kate than deal with being alone for the rest of lunch.

After the quiet and awkward walk to Ms. Kate's office, Ms. Kate gestured Phoenix to sit on the chair beside hers. Phoenix sat down, chewing on her lip nervously.

"So, Emma came up to me the other day to inform me she was quitting choir." Ms. Kate spoke, looking at Phoenix. "You're friends with her, do you think there's any particular reason she did that?"

Phoenix shrugged. "I don't know." She raised an eyebrow at the choir teacher. "Are you just talking to me because you want me to go back? Because I can't—"

"I'm not talking to you for that. I will accept you not wanting to come back, or Emma." Ms. Kate interrupted, casting a worried look. "I do, however, care about your well-being as well as Emma's. I've tried talking to her but she won't budge. And now I'm going to try one last time Phoenix …" she spoke sternly. "What's going on?" she said, softly this time. She seemed genuinely concerned about Phoenix. "I can only do so much if you do not tell me anything. I care about you Phoenix, and if there's something going on, you can tell me." Ms. Kate smiled softly at the girl.

Phoenix gulped, suppressing tears. "Whatever's going on, you are allowed to react to it. You are allowed to let those bottled up feelings burst. Because it's just you and me in this office, and I won't judge you on whatever comes out of your mouth." Ms. Kate assured, squeezing the girl's hand.

And just like that, Phoenix let everything go. Everything she's kept in for the past couple months, every feeling she suppressed, every smile she faked, everything…she just threw it out the window and stripped herself to a more vulnerable version of herself.

Ms. Kate wrapped her arms around the sobbing girl, rubbing her back and whispering consoling words to her the best she could.

Phoenix sobbed more than she had ever done in her life. Her eyeliner and mascara ran down her cheeks and clung onto her choir teacher as if Ms. Kate was her key to salvation.

And maybe she was.

Phoenix wiped tears from her face, sniffling. "I'm..." she closed her eyes, looking down. "I'm... homeless." She confessed, embarrassed. She opened her eyes and Ms. Kate nodded for her to continue. "My dad lost his job a couple months ago and we stayed at a family member's home but they kicked us out a month ago. I live in a homeless shelter with my parents and my younger siblings."

Phoenix pursed her lips. "I take care of them while my parents work. That's why I couldn't be in choir, I had to take on responsibilities my parents couldn't take." Her eyes welled up again. "It's just...*so* hard." Her voice cracked.

"I'm a kid...and now I can't be a kid...that's not...that's not fair!" she pounded her fists on her thighs. "Why can't I just be like everyone else who worry about school and boys and...and not that *plus* if my siblings are eating tonight? Or if I can pick them up from school on time? Or...if I'm ever going to have my own bed and my own room again? Why can't I have it easy?" Phoenix began crying again.

Ms. Kate looked at Phoenix sympathetically. "Life in itself is never easy." The teacher began as she wiped tears from the younger girl's face. "Think of it like…like rain." Phoenix looked at her quizzically and the teacher laughed. "This is a good analogy, I swear." She assured before continuing. "What happens when it rains?"

Phoenix eyed her, confused as she spoke slowly. "Everything is…wet…"

Ms. Kate nodded and smiled. "Yes, and doesn't it suck when it rains?" she questioned. "It's all foggy and humid and your make-up and your hair and your clothes are a *mess*. Not to mention the possibility of being sick. It sucks, doesn't it?"

Phoenix shrugged, nodding. "I guess…" she mumbled.

Ms. Kate smiled softly. "But do you want to know the beautiful thing about rain?" Phoenix looked at her expectantly. "No matter what, the sun is going to come out and everything dries up and suddenly everything is beautiful again. Like nothing ever happened. Like it wasn't wet and terrible just a couple moments ago."

The teacher wiped a tear from Phoenix's face. "Problems we face in life, Phoenix, they're like rain. It's horrible and unexpected and dark…but no matter what, the sun's going to come out and everything will be better again. It just takes time for it to dry up and become beautiful again. So just wait for the sun to come out again, okay?" she hugged the girl again. "And while the sun comes back, you have me to be your temporary sun."

Phoenix smiled softly at the teacher, hugging her tightly. "How are you going to be my temporary sun?"

"Whatever you need Phoenix, I will help you. Whether it's lending some money, or helping take care of your siblings so you can do your homework or you can go and spend time with your friends...I will always be a helping hand. Because like I've said before, you're so much more than just another student to me Phoenix ...you're like my little sister—yeah, I'm not comparing you as my daughter. I'm still young!" she chuckled, Phoenix joining in. "And I have your back, for anything."

In that moment, Phoenix felt the sun peak a little from the rain. And everything felt better. Nothing was perfect, but nothing was ruined just yet.

"I know you're here because Elena asked you to." Valerie spoke up, turning to Autumn who was writing lyrics messily into a sheet of paper and playing the piano.

"You're not wrong." Autumn said simply, pushing up her sunglasses. "I rather be spending time with my girlfriend, but no, she's in the other room while you and I are here. But I'd do anything for Elena, even help write songs for people I'm not fond of."

Valerie pursed her lips and nodded. "Right. Of course." She paused. "Just know I'm not after her, okay? I won't try anything on her, I just want her friendship."

"But you'd like something more, wouldn't you?" Autumn retorted through gritted teeth, tightening her grip on her pen.

"You're not wrong." Valerie confessed. "But she's your girlfriend, and I respect that. I'm not all that fond of you either, Autumn, but one thing that ties us together is Elena whether we like it or not. So we might as well try to be civil to one another, yeah?"

Autumn grumbled something under her breath before nodding. "Fine, whatever." She chuckled. "For the record, I'm sorry for calling you an ironic piece of shit."

Valerie raised an eyebrow. "You've never called me that."

"Oh, I know. I just always thought your last name was ironic because Elena tells me your skin is tanned and your last name is White. I hate irony and I hated you so…"

Valerie snorted. "Hailey would've loved you, I swear…"

"Who's Hailey?" Autumn asked.

Valerie's eyes widened. "Elena never told you about Hailey?"

Autumn raised an eyebrow before shaking her head slowly. "No…should I?"

Valerie cursed under her breath. "I shouldn't have said anything…just ask her later. No—ask her some other time."

"Is she someone important to Elena?" Autumn questioned.

"Yes." Valerie nodded. "And that's all I'm telling you. Let her tell you when she wants to. It's a touchy subject."

Autumn seemed to accept that answer for now. "Okay…so let's continue with this song you started." Autumn continued as they finished writing the fourth song since Autumn had arrived at Valerie's place. They continued working, throwing suggestions for lyrics and composition of the songs in general. Autumn and Valerie seemed to work well together when it came to writing songs, they soon realized.

Autumn suddenly put her pen down and spoke up. "Can we talk? I need to talk to you about something now that I know you're not an ironic piece of shit."

Valerie chuckled, nodding. "Sure, what's up?"

"I have cancer."

"I know that…" Valerie trailed off, raising an eyebrow.

Autumn nodded. "I know."

"Then why are you—"

"There's a high chance I won't go into remission." Autumn paused. "And there's a high chance I'll die instead."

"But the chemo—"Valerie stammered. "Didn't they catch the cancer on time?"

"It's spreading to other parts of my body." Autumn told her. "And don't tell Elena because I haven't talked to her about it yet...but...I'm considering stopping chemo."

Valerie's eyes widened. "Why?"

"Because what's the point? I'm dying. And the chances of me going to remission are—"

"But it's a chance." Valerie cut off. "Look, I'm not going to dictate your opinion but do you really want to die without vision? Don't you want to leave this world knowing you got to see every inch of it possible? Wouldn't that be a better way to leave? And think about your friends...your family...Elena. There's nothing wrong with being selfish and thinking of yourself, but they're on the same ship as you. And they're willing to support you."

"I just..." Autumn sighed. "I'm so tired..."

"Everyone is tired, Autumn, but no one wants to go to sleep."

"If I had a choice—"

"That's the thing, you *do* have a choice. You can die trying, or you can die quitting. Or you can live too. I know it's hard, but just take the chance Autumn. You never know what life can bring." Valerie advised.

Autumn's jaw clenched. "You don't fucking know my life and you don't know all the shit I went through. And I'm fucking done with it!" she snapped. "I don't want more chemo, I don't want to be blind, and I want everything to be easy…and it's not and I hate it because I can't do it anymore! So don't go fucking telling me that motivational bullshit about trying and not giving up, because you know what? I tried my fucking hardest since I was five years old, and what has that gotten me? Blind, angry, cancer-stricken, and—"Autumn groaned in frustration, pounding her fists in the piano keys.

Valerie stared at Autumn, biting her lip as she contemplated what to say next. "You're right…I don't know your life." She paused. "And I may sound selfish and really insensitive, but I don't really care." Valerie shrugged. "Elena has lost someone before, Autumn, and it would kill her to lose someone else who left by choice." She paused. "But I get it, I've talked to Elena about this before…I know this sucks for you. But I've seen Elena with you now and…she can't lose you. I know it'd be easier to die but she really needs you too, Autumn. You may think Elena's been the one helping you, but you have no idea how much you've helped her. She can't lose you too. So just—just *please* believe in miracles. They happen. They exist. And they can happen to you."

Autumn began to wonder who Elena lost, and how little she knew of her girlfriend's story. "I never thought of that…"

"Well you know now, so you need to try. I know dying is easier, because living is the hardest thing to do when your life is complete shit, but she needs you. She needs you so much, more than you'll ever know. Talk to her, you never know what could happen."

Autumn nodded. "I will." She paused. "I want you to promise me something, Valerie."

"Okay, what is it?" Valerie nodded.

"If I die— because whether I take chemo or not…that's still a lingering possibility—I want you to watch Elena for me, okay? Whether it's platonic or…or romantic…" she sighed. "Just take care of her for me."

Valerie smiled softly. "I will."

"Thank you."

In the other room, Elena was on her laptop watching Hailey's videos. She was torturing herself, she knew it. But Elena wanted to desperately cling onto a past she wished still existed in the present. She wanted to hold onto Hailey just a little longer, because it still hasn't hit her she was gone forever.

Elena watched videos of her past self and Hailey joking around with the camera. They looked happy. Hailey looked happy.

Present Elena felt tears running down her face and she quickly wiped them. Hailey promised her forever but only gave her 11 years. If Elena didn't feel guilty then, she surely did now.

"Where is she? I need to see her!" Maya exclaimed to the nurse at the desk. Her eyes flickered with panic and distress. "I need to see my mother, please!"

Doctor Rivera appeared from the hallways and grabbed the girl, directing her to her office.

"First, you need to relax before you can see *anyone*. Okay? You need to breathe. She's still with us Maya." Doctor Rivera said sternly, not being the kind of doctor to play around with.

Maya took a deep breath as she buried her hands on her face. "What's going on? My dad just called me saying something's wrong and I need to know—"

"What did I say?" Doctor Rivera cut off as she grabbed the younger girl's shoulders. "I need you to *breathe* and *relax*."

"How can I relax when something wrong with my mom and *you* won't tell me?" Maya exclaimed.

Doctor Rivera stared at her. "Relax." She said. "When you calm down, I will explain everything to you. Because I'm not telling you anything when you're like this."

Maya closed her eyes, steadying her breathing until she relaxed. "What's wrong with her?" she finally said in a whisper.

"Sit down."

Maya hesitantly sat down and looked up at doctor expectantly. "What's wrong?" she asked again.

Doctor Rivera leaned against her desk and crossed her arms. "I'm just going to come right out and say it…" she sighed. "The treatment isn't working as great as we expected. I started suggesting other possible treatments but your mother said she doesn't want any treatments anymore. She's done, Maya. She's going home Friday until she dies. She has about a month to live."

Maya's world crashed down at the words. Her mother didn't want to go along with treatment anymore. She was going to die. She wasn't going to have a mother anymore. Her eyes began to water as she looked up at Doctor Rivera.

"She wants to die?" her voice cracked.

"No, she wants to live before she dies. And she's not doing that being in this hospital Maya. You have to understand—"

"How can she be so selfish?" Maya snapped. "I *need* her! I need my mom! I can't go the rest of my life visiting her grave! I need my mom! I want my mom!" she said angrily as tears streamed down her face.

Doctor Rivera looked at the girl sympathetically. "Maya, she's always going to be your mom. There's no changing that. She will always be your mother, but she can't do this anymore Maya, it's too much for her. She rather get to spend time with you before she dies than spend time with you in a hospital bed. She's not afraid of dying, and you shouldn't be afraid of letting her go."

"I tried to find treatments why didn't they work? Maybe I can look—"Maya quickly began replaying in her mind all the treatments and their functions in her mind but was interrupted when Doctor Rivera placed her hands on her shoulders again.

"Stop that. Stop blaming yourself and stop looking for alternatives that aren't there. She's dying and you have to accept that.

You are not obligated to look for a cure, that's my job. Your job for now is to be a kid, Maya. I will admit I'm impressed with how smart you are. You have a promising career in the medical field. But that's later. Right now, you're 17 years old. You're 17 years old and you're still a kid. Keep being that. You've been trying so hard to mature and grow up, but don't do that to yourself. Hold onto this age and cherish whatever time left you have with your mother. Because she's not changing her mind, I'm sorry."

Maya listened to her words and wiped the tears away. She was still angry at herself that her hard work to help her mother failed, but Doctor Rivera was right.

"Can I see her?"

Doctor Rivera nodded. "She's in the same room as always." She paused before writing down her number on a slip of paper. "Whatever you need, call me or text me. I have a soft spot for you, Maya. You're a good kid." She smiled softly before sending her off with a hug. "Be strong."

Maya nodded as she slipped the paper in her pocket. She walked to the front desk where Toby was now and he looked up to notice his girlfriend with tears in her eyes. He quickly stood up and wrapped his arms around her.

"Hey, what's going on? Are you okay?" Toby asked, concerned.

Maya simply sobbed in his chest and Toby tightened his grip as he consoled his girlfriend. "Hey…it's okay. Whatever's wrong, it's going to be okay because I'm here. What happened?"

After Maya's sobs subsided she looked up at him. "I'm always in this hospital because my mom is here. She…" she sighed. "She has breast cancer and she's stopping treatment." Her eyes watered again. "She has a month to live." Her voice cracked before crying again. "Why is this happening? Why? Why *her* Toby? She didn't deserve any of this!"

Toby listened to his girlfriend's words with a sympathetic look. "I'm sorry about your mom. But she's still here, Maya. She's still here. So whatever time she has left, just cherish it and spend time with her. Time isn't scary, you know. There's something beautiful about time too." He told her with a soft smile. "Time means heals wound faster and happiness comes closer. Because all of this…madness? Yeah, madness." He chuckled. "All of this madness won't be forever. Everything is temporary. That's why time is such a beautiful thing. Because it moves you closer to where you want to be. So don't be scared of time, because your mom will be okay and so will you."

Maya pressed her lips on Toby's and sighed in content when she pulled away. "Thank you." She whispered. "Thank you for existing."

Toby smiled. "Thank you for letting me exist with you." He whispered back, kissing her forehead.

"I want you to meet her." Maya told him. "If you can right now…"

"I do now." Toby smiled, taking her hand.

Maya smiled as she led him to her mother's room. When they walked in Maya bit her lip and smiled at her mother. "Mom…meet Toby. My boyfriend."

Riley took a deep breath as he nervously stepped inside Emma's room. He really didn't want to do this, but he loved his sister. And this new version of her wasn't her. Riley wanted to help her because Emma has done so much to help him. He wanted to return the favor because she deserved to be helped too.

Looking around the neat room, Riley bit his lip as he walked more inside the room. Where did he even start? Rubbing his hands nervously exactly four times, he began carefully looking through

Emma's stuff. Through drawers, her closet, everywhere. He made sure to put everything back just the way it was.

After searching for half an hour, Riley sighed as he found nothing. He still hadn't looked under the bed though...

He crawled under the bed and took out a box that seemed suspicious. Riley bit his lip as he slowly opened the box and quickly frowned, his eyes watering with tears. Autumn was right.

Empty bottles, half-finished bottles, full bottles. Just bottles of alcohol that he knew Emma consumed. He wiped tears away as he closed the box and put it away and practically ran out the room in tears as he barged into his own, grabbing his phone with shaky hands as he dialed Autumn.

"Autumn?" Riley gulped as he wiped tears away from his eyes.

"Riley? What's wrong?" Autumn answered.

"You were right...she's...Emma's..." Riley's voice cracked. "She's not okay." He cried.

Autumn gulped and nodded. "Okay. It's going to be okay, Riley. We're going to make sure she'll be okay again. We're going to talk to your parents and then we'll talk to her with them. She's going to get the help she needs, okay? Don't worry. Emma's not going to stay like this."

Riley nodded and sniffed. "Okay…why did she turn to this Autumn? Why is she hurting?"

Autumn sighed, running a hand through her hair. "Sometimes…sometimes everything becomes a bit too much. It all got a little too much for her."

"Is it my fault?"

"Riley, don't you dare blame yourself." Autumn told him sternly. "It is not your fault."

But it might be hers.

CHAPTER TWENTY

Emma stumbled up the steps of her house and fumbled with the keys, dropping them a couple times and giggling at her clumsiness. She eventually opened the door and stepped inside, about to go to her room when a voice stopped her.

"Emma, come into the living room please." Emma heard her father.

Emma sighed and stumbled to the living room, her eyes flickering with confusion as she saw her parents, Riley, Ethan, and Autumn sitting in the living room.

"What's...what's going on?" Emma asked, her words slurred. That's when she noticed her mother's eyes tear up.

"Sit down, Emms." Her father, Robert, motioned the seat in front of them. Emma raised an eyebrow and sat down tentatively on the seat. She clearly looked a mess, her clothes wrinkled, her hair, and make up were a true mess.

"What's going on?" Emma asked.

Robert sighed. "This is an intervention, honey." He gulped, suppressing tears.

"For what?" Emma said, defensively.

"Your drinking." Ethan said this time. "It's getting out of hand..." his blue eyes watered. "I can't just sit and watch you drink into oblivion. I love you, Emma. You have to...you have to get help."

Emma quickly sprung from her seat. "I'M FINE!" she shouted angrily. "I'M OKAY!"

"Baby..." Her mother spoke up. "You're not, you're an alcoholic and you need to get help..."

Emma glared at her mother. "You wanted me to be your strong, big girl...didn't you? WELL HERE SHE IS!" she pulled on her clothes. "Isn't this what you wanted? You wanted me to take care of Riley and Autumn, well I did! ISN'T THAT ENOUGH FOR YOU?"

"You took care of us you forgot to take care of yourself, Emma." Autumn spoke up. Emma's head snapped towards Autumn's direction. "You can't do this to yourself."

Emma scoffed. "Like you fucking care, Autumn." She slurred angrily. "I've done *everything* for you. I crossed mountains and rivers *for you*. But it was never fucking good enough. I was just your fucking caretaker! *Not once* did you call me your best friend. *Not once* did you call me your sister. You stopped calling me that and you stopped caring about me. You *never* let me get close to you. EVER. And then Elena fucking comes along and suddenly you're this happy and giggly and smiley girl that tells HER everything." Tears began streaming down Emma's face as she tightened her fists.

"ALL SHE DID WAS MOVE HERE WHILE I TOOK CARE OF YOU AND WATCHED OVER YOU AND TRIED TO BE YOUR FRIEND. I TRIED TO BE **YOUR** EYES. BUT YOU NEVER LET ME!" she punched her thighs angrily. "But you let her...you let HER."

Autumn gulped as she listened to Emma, biting her lip. "And I'm sorry I did that. But doing this to yourself because I pushed you away doesn't help—"

"It does! Because I don't think about you or anyone. I don't feel anything. And feeling nothing is better than feeling everything..." Emma cut off.

"Ladybug..." Riley spoke up with a shaky breath. "Don't do this to yourself, please." His eyes watered. "I'm sorry I'm a lot to handle—handle—*handle* but I promise to be better. And I won't be too much for you—you—you. But please get help. Please..." Riley pleaded, rubbing his hands three times and then rubbing his neck four.

Emma looked at Riley and felt tears stream down her face at seeing her little brother so distraught. "I'm okay ducky, don't worry about me. Worry about yourself—"

"I can't worry about myself when my best friend—friend—
friend and my sister isn't okay." Riley cut off. "You have to stop.
Please stop…stop drinking. I—I—*I* want my ladybug back." He cried.

Emma looked at everyone as they kept talking to her about
getting help and shook her head. "Shut up!" she shouted. "Shut up!
Shut up! Shut up! Stop talking! I'M FINE. I'M OKAY."

"You're not—"her father spoke up.

"BUT THAT'S WHAT YOU WANTED ME TO BE. I'M
THE STRONG ONE. STOP…stop…" Emma wiped tears from her
eyes as she took a couple steps back. "stop making me the weak one.
I'm not weak…"

"No one said you were. But if you go and get help, you'll be
so much better—"Her father continued.

Emma covered her ears. "Stop!" she exclaimed. "I don't need
to get better!" she exclaimed. But she needed to drink. She quickly ran
out of the living room and opened the front door and left.

She couldn't take it.

There was too many people asking too much of her.

She already gave them everything she could, wasn't that
enough.

What was so wrong with drinking?

What was so wrong with forgetting?

What was so wrong with numbness?

What was so wrong with *her*?

Phoenix watched with a soft smile as Ms. Kate played with Noah and Penelope, laughing at the younger children's antics.

Ms. Kate had invited her to come to her apartment so that she could watch her siblings while she did her homework and have dinner. And that's exactly what she was doing right now.

She really couldn't thank Ms. Kate enough for her help she had given her, her lending hand and kind heart made things better.

"Thank you," Phoenix spoke up. She's probably thanked Ms. Kate a billion times. "Ms. Kate, honestly, things feel *so* much better now and—"

"Phoenix," Ms. Kate laughed as she carried Noah, balancing him on her hip. "Stop thanking me, I know you're thankful." She chuckled. "And call me Elizabeth. We're not at school." She chuckled.

Phoenix rubbed her neck and chuckled. "Sorry, I just…you've helped so much. You don't realize how much…" her eyes watered. "I'm smiling again. Like, *really* smiling…" she felt a tear slide down her cheek and quickly wiped it away. "I never thought I'd smile like that again."

The older woman put Noah down and quickly wrapped her arms around Phoenix. "I told you it'd stop raining, Phoenix." She smiled.

"You did." Phoenix smiled. "That's because you were my temporary sun, Ms.—Elizabeth."

Elizabeth smiled and nodded. "I'll always be the sun when you need me to be. I tell my wife that all the time and I'll tell you."

Phoenix's eyes widened. "You're *married?*"

Elizabeth nodded and chuckled.

Phoenix smiled softly. "So, how long have you been with your wife?"

"I'm 28 and we got together when I just got out of college. I was 22. We got married two years ago. But I've been with her for six years." Elizabeth told her with a smile.

"Wow, that's a while. Do you love her?" Phoenix face palmed. "Of course you do, you're married." She chuckled.

Elizabeth laughed. "Yes, I do love her. Very much." She smiled. "We're planning on having kids soon. We started looking at sperm donors. You're going to see me with a belly soon." She told Phoenix.

Phoenix perked up. "Really? Wow! That's so great! I'll help babysit, I'm a great babysitter." She said proudly.

"I'll take you up on that offer." Elizabeth smiled.

"How does your wife look like?" Phoenix asked. "Sorry, I ask too many questions." She blushed.

Elizabeth laughed and shook her head. "It's fine." She walked over to the living room where Phoenix's brothers and sisters were watching TV. She grabbed a picture of her and her wife and walked back to Phoenix, showing her the photo of the two on their wedding day.

"Wow, she's really pretty." Phoenix said. "Wait," she paused. "That's Loser's doctor!"

Elizabeth raised an eyebrow. "Loser?"

"Autumn. Piano playing Autumn Castillo." Phoenix clarified. "I went to chemo with her once when Elena couldn't. I met her doctor. Your wife." She paused. "You heard about Autumn, right?"

Elizabeth smiled sadly and nodded. "I have. My wife talks about her all the time. How is she?"

Phoenix sighed. "Well, she's not at school anymore. She can't take it since she's losing her mobility. She's going to be paralyzed from the waist down..." she trailed off with a frown. "And the chemo makes her really sick. It's terrible, because Autumn has gone through so much..." she paused. "You should be her temporary sun."

Elizabeth frowned. "I'll try. I tried getting her into that youth orchestra, but she wasn't very keen on it. She doubted her extraordinary talent. She's amazing on the piano." She sighed. "It's terrible what's happening to her. But we can't dwell on her sickness, we just have to keep our heads up for her. Because I'm sure she doesn't like to be reminded of something she already knows about."

Phoenix nodded, closing her textbook. "I feel like a lousy friend though, other than Elena, none of us have really tried being there for her. Elena's the only basically helping her out. Makes me feel like a shitty friend."

"Don't." Elizabeth shook her head, as Noah rested his head on her shoulder and Elizabeth rubbed his back. "You have your own issues to deal with, Phoenix. There's nothing to be guilty about."

Phoenix shrugged. "I guess...I'm trying. While trying to find my home at the same time. If I ever find it."

"Home isn't a place, home is a feeling." Elizabeth said to the girl. "It's the arms that hold you that makes you feel safe, who is that for you?"

"My mom and dad." Phoenix answered with a soft smile.

Elizabeth smiled. "Home is also the fit of laughter and smiles you get. Who is that for you?"

"My siblings. My friends. You." Phoenix smiled.

Elizabeth nodded and grinned. "See? Home isn't a location. It's the people you surround yourself with. You have a home, Phoenix. You have it here with me, you have it with your family, with your friends, with music..." she trailed off. "You may be physically homeless, but not in every aspect of the word. I assure you."

Phoenix smiled at Elizabeth's words. "Thank you." Phoenix paused. "Is there still a spot for me? In choir?"

Elizabeth smiled, patting the girl's back. "It never left."

Elena was looking outside the window of her living room and sketching the scenery in front of her. People strolling by bundled up in jackets, scarves, mittens, and hats, snow falling from the sky and coating the streets, and the simplicity of it all relaxed Elena.

Ana watched her daughter from the kitchen with an intense look. She had been concerned for her daughter. Elena was usually so cheery, but ever since Autumn's sickness came back and she received Hailey's package it was like seeing a different version of her daughter. A version she wanted gone.

"Elena? Do you think you can sit down for a moment? I want to talk to you." Ana called out to her.

Elena hummed as she did some final strokes with her pencil before putting down her sketchbook and turned around, sitting down in front of her mother. "What's up?"

Ana sighed as she grabbed her daughter's hands. "I don't want you to watch those videos Hailey gave you anymore."

Elena opened her mouth to protest but Ana put her hand up to stop her. "No, Elena, you need to listen to me right now. I'll let you speak after I speak." She paused. "Mija…you're hurting yourself. This isn't healthy. You've obsessively watched these videos more than once, you're clinging onto someone who isn't with us anymore. She's gone…Hailey's gone. And I understand it's all you have left, but you're only destroying yourself." She squeezed Elena's hands. "You don't smile anymore…not genuinely. You don't laugh. Joke around. You're not *Elena*. You're a different version of her. You're the grieving version. I understand Hailey meant a lot to you, she meant a lot to all of us, but you can't keep trying to live in a world where she's still here."

Elena listened to her mother's words and looked away. "You don't understand…"

"Then help me understand." Ana urged. Elena looked away from her mother. Ana frowned. "You don't have to be my strong girl right now, you know. You can be vulnerable to me, Elena. You know that. It's okay not to be okay sometimes, you just have to admit it yourself.

"I'm okay." Elena assured.

Ana shook her head. "You're not. Because if you were, you wouldn't be trying to hold back from crying right now."

Elena gulped and looked up at her mother's concerned, yet welcoming eyes. "I'll only cry if you hold me." Her voice cracked.

Ana felt her heart break at her daughter's words and immediately embraced her daughter in a tight hug. "I'll always hold you when you need me to." She whispered to her daughter as she kissed the top of her head. Elena immediately sobbed into her mother's chest, her body shaking as she clung onto her mom. Ana rubbed the girl's back as she kissed the top of her head again.

"It's my fault." Elena muffled in Ana's chest.

"What are you talking about?" Ana questioned.

Elena looked up with her teary face, guilt written in her features. "I didn't help her. I didn't help Hailey even when I knew. I knew she was depressed. I knew she was cutting. I knew she was bulimic. I knew every single thing. I knew it. But she told me to not say anything, so I didn't. I never did. But I should've." Her eyes watered again and tears streamed down her puffy cheeks. "If I said something she'd still be alive. And I'd still have a best friend and I wouldn't be so sad." Elena cried. "My fault...it's my fault."

Ana frowned as she lifted her daughter's chin and locked eyes with her. "Look at me, Elena," she said sternly. "It is *not* your fault. Hailey's death is *not* your fault. You did not put that razor in her hand or those pills down her throat. She did that. It wasn't your fault, and I'm not saying it was her fault either. She wasn't okay, and she didn't know how else to alleviate the pain. It wasn't the right choice, but she didn't know what to turn to." Ana sighed. "And you didn't know what to do either, you were stuck between fulfilling her wishes and fulfilling your own. I'm sure you tried helping her the best you could, but ultimately…her demons won. And there is nothing we could do about that now because she's gone."

Elena scoffed, sniffling. "Don't sugarcoat it, it was my fault. I could've stopped her. If I answered her calls the night before and I wasn't at that stupid art show…if I would've tried harder to fix her—"

"You can't fix people, Elena. You can't piece them together like puzzles. Humans are too complex to be fixed with ease. That's something they have to do on their own." Ana cut off.

Elena whimpered, taking fistfuls of her hair and crying. "It hurts…" she moved her hands away from her hair and pointed to her heart. "It hurts so bad. And I don't think it's ever going to go away. I let her leave and I'm never going to stop feeling guilty about that. Ever."

"I think you should consider talking to someone about this, Elena…" Ana said gently, rubbing her arm.

Elena quickly shook her head. "I'm NOT crazy!" she said defensively.

"No, you're not crazy. But thinking you can handle everything life hands you on your own is." Ana retorted.

Elena still shook her head. "I don't need to talk to anyone."

"Elena, your best friend committed suicide and Autumn was diagnosed with cancer again. You've gone through so much over the course of one year, it's okay if it gets to you. But you can't keep it to yourself. You can't pretend you're okay. You can't lie to yourself and keep acting you're this happy girl all the time when sometimes you're not." Ana told her. "Just consider it, talking to someone equipped could help."

Elena gulped. "I'll think about it." She mumbled. "Can I go up to my room?"

Ana sighed before nodding. "Okay." She agreed. "I'm serious though, you need to stop watching those videos."

Elena nodded. "Yeah, fine. Whatever." She said before rushing to get upstairs.

Ana frowned, running a hand through her hair. She was worried, Elena was shutting herself out. She wasn't dealing with her emotions correctly and she was afraid it'd affect her more than she thinks.

Upstairs in her room, Elena wiped away tears from her eyes. She knew her mother meant well, but talking about her feelings meant remembering. And she didn't want to remember, even though she remembered every day.

Elena was in her room as she dialed Hailey again after she didn't answer for the billionth time. She had left countless voicemails that terrified Elena. Most of them she was crying while apologizing over and over again for relapsing once again and harming herself again. It pained her that she wasn't able to answer at that time, but she had an art show to be at and didn't have time to answer.

But she did now and Hailey wasn't answering her calls or texts.

The last text Hailey left was just a simple, "I'm sorry, Lena. I'm so sorry." Nothing else. Just that. And it was sent a couple hours ago before Elena woke up.

Huffing, she slipped on her shoes and walked to Hailey's house. It was a five minute walk anyway.

She arrived to the house and was greeted by Hailey's mother who was basically her other mom.

"Can you wake up Hailey? She still hasn't gotten up yet, that lazy girl." Hailey's mother chuckled. "The pancakes are basically frozen now."

"I'll wake her up, don't worry. I'm the sunshine of her life." Elena laughed as she went upstairs.

"You really are." Hailey's mother smiled before going back to the kitchen.

Elena quickly burst into the room and Hailey was in her bed, appearing asleep.

"All right loser, get up." Elena laughed as she shook the girl. *But Hailey's body was limp and didn't even fidget. Instead, her head slid from the pillow and dangled slightly from the bed.*

Elena's eyebrows furrowed in confusion as she shook Hailey again. "Hails, wake up."

Nothing. No response from Hailey.

That's when the panic settled in as she shook her again.

"Hailey, stop fucking around and wake up!" she exclaimed, *her hands shaking Hailey again. She touched the girl's face.*

Cold.

This couldn't be happening right now. Elena's eyes watered as she suddenly noticed the empty bottle pills at her nightstand.

"Oh my god."

Elena noticed the razor blade, too, and she suddenly noticed her slit wrists with dry blood.

This had to be a dream. Hailey wasn't dead.

She grabbed Hailey's shirt in fistfuls and shook her lifeless body again. "Hailey wake the fuck up! Please! You're not dead, you're not..." she felt tears spilling from her cheeks. "HAILEY!" She sobbed as she shook her again, smacking her cold cheek. "Wake up, wake up!" Elena said desperately. "You can't leave me here...you can't leave me here!" she sobbed in Hailey's chest.

Hailey's mother walked in the room when she heard Elena screaming. "Elena what's going on—"

The woman stopped dead in her tracks when she noticed Elena sobbing in Hailey's chest while Hailey lied on her bed with her eyes closed and her wrists cut. The mother screamed as she ran to the bed and shook Hailey by the shoulders only to feel her daughter's cold skin.

Suddenly, Hailey's father barged into the room as did Hailey's brother. Everything after that was chaos. But Elena continued sobbing, guilt quickly hitting her because she didn't answer Hailey's phone calls. And she didn't reply to her texts. All because of a stupid, pointless art show.

All because of her.

Emma was many things. She was a sister, a daughter, a friend, a singer, a baker, a girlfriend…she was a lot of things.

But she was *not* an alcoholic.

An alcoholic drank alcohol like they couldn't live without it.

Emma could live without drinking.

She just chose not to. She chose to drink into oblivion. An alcoholic doesn't have that choice.

Emma does. She has that choice. She could stop if she wanted to. But she just doesn't want to. Why stop something that helps with the pain and pressure of life? Why stop something that made her feel nothing? Isn't that what everyone aimed for? To feel nothing? She has the choice to feel nothing, so she does.

And now, she chose to be in this apartment with people she didn't know. And she chose to be drinking by the windowsill and looking at the view of the skyscrapers.

Emma lived in a city filled with a bunch of different people, yet she's never felt more alone.

Taking another gulp of her vodka mixed with sprite, she closed her eyes as the bass of the music vibrated against the walls and shook her body slightly.

She didn't understand. Why would her parents, Ethan, Riley, and *especially* Autumn care about her habits?

They just needed Emma to be their happy and strong girl, and she was. She was strong...she was happy...

She was a liar.

Emma hiccupped as she tried getting up but her legs were jelly and they wobbled. She nearly felt herself fall but a pair of strong, but unfamiliar arms caught her.

"You look a little tipsy there babe, why don't we head to one of the rooms to sober you up?" the stranger's deep voice asked. Emma looked up, seeing double of the older man holding her. He was definitely older than 25.

"No..." Emma slurred out, trying to push him away.

"Come on baby...I'll show you a good time..." The man trailed off as he started kissing Emma's neck.

Emma weakly tried pushing him off. "No...get off me." She mumbled, starting to feel bile rush to her throat.

"You'll be too drunk to remember any of this, anyway." The man scoffed as he pushed Emma against a wall.

Emma protested, trying to push him off. "I said no!" she exclaimed as she felt his hands going up her pink dress.

The vomit came up her throat and she hurled into the guy's clothes. The man quickly backed away from her and looked at her with disgust.

"What the fuck man?" he shouted to her as his face scrunched up as the vomit intoxicated his nostrils, stinking up his clothes.

Emma wiped vomit out of her mouth. "Sorry…" she mumbled, her words incoherent.

The man growled, raising his hand and smacking Emma across the face. The younger girl yelped, clutching onto her cheek as tears spilled from her eyes.

"Fucking bitch…" he muttered before walking away, people laughing at him as he appeared with vomit on his clothes.

Emma held onto her stinging cheek and felt like puking again, pushing past a sea of people before finding an unoccupied bathroom and hurling against the toilet until her stomach was empty. She flushed the toilet and wiped her mouth again, rinsing her mouth with water before taking a look of herself in the mirror.

God, she was a wreck.

Her usually neat hair was disheveled, slightly greasy from not washing it for the past couple days.

Her make-up, usually done to the uttermost perfection, was runny. Her mascara and eyeliner were running down her cheeks and blackening the bags under her eyes. Her eye shadow was smeared as well as her pink lipstick.

And then her clothes. Her girly and, often neon colored, clothes were stained with alcoholic beverages spilled and god knows what else.

Her eyes watered at the sight, looking away. She was repulsed by her reflection.

Backing away from the mirror, she fell to her knees and sobbed.

She was a fucking wreck.

Who was she kidding? She felt pain. She felt anger. Sadness. Guilt. Every negative feeling poured onto her. It damaged her soul. It damaged every part of her.

Emma was damaged. She had been for years.

And *now* did people notice the slight cracks on her usually well-kept self. *Now* they noticed the brightness dimmed from her eyes. *Now* they noticed the tear-stained cheeks and runny mascara. *Now* they noticed the faint scent of alcohol. *Now* they noticed the damage done.

But they were too late.

Emma hunched over, hugging herself as tears spilled onto the white tiles of the bathroom floor.

"You're selfish. So selfish. YOU'RE crying? It should be Autumn who should be crying. She has fucking cancer and she can barely walk. What do you have to complain about? Nothing. You selfish bitch." The voice in her head taunted.

"Shut up." Emma muttered, rubbing her head.

"Riley is crying for you. He needs you. He's panicking because you've abandoned him. You abandoned him and he needs you. What kind of sister are you? A bad one. You don't even take him to therapy. You don't take him anywhere. You don't take care of him like you're supposed to. You're worthless."

"Shut up." Emma said, louder. She began rubbing her head forcefully, trying to get the bad thoughts away from her head.

"Ethan is going to break up with you soon. Once he finally realizes what a waste you are of a girlfriend. He'll find someone better. Prettier. SOBER."

Emma whimpered. "Shut up!" she exclaimed, hitting her head harshly.

"Your parents regret having you. Look at you, drunk and hopeless. Should've gotten rid of you while they had the chance. Because now they're embarrassed to call you 'daughter'. Just like Autumn is embarrassed to call you 'friend' and Riley 'sister' and Ethan 'girlfriend' and everyone else is even embarrassed to utter your name. Because you're a disgrace."

"SHUT UP!" Emma shouted, punching her head until it throbbed. "Stop telling me what I already know! I know!" she sobbed. "I know…"

Emma curled up against the cold, tile floor and wound up falling asleep until she heard the door pounding a couple hours later.

"Get out of the bathroom! I need to use it!" she heard a voice exclaim.

She got up, stumbling as she opened the door and the person pushed her out the bathroom and slammed it.

Emma staggered to the living room, noticing it was way past midnight. Where the hell did she leave her phone? She walked around the apartment in confusion until she remembered she left her purse by the windowsill. The purse still rested there and she grabbed it, looking through her phone and seeing messages and missed calls from Ethan, her parents, and even Autumn (surprisingly).

She had been dropped off here though. She didn't have her car. And she was definitely too drunk to drive.

But she didn't want her parents or Ethan to pick her up.

She didn't even know where to go. But she didn't want to be here anymore. With a sea of people she didn't know and a place she didn't recognize, she felt herself start to panic.

Her hands were shaking as she looked through her contacts, unsure who to call until she settled on someone.

"Emma...it's two in the fucking morning—"the groggy voice answered.

Emma hiccupped as she felt her eyes water again. "Can you please pick me up, May?" she pleaded in a small voice. "Please?" she definitely sounded drunk.

"Are you okay?" Maya asked, concerned. "Where are you? You sound drunk."

"No…" Emma sobbed. "I don't know…I just…I don't want to be here…please…" she rubbed her eyes.

"Give me the address. I'll take my dad's car. Are you okay? Did somebody hurt you?" Maya questioned.

Emma heard movement coming from the other line as she gave Maya the address.

"No…I'm fine…I think." She mumbled.

"I can't believe you're fucking drunk. I'd never expect it from you." Maya said, Emma hearing the jingling of keys and a garage door open.

"Me neither."

Maya sighed. "Stay on the line with me, okay? I'll be there in a few."

So Emma did, hearing the rumbling the engine of the car Maya drove and waited anxiously.

"I'm here Emms, go outside." Emma heard a faint beep coming from outside and quickly walked outside without a jacket. She couldn't find it anywhere.

She shivered as she stumbled outside, a sigh of relief at seeing a tired Maya waiting on the driver seat and yawning.

Emma stepped in and Maya quickly began driving back to her house. She wasn't about to send Emma back to her parents drunk.

They drove in silence for a while, Maya sending glances to Emma every so often while Emma kept her head down and fumbled with her fingers, obviously ashamed.

"What happened?" Maya spoke up.

Emma shrugged, mumbling incoherently.

Maya sighed, parking the car on the side of the road and turning to Emma. "Talk to me now. This is unlike you to call me *drunk* and like *this*." Emma stayed quiet, her head still down. Maya huffed before lifting the girl's head and forcing Emma to look at her. "Talk to me, Emma, I'm serious." She said sternly. "If you don't, I'm taking you straight to your house and you can explain all this to your parents. And I know you don't want that."

Emma stayed quiet for a couple more minutes before her eyes watered again.

"I hate being sober." Emma's voice cracked. "It just means I feel again."

Maya gulped. She wasn't expecting *that*. "Feel what?"

"How much I'm not enough…pain…guilt. Nobody sees me as nothing more than a support system…or a *caretaker*. But what if I need one?" Emma felt tears rushing down her face. "What if *I* need the support system? What if *I* need someone to take care of me? What about *my* needs? Don't *I* matter? Or am I just another insignificant person in a city with thousands of people? Am I just another person who needs a grave? With the way I feel…I kind of want a grave now."

Maya listened to the girl's words and felt her heart break. How had she not noticed this coming from someone she called "best friend"? It was funny how everyone called Autumn the blind one, yet everyone else was the blindest of all. She had occupied herself on one person in her life so much, she forgot everyone else existed.

Maya pursed her lips before speaking. "Emma…this isn't the first time you get drunk, huh?"

Emma nodded, ashamed. "No." she whispered.

"How long?"

"A year and a half." Emma confessed.

Maya nodded. "Okay." She said softly. "I want you to listen to me right now, okay? Can you do that?"

Emma nodded slowly, sniffling. "Yes." She whispered.

"Just because you're drunk, doesn't mean every reason you're hurting goes away. If anything, it multiplies it. Because the moment you're a bit sober again, everything you tried numbing away comes back to bite you in the ass. The numbness you feel when you're drunk is a temporary feeling, so you keep drinking to keep it numb. But you can't hide what you feel forever, Emma, I learned that now. You can't hide your feelings like they're nothing, because they're something. Your feelings matter and *you* matter. You're not just a support system or a caretaker…you're Emma Charlotte Brooks and you're enough, okay? You're so enough, Emma, you have no idea how enough you are."

At hearing Maya's words, Emma started crying and Maya embraced her in a tight hug. Emma clutched onto Maya as she cried.

Maya ran her hand through Emma's hair. "I may not have the exact same situation as you, but I know what it's like to be scared. I'm scared right now…" she trailed off before locking eyes with Emma who looked up at her. "My mother has breast cancer, and she decided to stop treatment. She's done. And she's going to die soon." Maya gulped. "I'm scared of what I'm going to feel after she leaves. I'm scared of how I'm going to go on without her. But I know I'll be okay. I don't know if it's going to be in a couple weeks, couple months, or couple years…but I know eventually I'll be okay and I'll breathe fresh air without my mother in it. And you will be okay too, Emma, I don't know when…but you will be okay soon. Everyone someday will be okay, some people just aren't patient enough to wait."

"I can be patient."

Maya smiled gently. "Do you want to stop? Drinking? Because you have to if you want to be okay again."

Emma bit her lip and shrugged. "I don't know…I don't want to stop."

Maya frowned. "I don't want to keep having to pick you up drunk, Emma. I don't want to have to keep seeing you like this. You have to help yourself. Ultimately, it's up to you whether you want to be okay again. I can't make that decision for you…"

Emma nodded. "I know…"

"I hope you make the right choice."

"Me too."

————————————————

Elena opened the door to Autumn's house and quickly stepped behind Autumn who held a tight grip to her walker as she walked small, tentative steps inside the house.

"Sorry I'm so…slow." Autumn mumbled sheepishly.

Elena shook her head, kissing her cheek. "Don't feel bad for something you can't control. Take your time, Autumn, I got you." She smiled softly.

Autumn smiled gently as she felt a sharp pain shoot up her legs and her legs stiffened. "Fuck…they really hurt today." She hissed.

Elena frowned as she closed the door behind them when Autumn fully entered the house. She quickly slipped off Autumn's sunglasses, smiling as she stared at Autumn's green, opaque eyes. Those eyes were one of her favorite things to look at.

"You're staring again." Autumn smiled as she slowly navigated to her room, Elena beside her.

Elena blushed. "Because you're beautiful to look at. There's nothing else I rather look at."

Autumn blushed this time. "I wish I could look at you too. But I don't need seeing eyes to tell you that you're beautiful. And that I love you very much."

"Can I kiss you?"

"You don't even have to ask." Autumn smiled.

Elena chuckled and pressed her lips against Autumn's, sighing in content when she pulled away. "I love you too." She whispered before they entered Autumn's room minutes later.

Once Autumn sat down on her bed, she panted heavily and clutched over her stomach. "Shit, that was a workout." She laughed.

Elena sat down beside her and rubbed her back. "You're okay though, right?"

Autumn nodded and hummed. "Yeah, I'm fine." She mumbled, rubbing her head.

"Why don't you lie down?" Elena suggested.

Autumn shook her head. "I'll be doing just that soon, I want to be on my feet for as long as I can be..."

"Don't be stubborn, Autumn, lie down. You're tired." Elena insisted.

Autumn groaned before listening to Elena and lying down, curling up in a ball and covering herself up with blankets. "Happy?"

Elena chuckled. "The happiest." She lied down beside Autumn and held her. "You should sleep, I'll hold you the whole time." She smiled.

"But I'm not tired." Autumn whined, pouting.

"Don't give me that pout and sleep." Elena laughed, kissing her cold hands. Autumn groaned as she cuddled into Elena's chest, her teeth chattering as she shivered.

"Are you cold babe? I can get you more blankets." Elena suggested.

Autumn shook her head. "I'll go get them." She mumbled, sitting up.

Elena protested. "No, you stay here and I'll get them. It's not a big deal."

But it *was* a big deal, to Autumn it was. "No, let me get it, Ellie."

Elena had already gotten up and out the room to get it and Autumn huffed as she grabbed her walker and lifted herself up, her legs feeling extreme pain. "Shit..." she hissed in pain as her legs barely moved an inch to walk.

Elena was looking through the closet that had extra blankets when she heard a loud thump and crash. Her eyes widened and she quickly dropped everything and ran back to Autumn's room to see the girl on the floor, groaning in pain.

"Shit, Autumn!" She exclaimed as she tried to help up her girlfriend but Autumn pushed her away.

"Don't help me!" Autumn snapped. "Just leave me here!" she said, her voice cracking.

"Autumn—"

"I CAN'T FEEL MY LEGS. I CAN'T MOVE THEM!" Autumn cut off, punching her legs and not feeling a thing. "They told me I had another month…"

Elena's eyes watered. "Baby—"she tried to say.

"I'm so fucking useless!" Autumn began crying. "I can't move, I can't see! It's not—it's not—IT'S NOT FAIR!"

Elena wrapped her arms around Autumn despite her protests. "It's okay…we're going to call your mom and we're going to take you to the doctor—"

"I don't want a doctor! I don't want anything! I just want…I just want to be able to live…but not like this." Autumn sobbed. "Not…not when I have cancer. Not when I can't move. Not when I can't see…"

This was the first time Autumn had finally addressed how much her diagnosis had affected her. This was the first time she cried about it in the months since she began chemotherapy. This was the first time Autumn was truly vulnerable in front of Elena.

"How can you love a fucking cripple, Elena?"

Elena kissed Autumn's temple, her heart breaking at the words. "Because I didn't fall in love with your legs Autumn…or your eyes. I fell in love with your heart. I fell in love with your mind…and just because your legs don't work anymore or your eyes…it doesn't mean my love for you will fade one bit. It's here to stay forever. I love you Autumn, and my heart belongs to you."

She felt a tear escape her eye. "And trust me, I hate that this is happening to you…I don't like seeing the girl I'm in love with suffer, but I refuse to leave you at your worst. I'm here to stay Autumn. I'm not leave. I'm going to help you as much as I could."

Autumn sniffed as she cried. "I'm sorry…I'm sorry for wanting to give up…"

"I know it's hard, but please don't give up. I don't want to lose you." Elena pleaded.

Autumn gulped. Remembering what Valerie had told her. "I won't. I'll try to stick around and keep messing up your entire life like always." She smiled gently. "I love you."

"I love you too." Elena smiled before kissing her hands again. "Promise me you'll tell me when something troubles you."

"I promise." Autumn whispered before sighing as she grabbed her legs. "I can't believe I can't walk anymore."

"I'll be your legs."

"Really?"

"Really."

CHAPTER TWENTY-ONE

Elena, Phoenix, and Maya we're sitting in Autumn's room. After Autumn's hospital visit, it was confirmed officially that Autumn paralyzed from the waist down. It took her a couple of hours of crying in Elena's arms to realize that there was nothing she could do about it. She just had to learn how to live with nonfunctioning legs.

Autumn was sitting up on her bed, coughing and wheezing into a handkerchief while Elena rubbed her back and murmured comforting words.

"Fucking hell." Autumn rasped out when her coughing fit finished. "I sound like a drug addict, don't I?"

Phoenix shrugged. "Well that chemo shit is drugs, might as well classify you."

"Phoenix, stop being a dumbass." Maya rolled her eyes before turning to Autumn. "You sound like the high class drug addict, if that makes you feel better."

"There's high class drug addicts?" Phoenix raised an eyebrow.

"Yeah, those rich kids that feel misunderstood in those shows and movies so they turn to drugs." Maya shrugged.

Phoenix snorted. "And *I'm* the dumbass."

"Well, you are." Autumn chuckled. "But that's okay, it's okay to be stupid. Trust me, I know a lot about being stupid."

"You mean your angstier days? They still exist Autumn, shut up." Phoenix teased. "Literally the other day weren't you complaining on the phone about how this—and I quote—"she cleared her throat.

"This bitch ass nurse doesn't know how to stick a fucking needle in my veins. This bitch is sticking poison in my body, yet *I* need to be patient. Let me tell you ,Phoenix Hale, I'll be patient enough to stick that needle up her ass." Phoenix imitated Autumn and smirked.

Autumn laughed loudly, coughing afterwards. "I was tempted to tell her that but Ellie taught me to 'whatever' things. So I did." She smiled. Elena blushed and leaned her head against Autumn's shoulder and Autumn rested her head on top of hers with a smile.

"Autumn Castillo has some serious character development going on." Maya chuckled.

"You know how people say bullshit like, 'Never change'? Poor things don't realize that change can be a wonderful thing sometimes." Autumn told her.

"We've all changed a lot since we all became friends, I think." Phoenix shrugged. "I mean…take me for example." She paused and gulped. "I've been homeless since New Year's. I live in a homeless shelter." She confessed, looking down at her hands. "I didn't think I'd be without a home, but you know what? That's okay."

Phoenix smiled softly as she looked back up to face her friends. "Ms. Kate told me that home isn't a physical place, it's an emotional one. It's the people that make a home, and that's you guys and my family...so yeah. I may be homeless but I'm not home *less* if you know what I mean." Phoenix laughed.

Maya hugged Phoenix and smiled. "You're never going to be homeless while we're around. You can crash at my place anytime if gets too much."

"Mine too." Elena chirped. "I know how obsessed you are with my room." She winked.

Autumn raised an eyebrow, blinking. "Are you guys having a secret love affair that I'm just discovering?" she chuckled.

"You caught us, Loser. Took you long enough. Now you can join our threesome." Phoenix joked.

"I can barely sit up." Autumn snorted.

"Aye, as long as everything still tingles down there you're good." Phoenix laughed.

"It does, if you're wondering." Autumn shrugged.

Phoenix looked at Elena and then Autumn. "Are you guys scissoring now? HOLY SHIT YOU BOTH HAD SEX, DIDN'T YOU?"

Elena and Autumn laughed. "No Phoenix, we have not had sex yet." Elena replied.

"*Yet.*" Phoenix smirked.

Elena and Autumn blushed while Phoenix kept teasing them. "All right, now that Phoenix has shared something...anyone else?" Autumn spoke up. "We're basically a support group now, let it out."

Maya gulped. "Well...I guess..." Maya trailed off, sighing. "This isn't easy for me, so bear with me."

The rest of the girls nodded as Maya took a deep breath. "I haven't really told many people. I told Autumn, Toby, and Emma. But yeah..." she paused. "My mom she's battling with breast cancer. And..." her eyes watered. "She decided to stop treatment and is at home now...she doesn't have much time left, so I'm taking whatever time I have left."

Autumn frowned at the news. "I'm sorry about your mother. She's a great woman. I met her once during one of my chemo sessions. She's really nice, and told me a lot about you." She smiled softly.

Elena looked at Maya sympathetically. "I'm sorry too. I know what it's like to lose someone, it's not fun." Autumn bit her lip at Elena's words, knowing Elena has lost someone but had yet to say anything about it.

Maya smiled back. "Thanks."

"Can we meet her?" Phoenix asked with a smile. "I mean, I've known you for years and I never met her. I want to know the woman who birthed your goddess self." She joked, trying to lighten the mood.

"Of course you can. I'm done hiding her." Maya paused. "I'm not even sure *why* I even hid her in the first place. I guess…I didn't want the sympathy. And I guess I didn't want to hear it from anyone else what I knew deep down: that she was dying. But I've accepted that fact now. It doesn't make it hurt any less, but at least my heart has accepted that nothing lasts forever. But I know she's always going to be there for me. I just won't be able to see it."

"She will be." Phoenix assured, squeezing her hand.

Maya nodded. "I know. And I started taking up dance again…I kind of let it go, but I realized time doesn't stop for anyone. I just got to keep going and do the things I love."

"Like Toby?" Phoenix smirked, wiggling her eyebrows.

Maya scoffed and whacked her arm. "Shut up." She blushed.

"She's blushing! Therefore they totally did it!" Elena piped up, laughing.

Maya blushed even harder and Phoenix's eyes widened. "Hold up...did you two *really*..."

"Maybe..."

"Heeeeyyyy!" Phoenix whooped. "Get that white chocolate May! How was it?"

"It was amazing. And that's all I'm telling you, I'm not some damn erotic novel." Maya joked. "And don't compare my boyfriend to white chocolate, he's not a damn Hershey's commercial either."

Elena laughed. "Good, I don't want to hear about you heterosexuals and your sex. It's repulsive to my Sapphic goddess self. "She joked.

Maya and Phoenix rolled her their eyes while Autumn chuckled. "You're such a goofball, Ellie." Autumn the side of her head. "But I love it."

Phoenix and Maya smiled softly at the interaction. They would've never expected many months back for Autumn to say that out loud. They never expected for Autumn to ever say what she felt out loud. But that was the beautiful thing about change, it made people happier.

"Do you guys know about Emma?" Maya spoke up, biting her lip.

Autumn quickly lifted her head from Elena's. "What about her? Is she okay?" she asked worriedly.

Maya shrugged. "I don't think she's okay. She called me a while back…drunk. I picked her up and she was a mess. It wasn't the first time she'd gotten drunk either."

Phoenix and Elena were surprised to hear that. "Are you trying to tell us that Emma's an alcoholic? *Our* Emma? Sunshine Emma?" Phoenix questioned.

"Unfortunately, yes. She's not okay and I don't know if you knew Autumn but—"

"I knew." Autumn whispered, bowing her head. "I know I'm the cause of it."

"That's not true—"Elena immediately spoke.

"It is. You guys all saw how I treated her. I was a bitch to her. I never gave her the recognition or the gratitude she deserved. She was nothing but a friend to me, but I was too angry and too closed off to see it. I was blind in more than one way, I guess." Autumn sighed. "Riley and I had an intervention with her parents and Ethan, but she snapped.

Like, really bad. I haven't talked to her since, even though I've tried to."

"Wow…" Phoenix trailed off. "We've all got shit going on, right?"

Elena smiled sadly. "You have no idea."

———————

Riley tentatively knocked on Emma's door exactly three times. She refused to leave her bedroom, and only would when she had to go to school (which she didn't really go to, she just hit whatever party was going on). Riley wanted his sister back and he wanted to try one more time to get her to understand she needed help.

"I'm sleeping." Emma's voice spoke from the other side of the door.

"Can I come in?" Riley pleaded. "Please?"

"I said I'm sleeping." Emma repeated, her voice hoarse.

"Emma…please?" Riley rubbed his guitar exactly eight times. "I just want to show you something—something—*something*."

"I don't want to see it."

"Please ladybug?"

It was silent for a couple minutes before Riley heard the muffled movements of Emma getting out of bed and opening the door. The girl didn't have any make up on and had on her pajamas. She had heavy bags under her eyes and she looked so *out of it*. It was like Emma wasn't even there.

"Hurry up." Emma deadpanned before lying back down on the bed, staring at the wall.

Riley nodded, biting his lip. "I…I wrote a song. And…I wanted to sing it to—to—*to* you."

Emma scoffed. "Okay, whatever." She mumbled.

Riley grabbed a chair and placed it in front of Emma and nodded. "I've only sang it in front of one other person, so bear with me—me—*me* if it's a little bad." He mumbled nervously. Emma didn't respond but Riley took it as his cue to sing the song. He took a deep breath before beginning to fingerpick the strings of his guitar and looked at Emma.

Emma had tears streaming down her face as well as she cupped a hand over her mouth in both shock and heartened from Riley's gesture. What struck her the most was that Riley wasn't displaying any of his ticks. He wasn't repeating every 14th word three times, he wasn't repeating *anything*. She hadn't seen him do that in years.

Riley was *trying*.

So why couldn't she?

When he finished the song, Emma quickly ran to Riley and wrapped his arms around her little brother and sobbed on his shoulder.

"Did you write that song for me?" Emma said in between sobs.

Riley was crying as well and nodded. "I'd write you a billion songs if it'd mean you'd be okay." He broke the hug and looked at Emma with teary eyes. "Please—please—*please* get help. I'll even go with you. I'll be there for you like you've—you've—*you've* been for me…just…please…I want to see you smile again. And sing—sing—sing. And bake. And laugh. I want to count how long it takes for you—you—you to stop laughing, I want to count how many jumps of joy you do—do—do when you're happy, I want to count how many annoying kisses you give me—me—me on the cheek, I want to count how many minutes you have a smile—smile—smile on your face. I want to count your happiness again…"

`Emma wiped tears away from her face as she saw the pleading look on her little brother's face. She took a deep breath as she kissed his forehead and hugged him tightly.

"Start counting."

Elena was at Valerie's apartment looking at a particularly emotional video of Hailey pouring her demons out to Elena. There were tears brimming in her eyes when suddenly her laptop was shut and her headphones were yanked out.

"What the—"Elena looked up to see Valerie clutching onto her laptop and putting it on the coffee table. "What the *fuck* Val?"

"You got to stop this, Elena. Do you think it's healthy? Watching videos of Hailey who's been dead for a year now? Do you really think it's normal to clutch onto the dead? Look, I get that she was your best friend—"

"*Is*. She *is* my best friend." Elena growled.

Valerie ran a hand through her hair. "Don't say that…you sound—"

"Crazy? Well maybe I am." Elena snapped, getting up to grab the laptop but Valerie stepped in between. "Give me back my laptop!"

"I'm not giving you anything, Elena." Valerie crossed her arms. "I promised Autumn I'd watch over you, and I'm starting now. I'm taking your flash drive and I'm not giving it back to you." She said as she turned around and yanked the USB out of the laptop.

"WHAT ARE YOU DOING?" Elena shrieked, trying to yank the flash drive out of Valerie's hands. "Give it back!"

"Elena, stop!" Valerie exclaimed as she pushed the girl away, the flash drive slipping from her hands.

Elena practically threw herself to retrieve the flash drive, but Valerie wanted to make sure she wouldn't get it. So she instinctively stepped on the flash drive with her heel.

Elena heard the crunching noise and her breath hitched. That's all she had left to remember Hailey by…to be able to remember how she sounded like. To remember her laugh. Her cries. Her *voice*.

Valerie and Elena locked eyes, the apartment completely *silent*.

Until Elena spoke up.

"YOU DID THAT ON PURPOSE!" Elena shouted, pointing at Valerie with angry tears spilling from her eyes as she picked up the pieces of the flash drive with her hand. "I can fix you, I can fix you…" she muttered to herself as she picked up the pieces. "I can fix you…"

Valerie looked at Elena and her heart dropped at the sight. Did she ever picture Elena this …broken?

Never.

She never would've associated "broken" and Elena Díaz together...but here she was, piecing it together.

"Elena, I am *so*—"

*"*Shut up!" Elena hissed, glaring daggers at the smaller girl. "Don't talk to me." She spat. "How could you do this? How can you take away my memories?" she snapped at the girl.

"Those aren't memories, Elena. That's not what you can force yourself to remember. You know what that is? It's a goodbye letter you keep rereading obsessively. And you need to stop—"

"I'M NOT STOPPING *ANYTHING*!" Elena snarled. "This was all I had left of her..." she whispered.

Valerie shook her head. "That's a lie. Are you completely forgetting every memory you made with her before she died? Before everything? You're destroying yourself, Elena. And the sad part is, you think you're so put together."

"I'm not doing anything—"

"Yes you are."

"No I'm not!"

"Elena, yes—"

Valerie yelped when she felt a hard slap collide with her cheek. Valerie clutched onto her throbbing cheek with wide eyes as she looked at Elena with shock.

Elena kept her hand up, feeling the stinging of how hard she hit Valerie with her hand. She let out a shaky breath at the realization of what she did. She *hit* someone. She'd never resorted to violence before.

The two girls stared at each other before Elena spoke up in a shaky voice. "I'm so sorry…" she whispered.

Valerie gulped as she hesitantly stuck out her shaky hand to Elena. "Give me the pieces." She whispered.

That's when Elena noticed she was gripping onto the broken, *sharp* pieces of the flash drive. Elena slowly opened her hand to see blood pooling in her hand.

"Elena." Elena looked up to see Valerie reaching her hand out. "Give me the pieces, please."

How was Valerie still trying to help her after what she did?

Slowly, Elena placed the bloody pieces of the flash drive in Valerie's small hand the girl quickly took the pieces and threw them in the trash can.

"Let's go to the bathroom. I'll clean you up." Valerie said softly, an inviting look in her brown eyes.

Elena let out a shaky breath as she followed Valerie into the bathroom. Valerie took out a first aid kit and motioned Elena to place her hand over the sink.

She turned on the water and Elena whimpered at the sudden pain hitting her palm.

"Sorry." Valerie whispered as she took out a gauze and antibiotic. "It's going to sting."

Elena hissed as the antibiotic hit her cut skin and suppressed the urge to tighten her hand as Valerie's delicate hands wrapped up her wound.

"Thank you." Elena mumbled, still not looking at Valerie in the eye.

"That's what friends are for."

Elena closed her eyes and let out a sigh. "You should ice that." Elena referenced to Valerie's red and already bruising cheek.

"I will." Valerie nodded.

It was an awkward silence as they both stood in the small bathroom. Both girls were unsure what to say after the events that unfolded in Valerie's apartment.

Valerie gulped as she decided to speak up again regardless of what happened. She promised Autumn she'd look out for Elena, and she would keep that promise.

"You can't keep shit to yourself and expect it not to get to you." She spoke up. Elena looked up and locked eyes with Valerie. "*Tell* someone. Talk to Autumn. You preach to Autumn about opening up about her feelings and being honest, yet you don't tell her anything. What kind of relationship is that?" Valerie questioned. "I'm sorry for stepping on the flash drive. But at the same time, I'm not. You can't live like this, Elena. You can't keep pretending you're okay when I see in your eyes how broken you are." She paused. "You spent so long trying to fix everyone...have you even tried fixing yourself?"

A tear streamed down Elena's face. "I'm not broken." Her voice cracked.

"It's okay not to be okay. It's okay to cry. It's okay to break down. It's okay to scream. It's okay to feel your emotions. Let them out, Elena. It's okay." Valerie assured.

And that's when Elena sobbed in Valerie's chest, clutching onto the girl that comforted her as her tiny voice spoke. "I'm not okay."

"I know."

"Am I going to be?"

"Yes."

At the doctor's office, Autumn and her parents were seated in front of Dr. Richards who had a dejected look on her face.

"I hate to say this…" Dr. Richards spoke up. "But I don't have good news."

Joseph and Cora tensed up at the news while Autumn gulped as she clutched onto the sides of her wheelchair.

"What is it?" Joseph spoke up, rubbing his hands together as he glanced at his daughter.

Dr. Richards sighed and stayed silent for a moment before glancing at the papers in front of her before piling them up and placing them in Autumn's folder.

"Just rip it like a band aid." Autumn said softly. "It's okay, I already have a feeling what it is anyway."

The blonde doctor gulped before nodding. "The tumors are completely gone from Autumn's eyes." That earned a sigh of relief from Cora and Joseph. "But, it really doesn't make a difference because the cancer's spread to her whole body…and there's no treatment that could put her in remission. I don't recommend anymore treatment, it won't help. Just…enjoy whatever time you have left."

Joseph was the first to break down into a fit of sobs at the news. Cora had tears streaming down her face, but she knew it was inevitable. She knew this would happen…but now it *was* happening. Now it *was* real. And reality has never been more terrifying.

"How long?" Autumn whispered, glad she was wearing her sunglasses so that no one could see the tears pooling in her eyes.

"A year…maybe less." Dr. Richards replied sadly. "I'm so sorry."

"No, don't apologize." Autumn shook her head. "Thank you."

Dr. Richards stared at Autumn quizzically. "For what?"

"For giving me a chance even when it was obvious there was none. You tried to save my life, and you did in some way…just by giving me your faith that I'd be okay." Autumn nodded. "And I'm okay. I am now. I'm not afraid to…to die. I'm just afraid to die in…darkness."

Dr. Richards felt her eyes water and quickly wiped them as she looked through her papers. "Actually, when I found out the tumors were gone…I decided to take it upon myself to look for possible surgeries to recover your eyesight." She smiled. "I did find one that looks very promising, Autumn." She told the girl. "You can spend your last days with sight."

"Are you serious? I'll be able to see again?" Autumn broke out into a wide grin.

Dr. Richards nodded. "It looks like it. I think you have a real shot here." She smiled as she began to explain the surgery and how it'd happen.

Autumn squeezed her mother's hand with a wide grin on her face. Sure, she was dying. But at least she'd get to see the world before she died.

She'd get to see Elena.

———————————————

Emma took a deep breath as she sat in a room with strangers that talked about their feelings and their struggles to other strangers.

She was doing this for herself. And for Riley. Because she knew she couldn't live like this anymore. Emma felt Riley take her hand and squeezed it exactly three times. She turned to him and he smiled at her reassuringly that this was a good thing she was doing. Emma smiled back and nodded.

"Thank you."

Riley nodded. "It's going to be okay." He whispered.

"I know." Emma whispered back before turning back to the man talking about his struggles with alcohol and how he'd been sober for two years now.

Emma had only been sober for two days and she already felt like she was losing her mind. But it wasn't so bad here, the people seemed inviting despite most of them being much older than her. She was definitely the youngest of the group here.

Once the man finished speaking, everyone clapped for him and the woman who ran the meeting stood up at the podium again with a warm smile.

"Thank you Greg, it's nice to know you're doing so much better. You've really come a long way." The woman said. Emma hoped deep down the woman would say the same thing to her in the future. "Now who would like to go next? Remember, this is a safe environment. A total judge-free zone. You have nothing to be afraid of."

The room was quiet for a moment and Emma licked her lips nervously. "You should go." Riley whispered in her ear.

"You shouldn't. What's the starting something we all know you're going to fuck up sooner or later? Because you're a failure." The voice in her head spat.

"You can do this." Riley encouraged.

*"You can't do this. You won't last being sober for long because you're **weak**."*

"You're strong—strong—*strong,* Emma. I know you are. Don't let no one convince you otherwise. It's a—a—*a* brave step you're taking right now."

"I'm strong." Emma repeated to herself as she pushed away the bad thoughts in her head.

Riley smiled and nodded. "You're strong." He affirmed.

Emma nodded with a smile as she raised her hand. "Can I go?" she spoke shyly.

The woman locked eyes with Emma and nodded with a bright smile. "Of course you can! Come…tell us whatever you want to tell us."

Emma stood up and walked to the podium as the woman went back to her seat in the front row. Emma looked at the group of people sitting and Riley waved at her and gave her a thumb up. Emma smiled before clearing her throat.

"Uh, hi." Emma greeted nervously. "My name is Emma." A few people greeted back with an encouraging smile and Emma couldn't help but feel touched by the gesture. She took a deep breath, pushing a strand of hair away from her face. "And... I'm an alcoholic. Obviously. That's why...that's why I'm here." She chuckled. "I started drinking about a year and a half ago. It was after a particular bad day. See, my best friend...Autumn."

She rubbed her arm at mentioning Autumn. "She's blind. She had cancer in her eyes and it took away her sight, so she can't see...she's like a sister to me. I love her very much. But she changed. She became angry...distant...cold." Everything Emma became too. "And it hurt that she pushed me away. But that day in particular, she said something very mean and it really hurt. So I was invited to a party by my boyfriend and that was the first time I got drunk. And I just kept getting drunk consistently afterwards..."

Emma took a deep breath before continuing, pushing away the bad thoughts in her head.

"My brother Riley...he's dealt with some issues since he was a kid." Emma locked eyes with Riley, and Riley nodded encouragingly as a signal that it was okay to talk about him. Emma nodded before continuing. "He has OCD and social anxiety. And my parents told me to be the big sister he needed. To be the happy and strong girl I always was. There was so much pressure from both sides. I had to care for Autumn and Riley, leave no room for me to care for myself. I grew accustomed to numbing my feelings with alcohol. So much, I just stopped feeling altogether."

Emma felt her voice crack and a tear slide down her cheek, quickly wiping it.

"My drinking got particularly worse this year. Autumn...she met someone. And the girl's great. She's been an amazing support for her. But what made me angry was how Autumn let Elena—her girlfriend—help her. Yet, she always refused for me to help her. It made me feel useless. Unwanted. A waste of space. So I drank more. To not feel unwanted. But I still did, who am I kidding? I still felt that way. No amount of alcohol could take away the stinging pain of being...rejected."

Emma pursed her lips before speaking again. "And then...there are these thoughts in my head. This...this voice that tells me mean and cruel things. I realized that was me. I told myself those things. I was cruel to myself. But I can't be anymore. I have to help myself because no one else will fully."

Emma smiled at Riley gently and he smiled back, tears brimming in his brown eyes.

"I may not be okay now, but I hold the strong belief that I will be now." Emma nodded. "I don't care how long it takes, I'll be patient now. And I'm not doing it for anyone else but me," Emma paused. "it's weird...I've never been this selfish before. But the good kind of selfish, the kind of selfish everyone doesn't mind." Emma breathed out a sigh of relief as she let all her feelings go. "You'll be seeing a lot more of me here. Because I'm going to get better. And...yeah." She chuckled, wiping away tears as everyone clapped for her and she sat back down next to Riley who hugged her tightly.

"I'm proud of you ladybug."

Maya was sitting outside her mother's bedroom as her father and grandmother were inside the bedroom talking with her mother. The doctor had come earlier because her mother felt particularly sick today. And she just knew right then.

It was time.

She accepted that reality already, her mother was dying. And as much as it broke her heart to know she had to spend the rest of her life without her mother, she'd have to anyway. She'd have to learn to live without her.

Her grandmother and father came out with puffy eyes from the crying they obviously did. Maya quickly stood up and both of them quickly wrapped their arms around her.

"She wants to see you. She doesn't have a lot of time left May." Her father told her sadly, kissing the top of her head.

Maya gulped and nodded. "I know." She whispered.

Her grandmother wrapped her arms around her and kissed her forehead. "It's going to be okay, you still have us. And you have her too, it just won't be in the physical form anymore."

Maya nodded and hugged her grandmother tightly before stepping inside her mother's room. Grace was lying on the bed with a tired look in her eyes. But despite being tired, she cracked a wide smile and her eyes lit up at seeing Maya.

"Hey there." Her weak voice greeted.

Maya's eyes watered and her mother quickly opened her arms for her daughter to embrace. Maya quickly ran to her arms and wept in her mother's chest, hugging her mother tightly and feeling her bones as she hugged her. It made her seem fragile. And her mother wasn't fragile. She was the strongest woman she knew.

"No tears, Maya." Her mother spoke. "That's what funerals are for. Funerals are to cry for the dead and I'm not dead yet, so wipe those tears and look at me."

Maya did as her mother told her and wiped away her tears and looked at her mother. "Sorry." She croaked.

"It's okay." Grace smiled, kissing her daughter's forehead. "I'm so proud of you, you know that? I tell everyone about you." She praised. "And I'll keep telling everyone about you up there with God. He's going to take care of me so don't you worry about a thing, because my job here is done."

"Your job? You spent years suffering through chemo only to wind up dying anyway. That's a pretty terrible job." Maya sniffled.

"It's not, Maya." Grace shook her head. "Want to know why? Because they tried treatments on me. And maybe one of those treatments will work on another woman. And maybe she's going to be able to live her life cancer-free. I save a life, Maya. And that's the best job God could give me besides the honor of raising you."

"But I still need you." Maya's eyes pooled with tears again. "I need you mom—"

"You don't. You got this, Maya. You are going to do amazing things with your life. This is just the beginning for you, you're going to live your life blissfully. And I will be smiling from up there."

"But I want you *here*."

"I know you do, and I wish I could be here too. I want nothing more than to see you become the amazing woman I raised, but life doesn't always work out that way. Sometimes, you can't get what you want. But just know that even if life gets rough, you can always cure it slightly with a good song and a good laugh. And you're going to have your amazing friends and your father and grandmother and Toby by your side to get through life without me. You'll be okay, I made sure to leave knowing you're taken care of." She smiled.

Maya smiled sadly before hugging her mother and kissing her cheeks. "I love you so much mom." She whispered. "I'm so glad I got you for a mother, I wouldn't want anyone else in the world."

"Not even Beyoncé?" Grace chuckled.

Maya chuckled. "Not even her." She paused. "But she can totally adopt me if she wants to." She joked.

The mother and daughter laughed before hugging again. "I'm going to miss you."

"Who says I'll be gone? You still have me here." Grace pointed to Maya's heart. "And here." She pointed to Maya's head. "I taught you how to love and I taught you how to think. I taught you everything you need to know, so you won't have to miss me. Because I'm still here through my teachings. You won't be alone, Maya. I'll always be your mother."

"And I'll always be your daughter. Your proud daughter." Maya smiled, kissing her mother's forehead before lying down on the bed with her mother.

Grace smiled at the gesture and rubbed her daughter's back as she hugged her. "And one more thing …" Maya looked up at her mother expectantly. "Make sure your coffee tastes amazing, Maya."

Maya smiled. "It will be the best tasting coffee life could make, I promise."

Grace smiled. "And that's all I want for you." She said. "The best."

Autumn was in the living room with Elena, resting on the couch while Elena sketched Autumn in her sketchpad.

"See? There are total benefits to me being paralyzed. Now you know for sure I won't move." Autumn joked.

Elena turned to look at Autumn and snorted. "That is a really bad joke."

Autumn laughed. "Well I'm laughing so it's a great joke."

Elena rolled her eyes. "That's because your sense of humor is the darkest thing ever." Elena said as she drew Autumn's eyes.

"Perhaps. But I also laugh at every lame joke you make." Autumn smiled.

"Hey! My jokes are a work of art!" Elena defended with a laugh.

"Sorry babe, but that's not the kind of art you should focus on." Autumn teased with a giggle.

Elena pouted. "Meanie."

Autumn smiled softly. "I know." She paused. "I have something to tell you. Two things. Good news and…bad news."

Elena stopped sketching and turned to look at Autumn, her heart pounding. "Okay…"

"Well, the good news is I'm getting surgery in my eyes…and it's very likely I'll retain my eyesight back." Autumn smiled.

Elena's eyes widened and she broke out into a wide grin. "Oh my god! Autumn!" she wrapped her arms around Autumn and laughed. "That's amazing! You're going to see again." She paused. "You're going to see *me*." Her eyes watered at the thought.

Autumn smiled and hugged Elena back. "I already see you Elena, but now it'll be in the physical form. But I see you. And you're beautiful." She whispered.

Elena blushed. "Can I kiss you?"

"Of course."

Elena smiled and pressed her lips against Autumn's cold ones. "I'm happy for you." She paused. "But what's the bad news?"

Autumn bit her lip as took Elena's warm hand and squeezed it tightly. "I'm so sorry. I wish this wasn't happening. But it is."

Elena felt her heart beat faster at Autumn's words. "Autumn...what's going on? You're scaring me here..." Elena trailed off, looking at Autumn expectantly.

Autumn took a deep breath before telling Elena the news she wished she didn't have to give her. "I hate to tell you this...but my fight is over." Autumn told her. "I'm terminal. I have maybe a year...or less. I don't know. But it's not much." She pursed her lips. "I'm so sorry."

Elena stared at her for a couple seconds before her eyes watered. "You're lying…" she croaked. "You're lying to me…this is some sick joke. You're not dying. You're not!" Elena exclaimed.

"Elena…"

Elena shook her head. "No! I can't! I can't lose you too!" Elena cried. "I love you…"

"And I wish that was enough to cure me Ellie, I really do." Autumn told her, hugging the girl. "But it's the end for me. But not yet. I still have time, and that time we're going to spend it well. And you're going to teach me more concepts like the amazing 'whatever'." Autumn chuckled. "And you're going to fix my entire life, remember? You already have. You already made such a big impact on me Elena. You're the best thing that's ever happened to me." She smiled. "Don't be sad…because I'm not sad. I'm not. I'm going to be okay. My death will be okay. I won't die miserably. I'll die the happiest girl alive, and *you* did that Elena Díaz…you did that."

CHAPTER TWENTY-TWO

At the news of Grace's death, Phoenix, Elena, Autumn, and surprisingly even Emma immediately wanted to visit Maya to comfort their best friend.

"Thanks for coming guys, I know how hard it is for some of you to come here." Maya spoke, glancing at Autumn and then Emma. Autumn was obviously appearing worse.

"It's…" Autumn took in some air before continuing. "… no problem Maya, we want to be here for you in this hard time." Autumn told her. Elena rubbed her back soothingly and Autumn smiled softly at the gesture. "Thank you." She whispered to Elena, knowing it was Elena's touch.

Emma smiled gently at Autumn, feeling terrible for having abandoned Autumn. But she was getting better now; she had been sober for almost a week now which was a huge accomplishment despite having the severe temptation to drink again at times. But she found ways to distract herself, she started baking again. It was a huge passion of hers and she wanted to get back to it. And she also wrote her feelings down in a journal.

Riley told her it was important for her to not be selfless and keep her feelings to herself. Emma had also started dabbling in photography, going for long walks with Ethan or Riley to take pictures. Ethan had shown her immense support with her decision to be sober and even stopped going to parties like Emma to avoid drinking. He wasn't an alcoholic, but he didn't want to tempt Emma by her seeing him drinking.

Things were going well for Emma, but she wanted to patch things up completely.

"Um, can I say something? I know this is about Maya, and I am incredibly sorry for the loss of your mother...but I want to patch things up between us. Because I know that we broke apart for a while due to personal issues we all were dealing with." Emma said.

Maya nodded. "Please say something, Emma. I'm not all for talking about death right now. And I think patching things up is a good idea right now. I've received too many flowers and condolences lately, so something different would be nice." She smiled to Emma and nodded encouragingly.

"Are you sure?" Emma asked, uncertain.

"Please open your mouth and get yapping, Brooks." Phoenix told the girl playfully.

Emma nodded before taking a deep breath and repeating the same story she's told countless times lately. She glanced at Autumn and Elena occasionally who were paying attention and Elena smiled for her to continue when Emma would pause. She let out a shaky breath she didn't even know she was holding when she was finished.

"But yeah…I'm doing so much better now." Emma told the girls. "Things are looking up for me and I want you guys to be around while I recover."

"Of course Emma, we'll be here for you every step of the way." Elena smiled with a nod, squeezing Autumn's hand. Autumn nodded as well, smiling shyly.

"Come here shorty!" Phoenix hugged Emma who laughed as she hugged the girl back.

"I missed you guys. And this…just…hanging out." Emma confessed with a smile.

"Same, and I think we all need this. It's good therapy to annoy each other." Maya chuckled, surprised to be in a good mood despite the circumstances of having lost her mother recently. But it was definitely better than hiding in her room and crying her eyes out.

The girls continued talking absentmindedly and Emma hesitantly stood up and walked to Autumn and Elena. "Hey…um…do you think I could talk to you, Autumn? Privately?" she asked.

Elena nodded. "If Autumn wants to, then by all means."

Autumn nodded. "Of course, lead the way Emma." She smiled softly as Emma pushed Autumn to the other room to talk to her.

"I feel like a pretty terrible friend, I didn't even know you were in a wheelchair now…" Emma said.

"It's okay, you know now." Autumn smiled softly. "And it's not all that bad." She paused. "I'm getting eye surgery in about a month or so. I'm getting my sight back."

Emma broke out into a smile. "Oh my god…that's…" her eyes watered. "That's really amazing."

Autumn nodded and smiled softly. "It is." She paused. "So…say what you need to say Emms."

Emma cleared her throat and nodded. "Of course, right." She gulped. "I just wanted to say I'm sorry. For…everything. For pushing you away when you got sick again…for resenting you while you resented the world. I just wanted to help you, and you wouldn't let me and that frustrated me. But I want us to start over. I want us to be what we've always been…best friends." Emma bit her lip. "I want my Autumn back, if you'd like to of course."

"I'll only forgive you if you forgive me." Autumn told her with a smile. "I've treated you the worst and I know I'm a huge reason to why you started drinking in the first place. So forgive me too. I want us to be not only best friends again, but sisters. Just like we use to be." She smiled. "I'll always forgive you, because you're my sister, Emma."

Emma nodded and felt a tear roll down her cheek before embracing Autumn in a hug. "Of course I forgive you Autumn. You're my sister too. And you always will be." She kissed Autumn's forehead before hugging her again.

"Good." Autumn quipped. "We should probably head back before they think I murdered you." She joked.

"That's a terrible joke Autumn, we *just* made up. Come on." Emma laughed as she pushed Autumn's wheelchair back to the living room.

"Oh good, you're back! I have news for myself to tell you. It's pretty exciting." Phoenix shared with an excited grin.

"Just tell us Nix!" Elena laughed. "She's literally been such a tease—in the most nonsexual way possible."

"But I bet you'd love it if it was sexual." Phoenix winked.

Elena rolled her eyes. "Sorry girl, I'm taken and you're straight as an arrow."

"Arrows can bend."

"Yeah, and then they break. Try again Phoenix, you're straight as fuck." Elena laughed.

Phoenix scoffed before waving her off. "Okay whatever. So…" she began. "as you guys know, I've been homeless." She smiled. "Well, dad got a promotion, and he's been making a lot more money…we're going to move into an apartment." She told them. "*And I'm getting my own room PRAISE IT!*" Phoenix exclaimed.

The rest of the girls broke into wide grins and cheered for the girl. "That's amazing!" Maya exclaimed with a grin. "Now we can go annoy you at your place."

"Yeah, Ellie and I will go have sex in your bed." Autumn blurted out with a smirk. Phoenix, Emma, and Maya's eyes widened as they burst into laughter at the girl's unexpected words.

"Autumn!" Elena blushed heavily, smacking Autumn's arm.

Autumn laughed. "I was just kidding!"

Phoenix smirked, laughing. "I am not letting y'all use my new mattress."

"We could break it in." Autumn smirked.

"AUTUMN!" Elena felt her face turn red while Maya and Phoenix were laughing uncontrollably.

Phoenix laughed. "More like *break it*. I know you lesbians go all or nothing when it comes to sex."

"Shut up, Phoenix." Elena threw a pillow towards her before smacking Autumn again. "And *you*!" she exclaimed before giving a goofy smile. "I love you." She giggled.

Autumn giggled and felt her face turn warm. "I love you too."

The rest of the girl's continued with their banter before Autumn called Maya over to her.

"What's up, Autumn?" Maya asked.

"For the funeral, do you think I can write a song for your mother and you?" Autumn asked softly. "I have a song in my head that I really think could help you while you grieve…" Autumn trailed off. "But if you don't want me to, I understand."

Maya smiled, touched by the gesture Autumn had in mind. "You really mean it?"

Autumn nodded. "Of course, I know this isn't an easy time for you and I want to help you in one of the few ways I can." She shrugged.

Maya bit her lip and nodded. "By all means then, you definitely can. Thank you, it means a lot to me…" she trailed off, feeling her eyes water. "You're a good person, Autumn Castillo."

Autumn shrugged before taking a deep breath. "I'm trying to be."

———————————

The day of the funeral approached and it was just like any other funeral, only a different dead person and a different pain. Everyone was wearing black and there wasn't a dry eye in the room. Elena squeezed Autumn's hand as the funeral went on until it was time for Maya to speak.

The girl had on a simple black dress and only mascara as make up as she stepped up to the podium. "My mom…" she began, turning to look at the casket. "She was the greatest woman to ever live. And I use to always joke and say it was Beyoncé—and she is. One of the greatest. But not *the* greatest. My mother, she loved me unconditionally, the kind of love every person strived to have. Despite her sickness, she always made sure to be there for me. She was my rock, she kept me together. And she still does. Because she's still here.

I know my mom wouldn't miss out on her own funeral, especially to make sure she looks good." Maya joked, causing a couple of chuckles in the audience.

Maya looked towards the audience with teary eyes. "The sad reality is…she's going to miss out seeing me grow up and become the woman she and my father raised. She's going to miss me graduate high school, college, medical school…she's going to miss my wedding…she's going to miss seeing me be a mother myself. She's going to miss the rest of my life. And that's the painful part. I won't have this amazing woman that I strive to be by my side. Just memories. I know she's still going to be here. She told me, but it won't be in the way I need her to be."

Her voice cracked. "You know I realized that when you lose someone, you lose yourself with them. A part of you is lost with them, and you don't get it back until you see them again. So, I hope you're waiting patiently up there mom." Tears streamed down her face. "Because I'll see you when I'm old and wrinkly, so don't make fun of my white hair when I get it. It's very chic." Maya joked with a laugh before wiping her eyes. "I love you so much, and everything I do from now on, I'll think of you." Maya said as she cried.

She composed herself after a couple minutes and wiped away her tears with her thumb. "Um…a friend of mine has written a song and she's going to perform it with my other amazing friend." She nodded to Phoenix and Autumn. "Take it away, girls." She said before walking off the podium.

Phoenix stood up and pushed Autumn's wheelchair towards the grand piano, moving the bench and situating Autumn by the piano keys. She sat down on the piano bench beside Autumn and grabbed one of the microphones handed to her before clearing her throat.

"Hi, I'm Phoenix. I'm one of Maya's best friends." Phoenix introduced herself before placing the microphone in front of Autumn's mouth. "Say something."

Autumn bit her lip. "Hi, I'm Autumn. And we wrote a song dedicated to Maya and her mother. I would sing, but singing in front of people terrifies me so Phoenix here will blow it out of the water." She wheezed. "So, Maya's mom...hi. I hope you're doing great and I hope you enjoy this song. Thank you for existing." She smiled softly before beginning to play the keys of the piano effortlessly.

Phoenix turned to her and nodded with a smile before bringing the microphone up to her lips. She took a deep breath and began to sing and looking directly at Maya.

Maya was already crying as she listened to the song that she immediately related to as she heard lyrics. She would give anything for more time with her mother, but she knew she had to go. And that was the hardest part, letting go of the things you care about.

Maya wiped away tears. Maya hoped she wouldn't forget her mother or anything that had to with her. She didn't want to forget how she looked like, how she smiled, how she laughed, how she cried, she didn't want to forget her words of wisdom, her humor. She wanted to remember it all. She wanted to remember her voice.

When Phoenix finished the song, Maya immediately jumped up and ran to Phoenix and Autumn and hugged them both.

"Thank you." Maya sobbed.

Elena watched the performance with tears streaming down her face. That's when it hit her. Looking around the funeral, she realized that soon this would be her reality too. Soon, she'd be the one crying over Autumn and desperately willing to give anything for more time with her. She'd be the one afraid to let go of her rock.

She gulped, getting up and running out of the funeral home and crying wretchedly in the front steps as she realized soon Autumn would die. Soon, Autumn would be in a casket.

Soon, she'd lose the love of her life.

"You left the funeral." Autumn spoke up, days after the funeral.

Elena turned to her, currently doing her homework at Autumn's house. "I had my reasons." She said simply.

"Then tell me them." Autumn responded, patting the spot next to her.

Elena bit her lip. "I don't know…"

"You can't expect anything to get better if you don't say anything Ellie." Autumn told her. "*You* told me that." She smiled softly. "Come on, talk to me. It's your turn to be helped."

Elena slowly put aside her homework and crawled next to Autumn, cuddling next to her and inhaling Autumn's scent. Soon, she'd forget it.

Autumn hugged the girl. "Just tell me everything, I'm all ears. I'm a great listener." She smiled gently.

Elena took off Autumn's glasses and put them aside as she looked into Autumn's eyes and bit her lip, her eyes watering. She'd forget what they'd look like too. "I can't lose you too." Her voice cracked. "Going to the funeral, it just reminds me that soon that's going to be me. *I'm* going to be the one crying my eyes out for *you*. *I'm* going to be the one with a hole in my heart because *you're* no longer going to be here to fill it. I'm going to lose you too." Elena started to cry.

Autumn felt her heart break at the words. It wasn't dying she was afraid of, it was the people she left behind to pick up the pieces left of her. "I wish I could say it's going to be okay, Elena. I wish I could say I'm not dying. But it's going to happen. I'm going to die. And I'm sorry there's nothing I could do to change that reality. Believe me, I want to live. I want to be with you and get married and everything. I want to do everything with you, but I can't. We don't have much time. But you know what? We're going to use whatever time we have left and make the most of it. Okay? We're going to have adventures and do everything and anything. I'm going to get out there and live, with you. Okay?"

Elena listened and nodded. "Okay…" she cried more. "I just can't lose you too…" she trailed off, biting her lip. "I can't go to more funerals…" Elena whimpered. Elena looked up to look at Autumn and Autumn smiled gently when she felt Elena looking at her.

"You can tell me." Autumn nodded, urging her to continue.

Elena gulped before taking a leap of faith and telling Autumn. "I hav—*had* a best friend. Her name was Hailey Gorman and I knew her for 11 years before she killed herself." Elena closed her eyes to resist the urge to cry more. "People are mean…they told her things. Mean things. It got to her too much. She started cutting…she started trying to lose weight by purging or starving herself. She was depressed. And then one day…she couldn't take it anymore and she took pills and slit her wrists. I found her dead. I had an art show and I didn't answer her phone calls. If I would've answered…she'd still be here. I'd still have a best friend…"

Autumn frowned at what Elena told her. "It's not your fault, you know. She chose to end her life and that's not because you didn't answer your phone. She was done, and you couldn't have stopped it. It's not your fault, you can't blame yourself for her choices."

"But—"

"Ellie." Autumn cut off. "It's not your fault. She chose to go. You need to give yourself that closure. You need to let this go. She's gone, and the only thing you can do is reminisce 11 years you had with her."

Elena shook her head. "I could've fixed her—"

"Elena, you can't fix people. You can't put together pieces on your own, they have to do for themselves. You can only push them in the right direction and hope they keep walking it. You tried, and that's that. You tried your hardest but she made the decision that enough was enough and ended her life and you can't hold yourself accountable for that, Ellie." Autumn told her.

"You don't understand…"

"Then help me understand."

Elena's eyes watered. "I want to fix other people because I can't fix myself."

"I'll send you to the right direction."

Later that night, Autumn lied in her bed and clutched onto Elena's letter that she had given her a couple months ago at Christmas. Elena said to read it when she felt like she needed to and at this point, she needed to.

She slowly opened the letter and pulled herself up, struggling for a bit before placing the letter on her lap and feeling the dots on her fingers. She began running her fingers as she read in braille Elena's letter.

Autumn,

It's snowing right now as I write this, my windowsill looks like a snow fairy came and sprinkled glitter and ice together. It's a pretty sight, I figured you'd like to think about that. It's nice to think about nice things sometimes, it makes you forget the bad things temporarily.

You know what snow also reminds me of? People.

I know that sounds weird, but snow reminds me of people. People can be the hard and dirty kind of snow, you know...the kind of snow you see on the street that can break your arm as you try to gather some or get you completely dirty with how mushy and gross it is. It's hard to touch, hard to get through. Not to mention it's cold as fuck.

But that's how people are sometimes, cold and hard to get through.

But snow can also be soft, like when it first falls from the sky and it's just sparkling. It looks like the most beautiful blanket of glitter before it becomes blemished. There's an innocent feel to fresh snow, because it hasn't been damaged yet. It has yet to be stepped on by people with their dirty shoes and or driven on by dirty cars or peed on by dogs...and people. And that's how people are at first.

Snow also melts eventually by warmth. And then spring comes and flowers bloom and leaves grow and sun shines and everything is perfect again.

But that's not the point, the point is...you remind me of snow sometimes, Autumn. When I first met you, you were the damaged kind of snow. The one I didn't want to step on and dirty myself with. But I took the chance anyway and eventually, fresh snow came in and replaced the dirty snow.

And now nothing can hurt you...

I thought anyway.

Before the cancer...

You know, I'm damaged snow too.

I'm dirty and messy and hard to get through. There's things in my life you don't know about that made me that way, and I think everyone at some point becomes dirty, hard snow that gets stepped on. The only thing hopeful about it that a fresh layer of snow replaced the dirty snow. And then eventually that layer is forgotten and you're okay again. But my fresh snow is taking a while to replace the damaged snow.

You help though, Autumn. And I know you think that I've helped you the most, but you don't realize the effect you've had on me. You've helped me too.

You make me feel like a work of art.

Like, I'm good enough to be taken a glance or two at.

Like I'm worth the time to be deciphered piece by piece until the meaning of who I am is uncovered.

Like I'm beautiful even if there was a wrong color painted on me or I was sculpted the wrong way or there was a tear or two in me.

You make me feel I'm a masterpiece. And all you had to do was tell me you were playing "Moonlight Sonata" by Beethoven when we first met. Even then, you made me feel acknowledged.

I didn't use to feel that way.

But you painted a fresh layer on me, you painted brighter colors in my soul. I'm rejuvenated, Autumn. And you did that. YOU.

You loved me by looking through the physical part of me and focusing on the emotional part. You see my feelings and yet you still find them beautiful.

And me? I learned to be blind, but not fucking stupid. I learned to look at you and not just see your physical beauty, but your beautiful mind.

I don't have to look at you to tell you I love you. Because those three words are not something you can see. They're something to express.

I learned how to say I love you in the way I kiss you, in the way I touch you, and in the way I speak to you. I don't need my eyes to tell you I love you because the rest of me has figured it all out. And that's because of you.

You don't give yourself enough credit, Autumn, because I think you've helped me more than I've helped you.

And I just want you to know that no matter what happens…my heart will always belong to you, it's yours forever. Even when my heart stops beating, it will still be yours. I'm yours, Autumn. There's no one else I want but you.

Even if you do die because of this wretched disease in your body, even if time is limited with you...my heart will be yours. And it will be for no one else but you.

So for Christmas, I not only gave you some vinyls...but I also give you my heart.

I'm yours forever, Autumn Castillo.

Your work of art,

Elena

Underneath the letter, Autumn felt a pop up heart. Autumn smiled, wiping away tears streaming down her face from reading the touching letter.

"My heart belongs to you too, Elena Díaz." Autumn whispered. "Forever."

———————————————————

After rereading Elena's letter multiple times, Autumn eventually fell asleep. It was way past midnight when it happened.

One moment, she was fine. The next, she felt like her lungs were on fire and smoke was closing up her airways.

It was a wretched pain, the kind of pain that makes you scream until you feel better. But the thing was, the more Autumn screamed...the worse she felt.

Autumn screamed out in pain as she clutched onto her chest, she gasped for her air...but she couldn't find any. She felt like she was suffocating.

Moments later, she heard footsteps run into her room. Her parents quickly attended to her.

"Baby, what's wrong?" Cora asked softly, trying to remain calm for her daughter.

Autumn only responded by gasping for air.

"She's turning blue, Cora." Joseph spoke, quickly picking Autumn up. "She can't breathe, we have to go to the hospital."

Cora nodded, biting her lip as she reached for Autumn's inhaler and placed it against Autumn's lips. She pressed it and tried to give Autumn some air which helped a little, but didn't help enough.

Dylan and Olivia rushed downstairs with worried looks on their faces as they looked at their older sister.

"What's going on?" Dylan asked, his voice cracking.

"Autumn can't breathe, we're going to the hospital. Stay here, we'll be back." Cora said before opening the door for Joseph as they rushed inside the car. Cora seated herself in the back with Autumn, placing her daughter's head on her lap.

Autumn screamed in pain, tears streaming down her face.

"Shhhh…it's okay." Cora whispered to her as Joseph sped off to the hospital. "You're going to be okay, baby." She placed the inhaler to Autumn's blue lips again. "This will all be over soon."

CHAPTER TWENTY-THREE

"Thanks for the scare, Loser. I knew I needed a heart attack or two this week." Phoenix spoke up as the girls visited Autumn after going to the hospital when she got an infection in her lungs that was taken care of.

Autumn chuckled. "You know I can't not give you guys a scare or two, it's all part of the Autumn Castillo package." Autumn joked.

Emma snorted. "You're an idiot, your jokes aren't funny." She teased before shrugging. "But honestly, as long as you get better…I'm okay with the tiny scares."

Elena bit her lip as she glanced at Autumn who had bowed her head. "About that…" Autumn trailed off. "There's something I need to tell you." She whispered.

Phoenix, Maya, and Emma all looked at each other with confused looks as they turned to Autumn. "What do you have to tell us?" Maya asked, having a bad feeling about this.

Autumn sighed, squeezing Elena's hand. "I'm dying." She admitted, biting her lip. "I have about a year or less to live…" she said, gulping.

The room grew silent, the silence they wish they didn't have to experience. "Are you fucking around with us? That's a really bad joke Autumn—"Phoenix began.

"It's not a joke." Elena spoke this time, squeezing Autumn's hand.

The three girls turned to Elena. "You knew?" Phoenix asked.

Elena nodded. "She told me...trust me, you guys are reacting to this better than I did." She replied.

Emma felt her lower lip tremble, just when things were getting better...just when she was regaining her friendship with Autumn...just like that. It just goes away.

Maya patted Autumn's free hand. "If it's better this way, then we just make the most of the time you have left. If there's nothing they can do, then we just have to live with the reality that no one ever gets what they want. But that doesn't mean we have to accept it with a frown, take it with stride. You can die with a peaceful mind. My mother did, and we'll make sure you do too." Maya smiled sadly, realizing she'd lose someone else soon.

Autumn smiled softly. "Thanks Maya, I plan on making the best out of what remains of my life. And think of it this way guys, my surgery is set to happen in two weeks. And then a month after...I get my sight back." She told them. "I'm going to die, yeah, but I'll die knowing I got to experience life with all my senses. I'll die seeing all of you guys, and that's a reassuring feeling knowing that I won more than I lost. So don't be sad, no tears. Save those for when you need them. But not for right now, I want fucking smiles, got it?" she said, playfully threatening them.

Everyone chuckled and Elena kissed her cheek with a smile. "All smiles." She whispered before the girls continued talking and hanging out until everyone but Emma left.

"So you're really going to die?" Emma spoke up after the two girls had a few simple conversations to pass the time. Her eyes watered at the thought of losing Autumn.

Autumn frowned, nodding. "Yes. I'm so sorry, you know I didn't want this. Of course I want to live, but I'm not afraid to die either. There's a mystery to death and it's something I don't mind discovering." She smiled softly.

Emma felt a tear roll down her cheek. "I can't lose my best friend Autumn…" her voice cracked. "Not when I just got you back."

Autumn reached her hand out to look for Emma's, clutching onto it when she found it. "Hey…you're not going to lose me. I'm your best friend and I'll never stop being your best friend. Fuck what I said about death, it can kiss my ass. I'll always be your friend and death won't come in between it."

Emma smiled softly at Autumn's words and chuckled. "You'll always be my best friend too, Autumn, that's never going to change."

Autumn smiled, opening her arms so Emma could hug her. Emma smiled and quickly hugged the girl tightly. "I love you, Emma. You're the bestest sister from another mister I could've had. And I fully intend on showing that from here on out."

Emma smiled, breaking the hug and kissing her forehead. "I'm glad." She whispered.

"Also, I have a surprise. For all of us." Autumn told her.

Emma raised an eyebrow, but nodded. "Okay…"

"What's the place I want to visit most in the world?" Autumn asked.

Emma thought for a moment. "Italy?" she guessed.

Autumn nodded with a smile. "Yup…"

"Okay, what are you going with this? Do you want go get pizza with the girls or something?" Emma asked, confused.

"Yes, in Italy." Autumn said with a smirk.

"Um…it's nice to have dreams, I guess. But we can't afford to go to Italy. Phoenix literally is just getting back up on her feet and—"

"I have a wish I haven't used. You know, the perks of being a cancer kid. They give you a wish to use before you die and I talked to this cancer foundation where they grant wishes and told them about my wish and they said yes." Autumn explained.

Emma stared at Autumn with a confused look on her face. "Okay, I'm confused."

Autumn chuckled. "We're going to Italy in four months. I'd start packing a bag."

Emma's eyes widened and she screamed. Autumn jumped when she heard the scream. "Holy shit! Will you chill?" she exclaimed, laughing anyway.

Emma squealed. "We're all going to Italy? As in—"

"My parents, Olivia, Dylan, Ellie, you, Maya, Phoenix, and me. Yup." Autumn nodded with a smile. It only caused for Emma to scream again in excitement and Autumn burst out into a fit of giggles at how excited her best friend was.

———————————————

Elena was in the art room at school working on a painting, the usual light in her eyes that flickered as she created an art piece was fading since Autumn's diagnosis.

The spark she use to carry as she created the art she use to take so much pride in was gone, now she was left with sadness and that's what she displayed in her paintings. Especially the one she was working on of a woman who appeared to be crying, her eyes red and puffy.

"So much sadness in her eyes." A voice spoke up from behind.

Elena turned around and saw Mrs. Freya standing behind her with her arms crossed as she observed the painting. "She's crying, obviously."

Mrs. Freya hummed. "I wonder if the person painting carries that same sadness the figure in the painting possesses."

Elena pursed her lips. "It's a high chance that the artist does." She said simply.

"Why?"

"I don't know—"

"What did I say, Elena?" Mrs. Freya interrupted. "Artists don't settle with 'I don't know'. You *do* know. You know your motives behind your painting. So explain them. I want to know what the painting is trying to give me."

Elena's grip on the paintbrush tightened and her jaw clenched. "She's sad and angry." She snapped. "She's pissed off at the world because it takes everything she loves away!" she yelled, angrily beginning to splatter paint into the painting, the detailed painting becoming covered in fresh, black paint. "And, and the world thinks she can handle it but she can't! She fucking can't! She's only breaking more and more and she won't be able to take it..." Elena started crying. "She won't..." she fell to her knees and started sobbing uncontrollably.

Mrs. Freya immediately kneeled beside her and enveloped her in a hug. She muttered comforting words to Elena while the girl cried until she looked like the painting she destroyed. Her eyes were red rimmed and puffy, having cried for a long time.

"Autumn's dying." Elena whispered.

"I know." Mrs. Freya whispered back, rubbing the girl's back.

"I'm going to lose her too."

Mrs. Freya shook her head. "You don't lose people, Elena. Losing people means you don't ever see them again, and you will see them again. You just have to wait until that happens. Losing things and gaining things is just a part of life, and it does suck. But it's life, and you have to keep living it. Autumn isn't gone yet, Elena. She's still here. You can't dwell on what's going to happen because it hasn't happened yet. People get so stuck in living in the past or the future, they forget that the present is right in front of them. Carpe Diem, Elena, seize the day. Live now."

"How do you expect me to keep living in the now when I know what's going to happen?" Elena told her, wiping away tears.

"Remember what I told you when we first met?" Elena nodded. "Well you need to live by that. You need to live, Elena. You can't focus your life on things that are sad. If we all focused on the sad things in life, we'd all be miserable. There's no space for misery when the world out there is too big, and too beautiful."

Mrs. Freya advised. "So, as much as I love that you express yourself through art, you need to use your words too, Elena. Because an artist needs to be able to show and tell, do you get me? You need to be able to create your art just as much as to be able to explain it. You should do that with your emotions. Show them, and tell them."

Elena smiled softly at the words. "You're right…" she whispered.

"Everything will work out in the end, Elena. Even if you think it's not going to, it will. It's a bump in the road I know you can overcome. And I'm sure Autumn believes you can do that as well. Just spend time with her and enjoy it. When the time comes she has to go, you simply have to accept it. But until then…get out there kid, *live.*"

Mrs. Freya stood up and went to her desk, coming back with a flyer for an art show. "You can start with this." She smiled softly. "There's an art show and every school gets to pick one student to present their artwork. There will be a lot of art critics and art schools there, and I am picking you to participate. I think if anyone can blow this out of the water, it's you."

Elena's jaw opened. "Are you serious?" she whispered.

"Do you think I just threw this shit out to everyone? Hell no, I pick people who won't embarrass me. And you won't do that with your art." Mrs. Freya joked, patting the girl's back. "You're capable of doing amazing things, Elena. I think it's about time you discovered it."

———————————————

Maya, Phoenix, and Emma were at a coffee shop working on a project and Emma glanced at her two friends and smiled. "Things are looking up, aren't they?" she spoke up.

Maya and Phoenix looked up from their work and smiled back at Emma. "I think so, yeah. I mean, look at us." Maya shrugged. "Just a while ago, we barely even acknowledged each other because we were so preoccupied with all our…issues. But now, now everything is good. We're all okay now, mostly, and I know things don't appear to be all that great, but it could be worse."

Phoenix nodded. "Like, Autumn. I mean, yeah, it's terrible that she's dying. But honestly, I hated seeing her suffering so much. I'm just going to make sure she has the best year of her life so that when she goes, it's with a smile on her face. Nobody should die sad, it's worse than dying itself."

Emma smiled sadly, looking down at her textbook. "I'm going to miss her so much…" she whispered.

"We all will." Maya reached over to squeeze Emma's hand. "But trust me, wishing for someone to stay because you need them is too selfish when they're suffering." She said. "I spent years researching and finding alternative treatment to save my mom's life. And I forgot that I wasn't the one dying most of the time, just because I needed my mom. And I still need her, but she's not suffering in a hospital bed anymore. And Autumn won't suffer anymore either. Look at her, she's in a wheelchair and her body is slowly dying…you can't tell me you want that for Autumn for the rest of her life."

"You're right…" Emma agreed. "I don't want to see Autumn suffer anymore." She paused. "I just…it's not fair that good people suffer the most."

"That's because good people can handle the suffering." Phoenix said.

"Look at you being wise and shit." Maya teased.

"Shut up, Maya." Phoenix playfully glared at her. "I'm plenty mature." She scoffed, flipping her hair.

Maya rolled her eyes and mocked Phoenix, flipping her own hair and scoffing. "Whatever." She mocked Phoenix.

Phoenix flicked her off. "Fuck you, okay."

"I have a boyfriend, sorry Phoenix. Maybe in another life." Maya laughed.

"Oh, white chocolate. Riiiiigggght." Phoenix smirked.

Maya rolled her eyes and threw a napkin at Phoenix. "Will you stop calling him that?" she chuckled. "He heard you call him that once and now he changed his contact name on my phone to 'White Chocolate'. You're influencing him, Phoenix. Stop."

"Well, what better influence than me?" Phoenix said cockily.

"I can think of a few people."

Emma laughed. "You two honestly…you're either bickering or proclaiming your love for each other."

"This is how our friendship works. If I don't make fun of Phoenix at least once a day, she'll think I'm being nice. We can't let that happen." Maya joked.

Emma snorted. "Well I'm glad we're all friends, teasing each other and all. I wouldn't ask for anyone else." She smiled. "I'm glad you guys decided to invite Autumn and me to sit with you guys when you did. If none of that ever happen, we wouldn't be as close and I don't know if Autumn and Elena would be dating."

Phoenix gasped dramatically, forming her fingers in a cross. "Don't say that satanic shit in front of me! Alena is much too blessed for that."

"And you wonder why we're embarrassed to be in public with you." Maya rolled her eyes.

"I'm hilarious, shut up." Phoenix elbowed Maya. "But honestly, Elena and Autumn is the cutest thing to ever exist. Autumn changed so much since she's been with Elena, she'd never say or do have the things she does. She's all cute and stuff, it's gross but still somehow appealing. I use to be afraid of that bitch, and now she makes me puke rainbows."

"Imagine how Elena must feel to lose all of that." Maya spoke, frowning at the realization.

The table grew quiet, all of them suddenly realizing the effect this would have on Elena. "Wow…you're right. Elena is so in love with Autumn…she's losing someone she gave her heart to." Emma sighed. "We have to be there for her when this all happens, we can't let her break. We have to all promise to be there for each other from here on out. We all have a special bond and we can't let that go again."

Maya and Phoenix nodded in agreement, crossing their hearts. "I promise." Both girls said in unison.

Emma smiled and nodded, crossing her own heart. "Me too." She whispered. "It's going to be hard when it happens, but we don't have to worry about that now. Right now, let's just enjoy time."

––––––––––––––––––––

"Ellie, where are we going?" Autumn giggled as Elena pushed Autumn into her house and to her art room. "Wait…I hear Celia Cruz playing…" Autumn trailed off and Elena rolled her eyes chuckling. Ana started to sing from her bedroom and Autumn giggled again.

"I hear your mom…we're at your house. But why I ask…why?" Autumn asked.

Elena laughed as she opened the door to her art shed. "We're going to have some fun." Autumn quirked an eyebrow and smirked. "Not that, you idiot."

"What did you expect me to think?" Autumn laughed.

"You're a 13 year old perv sometimes, I swear. Why am I dating you? Why?"

Autumn smirked. "Because you have a strange fetish for girls in wheelchairs." She replied, mustering up the most seductive voice she could make as she wiggled her eyebrows.

Elena laughed. "You're such a dork."

"But I'm *your* dork." Autumn pouted before pointing at her lips. "Now kiss your dork." She smiled before pecking her lips. "They're cold and blue and waiting for you!"

"I'm only going to kiss you right now because that was a clever rhyme, you clever son of a bitch." Elena joked before kissing Autumn's cold lips softly. "And because I love you, but that's extra information." She teased.

Autumn giggled before pulling Elena in for another kiss. "I love you." She whispered. "And I can't wait to see you." She smiled.

Elena smiled at Autumn's words. "And I can't wait for you to see me." She smiled. "But before you get your eyes back, let me be them one more time." She whispered.

Autumn raised an eyebrow. "What do you mean?"

"Let's make a painting, yeah?" Elena smiled.

Autumn smiled and nodded. "I'd love that." She whispered.

Elena nodded with a smile as she grabbed a fresh, white canvas and put it on her easel. She grabbed new paints and turned to Autumn. "We're going abstract, give me your hands." She said, grabbing the red paint and placing it on Autumn's hands. "It's red." She smiled.

Autumn smiled and nodded as Elena pushed her towards the canvas. "So what do I do?" she asked Elena as she felt the cold and sticky paint.

"Whatever you want. Just make the canvas come alive." Elena whispered to Autumn.

Autumn nodded with a grin before dipping her fingers in the paint and moving her red fingers all over the canvas, doing swirls with the red paint.

The feeling of the paint touching her fingers and her fingers touching the canvas made Autumn feel like she was doing something good, finally. She laughed and smiled as she splattered the remainder of the paint on the side of the canvas.

"Beautiful." Elena commented with a nod. "Absolutely beautiful."

"Come here." Autumn puckered her lips.

Elena laughed and leaned in to kiss Autumn again. Autumn giggled as she rubbed Elena's cheek with her paint-stained hand. Elena gasped and pouted. "AUTUMN ROSE CASTILLO!" she pretended to scold while Autumn laughed her butt off.

"Red suits you." Autumn teased.

Elena rolled her eyes before grabbing some yellow paint and pouring it on her hand and rubbing it on Autumn's cheeks and nose. Autumn protested while laughing. "Yellow suits you." She teased back before beginning to run her yellow fingers through the canvas.

Autumn laughed and reached her hands out before finding Elena's hips and pulling her down on her lap. Elena smiled and kissed her yellow cheek. "Our canvas looks pretty great."

Elena pulled the easel closer to them as she put more paint on Autumn's hands before guiding Autumn's hands and placing them on the canvas and moving her hands around.

"This is nice." Autumn smiled.

Elena smiled and nodded. "It is. I love being your eyes and describing everything to you."

"Well, you still are for the time being. How does our painting look?"

"There's a lot of yellow and reds and oranges." Elena started. "And there's a huge splatter on the side thanks to you. It looks like someone got shot, but whatever." She giggled. "And there are a lot of swirls and it looks like autumn when the trees are changing colors. And I find autumn to be a beautiful season because that's when I met you. I met you in autumn and fell in love with you in autumn and I will love you every other autumn after that. I'll love you in all four seasons." Elena smiled. "I think that's why you were named Autumn. I was meant to fall in love with a girl who reminded me of my favorite weather."

Autumn smiled at the words. "So we make orange, huh? It may be an ugly color, but it's my favorite color now." She said, intertwining her red hands with Elena's yellow ones and their paints mixing to make orange.

"We do." Elena whispered.

The two girls continued painting the canvas until every spot was colored in red, orange, and yellow. Elena smiled proudly at the painting. "We make a good team."

Autumn kissed Elena's shoulder. "We do." She agreed. "I love you. So much." She whispered.

Elena smiled. "I love you too."

Two weeks later, Autumn was in the hospital as nurses prepped her up for surgery. Her friends and family had come to support her and Elena held Autumn's hand the entire time. "Everything's going to be okay. It's going to go perfectly." Elena assured Autumn.

Autumn nodded. "I hope so. I can't wait to see all of you."

Phoenix smirked. "I don't know, I think once you see me you're going to be so mesmerized by my beauty you'll leave Lena over here for me." She flipped her hair.

"I'm blind, but I'm not stupid." Autumn teased, rolling her eyes while Elena mocked her and flipped her hair.

"She won't leave me. Once she sees my butt she won't." Elena smirked.

Autumn raised an eyebrow. "You have a nice butt?"

"Yes I do. It's the first thing Phoenix noticed." Elena laughed. "You have a very nice butt too." She smirked.

"I do? God, I don't even know how I look now. I just remember me being nine and weird looking."

"You still act like you're nine and you are a little weird looking." Cora spoke up with a laugh.

"Thanks mom, it's nice you show your support every step of the way." Autumn laughed.

"Oh but when *I* say something like that, you tell me to fuck off? Okay, I see how it is Autumn." Dylan scoffed.

"Dylan, language." Joseph scorned.

Autumn laughed as Joseph scorned Dylan. "And you're also Dylan, that's the difference." Autumn retorted. "And when I see you, I'm kicking your ass."

"Why?"

"For being Dylan."

"That seems fair." Olivia agreed with a laugh.

"Hey, you'll finally get to see how Lana Del Rey looks like." Maya added.

"I finally get to see my queen. Is she as beautiful as I imagine?" Autumn smiled.

"Calm down there, Autumn. Or Elena will get jealous." Phoenix teased.

Elena smacked her arm. "Do you really think Autumn will leave *this*?" Elena gestured to herself. "*Please!*"

"Okay, where is the sass coming from?" Autumn laughed.

"I woke up in a happy mood, okay? I'm excited for you." Elena smiled.

"Stop being cute, my doctor says I'm on the brink of diabetes because of you two." Phoenix teased.

"Good. You need some sweetness in your life." Elena smiled smugly.

"And you need some—oh wait Autumn's parental units are here. I can't say that." Phoenix zipped her lips.

Elena and Autumn blushed. "Phoenix, you're lucky I'm a cripple and I'm blind or else I'd shank you right now."

"Autumn!" Cora exclaimed.

"It's cool Mama C, when Autumn can see me. She's going to get it." Phoenix smirked playfully.

Cora laughed. "I might do it first."

"We can tag team so we both get a go at her."

"Sounds like a plan."

Autumn appeared offended. "So you'll hit a cripple? WHERE ARE YOUR MORALS?"

"Where yours are." Phoenix sassed.

"Shoot, let me call Satan. He has them. Along with my list of fucks I do not give."

"Please go under anesthesia. DOCTOR, GET THIS GIRL UNDER ANESTHESIA SHE'S ANNOYING ME." Phoenix exclaimed.

Everyone laughed at the witty banter between the two girls. They continued talking and joking around with Autumn until the nurses came in.

"All right Autumn, it's time to take you to the OR. The surgeon is ready for you." One of the nurses said.

Autumn nodded and everyone said their goodbyes before Elena turned to Autumn. "See you soon."

"Ditto." Autumn smiled widely.

Elena smiled and kissed her softly. "I love you."

"I love you too. And I can't wait to see you." Autumn told her.

"Ditto."

CHAPTER TWENTY-FOUR

Autumn thought of every possibility on how unsuccessful the surgery could be. She's had her share of disappointments with every alternative treatment or surgery for her eyes. And if by the time the bandages were taken off and she still saw the dark world she was accustomed to, it would just be another disappointment.

Disappointment was something she was quite accustomed to, especially in regards to her health. So she tried not to get her hopes up that the surgery would be successful.

But she did anyway.

And how could she not? Everything... it just felt right. It felt like it was all coming into place. There couldn't be room for disappointment, not this time around. She hoped. Autumn never hoped for anything, but *God*, she *really* hoped this surgery worked.

She wanted to see the world before she left. Autumn wanted to see the flowers bloom in the spring, the beauty of summer in the scorching heat, the leaves change colors and fall when autumn came, the white snow fall from the sky...

But more than anything, she wanted to see the most beautiful wonder in the world. The most beautiful work of art not even the most talented artist could recreate if they tried...

That, was Elena Díaz. The most beautiful masterpiece to ever come across earth.

Autumn knew she was beautiful, she didn't need eyes to see it. But she wanted to see the girl that changed her life for the better. She wanted to see the girl that showed her the concept of "whatever" and shared her many theories on life and just...loved her.

She wanted to see the girl she was madly in love with.

She wanted to see the girl that made her believe in true love because she found it. Autumn found true love with Elena and she'd never find it with anyone. Even if she lived to be 110, by some strange miracle, there'd be no one she could love more fiercely than Elena.

Elena was her person. She was the girl she talked to on the phone until three in the morning, and they'd have conversations about the importance of Oreos in society or something as ridiculous as that. But she was also the girl she could talk about the beauty of the universe or the beauty of life. She was the girl she could cuddle with but also laugh with until she was red. She was the girl that made her start singing again. She was the girl she wanted to write songs about forever.

Elena…she was *the* girl.

There was no one else for her.

Autumn was in the hospital room where she had stayed recovering for the past month. The bandages were annoying to have covering her eyes, but if at the end of the day they helped give her sight, she wouldn't mind the minor sacrifice.

"Are you ready, Autumn?" Autumn's ophthalmologist asked. Her friends, her parents, her siblings, and Elena were here with her to support her on this—hopeful—miracle.

Autumn nodded. "I've been ready for a long time…please."

Elena squeezed her hand and smiled widely, feeling anxious for Autumn's bandages to come off. She had a lot of hope at the moment, a lot of hope that this surgery worked. Autumn smiled at the squeeze. "I love you." Elena told her in a whisper.

"I love you too. I can't wait to see you." Autumn whispered back with a wider smile.

The ophthalmologist began to unwrap the bandages in her eyes and Autumn blinked when she didn't feel the bandages anymore. "Okay, I'm going to put some drops in your eyes and tell me if you start seeing anything." The doctor told her as he tilted her head up and placed the drops on both her eyes, Autumn flinching when she initially felt the cold liquid spill in her eyes. She blinked rapidly as she moved her head back down.

"Do you see anything, Autumn?" the ophthalmologist asked.

Autumn blinked again, suddenly everything starting to become brighter and shapes becoming clearer to see until she saw that it was *people*. It was still slightly blurry, but she saw. She was looking, she was *seeing*.

Tears formed in her eyes and she nodded, tears spilling from her eyes. "Yes." She choked out. "I can see...I can see!" Autumn started crying. "Oh my god, I can see..." she choked out.

Everyone else started crying along with her. "Autumn, can you see me?" Elena spoke up, tears streaming down her face.

Autumn turned to the side to where she heard Elena's voice. Autumn gasped. "Holy shit, you're beautiful." Autumn smiled widely, moving to touch Elena's face. "You're so beautiful, Ellie." She whispered, tears spilling down her cheeks.

Elena laughed and her lower lip trembled as Autumn *looked* at her. Autumn was *actually* looking at her. "You see me?" her voice cracked.

"I've always seen you." Autumn replied in a soft voice.

Elena started to cry as she enveloped Autumn in a tight hug. "Miracles exist, don't they?"

Autumn nodded as she broke the hug so she could look at Elena again, never wanting to stop looking at something so beautiful. So *breathtaking*.

"They do…" Autumn whispered, never looking away from Elena. "I see you and, God, you're so beautiful."

"Okay, but you haven't seen *me* yet, Autumn, so turn your head over here." Phoenix spoke up, laughing.

Autumn looked away from Elena, holding Elena's hand tightly, and turned to look at everyone else. She recognized Emma and she broke into a wide grin. "Holy crap, Emma you're so short." Everyone burst into laughter.

Emma rolled her eyes. "Really? That's what you notice?" she laughed as she walked up to Autumn.

Autumn opened her arms for Emma to hug and the girl immediately embraced Autumn. "You can see again…" Emma smiled widely, tears streaming down her face.

"I see you, and you're beautiful too. But your stature Emma…" Autumn teased.

Emma smacked Autumn's arm. "Shut up." She laughed.

Autumn laughed along and turned to see her parents standing there. "Wow, you guys look old. Did I stress you out *that* much?"

Cora and Joseph laughed. "No, that was all Dylan." Joseph joked before hugging his daughter.

Dylan protested. "Hey!"

Autumn laughed before turning to Dylan with a big smile. "You're tall as hell, Dylan." She said. "But I can still beat your ass." She teased.

Dylan rolled his eyes before hugging Autumn tightly. "I'm so happy you can see again." He whispered. "You deserve this more than anyone, especially happiness."

Autumn hugged him tightly. "Thank you." She whispered back.

Olivia hugged Autumn next, crying into her sister's shoulder. Autumn hugged Olivia tightly before breaking the hug so she could take a close look at Olivia. "You're so big and beautiful, Liv." She smiled. "You don't look like a kid anymore, wow." She laughed.

Olivia laughed before her mother hugged Autumn next. "I have nothing to say, but I'm just so glad you can see my eyes again.

They're the same eyes that I fell in love with the moment you were put in my arms." She whispered, wiping away tears.

Autumn smiled as she looked at her mother and hugged her tightly. "I love you too, mom." She whispered.

"All right, no sentimental bullshit for me. Am I hot or not?" Phoenix joked, doing a little turn. Maya rolled her eyes and smacked her arm.

Autumn turned to Phoenix and laughed. "You are very hot, Phoenix. But not as hot as Ellie, sorry." She teased. Elena smirked at Phoenix and flipped her hair.

"I told you the butt is too great to let go."

"Oh I haven't seen that yet, turn around." Autumn laughed.

"All right, that's it. I'm done trying to be attractive to lesbians, bye." Phoenix scoffed before turning to leave but then turning back around with a laugh.

Maya rolled her eyes. "Get ready, she's embarrassing visually too." Maya laughed.

Autumn laughed. "I can tell." She giggled before turning to Elena again. "Hi, beautiful."

Elena blushed. "Hi."

"Can I kiss you?"

Elena broke into a wide grin as Autumn used the same words she used. "You don't even have to ask."

Autumn leaned in and pressed her lips against Elena's, she sighed in content as she looked at Elena. "I love you so much."

Elena smiled. "I love you too."

Autumn smiled before holding her hand out for Elena to shake. "I'm Autumn Castillo, nice to finally see you."

Elena laughed and shook her hand. "Elena Díaz, the feeling is mutual."

"I was serious about the butt thing, turn around."

Elena rolled her eyes and hugged Autumn tightly. "I'm so happy you can see again." She whispered. "You deserve this more than anyone."

Autumn smiled and hugged Elena back before looking at her again. "No, I don't deserve this as much as the next blind person. I just got lucky. But I'm so grateful. I'm going to look at every little thing possible. Especially since I don't have another chance to see it again."

Elena frowned slightly at the thought that resurfaced once again. She was so consumed with happiness that she forgot that

Autumn's sight was only temporary as well as her life, she'd lose her soon.

Autumn noticed Elena's frown and kissed her lips softly. "No sadness. This is a happy moment, we need to make as many happy moments together as we can. You can save the tears for later, but for now, I want to see your beautiful smile on your beautiful face." She smiled. "Beautiful people smile, so everyone should smile."

Elena couldn't help but break into a wide grin at the words and nodded. "All smiles, no frowns." She said simply.

Autumn nodded, kissing Elena's cheek. "All smiles, no frowns." She repeated with a smile.

Autumn continued talking with everyone happily as she looked them all directly in the eye. She might have seemed intimidating looking everyone directly in the eye, but she wanted to make sure everyone knew she was looking and she was seeing and she was observing and she was listening and she was here.

Autumn looked at Elena and smiled widely as she took in her appearance. Elena was such a beautiful girl, she didn't even have to try hard to be beautiful. She had this beauty that was just there. There wasn't anything complicated about it.

She adored Elena's eyes. It was like looking into two cups of warm, inviting, and sweet hot chocolate.

She adored Elena's lips. They were pink and full and so god damn kissable. Her lips spoke beautiful, poetic words. Every word that came out of her lips made her fall more in love with her with every word. And the smile that could outshine even the sun itself made Autumn realize that there are more beautiful things in life that you often forget to notice.

But Autumn noticed everything about Elena.

From the way she threw her head back in laughter when someone told a funny joke, to the way her nose crinkled when she was concentrating on something.

If she had to pick to look at something for the rest of her life, she'd choose Elena. Something as beautiful as her should always have someone looking at her and admiring her beauty. It pained her that she didn't have a long time to adore and look at Elena.

But she'd love her as much as she could for the time she did have left. And she'd look at her every chance she had.

Happy tears formed in her eyes as she gave Elena an adoring look.

Autumn was never surer in her life that she loved someone.

By the time spring vacation arrived, Elena was disappointed to know that she had to go back to Miami to visit family for spring break. Any other time, Elena would be ecstatic to go home. But this wasn't the right time, it wasn't. Not when she had limited time with Autumn.

Granted everyone had limited time, because no one was destined to live forever. But with Autumn, she had a time limit. She had seconds counting down and days disappearing one by one. And with each passing day, the inevitable was closer.

But regardless of being forced to come to Miami, she did enjoy being back home. Especially getting to visit the beach. The warm sand at her feet, the cool water, the sun shining down at her…it was perfect. It was home.

And being that she was in Miami, Autumn told her it'd be a good idea to visit Hailey one last time to give herself the closure she needed.

It took a lot of convincing, but she managed to convince herself to go. She hadn't visited the grave since she left Miami to move to New York.

But now here she was, walking to Hailey's grave with white lilies, Hailey's favorite flowers, in her hands.

Elena took a deep breath as she sat cross-legged in front of the grave.

In Loving Memory of

Hailey Gorman

December 11th, 1996 to April 24th, 2014

Beloved daughter, sister, and friend

"The young die too soon because their young hearts cannot grow old"

Elena placed the white lilies in front of the gravestone and placed a kiss on the stone. "Hey there, Hails." She whispered, sitting back down.

"Well, I guess I should catch you up on my life…right?" Elena questioned.

"Um…New York is great, you know? It's very big. And bright. And beautiful…you would've loved it." Elena smiled softly. "I remember you said we'd both live in New York City together in a shitty apartment barely making it as two starving artists." She chuckled, wiping away a tear. "We could've had that, you know, we could've chased our dreams and done it together."

It remained silent for a couple minutes as Elena tried to formulate her thoughts.

"God, I should've done something Hailey…I should've said something. I should've tried harder, I should've—"Elena stopped herself as she stared at the grave.

"I couldn't stop it, could I?" she whispered. "I mean, there was only so much I could do…right? Autumn said I can't fix people. And it sucks you couldn't be the exception."

It became silent again as Elena smiled.

"Speaking of, I met a girl. Autumn. You'd love her. She's amazing. I mean, we started off kind of rough but eventually, everything worked out. We found each other and we've been…hopelessly in love ever since." Elena told her as she filled Hailey in on everything they went through and their entire tragic love story.

"So yeah, I fell in love with a blind girl. But she wasn't blind, because she could see right through me. She knows me well and I know her well. We know each other incredibly well. And even though she can see now, I still love her the same way I did when I met her. And I'll love her even when she joins you up there…" Elena's voice cracked.

"Hails, why do you lose the people you love? Is it some kind of sick test if you can live without them? I mean, I always say if you can learn to live without something…it eventually comes back to you. But you're dead, Hailey, I can't get you back. But I learned to live without you…slowly. Am I going to have to do the same for Autumn? Am I just going to have to learn to live without her? I can't learn to live without someone I fell in love with. I can't learn to live without waking up next to her or seeing her smile at me or hearing her tell me she loves me. How can you live without love? How?"

Silence.

Elena sighed. "The sad part is…you do. You eventually move on…but I don't want to move on. It means forgetting. And I don't want to forget. Forgetting means accepting your reality…and I don't want to. I don't want to accept that I lost one important person in my life and I'm about to lose another important person."

Silence.

"Maybe I don't have to. Who says I need to forget you and Autumn? Who says I need to forget the good memories? I'll keep them in my heart. Even the sad things, because if you don't have sad things in your heart…you won't remember what made your sad in the first place and you'll keep going back to the sad thing. So…I'll keep a piece of my heart here for you, Hailey." Elena smiled.

Elena's mind drifted to back to the good memories in her heart that she had of Hailey, and how happy they made her feel. Like when her and Hailey made stupid short films with each other, or when Hailey dared her to climb the tree at her old house and she ended up breaking her leg that summer. Or when they'd sneak off late at night to the beach and talk about everything and nothing at the same time while playing with the sand and looking up at the stars. Hailey would always talk about how one day she'd travel to the moon and take Elena with her so Elena could paint the stars in greater details and she could film them.

Elena kissed the tombstone again and stood up. "Until next time, Hails."

The girls were surprised when Autumn suggested going out somewhere, since Autumn tended to stay home most of the time. But since Autumn regained her vision, she wanted to be everywhere. So now, the five girls were all seated in an Italian pizzeria eating pizza and Italian ice.

Phoenix was quick to catch on.

"Loser, what the fuck? You don't go out, what are we doing here?" Phoenix spoke up. "And let's not mention that you so happened to insist we come to this pizzeria that was owned by an actual Italian person who also sold Italian ice *and* played Italian music…what is going on?"

Autumn smirked at Emma who had a smile on her face. Autumn pushed up her black glasses up to her nose. She had to replace the sunglasses with prescription glasses since her vision wasn't 100%, but with the glasses they definitely made her see clearly.

"Playing Sherlock now, are we?" Autumn laughed, raising an eyebrow.

Phoenix groaned. "Lenaaaa! Tell your girlfriend to get to the damn point!"

Elena laughed before turning to Autumn. "Babe, you don't want to meet impatient Phoenix."

"Maybe I do." Autumn smirked.

Phoenix glared at her. "Listen to me Loser, I will kick your ass if you don't tell me what's going on."

"Okay, fine." Autumn smirked. "Stiamo andando a Italia, Phoenix Hale." Autumn laughed. (Translation: We're going to Italy, Phoenix Hale)

"AND WHAT THE FUCK DOES THAT MEAN?"

Autumn giggled.

"Girl, I can't even do well speaking English! What are you speaking. It sounds like Spanish." Phoenix told her.

"It's Italian, dumbass." Maya spoke, laughing. "But seriously, Autumn, when the fuck did you learn Italian?"

"I'm a gifted kid." Autumn shrugged. "What I lacked in health, I made up for in brains."

"All right prodigy, let's not side-track here. What's the news?" Phoenix said.

"I already told you, it's not my fault you can't speak Italian." Autumn smirked.

Phoenix's eye twitched. "I'm going to kill you." Phoenix spoke.

"I'm not scared of you, Phoenix Hale." Autumn laughed.

"And I'm not scared of you. Let's agree on that and just tell usssss. I'm getting frustrated here and I will break a chair." Phoenix pouted.

Autumn laughed. "All right fine, I'll tell you." Maya, Phoenix, and Elena looked at Autumn expectantly while Emma only smiled smugly. "Emma knows already but...we're going to Italy in a two, months."

"Okay Richie Rich, and with what money?" Maya laughed.

"Some cancer foundation for kids. The cancer perks, you know?" Autumn shrugged.

Everyone stared at her. "Wait…you're serious? We're all going to Italy?" Maya's eyes widened.

Autumn nodded. "Yup, and my parents , Olivia, and Dylan." She said casually as she took a bite of her pizza.

"Okay, so Italy as in located in Europe, Italy. As in Lizzie McGuire went to Rome, Italy. As in WHAT?" Elena exclaimed, nearly falling off her chair.

Autumn giggled at Elena and nodded, kissing her cheek. "We're going to Italy."

Elena nodded slowly and looked at the rest of the girls before they all started screaming in excitement.

"CIAO MOTHERFUCKERS I'M GOING TO ITALY!" Phoenix shouted, dancing in her seat.

"I'd start learning Italian if I were you, Phoenix Hale." Autumn laughed as she rubbed her ears from the piercing screams.

Phoenix turned to her. "Yeah, sure. Okay." She nodded. "Fuck you." Phoenix told her in an Italian accent.

CHAPTER TWENTY-FIVE

Phoenix pulled the covers off Autumn. "Get the fuck up, Castillo."

Autumn's eyes fluttered open and she groaned. "In case you forgot, I can't get up." Autumn gestured to her legs.

Phoenix laughed. "Oh shit, right. Well tumble. Stop, drop, and roll. Do something, but wake the fuck up. We're going out."

"I fucking hate you sometimes, I swear." Autumn glared at her as she reached for her glasses and put them on.

"Love you too, four eyes." Phoenix smirked.

Autumn pushed herself up. "Vaffanculo." (Translation: Fuck you)

"Oh so we're going back to Italian? Well I hate you too, asshole." Phoenix smirked as she looked through Autumn's closet. "Okay, do you have anything remotely fancy?"

Autumn laughed. "Why do I need something fancy?" she asked.

"It's a surprise, I'm not telling you." Phoenix replied with a smug smile.

"Now how do I know this isn't a trap and you plan for me to die sooner?" Autumn raised an eyebrow.

"You're taking me to Italy, I'm not killing you yet."

"*Yet.*"

"I'll kill you once you sign over everything you own to me in your will." Phoenix joked, taking out a simple black dress Autumn had. "This makes me puke less. Jesus, do you have anything *not* black?"

"Who says I'm writing a will and who says I'm adding you in it?"

"Because you love me."

"Mm."

"And what does *that* mean?" Phoenix laughed, enjoying the banter between the two.

"I don't love you." Autumn scowled for a few seconds before smiling cheekily. "I lah you." She cooed.

Phoenix laughed. "Wow that was so lame. Go back to being a bitch, Loser."

Autumn rolled her eyes. "Last time I try being nice to you." She chuckled.

Phoenix laughed. "Good, the idea of you being nice to *me* sounds repulsive." She smiled.

Autumn smirked. "I wouldn't treat you any other way, Phoenix Hale."

Phoenix chuckled, looking at Autumn with a smile. The idea that she wouldn't be able to have bickering sessions like these with Autumn truly saddened her. She grew very close with Autumn and the thought of losing her made her wish time could slow down and she'd have more time with Autumn.

Everyone was wishing more time with Autumn, she wasn't the only one.

Phoenix helped Autumn get ready while Autumn kept being an asshole and playfully insulting Phoenix in Italian and Spanish while Phoenix returned the words in English. This quickly became their thing.

Once Phoenix finished helping Autumn get ready, she put on the fancy red dress she brought over to take.

"Phoenix, tell me right now…is this a date? Are you finally admitting how extraordinarily gay you are for me?" Autumn teased as she sat in her wheelchair.

Phoenix laughed. "I would *never*." She gasped. "But it's not, you'll see. You'll like it. Elena planned it out for you."

Autumn smiled widely at the mention of Elena. "Really?"

Phoenix nodded. "Yup, that girl loves you so much. It's insane. But cute." She shrugged.

Autumn smiled sadly. "I know…"

Phoenix frowned slightly. "Hey, this isn't the time to dwell on anything." She smiled again. "You're going somewhere with me and you're going to have a fucking great time. Okay?"

Autumn nodded and smiled softly. "Okay." She whispered.

Autumn eventually found herself going inside one of Julliard's prestigious theatres after taking the subway here. "What are we doing here Phoenix—"

She stopped herself when they entered the theatre to see her friends and family all dressed to the nines as they stood up and clapped for her.

Elena walked up to her, wearing a white dress and her hair done up. She pecked Autumn's lips. "Hey musical prodigy." She greeted.

Autumn raised an eyebrow. "Ellie…what is this?"

Elena smiled. "We want to see the best pianist in the world give us a final performance." She told her. "Think you can do that?"

Autumn's mouth gaped. "Here?"

Elena chuckled and nodded. "Yes, here. I had to do a lot of begging and some bribing to get us to open this space for us. We have it for an hour so let's get this started babe." She smiled as she pushed Autumn up to the grand stage and placed her in front of the gorgeous black piano. Elena kissed her cheek. "Have fun, rock star." She whispered before going to take her seat.

Autumn looked towards her small audience and smiled when Maya, Phoenix, and Emma practically screamed for her. Autumn laughed and smiled over to her parents and siblings before sending a wink to Elena.

She took a deep breath before she tapped the microphone. "Hey, so…this is a very unexpected surprise." She chuckled. "But a great one, so thank you. This is something I composed a while back, so I hope you enjoy it." Autumn nodded.

Autumn closed her eyes and placed her fingers on the black and piano keys before her fingers gracefully moved quickly across the piano. She smiled widely as she played, always getting lost in the music whenever she played.

Whenever Autumn played the piano, there was only one way she could describe it: magical. Maybe she spent too much time with Elena and her obsession with fairy tales, but that's what she truly felt playing the piano.

Perhaps some piano fairies sprinkled magical fairy dust on her fingers and her heart.

Perhaps Autumn defeated the most evil dragon and gained the strongest powers of all from it.

Perhaps Autumn started believing that magic existed again.

Perhaps Autumn defeated something stronger than a dragon or an ogre...perhaps she defeated her inner demons.

And now? Now she had her happy ending. And no one could tell her otherwise.

Her fairy tale ending took a while to come, but now it was here and she wasn't letting go. Even death comes for her, she will hold on to her happiness. She will hold onto her fairy tales because fairy tales aren't just for little children, fairy tales are for people who need to believe that they too can defeat something as strong as a dragon and they too can find their happily ever after.

Fairy tales are meant for believing, and Autumn believed now more than ever three very important things:

1. Autumn was pretty fucking great at playing the piano and writing music.
2. Autumn could love as fiercely as the next person, if not *more*.
3. Autumn could live.

So she thanked fairy tales and she thanked the person who made her believe in them again. Autumn opened her eyes and looked at Elena with a smile as she finished playing the song.

"I love you." Autumn mouthed to her.

Elena smiled and drew a heart in the air and pointed to Autumn. Autumn blushed as everyone cheered loudly for her and stood up.

Autumn nodded to them. "Thank you. I have a few more songs to play, but before I do…there's one song I wrote for Elena and would like to sing to her if you guys would let me." Elena bit her lip to contain the smile on her face.

Riley pretended to gag and Autumn glared at him playfully. "Well I'm singing it anyway so screw you guys."

"THAT'S ELENA'S JOB!" Phoenix exclaimed.

Autumn and Elena blushed. "Phoenix, do I have to remind you my parents are in the same room as you?" Phoenix shrugged and flashed an innocent smile to Cora and Joseph who laughed. Autumn rolled her eyes. "*Anyway*, this song's for you Ellie." Autumn smiled at her before beginning to play the piano. "Also, don't judge my singing if it's not as great." She chuckled before beginning to sing.

When Autumn finished the song she wiped away tears. Everyone stood up again and clapped for her, some with tears brimming in their eyes.

Elena stood up and ran to the stage, pressing her lips against Autumn's. "Thank you." Elena whispered.

"No, thank *you*." Autumn returned.

"For what?"

"For making me believe in magic again."

Elena smoothed out the invisible wrinkles of her blue sundress, biting her lip nervously as she stared at her art pieces hung up on the wall and then towards the crowd of people stepping inside. Her art show was today and to say she was terrified was an understatement, she hoped people found her art pieces good enough because she had doubts about her talents.

But one thing she didn't doubt for a second was the muse behind her art pieces.

Elena hadn't told anyone besides her parents about the art show, not wanting to draw so much attention to herself. So she only expected for her parents, Lily, and Mrs. Freya to show up.

Mrs. Freya approached the girl with a smile, standing still and staring at the pieces intently. There were four pieces that had made it in to the gallery. She called her art pieces, "My Beautiful Mess".

The first piece was a painting of Autumn in black and white. You'd think it was a pretty bland painting until you took a look at Autumn's eyes which were a bright, emerald green. It took Elena a while before she got the perfect shade of green. Elena put a lot of detail into Autumn's eyes and made sure they were the thing to capture your attention most.

The second piece was of Autumn standing with her white cane, back when she used it, and the background was black while Autumn was in full color. Elena worked especially hard to get Autumn's skin tone right and make sure every curve and every part of Autumn matched perfectly.

The third piece was a happier painting. She had taken a picture of Autumn laughing at something Phoenix did and Elena was glad to have captured that moment because it quickly became her favorite picture of Autumn. She radiated with happiness—practically *glowing*. And Elena never wanted to paint something so badly. So Elena recreated the picture in a painting filled with bright colors, there wasn't an ounce of sadness in the painting. It was definitely one of her favorites.

And, finally, the fourth piece. It was her most personal one because she was in it. It was of her and Autumn looking at each other and smiling. Inside Elena was an arctic fox while inside Autumn was an African bush viper. Their animals that at any other circumstance could never work out together, but in their case…it did. She and Autumn were the exception because she found love in a person she never expected herself to find.

"Very beautiful paintings, Elena." Mrs. Freya spoke up. "I can practically *feel* the emotions behind these paintings. Your muse definitely brings out something in you. Out of all your works, these are definitely the best. The transitions in your painting, they go from something dark and mysterious to joy and optimism. It's not just one feeling, but a variety of them. Feelings we can all relate to."

Elena smiled as she looked at her own paintings. "Thank you, I just wanted to show a girl I'm in love with."

"Well you did. Not everyone can portray love."

"Not everyone can portray love because not everyone can feel it." Elena told her. "Love is a concept people know of, but not something everyone can relate to."

"And that is why you're my favorite student." Mrs. Freya smiled. "Keep up the great work, I mean it. Don't let anything stop you from picking up a paintbrush. You're going to need art in your best times and your worst."

Elena nodded, aware of what Mrs. Freya was referring to. "I won't."

Mrs. Freya nodded before leaving to look at the rest of the artworks created. Her parents swung by and praised her art like they always did. Of course, like the embarrassing parents they were, Elena was forced to take pictures with her paintings so they could show off to their coworkers and friends.

"Lena, smile. Your parents are posting this shit on Facebook."

Elena looked away from the camera and broke into a large smile when she saw Maya, Phoenix, Emma, Valerie, and Autumn with smiles on their faces.

"How did you—"

"You thought you could keep this from us?" Valerie laughed. "Think again."

Elena walked up to hug them all and kissed Autumn's cheek. "Hey."

"Hey my little artist." Autumn smiled as she wheeled herself to get a closer look at Elena's paintings.

Elena blushed as she stood next to Autumn as Autumn observed the paintings intently, her eyes scanning around every inch of the canvases.

"They're not that—"Elena began.

"They're breathtaking." Autumn whispered, a big smile forming on her face. "Absolutely breathtaking. This is the best art I've seen from you to date…it's…wow."

Elena felt her face turn red. "Well…my muse made these paintings beautiful."

"No, the hand that created them made them beautiful." Autumn smiled.

Elena smiled. "God, can I kiss you?"

Autumn chuckled and nodded. "I'd want nothing more." She whispered before Elena pressed her lips against Autumn's.

"I love you my arctic fox." Autumn smiled, looking at Elena and squeezing her hand.

Elena glanced at the painting of her and Autumn before looking back at her girlfriend. "I love you too my African bush viper."

The city was far behind them and all the girls decided to take a little road trip out of the city before they ventured to Italy. Autumn wanted to see the stars and Elena would give her every single one if she could.

A couple hours from New York City, the girls had made a bonfire as above them illuminated hundreds—possibly thousands—of stars and Autumn looked up with a content smile on her face.

"I want to become a star when I die." Autumn shared as her green eyes were practically glowing at the sight of the stars. "That way you guys can come here and look up at the stars and know that one of them is me."

Maya smiled softly. "You'll be the brightest star, I'm sure of it."

Autumn hummed. "I refuse to be dark, I want to shine and be bright and colorful…" She chuckled. "I don't want dark colors anymore. There's nothing wrong with them, but I've lived with darkness for a majority of my life and I don't want to live more of them ever."

"You won't." Phoenix said softly, smiling. "If anyone here is shining brightest, it's you. You've come a long way since we met you…all of us have." Phoenix looked at her friends. "Change…it used to be something so scary to me. Because everything was changing in my life drastically and I had no control of it. But, you have control of change sometimes. Look at all of us, we weren't the people we were before. But we changed into better versions of ourselves and *we* chose to do that. And it's honestly made us so much closer."

Autumn smiled. "That was beautiful, Phoenix."

Phoenix flipped her hair. "I know, I try." She joked.

Autumn chuckled and looked at her friends and girlfriend. "Promise me you guys won't forget me."

"We couldn't even if we wanted to." Emma told her with a soft smile. "You have permanently placed yourself in each of our hearts, and we can't forget a person that in a way brought us together."

"Exactly, we're best friends for life." Phoenix stated with a nod.

Elena smiled, squeezing Autumn's hand. "Do you guys want to seal that statement?"

"Nah girl, I ain't doing no ritual shit." Maya joked, laughing.

Elena rolled her eyes and laughed as she walked to Emma's parked car and opened the car door, taking out her messenger bag. "I, um...this is going to sound super cheesy but I made friendship bracelets."

"Yes, that's pretty cheesy but I expect nothing less from you so continue." Phoenix laughed.

Elena glared at her before continuing. "*Anyway*, I braided five colors. Each of our favorite colors. So neon pink for Emma, lavender for Maya, orange for me, red for Phoenix, and blue for Autumn." She told them as she handed each girl their own bracelet. "It's a symbol of our friendship. And each color represents that no matter what, we'll always be connected just like these bracelets are."

Everyone put on their bracelets and smiled. "I'll never take it off." Emma smiled.

"None of us will." Autumn said softly as she ran her finger through the braided bracelet. "Thanks, Ellie." Autumn looked up at the starry sky and smiled. "Thank you...all of you. Really, you guys have given me the greatest days of my life."

"And you have given us the greatest memories." Maya told her.

Autumn smiled at her and looked back up at the starry sky with a hopeful gleam in her eye. "I don't know about you guys but this bonfire gives me kumbaya feelings and I want to group hug." She laughed. The other four girls laughed and quickly stood up and enveloped themselves in a group hug.

When the five broke their hug, they sat close by each other. Phoenix lifted up her hand up in the air where her bracelet was. "Long live us."

The girls smiled as they lifted their own hands with their bracelets. "Long live us." They said together.

Phoenix smiled. "And long live Autumn Castillo."

CHAPTER TWENTY-SIX

For two weeks, Autumn lived in heaven before even getting there. That is, if heaven truly existed, Autumn wasn't sure where she was going. But she hoped it was nice, and she hoped Elena would be there when it was her time to be.

Italy was everything Autumn imagined. Absolutely breathtaking. They visited as much as they could, but now they were spending their last few days at the place Autumn wanted to be at the most: Cinque Terre, Italy. It was even more beautiful than the pictures made it seem, and she enjoyed watching Elena paint sceneries from their hotel balcony.

Spending whatever time left she had with her friends, her family, and Elena made Italy even more beautiful. It was definitely a memory she would keep in her heart.

Even embarrassing moments like now.

"For the last time Phoenix Hale, we are not in Rome. Stop singing 'What Dreams Are Made Of' from that stupid movie." Autumn told the girl who was busy jumping on the hotel bed and belting out Lizzie McGuire's 'What Dreams Are Made Of'.

"LET ME LIVE!" Phoenix exclaimed as she sang into her hairbrush.

Autumn laughed as Phoenix clumsily jumped off the bed and got on her knees as she belted the song.

Autumn was pretty sure not even her oxygen tank could save her as she laughed even harder when Elena, Emma, and Maya barged into the hotel room.

Emma hopped on Phoenix's back and sang loudly as Phoenix pretended that Emma was the heaviest thing on earth.

This wasn't the first time they belted this song. And it probably wasn't the last, despite the many complaints they received from the hotel.

"Sing to me, Paolo!" Elena exclaimed dramatically as she pointed to Autumn, sitting down on her girlfriend's lap which was something she tended to do ever since Autumn started using her wheelchair.

Autumn giggled as she wrapped her arms around Elena's waist. "Okay, one, my name is Autumn. And two, I will not sing to you Lizzie McGuire's soundtrack."

Elena pouted before pecking Autumn's lips. "Party pooper."

Autumn smiled at the peck. "You know it."

"Ugh stop being cute, it's the most disgusting thing to witness." Phoenix teased.

"Watching you sing is the most disgusting thing to witness." Autumn retorted, sticking out her tongue playfully.

Phoenix threw a pillow towards the couple and both girls laughed. "Wow, what a weak throw." Autumn smirked.

"You're lucky you're already in a wheelchair so I can't put you in one." Phoenix smirked back.

"I can easily run you over with mine, don't test me." Autumn laughed.

"All right, all right lets relax and go to the beach! It's beautiful and we have yet to go!" Emma exclaimed.

Everyone quickly agreed to the suggestion and Elena smirked as she whispered in Autumn's ear. "I have a bikini I bought that I've been meaning to show you." She whispered before winking and getting off Autumn's lap and walking out the hotel room.

Autumn's face had turned red at the words and she was glad she had an oxygen tank at the time because she probably would've stopped breathing at the words.

After taking a while to get ready, the girls finally arrived at the beach and Autumn told her friends she wanted to sit in the sand instead of her wheelchair. So now she was enjoying the view of the beach while she held herself up with her arms, feeling the warm sand covering her hands.

However, right now her face was definitely warmer than the sand. Elena was being an absolute tease and Autumn hated it (and loved it).

She was wearing a red and white polka dot bikini and it was driving her crazy since Elena was right and her butt really did look great with it.

"Look Autumn, I get that you love looking at everything but can you make it less blatant that you're staring at Elena's ass?" Emma spoke up as she plopped down next to her.

Autumn looked away from Elena splashing away with Phoenix and Maya while purposefully making sure Autumn watching when she wiped away drops of water dripping down her chest at a painfully slow pace.

"What?" Autumn asked dumbly.

Emma laughed and shook her head as she looked up at the clear blue sky and then the clear blue water the beach had.

"Have you and Elena…" Emma gave her a suggestive look.

Autumn's eyes widened and she blushed, shaking her head sheepishly. "No."

"Have you gotten close?"

Again, Autumn blushed. "Yes." She mumbled.

Emma smirked. "And what's stopping you?" she asked curiously, enjoying seeing this bashful side of Autumn.

"Uh, I don't know. I guess when it feels right, we'll…you know." Autumn's face was beet red as she chewed on her lower lip.

Emma laughed loudly. "I'm just teasing Autumn, relax."

Autumn pouted. "I hate you."

"You love me."

"No I don't."

"Yes you do."

"Says who?"

"Says me."

"Shut up."

Emma giggled. "I'm going to miss this." She said without thinking. It grew quiet between them and Emma quickly felt guilty for saying the words. "I'm sorry...I shouldn't have—"

"I'm going to miss this too. I'm sorry I can't be your best friend forever." Autumn smiled sadly.

"On the contrary Autumn, you are my best friend forever. No matter what. You're my best friend forever and no one can replace you." Emma told her with a soft smile.

Autumn smiled. "You're my best friend too. Heck, you're my sister like I said. Now come hug me, you have me emotional now." Autumn laughed before the two girls embraced in a tight hug. "Don't forget about me, okay?"

"I couldn't even if I tried, Autumn." Emma whispered as she hugged her tightly.

"I really do love you Emma, all jokes aside. Thank you for existing as the same time as me." Autumn whispered.

Emma smiled. "I love you too. And I'll exist in any time as you if I have anything to do with it." She chuckled.

Autumn chuckled as well before noticing Phoenix, Maya, and Elena approaching them. "Let's go get wet, the waves aren't even too rough." Maya suggested.

"Yes, Maya, let's throw the paralyzed girl into the water. Genius idea." Autumn said sarcastically.

Maya rolled her eyes. "Retract the sass, Phoenix would pick you up and take you with us."

"Hell no, this bitch will drown me."

Phoenix scoffed. "Girl please, we all know the only thing you'll drown is Elena's—"

Elena's eyes widened and quickly covered Phoenix's mouth before shouting. "SO SWIMMING?" as everyone else laughed.

Autumn's laughs subsided and she eventually gave in, lifting her arms up to Phoenix. "If you drop me, I will hurt you violently." She said as Elena followed them.

Phoenix snorted as she easily picked up Autumn who clung onto Phoenix for dear life as they headed to the water. "You're in good hands Castillo."

"You're not car insurance, get out of here."

"Yeah? Well you're not a cup of sugar either, trick." Phoenix teased as the water reached her knees and she stopped, not wanting to go so deep for the sake of Autumn. "I'm going to move a little lower so the water touches you, is that fine?" Autumn nodded and Phoenix slowly lowered Autumn to the water so it touched her. "You good?"

"This water feels nice." Autumn smiled as her hands splashed the clear water at Phoenix who playfully glared at the girl in her arms.

Elena giggled and Autumn splashed her too, Elena pouting. "Now that was mean."

"You deserve it." Autumn teased.

"And what on Earth did I do?" Elena asked, feigning innocence.

"You know what I'm talking about." Autumn raised an eyebrow.

Elena only smirked while Phoenix rolled her eyes. "Look, I don't need to listen to your lesbian code language. I will drop you into this water, Castillo."

"I thought I was in good hands." Autumn recalled.

"Pff, go use Elena's. They seem more useful to you." Phoenix smirked.

"God, Phoenix, stop accusing us of having sex when we haven't even had sex." Autumn laughed.

"And that, is a punishment to society. Just get it on." Phoenix winked.

"You're sounding awfully contradicting for a girl who threatened to drop her paralyzed friend into the water for flirting with her girlfriend." Autumn told her.

Phoenix scoffed. "Details…"

Autumn eventually went back to her wheelchair and watching with a smile her friends splash around. Her parents and siblings eventually joined them at the beach and watched as they too had their share of fun at the beach.

"Hey you, come here often?" Elena winked as she approached her girlfriend, everyone having left but the two of them.

"No, but I just might now that I know you do." Autumn giggled.

Elena sat down on Autumn's lap and kissed her deeply. "I love you." She whispered when she broke the kiss.

Autumn smiled. "I love you too."

Elena wrapped her arms around Autumn's neck and nuzzled her neck as she watched the waves splashing, the sound of It comforting her.

But not as much as the comfort of hearing Autumn's steady heartbeat because as long as it kept beating, Elena knew she was alive and Elena knew she had some time still.

The two remained in comfortable silence as both of them watched the waves crashing and the blues and whites mixed in the water to create the beautiful color of the ocean.

"Thank you." Elena whispered, kissing Autumn's shoulder gently.

"For what?" Autumn smiled, turning to her girlfriend.

"For this. All of this." Elena told her, motioning around her. "This is our place now, right?"

Autumn smiled and kissed Elena's lips gently. "Yeah, it is. If I have a choice of where my ghost self or my soul can go, I'll be right here." She said softly. "So you know where to find me."

Elena stared at Autumn intently. "I don't regret falling in love with you. I will never regret anything that happens between us. You are my one and only love, there's no one else for me."

Autumn shook her head. "Don't say that." She whispered.

"No, but it's true—"

"Listen to me," Autumn interrupted, taking Elena's hand and kissing it gently. "Do not forbid yourself of love simply because your first one left. First loves were never meant to be forever Ellie, they were meant to be a temporary feeling of passion and bliss. But like all temporary things, they have to go. And there is nothing wrong with letting things go."

"But you're not temporary Autumn, you're my forever." Elena told her.

"I'm not. I'm your first love, but you're my forever. You're the only person I had the privilege of loving, and you're the only person I will ever belong to." Autumn kissed her cheek. "Promise me you're not going to deny yourself of doing one of the most beautiful things in the world: to love. Don't think because I'm gone, you disappear with me. You don't. You're going to be here, and you're going to become this amazing artist and then you're going to fall in love with someone who I know will love you as much as I do, if not more. And…you're going to marry them and have gorgeous children with them and grow old with them. Don't deny yourself that. Believe me, you deserve to love again. I'm not your forever, Elena, and that's okay because we made our little forever in the time we knew each other."

Elena's eyes welled up with tears. "I can't love someone the way I love you." She whispered.

Autumn cupped her face. "You can. Want to know why?" she smiled. "Because my heart is yours. As soon as I leave this earth, my heart will mix in with yours. So you'll have double the love in your heart. So much, you'll find someone to give it to. And that's okay, because I want that for you. I want someone to love you more than I ever could. And I want you to love someone more than you loved me. If you're happy, Elena, then believe me I will be happy. With or without me."

Elena nuzzled Autumn's cheek before kissing it. "As much as that comforts me to know you're okay with that, I told you my heart belongs to you. And it does. It always will belong to you. Even if love comes my way again, I will always be in love with you. First loves may not have been made to be forever, but they were the first and they will always be remembered. There's no forgetting your first love, and I'm not going to forget you."

Autumn smiled softly and kissed Elena's lips. Elena smiled and hopped off Autumn's lap and looked through her bag and took out her Polaroid camera.

"Let me take your picture." Elena told her.

"Why?"

"Because I want to remember this."

Autumn smiled and nodded. "Okay." She agreed softly.

Elena smiled and lifted the camera up to take Autumn's picture while Autumn smiled cheekily for the camera. Elena giggled as she took the picture and waited for it to come out. She smiled when the picture revealed itself and Elena showed Autumn the picture. "Beautiful."

Autumn blushed. "You're way more beautiful."

Elena chuckled and kissed Autumn's cheek. "Let's take a picture together. Because I want to remember this as well."

Autumn nodded and smiled at the camera before Elena took the picture. They took a couple more with silly faces and plenty of kisses before going back to enjoying the view of the beach in each other's arms.

"As cute as this shit is, we need to get you both ready." Maya spoke up as Phoenix threw Elena over her shoulder.

"Ready for what? And Phoenix get me down!" Elena whined.

Autumn smiled at her. "You'll see in…" she turned to Maya.

Maya chuckled and rolled her eyes. "One hour and 45 minutes." She said.

"For what though?" Elena asked, still trying to get down.

Autumn smiled. "You'll see, trust me." She said softly. "Phoenix and Maya will get you ready, and Emma and Olivia will help me out because God knows I need to look semi decent." She chuckled as Maya wheeled her away. "Make sure you wear something fancy!" Autumn turned around before she was a far enough distance that Elena couldn't hear her anymore.

"Spill, Nix." Elena told her when Phoenix put her down.

"You'll find out in…" she checked her phone. "One hour and 42 minutes." Phoenix smirked as Elena groaned and kicked the sand as she followed Phoenix back to their hotel to get ready.

Elena walked to the lobby in a pink dress that zipped in the front with her hair tied back with a pink bow. She had kept asking Maya and Phoenix what was happening but the two girls wouldn't budge and instead got her ready upon Autumn's request.

Elena stood at the lobby and pursed her lips as she looked around, waiting for Autumn to show up.

That is, if she *was* showing up. Autumn didn't really assure her she'd be here for whatever surprise she had.

Her worry didn't last very long, however, because right then Autumn wheeled towards her in a maroon colored dress and her hair down in a natural state. She looked absolutely stunning. Then again, Autumn was *always* stunning.

Autumn smiled as she finally made it to her girlfriend. "Hi beautiful." She greeted, looking at Elena. "You look gorgeous."

Elena blushed. "Have you seen yourself? You clean up nice, Castillo." She teased as she pecked Autumn's lips. "Now what have you planned you sneaky devil?" Elena giggled.

Autumn laughed. "Just push me and we'll walk there. I'll tell you where to go." She told her. "But before I do that…" Autumn wheeled herself to the person at the front desk and Elena watched with a raised eyebrow before Autumn came back with an arrangement of colorful flowers and a proud smile. "For you my beautiful girl." Autumn told her as she handed Elena the colorful arrangement.

Elena grinned widely as she took the flowers and kissed Autumn's lips before pulling away and smelling the sweet scent of the variety of flowers. "They're beautiful, thank you baby." Elena kissed her again.

Autumn smiled at her. "Anything for you." She whispered.

Elena kissed her again before the two headed to wherever Autumn was planning on taking her. After a short walk, Elena and Autumn went inside an incredibly fancy restaurant that Elena *knew* was not only incredibly fancy, but incredibly expensive.

"Autumn, this place looks like somewhere I'd probably work at, not eat at." Elena told her.

Autumn chuckled. "Don't worry about it, just go with the flow." She told her girlfriend.

Elena nodded as Autumn said something to the hostess and the two were taken to a more secluded area of the restaurant where the beach was at their view. The two were seated and Elena looked around.

"Holy shit the fanciest I've ever gone is probably Olive Garden." Elena told her as she looked around in awe." This place is beautiful." Elena whispered as she looked up at the twinkling lights illuminating above them. It was like having a galaxy looking down on you.

Autumn giggled at Elena's astonished face. "Well Olive Garden is great but nothing compared to this place, so get ready. I heard this place is really good."

"How could you afford it?" Elena asked.

Autumn shook her head as she placed her hand over Elena's on the table. "Don't worry about that. Let's just enjoy tonight." She whispered before kissing Elena's hand.

"But—"

Autumn giggled. "How about we whatever this?" Autumn suggested.

Elena pouted before smiling. "Okay."

Autumn smiled. "Whatever."

"Whatever." Elena said softly.

"Say it louder." Autumn told her. "Whatever."

"Whatever." Elena said, a little louder.

"Do you hear yourself, Ellie? Come on, you could do better than that!" Autumn laughed. "No one's here anyway."

Elena chuckled before clearing her throat. "Whatever!" she exclaimed.

Autumn smiled. "That's right." Autumn nodded. "Whatever."

A waiter dressed in a white button up with a red bowtie and black slacks approached them with menus. "Good evening ladies." He greeted in a thick, Italian accent. "Is this your first time here?"

Autumn nodded. "Yeah, we're from the states." She told the waiter.

The waiter smiled. "Then I will make sure you have a magical evening here." He assured with a nod. "How about some champagne?" he suggested.

"Well, we are celebrating our love so yes. Give us the best champagne you could get us." Autumn told him with a nod and a smile.

"It would be a pleasure, I'll be right back." The waiter smiled before walking away.

Elena looked at Autumn with a quirked eyebrow and Autumn looked at her with a laugh. "Why are you looking at me like that?"

"Because your surprise me every day." Elena told her.

"Oh really?"

"Yes, really. You brought me here on a date to a fancy restaurant with the beach right beside us and stars shining above us and lights illuminating around us. This is perfect, I don't even know what to say..." Elena trailed off.

"You deserve this and more. I want tonight to be magical for the both of us. Because you're my piece of magic and I want you to become an even bigger piece. You're my beautiful girl and you deserve beautiful things." Autumn said softly, squeezing her hand.

Elena smiled at Autumn before the two started to look through their menus. "I literally do not understand a thing that it says on here." Elena giggled.

"Well you're lucky I'm fluent in Italian." Autumn told her as she explained all the dishes to Elena.

"Okay, well I'm going to go with the dish that sounds prettiest so…" Elena pointed to one of the dishes to Autumn.

Autumn chuckled. "You're cute." Autumn told her.

"You're cuter." Elena replied.

"I know." Autumn joked, winking at her.

Elena giggled as the waiter came back with the bottle of champagne and served them both a glass. "I had the chef pick out the best bottles she could think of. She says this bottle tastes like magic, and that the magical part of it is that only people who drink from this bottle should be two people in love. That's why it tastes amazing." He explained. "Love is what makes it taste amazing."

Elena and Autumn looked at each other before smiling and raised their glasses to each other, clinking them slightly. "To magic and love then, two of the greatest combinations ever created." Autumn said softly before the two of them took a sip of the supposed magical champagne.

Autumn stared at the half full glass of champagne with wide eyes. "Whoa." She managed to say. "That is *so* good." She exclaimed.

Elena nodded in agreement. "Wow, magic tastes amazing." She whispered.

The waiter laughed. "The chef made a wise choice then." He smiled before listening to what both girls wanted and walking off.

"Our love must be pretty magical." Elena told Autumn, holding Autumn's hand on the clothed table.

"It must be." Autumn whispered. "Who knew playing Beethoven's 'Moonlight Sonata' would get us here? Who knew I'd have the privilege of falling in love with you? I think that's the beauty of not knowing the future, because you're met with the biggest surprises. Whether it's good or bad, it's there. And you're definitely my biggest surprise. My most beautiful surprise."

Elena smiled, feeling bittersweet over the words and everything that was happening now. This was only temporary, Autumn was only temporary. But the feelings Autumn gave her despite everything, that was not temporary, that was forever.

A musical group played in the streets at night. Elena thought it was incredibly cheesy they picked a song from Disney's *Lady and the Tramp* but it attracted people. Including her and Autumn. She was on Autumn's lap as they listened to the Italian men harmonize.

Elena kissed Autumn's cheek. "I love you." She whispered in Autumn's ear.

Autumn smiled as she pulled Elena in for a kiss. "I love you too." She whispered in Elena's ear.

"This has been the greatest night of my life." Elena smiled. "It couldn't have been more perfect."

"Well, it hasn't ended yet." Autumn told her, looking at Elena and tracing her lips with her finger.

Elena raised an eyebrow. "What do you mean? Do you still have more plans in store?"

Autumn hummed. "I have a couple." She whispered, kissing Elena's cheek. "But first, take me to the nearest grocery store with a gumball machine."

"That is the most random request I've ever received."

Autumn laughed. "Just take me." Autumn pouted.

Elena was never one to resist a request from Autumn so they ventured off to the nearest grocery store and Autumn wheeled toward the gumball machine with plastic rings inside.

"Give me a quarter."

Elena raised an eyebrow. "Why?"

Autumn turned to her. "Well, I guess I should ask first."

"Ask what?" Elena tilted her head.

"For you to fake marry me." Autumn chewed on her lip nervously.

Elena stared at her. "Are you serious?"

"Damn it, I shouldn't have asked—"

"Yes."

Autumn's eyes widened. "Yes?"

"Yes."

"Yes as in, yes you'll fake marry me?"

"Yes."

"Can I have a quarter then?"

Elena giggled. "But you proposed to me!" Elena exclaimed as she reached into her bag anyway.

"Yeah, and I just took you to an expensive restaurant."

Elena handed Autumn the quarter. "Touché."

Autumn smiled cheekily. "Yeah, think you can spare another quarter?"

"You think I'm rich or something, Castillo?" Elena joked as she gave Autumn another quarter.

Autumn stuck her tongue out playfully before putting a quarter into the gumball machine and twisting it until a plastic container with a toy ring came out and did it again so she'd have two rings. One had a blue rock and the other an orange— a wonderful coincidence, Autumn thought.

"Are we really going to get fake married in a grocery store?" Elena raised an eyebrow.

"An *Italian* grocery store, there's more sophistication to it." Autumn retorted as she handed Elena the orange toy ring.

Elena chuckled. "Okay, so...I guess we should say our vows then." She smiled.

"Okay." Autumn smiled.

Elena blushed before looking down at the plastic container. "I vow to love you beyond the time you have left. Because I can't learn to unlove a person who made me feel like art, and made me feel like I was worth everything even at my worst. I…I love you so much Autumn Castillo, and I'll love you when skies are grey and when skies are blue and when skies are a mix of the two or even the brightest colors a person can ever witness. "

Elena continued. "You painted my world, Autumn, even when you only saw darkness. You painted me every color in the world, and I can never forget a person who made my world colorful. You did that Autumn, you brought color into my life when it was sad and now I paint the colors of happiness thanks to you. And even when you leave, I'll find my way back to those happy colors because I know you would want that."

Elena's eyes welled up and she squeezed Autumn's hand. "You're my beautiful thing, my art piece that existed outside of a portrait. And I hate the fact that there's going to be days I won't wake up next to you. There's going to be days I'll paint something or draw something or sculpt something and you won't be there to admire it with me. There's going to be days when it rains or it snows or leaves fall or the sun shines and you won't be there with me to see it. I won't get to wake up next to you anymore. I won't get to spend the rest of my life with you, but I am happy to say I spent part of my life with you and I was the happiest person alive." Elena told her, kissing her cheek.

"You are the best thing to ever happen to me and I love you so much. More than the moon loves its stars, more than peanut loves butter, more than Maya loves Beyoncé…" Elena and Autumn giggled. "More than anything in the world, I love you. And I will love you no matter what."

Autumn smiled widely at Elena's words. "God, how can I top that?" she chuckled before biting her lip. "I'm not good with words. But…I am good with music. So…I'll use that." Autumn took a deep breath. "When I look at you it's like the song 'And I Love Her' by The Beatles. Your eyes remind me of the song 'Ebony Eyes' by Stevie Wonder. Your smile reminds me of the song 'Fallingforyou' by The 1975. Kissing you reminds me of 'Kiss Me' by Sixpence None The Richer, but The Fray's cover because songs mean so much more when they're slower." She smiled. "

When I think of you in a cheesy montage I think of 'Wouldn't It Be Nice' by The Beach Boys." She giggled. "And when you're not okay but you don't want to admit to me, you remind me of Ed Sheeran's 'Even My Dad Does Sometimes'." Autumn said softly. "Your personality…it reminds me of 'Crazy Beautiful' by Andy Grammer because you're crazy and you're beautiful." Autumn teased as Elena smacked her arm while laughing.

"The love I feel for you reminds me of Journey's 'Open Arms." She whispered. "And the way you make me feel reminds me of

'Home' by Edward Sharpe and the Magnetic Zeroes." Autumn smiled. "But despite it all, you're the greatest masterpiece that not even I can compose. The music of your soul and the music of your beauty is a symphony and you make my heart feel like a melody. You are the best music I ever got to hear when I was blind and you are the best music I got to see when I wasn't."

Elena wiped away a tear. "That was the most beautiful thing I've ever been told at a grocery store at 9 pm." She giggled.

Autumn giggled as she wiped away tears of her own. "I guess we should exchange rings now." Elena nodded as she opened the plastic container in her hands and Autumn did the same.

Elena placed the toy ring in Autumn's finger. "I do." She whispered.

Autumn smiled at Elena as she placed the toy ring in Elena's finger. "I do."

"Can I kiss you?" Elena whispered, smiling.

"I'd love nothing more." Autumn whispered back.

Elena pressed her lips against Autumn's and kissed her passionately, Autumn quickly returning it. "You know, now that we're fake married we can…" Elena trailed off suggestively.

Autumn's breath hitched. "Do you…you want to?" she stammered.

"Only if you do." Elena whispered.

"Well I sure as hell don't want to die a virgin."

———————————

When Elena and Autumn made love to each other, Elena pretended she was painting a beautiful painting on a canvas and the canvas was Autumn's body. Autumn pretended Elena was a piano and she was creating the most beautiful song.

Elena was her favorite song.

Both girls were panting (Autumn mostly wheezing) after they made love to each other. It was awkward, with mostly awkward touches and a billion questions, but it was perfect. To them, just loving each other in a more intimate way was special enough. And no awkwardness could ever ruin that for them.

"Hi." Autumn smiled as Elena rested her chin on Autumn's chest.

"Hi." Elena whispered tracing random patterns on Autumn's arms.

"I love you." Autumn told her, kissing Elena's cheek.

"I love you too." Elena whispered.

"That was magical."

"Everything with you is magical." Elena kissed her chest softly before staring at Autumn with a loving look.

Autumn smiled and the two lied in comfortable silence, their breathing and rapid heartbeats the only thing moving.

"I wish I could stay."

Elena looked at Autumn. "I wish that too. But it's okay."

Autumn's eyes watered. "Don't forget me."

Elena shook her head and kissed Autumn's lips. "Never." She kissed them again. "Never ever. You are forever engraved in my heart, no one could take you from there."

Autumn kissed Elena back. "I'll see you again."

"I know."

CHAPTER TWENTY-SEVEN

Autumn lasted longer than she was expected to. She got to spend another Halloween, another Thanksgiving, another Christmas, and another New Year's. She got to celebrate Elena's 18th birthday, she got to celebrate her best friends and her girlfriend graduate high school, she got to celebrate her friends and her girlfriend's excitement as they were accepted to their dream schools.

Phoenix was going to be attending Juilliard for voice performance in the fall, full ride. Maya was going Georgetown University in Washington DC to study pre-med and Harvard's prestigious medical school was already eyeing her even though she hadn't started yet. Emma was going to the Institute of Culinary Education and was going to study pastry and baking arts, assuring Autumn she'd send her best pastries to heaven specifically for her.

After a lot of convincing on Autumn's part, Elena applied to several art schools across the country and even applied to a school that was a long shot: Royal College of Art in London. But she got in. And she was going there too.

Autumn couldn't have been more proud.

Now, it was July. Autumn made it past even her own birthday, but she knew she wouldn't make it to the next one.

The day before, Autumn felt it. She just knew her time was coming now. So when she woke up with blood gushing out of her nose and gasping for air, she knew there wouldn't be a next day for her.

Autumn lied on the hospital bed, obviously weak, obviously close to leaving, and obviously with no time left. But she did have time left to say goodbye to the people who mattered most to her. She'd make sure she would have time.

Phoenix stepped inside the room, obviously had been crying earlier at hearing that Autumn was in the hospital.

"Hey, Loser." Phoenix greeted with a smile.

Autumn smiled weakly, heavy bags in her eyes and her skin even paler than usual. "Hey." She greeted as Phoenix sat on the chair beside her bed.

"So…this is it, huh?" Phoenix asked, her voice cracking. "You're really going?"

Autumn smiled sadly. "It's time, Phoenix Hale. But I'm not scared. I'll be okay." She said softly, patting Phoenix's knee gently. "You're going to be famous. And I'll be jamming to your music, it's going to be great."

Phoenix smiled. "I'll make sure to dedicate my accomplishments to the best musician I ever knew, you." She told her.

Autumn chuckled. "Thanks, I appreciate it." She paused. "I always found you to be my musical soul mate. You always knew what I was looking for in a song. And you always helped make my songs better." She breathed out. "That's why I'm giving you my songs."

Phoenix stared at her, eyes wide. "What? No, Autumn, they're yours."

"They are, yes, but why keep them stored somewhere to collect dust when they can be brought to life by your talent?" Autumn retorted. "I have notebooks filled with songs. Probably over 20 notebooks. They're under my bed. Get them and keep them. They're yours."

Phoenix nodded and wiped away a tear. "Thank you."

Autumn shook her head. "No, thank *you*." She smiled. "I'll be remembered when people play your songs."

Phoenix squeezed Autumn's hand. "No Autumn, *our* songs."

Autumn smiled. "Even better." She whispered.

Phoenix smiled. "You're the best person I ever got to know. I'm never going to forget you. Especially if you decide to haunt my ass if you can. Try not to scare me too much, but you're bitch ass will be throwing plates to my head and shit." She joked.

Autumn laughed. "Oh please, throw plates?" the girl scoffed. "That's for amateurs, I'll grab a can of hairspray and a lighter and light it up and go to your room to scare you."

Phoenix laughed. "I'll be waiting for that."

Autumn smiled. "Good." She whispered before squeezing Phoenix's hand. "Phoenix, can you do me a favor?"

Phoenix chuckled and nodded. "Yeah, what's up?"

"Can you sing for me?" Autumn whispered.

Phoenix nodded. "Of course, I'd love that." She smiled softly.

Phoenix sang a song and wiped away tears when she finished, smiling at Autumn. "Bye Autumn."

Autumn smiled back. "Bye Phoenix."

———————————

Maya sat next to Autumn and smiled at her. "I'm not sad you're leaving, you know." Maya told her.

"Good. I don't want anyone to be." Autumn whispered.

"You're going to be okay." Maya assured with a nod. "Make sure to say hi to my mom for me if you see her, all right?"

Autumn smiled and nodded. "I will. We'll be cheering you on as you become the best doctor the world could ever have."

Maya's eyes teared up. "After seeing you and my mom suffer because of cancer, I made a promise to myself. I'm going to make sure that I find a cure for cancer, I will never stop trying. Because I don't ever want to see another person suffer under the hands of it."

"Good, that's really good, May. I know you can do that."
Autumn smiled. "You're going to accomplish so much. You're a
certified genius."

Maya chuckled. "Thanks."

Autumn nodded. "Make sure to add cream and sugar to your
coffee, May, okay?"

Maya's wiped away a tear and nodded with a smile. "I will.
It'll be the best tasting coffee in the world."

"And share your coffee with everyone else, so their coffee can
taste great too."

Maya nodded. "I'd want nothing more."

Autumn smiled faintly. "I'm sorry you had to lose two people
to cancer in the course of one year." She whispered.

Maya shrugged. "Shit happens."

Autumn chuckled and opened her arms. "Hug me, May." She
pouted.

Maya chuckled and hugged Autumn tightly, finally letting go the small sob that wanted to escape. "I'm going to miss you so much." She cried.

"Me too, May, me too." Autumn whispered, her eyes watering. "I can never thank you enough for sharing your wisdom with me. If you hadn't told me about my coffee, I wouldn't have Ellie. I wouldn't have you guys. I probably wouldn't even have my sight. It's amazing how much words can have an impact on a person's life. And your words made an impact on mine. You're already changing lives, May, and you're not even a doctor yet." She smiled, wiping away Maya's tears.

"And you changed mine, Autumn. All of you guys did. Thank you for existing. It sucks you can't stay longer, but just know having you here was a blast." Maya told her.

"Yeah?" Autumn smiled widely. "Well I had the best time here too, and my coffee tasted amazing thanks to you guys."

Maya smiled as she hugged Autumn again. "Bye Autumn."

"Bye Maya."

———————————

Autumn watched as her parents, Dylan, and Olivia tried to keep it together without bursting into tears.

"You can cry, but it won't change anything, you know that." Autumn whispered.

"We just don't want you to go, Autumn." Olivia told her, kneeling beside Autumn and squeezing her sister's hand. "I just want one more day with you. I just want my sister for a little bit longer." Olivia cried as Dylan hugged Olivia, placing his hand on top of Autumn and Olivia's.

Autumn nodded. "I know Liv, I know. But all you get is right now, and I'm so sorry for that."

"I love you, Autumn." Olivia whispered as Autumn wiped away her little sister's tears.

"I love you too, Liv." Autumn smiled. "I'll always be your big sister. And if you do anything stupid I'll come back as a ghost to kick your butt." She giggled, making Olivia giggle. Autumn smiled. "That's what I wanted to hear." She whispered, kissing her sister's forehead.

Dylan sniffled. "I enjoyed annoying you for 16 years." Dylan told her.

Autumn chuckled. "I didn't." Autumn playfully glared at him before laughing. "I'm kidding, I enjoyed your annoying self too." She squeezed Dylan's shoulder. "Be good, okay? Don't be such a douche. It's a bad look on you." She teased.

Dylan chuckled. "And don't piss of God or Buddha or whoever's up there or they'll send you straight to hell—"

"Dylan!" Cora scorned.

Autumn giggled. "It's okay, mom. I have a VIP section in both places." She joked.

Cora smiled and kissed Autumn's forehead. "I want you to know you were the best blessing God gave me. Even when you wouldn't let me in, even when you were hard to handle…you were still my blessing. And you'll always be in my heart baby, because you've been in there from the moment I held you in my arms and you looked at me with your beautiful eyes." Cora wiped away the tears from her eyes. "And you will forever have that impact on me."

Autumn felt tears of her own slide down her cheeks. "You'll always be in my heart too mom. All of you guys." Autumn whispered. "I couldn't ask for a better family."

Joseph hugged his daughter and kissed her forehead. "And we couldn't ask for a better daughter." He told her. "You won't ever be forgotten in our family, because you made such an impact. You were the best Castillo to ever exist. There is no better Castillo out there honey."

"Well, not to toot my own horn…" Dylan trailed off.

Joseph and Autumn laughed as Joseph ruffled his hair. "Dylan, you're ruining the moment."

"Like he always does." Autumn teased before turning to her father. "Thank you dad." She whispered.

Olivia wiped away tears. "Can we all just hold each other for a little bit?"

Autumn smiled. "I'd love that."

The Castillos all gathered on Autumn's bed and held onto each other, tears being shed and smiles being exchanged as they bonded one last time as a family.

"Bye Autumn." Olivia whispered.

"Bye Olivia."

Dylan squeezed Autumn's shoulder. "Bye Autumn."

"Bye Dylan." Autumn whispered.

Joseph and Cora kissed their daughter's forehead. "Bye honey." Joseph whispered as Cora cried.

"Bye mom, bye dad." Autumn's eyes watered. "Bye."

Emma held Autumn's hand as she sat on the edge of the bed with tears streaming down her face.

This was it.

This was all the time she had left with her best friend. Autumn would be gone soon, and she couldn't stop it. She couldn't ask for one more minute or one more day with Autumn. This was all she had left.

"…and that is why you should name your bakery after me." Autumn finished her ongoing argument with Emma as to why Emma should name her future bakery after her.

Emma laughed. "I'll take all of that into consideration when the time comes Autumn." She promised the girl.

Autumn chuckled and nodded, appearing weaker than she had with everyone else. "That's all I ask for." She whispered.

"I'm going to miss you so much." Emma whispered, tears streaming down her face.

"Me too, Emms, me too. Don't forget me." Autumn told her.

"Never." Emma told her.

Autumn nodded and smiled as she fixed the cannula in her nose that helped her breathe. "I want you to promise me something."

"Anything." Emma nodded.

"When I die, don't you dare touch a drop of alcohol. Do not mourn me that way. Do not mourn me *at all*. I do not want that for you ever again. Do not ever numb your pain away, I want you to say what you feel and to never be afraid of it. Please try to be happy, and when you remember me…please smile and don't cry. Because you're my best friend, and while I didn't treat you like that for a long time…the time I did I want you to remember me by. I love you so much Emma…" Autumn didn't bother wiping away the tears that streamed down her face. "And it was a privilege to get to be your friend." She whispered. "So promise me, that you'll try and live the happiest life out there. Because you, out of everyone in the world, deserve that. And so much more." Autumn told her. "So thank you, for being there when no one wasn't."

Emma was crying at Autumn's words and nodded. "I promise, A, I promise to make you proud of the life I will live. And I promise that I will never touch a drop of alcohol ever again. I don't need it anymore because I am not afraid to feel my emotions. I am not afraid to feel sadness, to feel anger, to feel happiness and joy and frustration and every feeling in the dictionary. It is not bad to have emotions and it is not bad to react to them, I know that now."

Autumn smiled and nodded. "Good, I'm glad you know that. I want you to be happy, Emma." She said softly.

"I want to be happy too." Emma smiled.

"You will be." Autumn nodded. "I know you will be."

Emma quickly crawled to Autumn and sobbed into her chest as she hugged her best friend tightly. "I'm going to miss you so much." Emma said in between sobs. "Please stay."

"I can't."

"*Please, please* stay." Emma pleaded.

Autumn cried with Emma. "I wish I had that kind of power Emms, but I don't. I have to go. But I'll be right here." She pointed to Emma's head. "And here." She pointed to Emma's heart. "And I promise to haunt you as ghost at your bakery. Maybe you can give me a job." She joked, trying to lighten the mood.

Emma chuckled. "I'd really like that."

"Take care of yourself, Emma, and I wish you the best in the world. You'll make the best baker in the world. The world doesn't know the storm that's coming." She smiled.

Emma smiled. "Thank you."

Autumn nodded and the two held each other while they cried, knowing this was goodbye for them. But never for their friendship.

"Goodbye Autumn." Emma whispered, kissing her best friend's cheek.

Autumn looked at Emma and smiled softly. "Bye Emma."

Elena took a deep breath, the day she dreaded most having finally arrived. Elena wasn't good with goodbyes. She wasn't good with losing the people she cared for most. And she wasn't good at letting go. But here, she didn't have that choice. She had to let go of Autumn whether she liked it or not. Not even the strong love she had for Autumn, the love of her life, could save her. She couldn't save Autumn, and that was the worst part.

Elena stepped in to see Autumn, looking so small and so delicate in her hospital bed. But despite Autumn's desperate want to let go, despite the obvious need to go…she held on with a smile for Elena.

"Hi Ellie." Autumn's raspy voice greeted, sounding weaker…almost non-existent. What Autumn would soon become in this world.

"Hi Autumn." Elena smiled back.

Autumn tapped the spot next to her bed, signaling for Elena to join her. Elena quickly walked to Autumn and climbed onto the hospital bed. "Does it hurt?"

"What hurts?"

"Dying."

Autumn shook her head. "No." she whispered. "I'm in absolutely no pain baby, I promise." She assured her girlfriend.

"Good." Elena whispered.

"I love you so much." Autumn whispered to her.

"I love you too." Elena smiled softly as she nuzzled Autumn's chest. "I'm always going to love you."

"You shouldn't."

"Well good thing I don't listen to you." Elena chuckled, kissing Autumn's cheek before staring intently at Autumn, wanting to memorize every part of Autumn.

"Why are you looking at me like that?" Autumn asked.

"I want to remember you." Elena told her.

"Don't do this to yourself, please." Autumn whispered.

Elena started crying, tightening her grip on Autumn. "But what if I forget about you, Autumn?" Elena managed to say. "What if I forget the way your nose crinkles every time I poke it, what if I forget how you smell like vanilla, what if I forget the color of you forest eyes, what if I forget how your voice sounds like in the morning, in the afternoon, and at night? What if I forget everything I fell for, Autumn?" Elena cried as she clutched onto Autumn for dear life, as if holding her would make a difference. As if holding her would give her more time. "I don't want to forget you."

Autumn held onto Elena tightly, rubbing her girlfriend's back and kissing the top of Elena's head as tears of her own fell. "Remember how I said I'd be forgotten? That I didn't want to be remembered? Well remember me, Elena." Autumn told her, smiling softly. "Remember me." She whispered. "You will, I know you will. You have pictures of me in case you forget how I look like, you have CDs of my voice in case you forget how I sound like, and you have pieces of clothing I left in your room that still smells like me. Keep them. Keep them all and that's how you'll remember me."

"But what if I lose all of that? What will I do then?" Elena asked, crying even harder.

Autumn kissed Elena's forehead as she looked into Elena's brown eyes. "You'll see me in your dreams. And you'll feel me. And smell me. And hear me. I'll sing to you in your dreams. You'll hear my voice in your dreams so you'll never have to forget me, Elena." She whispered. "I'm yours forever."

Elena cried and Autumn wiped away her tears. "I love you so much." Elena managed to tell Autumn.

Autumn wiped away tears and nodded to her girlfriend. "I know baby…I love you too. I love you so much my beautiful girl." She whispered.

Elena cried and Autumn held her silently, rubbing her back soothingly despite knowing that nothing she did would soothe Elena's pain. She just let her release it all, because that was all she could do."

"I wrote you one final song Ellie." Autumn told her. "Do you want me to sing it for you?" Elena nodded and looked up at Autumn expectantly.

"Please."

"I could never say no to you." Autumn smiled before taking a deep breath and singing, despite her voice sounding weak.

Elena was in tears by the end of the song and looked at Autumn. "Can I kiss you?"

Autumn nodded. "I'd want nothing more."

Elena kissed Autumn passionately, making sure this to be the kiss she'd always remember. The last kiss she'd ever give to the love of her life. When Elena pulled away she kissed Autumn's cheek before hugging Autumn tightly.

"Goodbye Autumn."

"Goodbye Elena."

CHAPTER TWENTY-EIGHT

Autumn Castillo died in her sleep at the arms of Elena.

Elena liked to think that was a good thing, that Autumn felt no pain. But now, Elena felt pain. And unbearable pain like no other. Autumn was just…gone, lifeless. Elena woke up to cold corpse and an even heavier heart.

When you lose someone, it feels like the thing that tethered you together was cut off by a pair of scissors. And the worst part was that the living kept the pieces while the dead carried on.

Elena knew everyone was hurting over Autumn's death, she knew.

But no one lost the love of their life.

Yes, they lose a best friend, a sister, a daughter…but they didn't have to face the tragedy of losing the person you planned to spend the rest of your life with.

Elena, she had to start all over. She had to move on as if Autumn was just a faint memory, but Autumn couldn't be faint memory to her. She couldn't, not when she splashed in color in Elena's eyes.

So, Elena cried in her mother's arms as the funeral went on. People talked about Autumn, as if they knew her the way she did. As if it pained them the way it pained her. They all called her, "an angel that left too soon" which Elena called bullshit.

Autumn was not an angel. Autumn was her African bush viper. Autumn was the person she never expected to find love in, Autumn was the person she never thought could work out but she did. Autumn was her beautiful surprise, her beautiful mess.

But now she was gone.

The thing about mourning was, it was a temporary feeling to most. It hurts at first, but eventually you find a way to go to sleep at night and wake up in the mornings without feeling like crying until your heart bleeds.

But how can you do that? How can you wake up one day and just be okay? How can you move on from someone you cherished most? How can you not spend every waking day thinking of them and every dreaming night seeing them in your dreams? Elena couldn't understand this, how can you forget a person that gave you so much to remember?

"Hello, I'm Emma. And this is Phoenix." Emma's voice spoke up as the funeral was close to coming to an end and then the burial would take place. Where the goodbye would truly be forever.

"Autumn was our best friend." Emma told everyone, her eyes puffy and red from all the crying she'd been doing. "And we loved her so much, but God had other plans for her. I like to think she's watching her funeral to make sure no one is being too dramatic." She chuckled. "So if you are watching, Autumn…" Emma looked down at her friendship bracelet that she had with four other girls that changed her life.

Emma felt a tear slide down her cheek and she took a deep breath. "We hope to see you again. Take care, my friend and I hope you enjoy this song that Phoenix wrote for you." Emma nodded to Phoenix and the girl quickly began playing the piano and sang a song in memory of Autumn.

Writing this song felt like her heart would burst at any second from all the pain of losing someone you felt was your best friend. But Autumn deserved this song, she deserved to be remembered through music. Just like Phoenix knew she would want to.

Phoenix looked at Elena, making sure the girl knew this song was for her too. She knew her best friend was hurting, and would do everything in her power to make sure she wouldn't hurt too much. Elena locked eyes with Phoenix and felt her eyes well up even more, starting to cry all over again.

When they finished the song, the two girls looked up at the ceiling and smiled softly. "Long live, Autumn Castillo." Phoenix whispered to herself.

Crying: to produce tears from your eyes often while making loud sounds because of pain, sorrow, or other strong emotions.

Elena's heart wrenching sobs echoed through the cemetery as she gripped onto the dirt that buried Autumn.

Autumn Rose Castillo

June 27th, 1996-July 29th, 2015

Loving daughter, sister, and friend

Elena sobbed uncontrollably, placing her hand on the tombstone and feeling her heart clench. "Come back…please come back. Please…I still need you here." Elena pleaded. "You can't leave me Autumn, please come back. The world is too beautiful to spend the rest of my life without you, come back." Elena cried. "Stay with me…" Elena begged to the tombstone that wouldn't ever respond to her.

Valerie walked up to her, having attended the funeral to pay her respects. Her heart broke at the sight of Elena's broken state, there was no denying she lost someone important to her. The entire cemetery knew this.

"Hey…" Valerie kneeled next to Elena. "Come on Lena, let's go."

Elena shook her head. "I'm staying."

"Don't do this to yourself." Valerie told her. "She wouldn't want this."

"SHE is Autumn!" Elena yelled, making Valerie jump. "DON'T pretend like Autumn's forgotten already. Because Autumn isn't…my Autumn isn't gone." Elena sobbed.

Valerie frowned. "I know you're mourning, but Lena you're hurting yourself. Come with me, I'll take you home."

Elena shook her head, hugging herself. "I'm staying with Autumn. "She whispered.

Valerie sighed. "Lena please…"

"Please let me stay with Autumn…please…" Elena wailed. "Don't take her away from me…please…I need her."

"Lena come on, you can't stay here." Valerie told her. "You've been here for hours."

"Then leave!" Elena snapped. "I didn't ask you to stay here. Leave me alone with Autumn, go!" Elena exclaimed to her, glaring at the girl.

Valerie took a deep breath, but nodded. "Okay." She said before leaving Elena by herself at Autumn's grave.

Elena sobbed as she curled up to the tombstone, crying into her knees. "Come back…" Elena pleaded in a whisper.

Elena continued crying and Phoenix, Maya, and Emma approached her and sat beside her. Elena looked up and Emma smiled sadly at Autumn. "Come here." She whispered to Elena, opening her arms for Elena to embrace in.

Elena quickly hugged Emma tightly and sobbed grossly into Emma's chest, her tears quickly staining Emma's shirt. Emma held onto her and felt tears of her own escape. "I know, Lena, I know. It's going to be okay."

Phoenix wiped away a tear and nodded. "Yeah, Autumn's still with us making some dick comment about how dramatic we're being." Phoenix chuckled, trying to lighten the mood. "A's fine up there. She's doing good so we'll do the same."

Maya rubbed Elena's back. "Autumn's not gone, Lena, she'll always be in our hearts. She won't ever truly die because we'll keep her spirit alive. The dead don't always have to be forgotten." She said softly.

Elena nodded as she kept crying in Emma's arms. Emma looked at Maya and Phoenix, the two girls nodded. "Hey, let's go somewhere."

Elena shook her head. "I don't want to leave—"

"Trust me, Autumn would be there too." Emma assured as she helped Elena up and took her to her car, Maya and Phoenix getting in as well.

"Where are we going?" Elena rasped, her voice hoarse from all the crying.

"To see the stars."

The four girls lied on the ground as they stared up at the starry sky they had gone to with Autumn numerous times when she was alive. They did what they usually did, talk about everything their minds could come up with as they looked up and admired the illuminating sky.

"Where's Autumn?" Elena whispered as her eyes scanned over the hundreds of stars.

Maya tilted her head slightly. "Which one is the brightest one?"

Emma smiled as she pointed to the brightest star in the sky. "There she is." She told her friends.

"Sup, Loser? Have you met Michael Jackson yet? That'd be cool if you did." Phoenix chuckled.

"Nah, she'd want to meet Kurt Cobain first. Or John Lennon. Or Bob Marley." Maya told Phoenix with a smile.

The girls kept on talking, sharing favorite memories of Autumn and reminiscing the times they spent with the girl.

"Autumn's favorite song in the whole wide world was 'You Get What You Give' by New Radicals." Elena spoke up randomly.

Emma smiled. "It was. She'd dance to it when we were younger." She told her friends.

Elena hummed. "Put it on. Let's jam out to this for her." Elena told them. "For Autumn."

Phoenix and Maya nodded with a smile. "For Autumn." The two agreed.

Emma quickly ran to her car and plugged in her phone and blasted as loud as it could go the song.

The girls all got up and sang on top of their lungs, even if they didn't know all the lyrics to the song.

The four girls sang at the top of their lungs as they jumped around and danced, laughing at their embarrassing antics.

It was then they realized Autumn was here with them sending them a message to not be afraid to live even if she is gone.

By the end of the song, they were panting and out of breath. They all looked at each other and the four laughed.

"Promise me one thing." Emma spoke up as everyone tried to catch their breath. "Every year, on this day, we come here and we jam out to this song and we celebrate Autumn. This day doesn't have to be sad. Or the day we lost her. It doesn't, because she impacted all of us in a good way…and we should remember her with smiles." Emma told them with a softly smile. "So can you promise me we'll come here every year and do this?"

Phoenix quickly nodded. "I promise. Autumn's our girl, she deserves to see us like this than in tears."

Maya agreed. "I promise too. We said we'd remember her, and this is the best way to remember her." She nodded. "She deserves that."

The three girls turned to Elena expectantly and Elena bit her lip before nodding. "You know I'd do anything for Autumn." She whispered with a sad smile.

The girls smiled and quickly enveloped Elena in a tight hug. "Everything is going to be okay." Phoenix told Elena.

Elena simply nodded. "Before I forget." Emma spoke up as she walked back to her car and got out four lanterns from the trunk. "Autumn always wanted to do this, but we never got the chance to do it…so…for Autumn."

Each girl took a lantern and lit it up with a lighter Emma provided with before looking at each other. "Take care of us Autumn, will ya? Make sure to haunt our asses if we get into some trouble?" Phoenix looked up with a smile.

"Mostly you then." Maya retorted with a smirk.

"Whatever, jerk." Phoenix chuckled.

Emma chuckled before looking up and smiling softly. "We love you, Autumn." She said softly before the four girls released the lanterns.

Elena looked up and watched the lanterns float up until they were out of sight. "I'll see you in my dreams, Autumn." She whispered to herself. "I love you so much my African bush viper." The four girls hugged each other, seeking comfort in each other as they mourned and celebrated the tragic loss of Autumn Castillo.

EPILOGUE

10 years later…

Moonlight Sonata hadn't stopped playing in her dreams for the past 10 years. It's a strange comfort, because it reminds her Autumn kept her promise. But it also reminds her Autumn's dead.

Elena stretched as she got out of bed, and walked to the bathroom of her spacious apartment in Cinque Terre, Italy. When Elena attended Royal College of Art, she was the talk of the town. Her art became a big deal around the school, because she quickly became known as the "quiet girl with a story". Elena had a story all right, but she could only share it through paintings.

After she graduated from Royal College of Art, she made her money from auctioning her art that went dramatically from famous at her college to famous to all of London and then the world.

Elena became the Edgar Allen Poe of art scene, people said. Elena laughed at that, because Autumn loved Edgar Allen Poe. But then she cried because she remembered *Autumn* loved Edgar Allen Poe. Autumn would've loved to know her girlfriend was the Edgar Allen Poe of art.

Autumn would've liked to hear a lot of things.

Now, Elena made her money from selling her art. Just one painting on its own was worth thousands so Elena lived comfortably.

She bought an apartment and lived by the beach, Elena would've loved to have shared this apartment with Autumn.

Elena would've liked a lot of things.

Elena really did try (well, her friends tried. Elena just reluctantly went) to get back into the dating scene. But they either reminded them too much or too little of Autumn, Elena didn't know which feeling was worse.

Stepping into her art studio, she did her hair up in a ponytail as she finished painting her latest piece. It was of Autumn, of course, and it was from a dream she had of Autumn. Autumn was in a field of sunflowers and Elena's hands reached out for the girl wearing white and with the greenest eyes she'd ever encountered. But Autumn would only giggle and keep walking a couple feet away from Elena as she threw her petals from the sunflowers.

Elena smiled as she stared at the painting of Autumn, not even feeling the tear that slid from her cheek as she painted in Autumn's emerald eyes in.

"Mrs. Russo hates me, I swear." Elena spoke, as if someone was in the room. She liked to think that Autumn could hear her, she never replied, but she hoped she at least heard her. "She complained about me playing your songs too loudly." Elena chuckled. "The old hag doesn't know good music, I tell you." She scoffed as she finished the painting and continued talking about anything her mind could come up with.

Elena probably scared the crap out of her neighbors when she talked and no one would reply but she'd continue talking anyway. They thought Elena was crazy and perhaps she was.

Love had a crazy way of making you, well, crazy.

Losing love simply made you mad.

Elena thought so anyway.

Elena titled her head as she observed the painting from afar. "You look beautiful, Autumn." Elena spoke softly. "You always look beautiful."

Elena walked to the kitchen and served herself a cup of coffee and then walked out to her tiny balcony and stared at the beach with people and the ocean waters crashing into the shore. She hated looking at the water.

Because it was blue.

Autumn liked the color blue.

Elena cried to herself every time she saw the crystal blue ocean the first couple weeks she moved to Cinque Terre. Eventually, she learned to cry on the inside like everyone else.

Elena ate some of the cookies she brought from the nearby bakery with her coffee and kept watching the waves crashing onto the shore.

Today marked 10 years since Autumn passed away.

In four days, she'd be back in New York to release lanterns and listen to "You Get What You Give" by New Radicals.

In four days, it would be like every other year. Full of pain, full of laughter, full of smiles. Because Autumn made her feel all of that and more.

Elena sighed before rubbing her eyes. "Remember that song you had me listen to once? It was called *Give It All* by Train. You know that song? You had me listen to it before you…left." Elena said aloud. "It would go like…" Elena thought for moment. "I'd give it all for one more night with you…" Elena sang out loud.

"Well…I would." Elena got up and washed her mug before going back into her art studio and painting the day away.

———————————

Maya, Phoenix, Emma, and Elena sang at the top of their lungs. It was the 10th visit they'd come to.

To the exact same spot they would go with Autumn to see the stars and jammed out the same song and would release lanterns. And most importantly, there would always be a star shining bright.

Autumn, they liked to believe.

Emma and Maya crashed into each other and laughed loudly as Phoenix and Elena danced like total idiots.

At the end of the song, the four girls were out of breath like always. "I'm 28, I'm getting too old for this shit." Maya panted.

Phoenix laughed. "The irony is that you're a fucking doctor, shouldn't you be the healthiest out of all of us?" she teased. Maya answered that question by flicking off Phoenix.

Emma and Elena laughed as they tried to even out their own breathing. "Retract the claws, girls." Emma chuckled.

"You know damn well Autumn would film our cat fight if she was here." Phoenix chuckled, smiling softly.

Elena smiled sadly as she lied down and looked up at the starry sky. "Yeah…" she trailed off. "Autumn would."

Maya, Phoenix, and Emma joined Elena on the ground and looked up at the bright-lit sky themselves.

They were still close after all these years, and all of them still kept their friendship bracelets and never took them off for anything. Maya and Emma even wore them on their wedding days, never even dreaming about getting married without them.

Emma opened up a popular bakery in New York when she was 25 and had worked as baker at a bakery for a couple years. It was the best tasting bakery in New York, at least Emma liked to say. Emma did take Autumn's argument into consideration and did name it after Autumn.

She named it *Autumn Leaves.*

And on June 27th all of her cupcakes had blue frosting, in honor of Autumn's birthday. Emma married Ethan when they were 26 years old and they had a daughter a year later, they named her Autumn. Emma couldn't think of a better name, especially when her little girl opened her eyes and were a hazel color. Combined with the colors brown and green, Emma knew this was no coincidence.

Emma also started a youth group for teens dealing with alcoholism, because she never touched a drop of alcohol and she wanted to make sure no teen ever would deal with pain the way she did.

Maya was the star of Georgetown University's pre-med program and dominated Harvard Medical School. She became a pediatric oncologist and worked with children who suffered from cancer.

She worked her hardest to make sure she could help every child at her reach to spare the pain of losing them like she lost two important people in her life. Toby and her married eight months ago, and were living in an apartment in New York, talking of having children soon.

Maya also started a charity for women with breast cancer and named the charity after her mother, thanks to Elena, Emma, and Phoenix for promoting it constantly, it made enough money to help.

Phoenix soared at Juilliard, captivating everyone with her angelic voice. It was no surprise when record labels started eyeing her, desperately trying to get her to join their record company. She signed with a record label and with Autumn's songs and of her own, she dominated the charts with the heart-wrenching lyrics with a powerful voice behind it.

Like Autumn predicted, Phoenix became popular in the music industry. But Phoenix didn't discredit the people that believed in her, she always took the opportunity to speak highly of her best friend that wrote songs.

Autumn Castillo was a name people knew, and Phoenix knew no one would forget it. Phoenix also became a known philanthropist, donating money for the homeless, helping build shelters, funding research to help cure blindness, and donating to cancer research.

"There she is." Phoenix spoke up, pointing to the brightest star in the sky.

"Yeah…" Emma smiled, her eyes watering. "There she is." She whispered.

Maya smiled sadly. "Should we light up the lanterns?"

Everyone nodded and Emma got the four lanterns and the lighter from the trunk of her car and walked back to them.

The four women lit up their lanterns. "Hope you're doing all right up there, Autumn." Maya told the sky. "Our coffee tastes great down here." She smiled softly.

"We love you, Autumn." Emma said next, smiling.

"Better be bragging about me up there." Phoenix chuckled.

Elena looked up at the starry sky before whispering. "I love you so much my African bush viper."

The four women let go of their lanterns and watched the lanterns float away until they were out of sight.

"10 years…" Phoenix trailed off as she put her hands in her pocket. "Has it really been that long?"

Emma nodded as Maya had her arm around Elena's shoulders. "It has…it still feels like it just happened."

"Because she's still alive, we kept her alive in our hearts." Maya told them, smiling softly.

The women kept talking as they walked back to Emma's car, Emma stopping Elena as Phoenix and Maya walked ahead.

"I have something for you." Emma told her. "It's in the trunk."

Elena raised an eyebrow. "What is it?"

Emma bit her lip. "I found them, in Autumn's room. I kept it to myself because I wasn't sure whether you were well enough to get them but... it's a CD from Autumn for you with a letter." She told Elena.

"I put them in a box with a couple other things like her journal. The one she kept to herself. I figured you'd want them." Emma shrugged. "I think it would help you."

Elena's eyes widened and she nodded. "Oh…thank you." Elena hugged Emma, smiling softly at her. "It means a lot." She said, her heart pounding as she thought about what the letter, CD, and journal contained.

Emma nodded. "Yeah…come on." She tugged on Elena's arm. "Let's go get cupcakes from my bakery, I know how much you love them." She smiled.

Elena smiled. "That I do." Elena chuckled as she followed Emma to the car and drove back to New York City, Moonlight Sonata playing in Elena's head like always.

A week later, Elena was back at her apartment in Italy. She had to resist the intense urge to open the box. But she vowed to wait until she was back here. It felt right to do so in Cinque Terre, her and Autumn's place.

Elena took a deep as she ripped open the cardboard box, taking out the contents and bursting into tears.

Her red infinity scarf with white polka dots that Autumn "stole" from her. She smelled the scarf and was hit with the vanilla scent that belonged to none other than Autumn Castillo.

Elena cried even harder.

She kept looking through the contents of the box, finding pictures and drawings from Autumn that were for her. Elena cried through it all.

But when she got her hands on the CD with "For Elena" scribbled on it, that's when her heart began pounding.

Elena sat down on the couch in the living room, her hands still clutching onto the scarf, and popped in the CD into her laptop. She let out a shaky breath before pressing play.

There was a static noise and then suddenly the voice she fell in love with years ago spoke.

"Hi Ellie."

Elena burst into tears again, two words in and Elena was already on the verge of a breakdown.

"I, uh, I don't know if you'll ever get this. But if you do, I just want you to know how much I love you. This song I'm about to sing, I wrote it after I found out I was dying. So...yeah." Autumn sighed. *"Believe me, I don't want to go. I want to stay. I want to stay with you..."* Autumn's voice cracked. *"But we can't always get what we want, huh?"*

Elena wiped away tears. *"You know, music became even more beautiful to me when you started to become the reason I even wrote it.*

Music…it's beautiful when you have a reason to write it. Others write it for themselves, for the world…me? I write it for you." Autumn took a deep breath.

"Riley taught me how to play this on the guitar, so Riley," Elena chuckled when she heard a faint "Yeah?" in the background. *"Get out, you're no longer needed."* There was some speaking in the background. *"Okay, fine. We can go get sushi after this, YES sushi. Oh? You're allergic to sushi."* Autumn sighed while Elena giggled. *"We'll go get Burger King now get out dude, I'm trying to sing a romantic song I composed to my girlfriend."* Elena heard Riley teasing Autumn and Autumn must've thrown something because she heard a loud bang and the door slam and footsteps become faint.

Autumn chuckled. *"As I was saying, he taught me how to play my song and now I'm going to play it. I love you my arctic fox."*

Elena smiled and heard guitar strumming, her eyes immediately watering as Autumn played the guitar, knowing the girl was fully concentrated as she played the song. She then heard Autumn singing the touching song for her. The last song she ever wrote for her. Elena cried even harder.

Elena was sobbing after the song finished but it was quickly replaced with sobbing and laughter when she heard Riley's voice boom. *"DID YOU MAKE SURE THE RED LIGHT WAS OFF WHEN*

YOU FINISHED BECAUSE YOU—YOU—YOU ALWAYS FORGET EVEN THOUGH YOU CAN SEE NOW." Elena laughed loudly.

"*I was getting to that!*" Autumn exclaimed before grumbling something under her breath. "*If you listen to this part Elena, I hope the romance outweighed the obvious production of this song.*" Autumn chuckled. "*I love you and I'll see you soon.*" And the audio went static.

Elena replayed the CD more than 15 times until she decided she'd produced enough tears (and because fucking Mrs. Russo started complaining about the loud music and her loud wailing). Elena closed her laptop and went back to the opened box.

At the bottom of the box was an envelope.

To: Elena

From: Autumn

Elena picked up the envelope and bit her lip as she opened it carefully, opening the letter and her eyes welled up with tears when she saw Autumn's handwriting.

Elena,

When I read your letter, needless to say I was a sobbing mess. Yes, you read it here. I, Autumn Rose Castillo, was a sobbing mess because of a pile of combined words that turned out to be something beautiful. Something I will keep in my heart forever.

I'm dying. You know that.

I don't have much time left despite having made it past my time. I'm going to leave soon.

But before I do, I want you to know 12 things.

1. *I have loved you for 1 year, 7 months, and 3 days. And if I don't reincarnate into a new being, then I will spend the rest of eternity loving you.*
2. *The color of your eyes is, in fact, not brown. They're a special color I am inventing right this instant...teddy bear. Yes, teddy bear. Because a teddy bear's fur is typically brown. But so much sweeter, tenderer, and obviously cuter than the regular old brown. So, please, never say your brown eyes anything less special than the color teddy bear.*
3. *Your art will be worth thousands of dollars and everyone will know your name. You will not be forgotten like you feared, my dear (that rhymed, ha).*
4. *There is nothing wrong with falling in love again. And by that, I mean...find someone else to love you I never could. (Just saying though, Valerie's single from what I hear. She's pretty cool, GAY, and not a hoe like I said when I met her...JUST SAYING I GIVE YOU MY BLESSING.)*

5. *You changed my life and opened up my eyes, I saw before my sight was ever coming close to coming back. And YOU did that.*

6. *The definition of soul mate is "a person ideally suited to another as a close friend or romantic partner" and you are mine.*

7. *When hippos are upset, their sweat turns red. Random fact, but I just wanted to point out thank god humans don't turn different colors based off emotions because I'd be red permanently. WITH LOVE. But mostly anger. BUT LOVE TOO.*

8. *I am glad you snuck up on me the first day of school to listen to me play Moonlight Sonata. That became my favorite song to play.*

9. *You are not "whatever" to me.*

10. *I love peanut butter cookies and you.*

11. *I was made to love you.*

12. *If I reincarnate, I hope I'm an African bush viper.*

I've constantly asked myself what the definition of love could possibly be. I've pondered this question since I fell in love with you. And I finally came to a conclusion of what love is.

Love is three in the morning phone calls where both of us are tired as heck, but we want to stay up to listen to the calm breathing of one another.

Love is teddy bear eyes and brown hair dancing around in her underwear as she paints the world through her colorful eyes.

Love is looking at someone and realizing the world gives little blessings in the form of people.

Love is sharing my peanut butter cookies with you and trying not to be mad when you finish most of them (still mad at you).

Love is the color orange, it means happiness which is equivalent to love and that is what I feel for you.

Love is starting to whistle again when you stopped.

Love is finding a whole world inside a person and wanting to discover everything there is to see.

Love is...you.

When you miss me, listen to Moonlight Sonata and stare up at the starry sky. I will be the brightest one smiling down at you.

I love you.

Your beautiful mess,

Autumn

That night, Elena fell asleep outside looking at the brightest star in the sky and listening to Moonlight Sonata.

"I'm glad I snuck up on you to listen to you play Moonlight Sonata too, Autumn. I'm glad too." Elena said to the sky.

"Why am I holding a toy piano you ask?" Elena asked the tombstone. "I bought one at Target and spent two weeks learning how to play Moonlight Sonata." She chuckled. "See what you do to me, Castillo?"

Elena bit her lip. "After reading your letter…I realized no one can love me as fiercely as you did. But I can't deny myself the right to move on…so I started willingly going out on dates." She said. "I know, shock of the century," she laughed. "If I find someone that I develop feelings for, I promise I'll try to make it work. It'll be hard…but I know this needs to happen. You'd want this for me and I want this for me."

"But I promise you one thing," Elena paused. "I will never stop painting you. I paint things that impact me most and you…you have been my greatest impact. You are my muse, and there is no beautiful mess I rather paint than you."

Elena stood quiet for a couple minutes before speaking up again.

"Do you want to know my definition of love?"

Elena stayed quiet again for a few minutes before speaking up again.

"Love is...is when and you draw a circle. And you have no idea why you drew it, or what the point of it was. But all you know in that moment is that you *feel* something. And it feels nice, because a circle is full. There are no corners, but just a big space that you can fill whatever you want in. Love, is choosing to fill bright colors in comparison to dark ones. Love is wanting to paint a person's world bright colors in hopes you change their world. And I hope I did that for you, Autumn. I really do hope I could have been that person to you. Because you were to me. You will always be the person that person to me."

Elena wiped away tears and kissed the tombstone. "I love you so much, Autumn Castillo. And no one can change that. So thank you for loving me back." She sniffled before sitting down in front of the grave. "Now, let me play you the shitty version of Moonlight Sonata because I have this weird feeling that I need to do this in order for us to come full circle. So I can be okay again to move on."

Elena smiled softly before playing the worst interpretation of Moonlight Sonata to date. It was so bad, Elena was sure Beethoven himself was glad he was deaf.

When she finished playing the song on the toy piano she threw the piano to the side. "And *that* is why I stick to being an artist." She giggled.

Elena stuck around for a while longer talking to Autumn in hopes she listened before getting up and taking her messy messenger bag and toy piano and walking into the busy streets of New York City.

She took out Autumn's journal, the messy, clattered one Autumn always kept but never read. She opened a random page as she walked and it landed to an important date.

09/05/14

That was the day her and Autumn met.

Curious, Elena continued reading the journal entry.

Day 2,123 of being stuck in the dark. If I'm being honest, today is one of the rare days when being blind is not a bad thing.

Someone listened to me play the piano today. ME.

No one ever takes the time to listen to a blind girl play the piano, especially not a bitchy one. But this person...whoever she was actually cared to stop and listen. I felt...important. Like I mattered.

Of course, I scared her off by being, well, ME. So I probably won't ever hear of her again. She seemed nice. Her voice sounded like a really good song. You know, the kind you have to close your eyes for because keeping them open won't suffice. That's how her voice sounded, it was...magic.

Yeah, magic.

Wow, I sound like I'm in love with this girl. I should stop…

BUT I CAN'T.

Because someone cared for once, you know? Someone cared enough to listen. Not necessarily me, but listen to what I head to say through the music.

Whoever this girl was…I wish I hadn't scared her off. It would be nice to have someone listen to me once in a while.

She just (there I go again, ranting about this mysterious stranger with the pretty voice)…she seems like the kind of person I wouldn't mind if she messed up my life a little. Maybe shed some light, I don't know. I sound delusional now.

Oh well, whoever this mysterious stranger was…I thank her. Because I felt like the world was on my side today and it was because she balanced it out for me.

I hope she has a good day today.

-Autumn

Elena closed the journal and smiled, hugging it tightly. "I did have a good day, Autumn…I did."

Acknowledgements

Let me just start off by saying I never even thought I'd ever publish a book of my own. It's still a surprise to me but I'm incredibly thankful for it.

I'd also like to thank the readers, you wonderful humans got it to this point. So whatever successes this story brings, it's all thanks to you.

I'd also like to thank Andy who made the drawing of the Arctic Fox for the book cover. It's a beautiful drawing and he's very talented.

Also very special thanks to Scott SantAmour who contributed to the beautiful book cover. His African Bush Viper is amazing, he's an amazing artist you should check out.

And to the person who created the book cover in general, @SLOTHTATO on wattpad and @make_covers on Twitter. Thank you for the incredible book cover you made. There wouldn't even be a book if you didn't agree to making it so thank you so much for helping me accomplish this.

Also, I don't want to get sued so…the cover of the book has some things that comes from Iconfinder and Webweaver…so don't sue me please. I am a struggling college student.

Finally, a thank you for everyone who told me this couldn't be accomplished. You encouraged me to make sure it did.